SANDS OF MEMORY

COMPANY OF STRANGERS, BOOK 5

MELISSA MCSHANE

Night Harbor Publishing

Map by Oscar Paludi

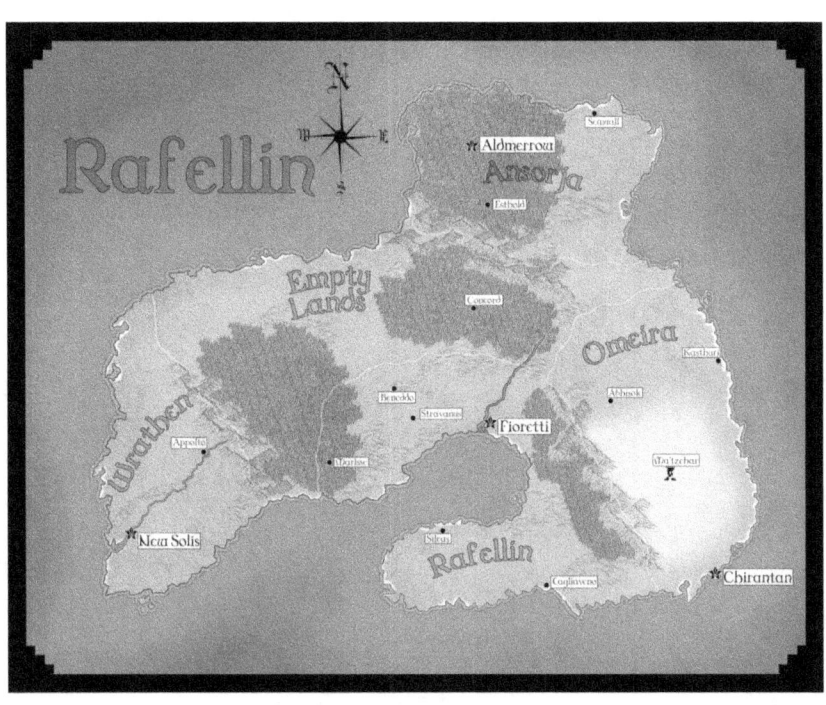

Dedicated to the Saturday Night Gaming Group,
which has survived thirty years of adventures, including:
unicorn obliteration,
exploding priests,
plans that are just the shotgun,
and splitting the party to hilarious results.

There's always another dragon.

1

Sienne knelt on the worn, scuffed floorboards of Mistress Elodie Givvani's office and tickled the copper-red puppy's nose with her knotted handkerchief. The little animal growled, a high-pitched sound closer to a purr than the deep-throated grumble of a dog, and fastened his tiny teeth in the knot. Sienne tugged against his grip and smiled as the pup's hind legs skittered on the floor. The worn wood was the only sign the room hadn't been constructed yesterday.

Anywhere else in the university, she would have worried about the dog wrecking carefully constructed piles of books or shelves full of artifacts, but Mistress Givvani displayed the kind of cleanliness Sienne normally associated with a professional laundry, though without the smell of boiling water. Nothing disrupted the well-scrubbed surface of her desk, the one bookcase was practically empty, and the only chair in the room was the one Mistress Givvani was currently sitting in. It was the only room Sienne had ever been in where the fragrance of soap was strong enough to be called a stink.

"You're sure the spell doesn't summon real animals?" she asked, teasing the pup by brushing the handkerchief across his nose again.

"Positive," Mistress Givvani said. Her short gray hair flew in wisps around her face from the many times she'd run her fingers through it since Sienne had entered the office. It was the only disorderly thing about her and reassured Sienne that she was a real woman and not a marble statue. "They're realistic, granted, but they're creatures of magic, given form by the spell and released at the end of its duration."

"So why can't the duration be permanent?"

"That would usurp the power of God. Our best theorists believe She grants us this limited exercise of the power of creation to give us greater empathy and an understanding of Her nature. Bringing life into being...it's humbling, even if the being is something monstrous." Mistress Givvani ran her fingers through her hair again. "You'll notice none of those creatures have human intelligence. Nothing we can summon does."

"But these creatures all seem to understand what I ask of them. Even the frog will take simple commands."

"That's another reason we know they're not real creatures summoned from somewhere else in the world. The magic creates a link between summoner and summoned that makes the summoned creature inclined to obey. It goes both ways, too— you've no doubt noticed you understand their nonverbal communication."

"I do, a little." Sienne let go of the handkerchief and giggled as the puppy rolled backward tail over ears from the sudden absence of pressure. "It's a relief to know there isn't some child in tears somewhere hunting for his puppy."

"That would be cruel, yes." Mistress Givvani bent to scratch the puppy's head. It looked up at her, yipped once, and vanished with a faint *pop*. "You'll also find the more often you cast the spell, the longer the duration will become as your reserves stretch to meet it. As is true of most spells with a limited duration."

"That's good to know. Thank you for your time."

"It's no trouble. You did recover the spell, after all, and provided us with a new line of investigation. Who knows what other spells have a versatility we haven't discovered yet?" Mistress Givvani laughed. "Probably not many, given the propensity of students to mispronounce the spell languages when they're learning. But it's a pleasant possibility."

"I never thought I'd be back in academia, when I became a scrapper a year ago," Sienne said. The office looked nothing like those of her teachers at her old school in Stravanus. Those had been packed with books and artifacts, not cleaned to within an inch of their lives. But it had the same feel to it, the sense that here was a place where knowledge happened.

"Life does take us unexpected places," Mistress Givvani agreed. "Like Omeira, apparently."

"Like Omeira." An odd thought struck her. "I don't suppose you know why there are no Omeiran wizards?"

Mistress Givvani's brow furrowed. "Aren't there?" Her eyes grew distant, and she tapped her fingers on her desk. "You know, I've never thought about it, but it's true we've never had a single Omeiran student in the wizardry school. Plenty of them in the other colleges, of course, but...well, that doesn't mean there are *no* Omeiran wizards."

"My companion Kalanath says there aren't. But he doesn't know why, either. I can't believe Omeira doesn't have any children born wizards. Even the southern continent has wizards."

"And no more nor fewer than we have up north," Mistress Givvani said. "I suppose it's something you could ask about while you're there. If it matters. I don't know that it's more than a curiosity, though some of my colleagues—the ones obsessed with theory, though you didn't hear me use the word 'obsessed'—would disagree." She stood and stretched like a cat, unselfconscious and relaxed. "Shall we see about the other matter?"

"Please."

Mistress Givvani's office opened off her private lecture hall, which at the moment was empty of students. It was as tidy as her office, if more thoroughly furnished. Chairs and desks aligned at precise right angles to the walls and each other filled the high-ceilinged space, which was over-warm due to the sunlight pouring through the tall windows. The glass was thick and bubbly, not the thin modern glass sheets of the mathematics building across the courtyard, and it showed the world in colorful smears, some of which moved as students crossed the courtyard from one building to another.

The sight took Sienne back in time again, to years past when she was a student sitting at a desk like these, though the room she remembered had no windows and was always cold even in the heart of true summer. Perhaps all schools were alike on some level despite their physical differences.

The halls of the wizardry school of the University of Fioretti were thronged with students, all of them wearing the lightweight blue gown that marked their school. They walked in groups of three or four, chattering away in conversations Sienne couldn't make out. Words came to her ear, fragments of sentences that together made no sense: *activated the hummingbirds in I asked for dinner*. She caught a few curious glances directed her way, assessing her trousers and shirt that said she was a scrapper, but no outright stares. She didn't look *that* out of place.

They passed through the rotunda, a tall, domed room from which corridors radiated like the spokes of a wheel, and down a new hall. This one was somewhat less packed with students and had no windows, instead being lit by giant versions of the lights Sienne could summon with a thought. The lights hung from the ceiling like moons in an alien sky, cold-white and casting sharp-edged shadows on the floor and walls.

Mistress Givvani opened a door about a third of the way down the corridor. "I'm as ignorant as you are about the thing," she said. "Let's see what they've discovered."

This room looked like a wizard's chamber, with its high ceilings and narrow windows whose glass was yellowed with age. Bookcases crammed with ancient tomes made a maze of the room, and more books piled on mismatched chairs made the path through the maze narrower. Sienne swept a hand across the surface of the nearest pile and sneezed at the cloud of dust that went up from it. The room smelled of dust and dry paper and, astonishingly, fresh apples. Sienne dusted her hand off on her trousers, leaving a pale smudge, and followed Mistress Givvani, who walked with a confidence Sienne didn't think the maze warranted. She felt she might be lost in this room forever.

"Vincentius? Joanna?" Mistress Givvani called out. "Don't tell me the books have finally engulfed you."

A thump, then a patter of louder thumps, sounded somewhere in the distance. Someone cursed loudly, making Mistress Givvani blush and say, "Sorry about that. Master Vitali isn't always careful about his language."

"I don't mind," Sienne said.

They came out of the maze into an empty space about ten feet in diameter, hedged in on all sides by stacks of ancient books and a desk big enough to seat ten to dinner. One of the piles had fallen over, and a thin, gangly man with a prominent chin knelt beside it, still swearing, but softly now, and stacking the books untidily. "There has to be a better way," he muttered.

"There is. It's called 'organization,'" Mistress Givvani said with some amusement.

"I can't be having with your organization, Elodie. It stifles the mind." The man looked up. "Who's this?"

"This is Sienne Verannus. The owner of the artifact I asked you to investigate?"

"Oh. You," the man said, as if Sienne were an unexpected, unwanted guest. "You're not planning to donate the artifact to the university, are you?"

"Um...no?"

The man grunted. "No one ever does, more's the pity. At least not until they're dead. Could I convince you to make the bequest in your will?"

"I...I don't have a will."

"No? And you a scrapper? At least I assume from your dress you're a scrapper. You of all people ought to have a will."

"Sienne's not here to discuss inheritance law, Vincentius. She wants to know what you learned about the artifact," Mistress Givvani said.

Vincentius rose to his full ungainly height. He looked like a stick insect unfolding, one slow joint at a time. "It's here somewhere," he said. "I'm sure it's here somewhere."

Sienne cast an eye on the piles of books, on the clutter covering the desk, and tried not to feel anxious over the fate of the hazard deck she'd given over to this man's care. It was in a bright red box, for Averran's sake, it ought to be visible!

Behind them, in what Sienne thought was the direction of the door, another sliding thump and a curse echoed through the room. "Joanna!" Vincentius called out. "Where's that artifact?"

"You'll have to be more specific," a woman replied. "Why do you have all these books, anyway? They should be in the library."

"Don't tell me my business, woman!" Vincentius roared.

"Don't call me 'woman' again or so help me I'll let you have one right round the ear!" the unseen woman shouted back.

"Treacherous whore!"

"Ignorant ass!"

"Maybe we should come back later," Sienne murmured, shifting uncomfortably in the direction of the maze.

"Don't worry, they talk to each other like this all the time," Mistress Givvani said. "Personally, I think they should just sleep together and get it out of their systems, but they seem to prefer the unresolved tension."

"Sex is a distraction from the essentials," Vincentius said, startling Sienne, who hadn't thought he could hear them over the shouted invective he was trading with his...colleague? "Joanna, come meet our guests."

A woman as round as Vincentius was thin emerged from the maze clutching an oversized book to her chest. "Guests? What guests? Nobody ever comes here. It's why I like your office better than mine."

"The owner of that artifact. You didn't take it, did you?"

The woman, Joanna, examined Sienne as Vincentius had. Sienne was growing tired of being stared at like a museum exhibit. "Of course not," Joanna said. "It's probably exactly where you left it." The clutter on the desk shifted without being touched, pieces of artifacts and small books rising into the air and shuffling into piles so the center of the desk was clear.

"You're a wizard," Sienne said.

"I am. I specialize in studying the magic of the before times, which is why Elodie gave me your artifact."

Sienne glanced at Vincentius, who gave his stack of books a final nudge to keep them from falling. "And...Vincentius...is a wizard, too?"

"No, an historian," Mistress Givvani said. "Oftentimes we learn more about artifacts from the histories than from arcane investigation. It's safer than working out an artifact's function by trial and error."

Something red caught Sienne's eye. Vincentius picked it up. "Here it is. Right where I left it. I told you that's where it would be."

Joanna rolled her eyes and let the rest of the mess return to the desk. "This is a powerful artifact. I don't suppose you want to donate it?"

"I already asked," Vincentius said. "She doesn't even have a will."

"I promise I'll draw up a will immediately," Sienne said, cutting off Joanna, who looked about to start in on a lecture. "What does it do?"

Vincentius shoved a pile of artifacts to one side and sat on the desk. His long legs swung gently, the soles of his feet brushing the floor. "There are records of hazard decks like this one occurring as recently as five hundred and forty-five years ago. They were never common, even among the ancients. Mostly they were used as divination tools in the time before the avatars, when God's voice wasn't as clear as it is today. So that's one use, if you know how to read a hazard deck."

"But that would be like using a cannon to swat a fly," Joanna said.

"*I'm* explaining it, harpy."

Joanna scowled at him and raised one hand for a prodigious slap she didn't deliver. Vincentius ignored her. "The real use, the magical use, took some doing to figure out, because the histories only referred to what it could do, not how to make it do it." He removed the lid and displayed it, with its black angular characters burned into it. "I couldn't find out what the symbol means, but based on other evidence, I think it's a name, or a house name—something identifying the owner."

He tipped the cards into his hand. His long, bony fingers curled easily around the deck. "First, shuffle the deck three times." He did so, the cards riffling through his fingers with a faint snapping sound. "Then cut three times, like this." He set the deck on the desk and cut it into three piles, then picked up the center pile, stacked it on the left-hand pile, and put both atop the right-hand pile. "Then you draw a card. No, not you. The person who shuffles draws a card. Otherwise the magic doesn't work. Each person can do it once every twenty-four hours."

Sienne waited. Vincentius continued to hold the deck loosely in one hand. "So...why don't you draw a card?" she finally asked.

Vincentius snorted. "Every card has a different effect, and not all of them are positive. I'm no gambler."

"Can I try?" Sienne asked.

"It's your artifact. Go ahead," Vincentius said, handing her the deck.

Sienne awkwardly shuffled the cards, which were almost too big for her hands, then cut the deck as directed. With only a moment's hesitation, she drew the top card from the deck and turned it over. Three staves against a golden background looked back at her. "I don't —" she began, then blinked. Everything had taken on crisp, sharp edges, like shadows on the brightest day in true summer. "Thirty-eight books on that shelf," she said. "Forty-two on that one. There are seventeen artifacts on the desk—I only looked at it once and I remember everything."

"Staves is the suit associated with intelligence and memory," Joanna said. "This one seems to have enhanced yours."

"And you just know that?" Vincentius said.

"I dabble in hazard reading."

"So how long will it last?" Sienne asked. Everywhere she looked she was conscious of numbers: numbers of books, numbers of nail heads in the floorboards, numbers of hairs on Mistress Givvani's head. It didn't dizzy her or make her feel overwhelmed; in fact, she felt her mind clicking along like a hummingbird's wings, zipping from thought to thought. It felt incredible.

"No idea," Joanna said. "We only know it's not a permanent effect. And that it seems to draw not only from the five spell languages, but from divine power as well. That is, the few effects the ancients recorded either duplicate a wizard's spell or priest's blessing, or do something related to those."

"I know priests can invoke blessings to enhance memory," Sienne said, recalling that Perrin had done something like that for Alaric once.

"Exactly," Vincentius said. "There's an implication, too, that the shuffling—randomizing the deck, as it were—allows God the opportunity to choose something most helpful to the wielder of the deck at that time. I don't know if I believe it, but it's an interesting theory."

"Wait," Sienne said. "You said *five* spell languages."

"All five," Joanna said. "Including charm. Another reason to be careful with it. It doesn't contain actual spells, so it's not banned, but you should take care how you use it."

Sienne nodded, torn between nervousness at handling such a powerful artifact and excitement at the possibilities. Charm...it was devastating, as she knew from personal experience, and she had no desire to cast *dominate* on anyone, but suppose the deck let her put enemies to sleep? Or frighten them away? Surely even the most rules-bound wizard could see the benefit to that.

Vincentius opened a desk drawer and dug around in it for a bit, coming up with a palm-sized notebook. "I've written down the effects I was able to uncover in my research. You can add to the list as things come up. It might not matter, since you can't invoke an effect by searching the deck for the card you want, but you might be able to see a pattern and decide if the odds are in your favor."

Sienne opened the book. Vincentius had remarkably neat handwriting for someone whose office looked like the aftermath of an earthquake.

Five of coins—creates small gem. Records say it doesn't disappear.

The Seer—record of talking sword, giving advice about the future

King of swords—companion appears to fight for invoker —impossible?

"None of these seem bad," she said.

"I couldn't find specific evidence of cards that had a negative effect, true," Vincentius said, "but there's plenty of records of people referring to these decks as cursed, or of destroying them out of fear of what they might do. You should be careful."

"I will." Sienne put the cards into their box and tucked it away in her pack. "Thanks for everything."

"Don't forget about your will," Joanna said. "You scrappers all think you're immortal, but death takes us all, in the end."

"Don't frighten the girl, shrew," Vincentius said.

"Don't call me a shrew, you worthless excuse for a man!"

"Vixen!"

"Louse!"

"We can go now," Mistress Givvani murmured. Sienne was grateful to make her escape.

They walked together as far as the rotunda, where Mistress Givvani said, "Good luck to you. And feel free to return any time you have an artifact you need identified."

"I will. Thanks again. I don't know that the hazard deck will be useful to us, but we never turn down magical assistance."

She bade Mistress Givvani farewell and strolled across the courtyard to the gate. Unlike the halls, the courtyard was virtually empty at this early hour, and the sound of Sienne's footsteps on the cobbles echoed off the walls of the surrounding buildings. Their cold, forbidding façades made her grateful she wasn't a student at the university, constantly watched over by the marble bas-reliefs carved into every conceivable surface.

Now she looked around for a quiet place to *jaunt* home from. Maybe it was an indulgence because being able to *jaunt* amid distractions was more useful to her team, and she ought to look for opportunities to practice, but *jaunt* took long enough to cast she didn't like being stared at while she did so. The portico of the library was empty; that would do as well as anywhere.

She tucked herself away in a corner of the broad, imposing portico and opened her spellbook. Transport spells were all long and cut her mouth to ribbons, which was why she rarely used them. Today, she was in a hurry.

She began reading the spell and immediately tasted blood. Swallowing, she read on. A quivering tension began in her stomach, radiating gradually outward until she felt something was gently pulling on her in every direction. The tension grew more intense until, spitting out the final syllable, she released it all at once and found herself in her own bedroom, breathing heavily. She swallowed more blood and closed her eyes as she recovered—another indulgence, since if she had to do this under pressure, she wouldn't have time to recover. Then she dropped her pack on the bed and headed downstairs to the sitting room.

The normally peaceful sitting room, rented from their landlord at a better than reasonable price, overflowed with backpacks and canvas bags. Dianthe sat on the sofa and studied the contents of one of them. "We have to reduce," she said. "This will cost far too much to ship."

"I thought we had enough money not to worry about that anymore," Sienne said, taking a seat next to her.

"No reason we can't still be frugal, as I believe *you* pointed out. And we still have to carry this lot." Dianthe leaned back and blew out her breath. "*And* we'll buy supplies for the actual journey in Chirantan, so you can multiply what you see here by five."

Three sets of footsteps sounded in the hall. "You're back," Alaric said. "Did they know what the hazard deck was?"

"Yes. It's exciting. Random, but exciting. I don't know how useful it will be."

"I prefer stability, myself," Perrin said, pushing his long hair back from his face. "Uncertainty may be the spice of life, though I am not certain that is the saying, but how much better to know one's path."

"You don't like surprises?" Dianthe said.

"Not at all."

"I agree," Kalanath said. "Surprises can be not pleasant."

"Or they can be exciting!" Sienne exclaimed. "I had no idea you two were so stodgy."

"It is not stodgy when surprise means, 'hello, I am here to kill you,'" Kalanath said.

"That almost never happens."

Distantly, she heard a knock at the back door. "Are we expecting company?" Alaric asked.

"I don't think so," Dianthe said. "I hope it isn't someone looking to hire us. I hate having to turn people down."

Kalanath turned and disappeared down the hall. Perrin entered the room and sat on the chair across from Dianthe. Alaric went to Sienne's side and leaned down for a kiss. "So, can you be more specific about the deck?"

"Well, each card—"

Kalanath returned, his eyes wide. "Perrin," he said, "it is a surprise for you."

Perrin looked up, startled.

"Papa!" two small voices shrieked.

Delphine and Noel Delucco dashed into the room and flung themselves at their father. Perrin's arms reflexively went around them, surprise deepening to stunned amazement.

"Children," he said, "what are you—"

Another figure entered, more sedately. One look at Cressida Delucco's face, though, told Sienne she was anything but serene. "I'm sorry, Perrin," she said in her husky alto, "but we had nowhere else to go."

Perrin rose awkwardly, hampered by the two children clinging to him. "Why should you need to go anywhere?"

"Because your father intends to take our children away from me," Cressida said.

2

"Children, quiet," Perrin said. Delphine and Noel subsided, though their radiant faces said they, at least, thought this surprise the most wonderful thing ever. "What do you mean, take the children away?"

Cressida's hands were clasped tightly in front of her as if they might otherwise fly away. "He discovered what I was doing," she said, "having the children pray to Averran nightly on your behalf. He…was most displeased." She didn't seem aware that she was crying.

Perrin took a step toward her, then subsided. "Did he strike you?"

"Father Delucco never sullies himself with physical violence," Cressida said with a bitter smile. "Words were quite enough. After explaining in some detail why I am an unfit mother, he declared that he would take steps to have my parental rights invalidated, on the grounds that I was corrupting his grandchildren."

"He can't do that," Sienne exclaimed. "I don't care if he's the patriarch of the family, there's no room in the law to allow that."

"The law is much crueler than you believe," Cressida said. "Things are changing, yes. Family heads no longer have the power they once did. But there are still corrupt judges, and venal law-speakers, and he needs only find those and convince them it is in their best financial interests to declare the worship of a particular avatar detrimental to the well-being of the family. I had no choice. I took the children and walked out of the house an hour ago."

"And you came to me." Perrin pinched the bridge of his nose as if his head ached. "Cressida, what can I do? I have no parental rights to our children. I cannot bring action against my father because he is within his authority."

Cressida held her head high. "You are their father," she said, "and you care more for their well-being than Lysander Delucco, who sees them only as dynastic spoils. You know he is a tyrant. If you ever loved me, if you care at all for their needs, help me escape him."

No one spoke. Perrin stood still, his face frozen in astonishment. Dianthe finally stood, clearing her throat. "Why don't you sit," she told Cressida. "You look as if you're about to fall down."

Cressida did look exhausted, her eyes hollow and bruised-looking, her mouth quivering as if she were close to shedding more tears. She let Dianthe guide her to the sofa, though her eyes never left Perrin's. Kalanath said, "Should we go?"

"No," Alaric said. Perrin jerked and turned to look at him. "I know, this is a personal thing, or should be," Alaric went on, "but I think you'll need our help."

"I cannot involve you in this," Perrin said. "My father is powerful and vindictive. I will..." He stroked Noel's hair without appearing to realize his hand had moved. "I will not be able to accompany you to Omeira."

"You're going to Omeira?" Cressida said.

"Not anymore." Perrin turned back to Alaric. "I am truly sorry, but if I am to take my—Cressida and the children to safety, I cannot simply give them money and hope for the best."

"Then we'll all go," Sienne said. "Omeira can wait."

"Stop a moment and think," Dianthe said. "We don't have the resources to hide the Deluccos indefinitely, and it would have to be indefinitely because I doubt Lysander Delucco will give up on searching for them when it turns out they've disappeared. And—no offense, Cressida, but I doubt you're equipped to support yourself and your children. You'll need protecting."

Cressida's lips quivered harder. "You are correct," she said. "I apologize. I should not have imposed on you." She rose from her seat.

"I didn't mean we wouldn't help," Dianthe said in some exasperation. "Just that it's not as simple as taking you to a safe house, or even to another dukedom. We need a permanent solution, one that legally frees you from Master Delucco's grasp."

"Legal," Sienne said. "We need a law-speaker willing to find a way around an unjust law. And we need a place where they'll be safe and protected while that happens." The beginnings of an idea took shape in her mind. If they could be persuaded...it would be a risk, but not nearly as big a risk as it would be for Sienne and her friends...

"But you have plans—I've interrupted—I didn't think this through. I didn't stop for anything this morning, I just ran. We have nothing but what we're wearing." Cressida sank into her seat, this time as if her legs wouldn't support her. Dianthe put an arm around her shoulders.

"We will help," Kalanath said. "You should not cry. We do not like Lysander Delucco at all. He is...it is what you say when someone enjoys hurting others."

"A rat bastard," Perrin said. "Cressida, I will not allow him to take the children away, do you understand? My friends and I have resolved worse problems."

"We just need to find someplace far enough away, and protected enough, that he won't be able to follow you," Alaric said.

"And I think I know the place," Sienne said.

———

NUMBER FOUR, PLAZA OF SIGHS, WAS IN AN UPROAR. SIENNE WAS USED to the chaos her large family necessarily traveled in, but it still surprised her that any family could need quite so many trunks. She waited for a footman to carry one of those trunks to the waiting line of carriages, then ducked inside the house.

Stacks of luggage waiting to be loaded made the oversized entry chamber feel cramped. She could still smell the remains of breakfast, sausage and eggs and ham, making her stomach quiver—rich food too early in the day nauseated her. Someone was having a loud argument deeper in the house, probably her sisters by the high-pitched voices. *That* wasn't something she missed about her family.

She climbed the stairs and went in search of her parents. At this point in the process, her mother would have succumbed to the blinding headache she always got, and her father would be off rousting her brothers to make sure they hadn't left anything behind. Another thing she didn't miss. So much nicer to be part of a scrapper team, able to drop everything and go at a moment's notice. Well. Except for their current trip to Omeira. But even that had been accomplished with less fuss than it took to get eight people and their belongings from Fioretti to Beneddo. Add to that ten days on the road in a closed carriage with her sisters...no, even walking through the wilderness was better than that.

All the doors on the second floor were open. She entered the only one from which no light emerged. Her mother lay on the four-poster bed with her eyes closed. Green light shone behind her eyelids as Lorne Macchari, her mother's personal priest of Kitane, completed an invocation to his avatar. Sienne waited silently by the door for them to notice her. Lorne looked her way first. He was short and compact, with an elegant face and long black hair he wore tied back at the temples. "Clarie," he said in his quiet voice, "Sienne is here."

Mother made an abrupt movement to sit, then subsided. "My head still aches," she whispered. "Come here, Sienne."

Sienne moved to sit on the bed and take her mother's hand. "Did you come to say goodbye?" Mother said. "I'm afraid everything's in chaos at the moment."

"I did, but I had another reason, too," Sienne said. "I have a favor to ask."

"Oh?"

"It's...a big favor. But you could save three lives."

Her mother's eyes remained closed, but her eyebrows went up. "Dramatic."

"It's a dramatic problem. You know about Lysander Delucco, yes?"

Mother frowned. "He disinherited his son, didn't he? Your companion Perrin?"

"Yes. Perrin's wife—former wife—has challenged his authority, and he's threatened to take her children away from her."

Mother's eyes flew open. "He can't do that."

"Cressida thinks he can. At the very least, he can make her life miserable. She came to Perrin for help."

"And by extension the rest of you. *Is* there anything you can do to help? They can't stay in the city."

"I know." Sienne took a deep breath. "I was hoping there was something *you* could do to help."

"I see." Mother smiled. "You want us to give them sanctuary in Beneddo."

"Lysander Delucco is powerful and wealthy, but he's not noble. There's no way he could get at Cressida and the children if they were under your protection, yours and Papa's."

"By law, the children still belong to him." Mother's face tightened in a scowl. "If he brings suit against us, we'd have to give them back."

"I have faith that you'd be able to stall him while Alcander works out a counter-challenge."

"Alcander? He's still a student, not a full law-speaker."

"True, but he has a thirst for justice, and he's smart. I don't doubt he'd enlist some of his teachers in solving the problem. Everyone knows taking children from their mother is wrong—the law just needs to reflect that."

Mother was silent. "Please, Mother, help them," Sienne said. "You didn't see Perrin when they showed up on our doorstep. He's devastated to be so powerless. I think he still loves his wife, and he's devoted to his children. You can't let a rat bastard like Lysander—"

"Language, Sienne." Mother sighed. "Though I agree he is a rat bastard. Very well. Let me speak to your father. This is something he'll need to agree to."

"But you'll convince him, yes?"

"Sienne, a strong marriage means two people working in accord toward the same goals. It isn't one spouse manipulating the other. Though I'm not above couching my arguments in the most... convincing way possible. Why don't you find Alcander and put your proposal to him?"

Sienne ran Alcander to ground in the mansion's library, a small, boxy room that smelled of lavender. Its contents ran to job lots the mansion's owners had bought because the spines all matched. Alcander was reading a book whose leather binding was shiny with age, one Sienne recognized as belonging to him. "Sienne!" he exclaimed, setting the book down on its face. "Come to see us off?"

"You'll break the spine if you do that, heathen."

"It's already broken. Sit, and tell me what the king is like. I can't believe neither of us has to rule Beneddo someday. I would have sworn the king changed his mind for no one."

"He's intense and clever, and very intelligent. Driven, maybe. Not kind, but that's probably not an important characteristic for a king. I thought I hated him, but now I'm not sure." Sienne shook her head. "That's not why I'm here. How would you like to make legal history before you're twenty-two?"

Alcander's eyebrows went up. "You're not thinking of suing me, are you? Because I can't believe you have grounds for that."

"No. I want you to overturn an unjust law." She summed up the Deluccos' situation, not giving him the opportunity to interject irrelevancies, and ended with, "We need a way to keep Cressida and her children out of his clutches permanently. They can only hide in Beneddo for so long."

"You don't ask for trifles, do you?" Alcander said. His eyes were distant, focused on something not in that room. "I don't know, Sienne. We're talking about weakening the legal protections of a patriarch. There are plenty of judges who benefit from those protections and won't want to see them removed."

"But it's unfair. Perrin lost his marriage and his children just because he decided to worship a different avatar. Now Cressida is in the same position. Isn't that, I don't know, like saying some avatars are better than others?"

"That's the line of reasoning that occurred to me. The problem isn't that the heads of families have power, it's that they have too much power. Maybe it's valid that they can annul marriages—"

"I'll never believe that!"

"I said 'maybe.' They at least ought to have to show a better reason than changing one's faith." Alcander focused on Sienne. "I think it's possible. And I have a professor who will see it as a challenge." He grinned. "I might even turn it into a thesis."

Sienne hugged her brother. "Thank you. Perrin thanks you too."

"I can't imagine how hard it would be to lose your family. Though this won't restore his marriage. Is that something he wants?"

"I don't know. I can't tell. I think he still loves his wife, but they hurt each other badly. It's going to take more than a change in the law to fix what's broken between them."

"Well, it starts with changing the law. The rest is up to him."

They walked back up the stairs and met their father coming down. "Sienne," Papa said, embracing her. "Your mother put your surprising proposition to me."

"And?"

"We shouldn't interfere in another family's dispute," Papa said. "On the other hand, I don't believe children should be separated from their parents, no matter the legal right of a patriarch to do so. And, not to be proud, but I am duke of Beneddo and far more powerful than some upstart nobody with more money than sense."

Sienne threw her arms around her father again. "I'm so glad."

"We'll be leaving in two hours. Will you bring them to us, or use magic to take them directly to Beneddo?"

"I thought about taking them directly to Beneddo for safety, but that leaves them at loose ends in the city while you're on the road. Will you mind accommodating them in your caravan? They'll have money to pay their way."

"Nonsense. They'll be our guests. Our financial situation is not as precarious as it once was, since the Lanzanos chose not to ask for the marriage settlement back. I don't suppose you know anything about that?"

"Ah...I might have blackmailed Rance just a tiny bit."

"Say no more. At any rate, we're happy to host them for as long as it takes." Papa kissed her forehead. "Bring them here in two hours. I have to say I feel energized at the idea of helping someone escape an unjust situation. And Liliana will be thrilled to have her friend join us. Anything that keeps Liliana occupied on the road..." He exchanged knowing glances with Alcander, who grimaced.

"I'll be back, then. Is Felice still here? I wanted to ask where she'll be living."

"She left already. I can't say I'm thrilled to have her gone, but she seems happy enough, and I wouldn't stand in the way of that." Papa smiled. "In the way of any of my children's happiness."

Sienne thought about *jaunting* back home, realized she would need all her reserves to bring the Deluccos to her parents' mansion, and trudged back through the streets, cursing yet again her lack of *transport*, which would convey several people at once. Back at Master Tersus's house, she went looking for Alaric and found him in their bedroom, packing his clothes into a large canvas bag. "Did they agree?" he said.

"They did. I'll tell Cressida. I was thinking I should *ferry* them directly to my parents' mansion, in case Master Delucco has men out searching the streets for them. He has to know they're missing by now."

"Dianthe went out to buy them clothes for the trip. They really did leave with nothing. I think Perrin is grateful for our last salvage expedition, because he's got more than enough money to care for their needs."

Sienne put her arms around his waist. "Can you imagine being forcibly separated like that? Somebody else dictating whether you can be with the one you love?"

"That nearly happened to us only three days ago. Of course I can imagine it."

"That's true. I've been trying to forget."

Alaric sat on the bed and drew her onto his lap. "It won't happen again, sweetlove. And if we're lucky, we'll give Perrin a second chance."

"If he wants it. I'm not sure how he feels."

"Then you're not watching closely enough. He looks at Cressida like she's water in the desert."

Sienne kissed him. "You mean, like this?"

"I mean exactly like this."

She rested her head on his shoulder, and they sat like that for a while. It was painful to remember she'd nearly lost Alaric, nearly lost all her friends and the life she loved so much, thanks to Rafellish inheritance law and the whim of the king. She closed her eyes and breathed out a silent prayer of thanks to every avatar there was.

Far away, she heard the back door open and shut. "That'll be Dianthe," Alaric said, helping Sienne stand. "Let's tell everyone the news."

Delphine and Noel sat at the long kitchen table, eating soup under Leofus's watchful eye. Cressida sat beside them, her bowl untouched. "It's going to be all right," Sienne said. "They'll take you."

Cressida closed her eyes and let out a sigh. "It is most generous of them. I hope you told them we will provide for ourselves."

"You can tell them, but my parents insist you're their guests. They won't take a centus from you."

Cressida smiled. "It's not as if it's our money. Perrin has been generous as well. I am not accustomed to receiving charity, only to giving it."

"Nothing wrong with that," Dianthe said, setting down a bulging sack. "Nightclothes, a change of dress for each of you, assorted toiletries. I think I guessed right on the sizes, but maybe Sienne could fit them more closely to you."

"I should conserve my resources," Sienne said. "I'll need to *ferry* all three of you to my parents' house, to keep you off the streets and out of sight. But once you're with the Verannus horde, you'll be safe. My parents won't let Master Delucco take you."

"Thank you," Cressida said. "I owe you everything." She spoke to

Sienne, but she was looking at Perrin, who stood silent in the corner. Despite what Alaric had said, Sienne couldn't see a trace of love or longing in his face. Without a word, he left the kitchen, brushing past Kalanath, who looked startled at his abruptness.

"Are we going to visit Liliana?" Delphine asked into the sudden silence. "I like Liliana."

"You like her brother Giles," Noel said in a sing-song, teasing tone of voice.

"I do not!"

"Delphine. Noel. That's enough," Cressida said. She rose from the table. "Behave yourselves. I need..." Without finishing her sentence, she left the room, turning left to follow Perrin. Sienne wished desperately she had some excuse for following them. She knew eavesdropping was wrong, but that had never stopped her before.

Alaric cleared his throat. "We should eat. And then we need to make a decision."

"About what?" Dianthe asked, taking a seat next to Delphine.

"About whether we're going to Beneddo, too."

"Should we?" Kalanath asked. "If they are safe with Sienne's family...but if something goes wrong, and we are not there, it is bad."

"We can't go," Dianthe said. "We need to draw attention away from Cressida."

"Wouldn't it be better if all of us disappeared?" Sienne said. "I don't mind drawing Master Delucco's attention if we have to, but that doesn't mean I want him breathing down my neck. He's vindictive enough he might take out his wrath on us, and then we'd have to fight his minions, and *somebody* would end up in jail. I don't like the chance that it might be us."

"If we disappear, we cede control of the search to him," Dianthe said. "Not having any leads to pursue, he'll follow up on every possibility, and that includes Sienne and Beneddo. Which means he could fall into the truth by accident. If we stay here, or go elsewhere but leave a trail, we'll control where he searches. Especially if we can make him believe we either have Cressida, or know where she and the children went."

"That sounds like you again wish us to go to Omeira," Kalanath said.

"It seems the best option, yes. He'll likely believe Perrin is trying to—" Dianthe glanced at the children, who were listening avidly. "That is, leaving the country will make the ploy more believable."

"Isn't Papa coming with us?" Delphine asked.

"It's not safe for him to do so," Alaric said. "Not safe for you, that is."

"But I want to go with him! Why can't we go to Omeira with you?"

"That is not safe either," Kalanath said. "We go to the desert. We do not take children."

Delphine threw her spoon into her empty bowl, making it rattle. "It's not fair!"

"No, it isn't," Dianthe. "It's just the way things are."

Sienne said, "Someday—" and closed her mouth, trapping the rest of her words. She had no business promising these children they'd one day have an intact family again, much as she longed to.

Perrin and Cressida remained in the sitting room almost until it was time for Sienne to take them to join her family. She helped entertain the children with minor magics, wishing she knew what kept their parents occupied. Wouldn't it be wonderful if they were making things right, resolving their differences, maybe kissing until they couldn't breathe? But when they finally returned to the kitchen, they didn't look like two people in love. "Children," Cressida said, "say goodbye to your father."

Both children ran to him, Delphine in tears. "We can go with you, can't we?" Delphine said. "We'll be good. We won't be any trouble."

Perrin looked at Alaric. "Go where?"

"Omeira. Dianthe will explain later."

"Delphine, my sweet, you must go with your mother," Perrin said. "She needs your help to look out for Noel."

"I can look out for myself!" Noel declared. "I'm six now!"

"And you will both need to take care of your mother," Perrin said, deflecting this handily. "Promise me you'll obey her, and...I will see you again soon, in Beneddo."

He exchanged looks with Cressida, whose face was expression-less. "I will contact you as we discussed," Perrin said. "The duke and duchess will protect you until I return, and then...we will make further plans once we know whether Alcander Verannus has been successful."

"I mean no offense, Sienne, but I am leery of entrusting my future to a boy who is not even a law-speaker yet," Cressida said.

"Don't worry about it," Sienne said. "We won't let Master Delucco take the children, whatever it takes."

Dianthe made a pained face, but said nothing. Sienne extended a hand to Cressida. "Come with me, and I'll introduce you to my parents."

It took nearly ten minutes to transport the three Deluccos to where the Verannus horde, as Sienne called it, waited outside the mansion. Most of this was the delay Noel caused when he realized his father would not be coming with them to see them off. Finally Alaric persuaded Noel to take Sienne's hand, and she cast *ferry* once more. Cressida waited with Mother and Papa at the front door, sweating in the afternoon sun. She took Noel's hand and bowed low to Sienne. "Tell your friends I am in their debt," she said. "As I am your parents'."

"It's our pleasure," Papa said. "And now I think we should be on the road. Mistress Delucco?" He gestured toward the carriage at the head of the line.

"We'll join you in Beneddo when this job is over," Sienne said, hugging her parents one at a time. "Good luck."

She waved the carriages out of sight, then began the long walk back home. She felt dizzy and a little sick the way she always did when she pushed the limits of her resources. If she'd known she'd have to *ferry* three people today, she wouldn't have *jaunted* to and from the university. Well, there was no sense dwelling on should-have-done when it was in the past.

It was interesting, though, how her ability to do magic had grown the more practice she got. Only a little over a year ago, she'd been a fugitive from her family, desperately looking for work, with barely a dozen spells in her spellbook and the ability to cast only a handful of them before reaching her limit. She recalled the first challenge to her magic after becoming a scrapper, tricking another scrapper team so hers could retrieve a stolen artifact. What had taken about half her reserves then would barely tap them now. And there was no reason to think she'd reached the limits of her power. It was a cheering thought.

She kept a careful eye out for anyone who might be following her. What they didn't need, at this point, was for her to be snatched by Master Delucco's thugs when she was in no condition to defend herself. But the throngs filling Fioretti's golden streets were as indifferent to her as they always were. It was one of the nice things about living in a big city; people tended to mind their own business. It could be an unpleasant thing as well, if you were being attacked and needed someone to run to your rescue, but in general Sienne was satisfied to pass unnoticed.

She turned the corner onto Master Tersus's street and climbed the shallow incline to his back door. "I'm back," she called out.

"Sienne," Dianthe said. "Everything went well, right?"

Sienne entered the kitchen, where her friends were seated around the table. Bags filled the space between the table and the windows. "Of course. Are we ready to go?"

"Just waiting for the wagon to drive us to the port," Alaric said. "Sit. You look like you pushed yourself too hard."

Sienne sat next to him and leaned against his shoulder. "A little. I'll be fine. Just don't anybody need a spell cast in the next several hours."

"This is intolerable," Perrin said, shoving abruptly back from the table. "I cannot bear it. My father cannot be allowed to continue in this madness."

"Perrin," Alaric said, "we've been through this. There's nothing you can do."

"I have two good fists," Perrin said. "I can beat him senseless. How dare he treat my children like his property? And hurt Cressida? It is unjust, and more, it is wrong."

"We're doing what we can," Dianthe said. "The only way is to change the law. Beating Master Delucco is just a temporary pleasure, and it will get you thrown in jail. How can you help Cressida if you're locked up?"

"It seems I am incapable of helping her when I am free." Perrin bowed his head so his hair was a dark curtain across his face. "I could do nothing for her but hand her a purse and bid her farewell. It is hardly the act of a husband."

Sienne almost pointed out that he wasn't Cressida's husband anymore, but Alaric's heavy hand on her knee silenced her before she could be stupid out loud. Alaric said, "Is that what you care about? Looking like a hero?"

"Of course not. I simply…" Perrin's voice trailed off. "I should have gone with her. Anything might happen."

"Going with her would only draw attention to her," Dianthe said. "Perrin, this is the best way."

"I think she knows how you feel," Kalanath said.

Perrin looked up. "And how is that?" he asked, dangerously calm.

Kalanath didn't flinch. "You do not stop loving just because you cannot be together," he said. "My mother taught me that. I think she is right. I hope it is true."

Perrin closed his eyes and let out a long, slow breath. "Averran help me," he said quietly, "it is true."

"Then the way to show that love is by leading your father away from them," Sienne said. "We'll go to Omeira, be decoys, and find the lost city of Ma'tzehar. And when we return from Omeira, we'll go to Beneddo and Alcander will have a solution for you." She didn't dare say *and then you and Cressida can be together*, but she held the words in her heart and hoped they could become true.

"Very well," Perrin said. "You speak the truth. But I hope my father's minions attack us, because I would dearly love to bloody my fists on their faces."

"*I* hope it doesn't come to that," Alaric said. He rose, and shouldered three of the bags. "Let's wait for the wagon outside. I feel the need for fresh air."

Sienne lifted her own bag, felt the room spin around her, and was relieved of the bag by Kalanath. "Do not become sick," he said, "because it is an ill omen for the trip if you do."

"You haven't had any dreams about it, have you?"

"None. But the journey has not yet begun. There is time still." Kalanath looked grim. "I hope it does not happen."

"I hope so, too." It wasn't entirely true. Kalanath was prone to prophetic dreams, and Sienne welcomed anything that might help them find the lost city. But she knew how they disturbed him, and in that respect, she didn't want that for her friend.

She followed him outside and down to the corner where the others waited. Regardless of what Kalanath had said, she couldn't help feeling that this, now, was the start of a journey that would take them to places far stranger than any they'd seen before. So long as it also gained them their goal, she was willing to go just about anywhere.

3

The harbor bustled, as it always did, with men and women engaged in loading and unloading cargos, boarding boats to be rowed out to the tall ships thronging the harbor's mouth, arguing tariffs with the harbormaster, and hailing friends or even chance-met strangers. The cries of the seabirds cut across the rumble of a thousand conversations all being carried on at top volume. Jouncing along in the wagon, Sienne watched the excitement in fascination. So many people, going so many places! And she was one of them.

"Do we need to make a fuss about leaving? Repeat where we're going in loud voices?" she asked.

"We did most of that while you were gone," Dianthe said, "but it won't hurt to announce it to everyone we meet. We want Master Delucco to have as little trouble as possible following us."

"Maybe not literally," Alaric said. "I don't know if even he has the resources to send thugs to Omeira after us." He grinned. "Though if he does...well, nobody there will make a fuss if we have to beat those thugs bloody."

"A possibility I await with great enthusiasm," Perrin said.

The wagon trundled to a halt at the head of the pier. Alaric helped Sienne out and refused to let her carry her bag. "Rest," he reminded her. "Do you get seasick?"

"I don't know. I've never been to sea before."

"Well, it can be unpleasant the first couple of days, and if you're prone to it, you don't want to add to it by exhausting your magical resources." He threw several bags over his broad shoulders and nodded at the end of the pier. "We're looking for the boat for the *Wave's Crest*."

Sienne trod down the pier in front of him, squinting at the names painted across the boats' hulls in the bright afternoon sun. Heat radiated from the pier steadily, making Sienne grateful she wasn't hauling anything; sweat prickled under her arms and beneath her breasts as it was.

She didn't know the proper name for the little boats that lined up along the pier, so different from the ships at anchor in the harbor. The boats had no masts nor sails, though some of them were big enough to carry a dozen people and others looked too small to hold more than two. Some were unattended, but most had two or three sailors loading bags and boxes into them, arranging the cargo neatly regardless of the varying shapes of the packages. It made sense—you wouldn't want cargo shifting in bad weather—but Sienne couldn't help wondering how long you'd have to work at being a sailor before you could stack things so perfectly.

She saw a boat painted a weathered blue and purple with the words WAVE'S CREST painted on its rear. That was another thing that no doubt had a name beyond "back of the boat." A woman reclined across its bench seats, a large hat pulled over her face. Aside from her, the boat was empty. "Over there," Sienne said, pointing.

Alaric laid his burden down beside the boat. "Five passengers for the *Wave's Crest*," he said.

The woman sat up and flung the hat away, squinting up at them. "About time," she said. "Load up. The others went out already."

"You've been waiting long?" Alaric said, in the overly polite tone he used when someone irritated him.

"Ages. At least ten minutes." Her accent was smooth and rippled like the waves, though she looked Rafellish. "I hate waiting for anything. Sleep only gets you so far."

Sienne stepped into the boat, wobbled, and the woman grabbed her elbow to steady her. "New to the ocean?" she said. "You'll get used to it soon enough. I'm Brigit."

"Sienne," Sienne said. "Thanks." She let Brigit help her to a seat near the front of the boat, thought about asking what the front of a boat was called, and decided she didn't want to draw any more attention to her ignorance than she already had.

Alaric took a seat on the bench opposite her. "Still excited?"

"Of course." She reached out and trailed her fingers in the water. It was warm and, when she sniffed her hand, smelled of salt and something else she couldn't identify.

Brigit finished arranging their belongings wherever they'd fit, and said, "You've certainly got enough to be going on with. Long journey?"

"All the way to Omeira," Alaric said. "I understand your ship goes farther than that."

"We're making the run to Seawall now. Stay aboard long enough, and we'll take you home to see your kin, Ansorjan." Brigit shielded her eyes and looked off across the pier. "And now we wait...no, there he comes."

Sienne couldn't figure out who Brigit meant, what with the crowds, but eventually a tall, dark-skinned Omeiran man strode toward them. His shaved head gleamed in the sunlight and contrasted strangely with his full red beard. Sienne realized she was staring and averted her eyes, looking instead toward the ships moored farther out in the harbor. Which one was the *Wave's Crest*?

"Brigit. Sorry to leave you with all the work," the man said. His Omeiran accent, while still as sibilant as Kalanath's, was more fluid, the accent of someone who'd spoken a second language long enough to be comfortable with dropping pronouns and using contractions.

"Lazy," Brigit said without animosity. She jerked her head. "Take your oar, man, and let's away."

The man jumped down into the boat, making it rock and causing

Sienne to fling her hands to either side for balance. The man either didn't notice or didn't care, taking a seat in the middle and picking up one of the two giant oars. With a minimum of fuss, the two sailors maneuvered the boat away from the pier and into the open water.

Sienne, facing backwards from the boat's forward motion, saw only the pier receding from view and, nearer to hand, the rowers. The ocean breeze cooled the sweat around her hairline, bringing with it more of the salty scent and the bitter tang of hot tar. "Do you want to change seats so you can see where we're going?" Alaric suggested.

She didn't want to admit she was afraid of falling out if she stood. "That's all right, thanks," she said. "Do you know how long the journey will take?"

"To Chirantan?" Brigit said, though Sienne had addressed Alaric. "It's a good week's travel, barring storms or kelpie attacks."

"Kelpie attacks?" Sienne exclaimed.

"She's teasing you," Dianthe said. "Kelpies don't attack humans. Seals are their natural prey."

"Kelpies will defend themselves if humans attack first," the Omeiran said. "But it's true, they're not dangerous. It's the sea serpents you have to watch out for. Thirty feet long, with spiny backs and teeth like daggers...they follow the shipping lanes, looking for easy prey."

Sienne shuddered. "Are you teasing me, too?"

"Ajhital doesn't tease. He's too literal," Brigit said. "But don't worry, miss, our ship is too big for them to tackle. Unless one of those deep-sea beasts comes in close."

Sienne closed her fingers on her spellbook in its harness. "I'm not worried so long as they're not immune to fire."

"Fire?" Ajhital said in alarm. "You're not a wizard, are you? Best not be casting spells aboard ship. Especially not fire. Could kill us all."

"I wouldn't do that!"

"Don't like wizards," Ajhital murmured. "Got jumped by a wizard once. Took my purse and left me chasing wisps all night."

"I wouldn't do *that*, either," Sienne protested. "Not all wizards are the same."

"As you have famously told me on more than one occasion," Alaric said with a grin. Sienne kicked him on the knee, not hard enough to hurt, and he grinned more widely. Then he looked past Sienne's ear and said, "That looks like the ship."

Sienne slewed around in her seat to watch the *Wave's Crest* approach. It was of average size, based on the other ships in the harbor, with sails furled to give the masts the look of tall pines stripped of their needles, bare to the sun. With a minimum of maneuvering, Brigit and Ajhital brought the boat around, barely bumping the side of the ship, and hollered up to a couple of men looking down at them.

Sienne gasped and ducked as something came flying toward the boat. It turned out to be a rope ladder whose end puddled in the bottom of the boat. Alaric steadied it. "I'll go first," Dianthe said, and clambered up the ladder as nimbly as if it were made of sturdy wood and not loose, twisting fibers and sticks.

"Sienne?" Alaric said. She swallowed and took hold of the first rungs, wishing she hadn't overextended herself—*jaunt* would be so much more graceful, and wouldn't require her to dangle who knew how many feet in the air over the ocean in front of all these sailors. Gritting her teeth, she made her slow ascent. The rope ladder twisted uncomfortably with every step. In midair, the ocean breeze felt more like a wind, shaking the ladder further.

She was so focused on where her feet went it startled her when someone grabbed her wrist. Her foot slipped, not much, but enough to set her heart pounding. "Just crawl over the rail," Dianthe said, holding her tightly. Sienne did so, ungracefully, nearly falling over the rail to the deck and managing at the last minute to get her feet under her. "Not so bad, right?" Dianthe said.

"Next time, I'm using magic," Sienne said.

She paced the deck while she waited for the others to climb up, getting used to the movement of the ship beneath her feet. It wasn't as bad as the boat had been, probably because the ship was so much bigger it wasn't as disturbed by the waves lapping against it. When her friends were all aboard, she leaned against the rail and watched the sailors hook chains to the boat and haul it up, dripping, to dangle above the deck on one side of the ship. Its bottom was dark with water and a greenish scum that turned the blue and purple of the paint gray. It was hard to imagine it had ever been new.

Compared to the docks, the ship was remarkably quiet. Sienne had always imagined, when she thought to imagine it, the shouts of sailors filling the air from the tops of the masts to the depths of the cargo hold, but almost everyone talked at a normal volume. Even the sailors dangling from the ropes woven around the sails and between the masts were quiet, though in their cases it was likely because the wind carried their voices away.

"Captain," Brigit said, and Sienne turned away from her contemplation of the sailors to see who she'd addressed. There were any number of sailors crossing the deck, doing mysterious things with rope, but only one who looked like Sienne's idea of a sea captain, if a short one—the woman who approached was barely five feet tall, and some of that was the high heels on her boots, shiny with wear. She wore the same clothes as the other sailors, cotton twill trousers and a cotton shirt open at the neck, but had flung over it a red coat, trimmed with gold braid and buttons, that was much too warm for true summer. Her three-cornered hat bore an ostrich plume that added another two inches to her height. Wrinkles from years of staring into the sun nearly buried her gray eyes, but despite that, and the gray in her dark brown hair, she didn't look old so much as distinguished.

Sienne's eye was drawn to the knife thrust through her belt. It was no utilitarian blade, but ornamented with jewels and gold, the kind of treasure scrappers dreamed of finding. Normally that meant the knife itself was worthless as a weapon or even as a tool, but looking at the captain, Sienne found it hard to believe she would carry anything simply for vanity's sake.

"Like it?"

Sienne, startled, looked up to find those gray eyes regarding her

34

with an uncomfortable directness. "Just wondering how well it holds an edge," she blurted out.

"Because it looks like a bordello whore's nightmare?" The woman laughed and extended her hand to Sienne. "It's sharp enough for my purposes. I'm Sylvie Talvanus, captain of the *Wave's Crest*. I take it you're the rest of my passengers."

"We are," Alaric said, shaking hands. "Alaric, Sienne, Dianthe, Kalanath, and Perrin."

"Welcome aboard. We have a few rules for passengers. Stay out of the way of the sailors. If you can't do that, stay below for the duration. If I tell you to do a thing, you do it, for all our safety. No fraternizing." She eyed Sienne and Dianthe as if questioning their morals. Sienne opened her mouth to be outraged that the captain didn't think the men might be inclined to fraternize, but Talvanus rode right over her. "Everything but the deck, the mess, and your quarters is off limits. We're a cargo ship and most of what's here is none of your business. You'll address me as Captain. I'll probably address you as 'you there' until I learn your names, and since you'll only be with us for a week, that might not ever happen, so no offense intended. Any questions?"

"What is the 'mess'?" Perrin asked.

"It's the common room where we all eat. Hope you're not fussy, because you get what the rest of us do."

"We're not looking for special treatment," Alaric said.

The captain looked him up and down. "Scrappers, are you?"

"Yes."

"You willing to fight for the ship if it comes to it?"

Alaric's brow furrowed. "You think that will happen?"

Talvanus shrugged. "Pirates have been known to attack lone ships even along this well-trafficked path. And there are other threats at sea. I doubt it will be a problem. I just want to know if you'll be a liability."

Alaric moved his shoulders so the hilt of his sword shifted, catching the sun and gleaming like polished silver. "We never have been before," he said.

A smile touched Talvanus's lips briefly. "Well said, Ansorjan whose name I've already forgotten."

"Alaric."

"I'll try to remember." She put two fingers to her lips and blew a shrill whistle. "Ajhital! Show these scrappers to their quarters. We set sail in one hour," she told them, and walked away toward the front of the ship.

Ajhital, who'd been supervising the removal of their belongings from the boat, came toward them. "This way," he said, gesturing toward a hole in the deck and a steep staircase that was practically a ladder. Ajhital descended it backwards, as if it were a ladder, so Sienne followed suit, her spellbook banging against her hip.

The dimly-lit space below smelled of unwashed bodies and tar, and Sienne held her breath, suppressing a sneeze. Most of the light came from a larger hole than the one they'd entered by, through which a net filled with crates and sacks was descending, but there were dim magical lights affixed to the walls. Without thinking, Sienne made them glow brighter, then glanced at Ajhital to see if the Omeiran had noticed. How presumptuous of her! But he was already walking away toward another hole in the deck below the first one.

"We cover the hold when we're underway," he said, gesturing at the net, which continued its descent into the belly of the ship. "You're not to enter the cargo hold. Nothing down there worth looking at, anyway. This is where we mess." He pointed at a couple of doors. "Galley—that's where the food is cooked—and the head. For relieving yourself," he said, in response to Sienne's confusion. Why couldn't they just call it the privy? "And back that way is captain's quarters," he added, pointing at a door in the opposite direction.

"Where do we bunk?" Alaric asked.

"Passengers get these cubbies," Ajhital said, waving a hand toward a couple of other doors in the direction of the captain's quarters. "Not much privacy aboard ship, if you were wondering. Hope you brought bedrolls."

"We did. Thanks. We're used to sleeping rough."

"Guess you would be, being scrappers and all." Ajhital nodded.

"Bells ring for meals and at midnight. You'll hear them. Any questions?"

"Are there any other places we should avoid?" Dianthe asked.

"Aft of the weather deck, mostly. Where the wheel and capstan are. If you stay out of the way of the sailors, you'll be fine." He nodded again and retreated up the ladder.

Alaric opened the door Ajhital had indicated. Inside was a stuffy small space, unlit, that smelled of damp and tar. He dropped his burdens on the floor—the deck?—and stepped aside for the others to do the same. "Where do the sailors sleep?" Sienne asked.

"They sling hammocks in the big room," Alaric said, "and I'm sure some sleep in the cargo hold when they sail in cold weather."

"Look at that," Dianthe said, pointing at the rafters of the mess room. A flattened pallet of weathered wood pressed against the ceiling, held there by ropes. There were several of these, Sienne saw, at regular intervals across the ceiling. "Those are tables with benches," Dianthe said. "They lower them at mealtimes and tie them away all the rest of the time, or when it's stormy, so they don't take up deck space and they aren't free to fling themselves all over the place. It's clever."

Sienne couldn't help wondering what happened if the ropes broke. "Clever," she agreed, and sat down on her bundled bedroll. "Do you ever get used to the smell?"

"It will pass," Alaric said. "Let's arrange our things, and then I think you should lie down for a while, before we get underway."

"I'd rather be up top. It's stuffy down here and I feel a headache coming on."

"All right. Let's find a place we can watch from."

They arranged their bags and bedrolls, then returned to the upper deck. No more cargo was being lowered into the hold, and a net woven of fat ropes had been slung across the upper hole so no one could fall in. Sienne gave it a wide berth nonetheless, fearing superstitiously that she might trip and fall regardless.

She followed Alaric to the front of the ship, past where the sailors worked, all the way to just behind the figurehead. The mermaid, bare-breasted with wildly flowing hair, faced the sea fearlessly for someone so exposed to the elements. Years of sun and wind had scoured the paint from her body, leaving her age-darkened and smooth. Sienne wanted to touch her, to see if she was as smooth as she looked, but doing so would have meant either climbing over the side of the ship, or casting *float*, and neither of those was possible.

Alaric put his arm around her, and they stood watching the waves lap against the ship's nose far below. "It's not called the nose, is it?" she said.

"Hmm? Oh. No, it's the prow. And this end of the ship is called 'forward' and the back is 'aft.' That's about the limit of my nautical knowledge, I'm afraid."

She leaned into him. "When did you last go to sea?"

"Three years ago. From Fioretti to New Solis in Wrathen."

"It was four years ago," Dianthe corrected him. "That salvage job outside Appolto."

"Was it? It feels like only three." Alaric smiled. "That was an interesting job."

"With an interesting client," Dianthe said.

The way she emphasized "interesting" made Sienne say, "What was so interesting about him?"

"It was a her," Dianthe said, "and it was the kind of interesting he probably wouldn't want to share with *you*."

"Ohhhh," Sienne said. Alaric's face was redder than his usual true summer sunburn. "You slept with a client?"

"You don't want to hear about my past romantic entanglements."

"Ah, but when they are clients, my curiosity is piqued," Perrin said with a grin. "Forgive me, but is that not unprofessional?"

"She must have been remarkable," Kalanath said.

"She was," Alaric said, "and I was carried away. It wasn't more than a dalliance," he assured Sienne.

"Alaric, you've never held my previous romance against me, I don't see why I should make a fuss over something that happened four years ago."

"But it is awkward still," Kalanath said.

"Right." Alaric hugged Sienne more tightly. "And yes, it was unprofessional, and it's the only time I've ever done anything like it. Besides, Dianthe has done it, too. Remember Marisse?"

Dianthe slugged him on the arm. "That's low, bringing up my past to avoid talking about yours."

"I assume this was before Denys," Sienne said.

"Of course. There was a man in the Marisse city guard...hmm, it occurs to me I might have a type. Anyway, every time we passed through there, he and I, um, met. But he was never a client, so it's not the same at all."

"It is interesting to me, the ways men and women come together," Kalanath said. "I have no such stories."

Sienne, her mouth open to tease Alaric further, gaped at him. "None? You mean, not ever?"

Kalanath shrugged. "It is not something I care about. It is...when the divines wanted me to have many children, it felt wrong. To treat sex as not a thing that binds you to another, I mean. I do not think I am interested."

"I can hardly blame you," Dianthe said. "But you never know. I swore I wasn't going to marry, and now...it's the right time for me, I suppose. Not that I want to tell you your business. If you're not interested, I don't think anyone should try to change your mind."

"I understand." Kalanath turned and leaned against the rail. "I think we are underway."

Sienne followed his gaze. The sailors' actions were as impenetrable to her as ever, but they did seem to be moving with greater intent. The dun-colored sails had come unfurled like drab butterflies, catching the wind with the sound of someone beating a rug, *whop whop whop*. The shore, already distant enough that the people scurrying around it looked like two-legged beetles, now drifted past too slowly to dizzy her, but fast enough the movement was obvious. Sienne sucked in an excited breath. Finally, their journey had begun.

4

When the others went below, Sienne stayed on deck with Alaric, watching the ship break the waves, churning up a froth of foam that boiled around the prow. Occasionally, she looked back at Fioretti, dwindling into the distance, until it was nothing more than a brown scum on the water's surface. Then she watched the waves again. "I hope we see kelpies," she said.

"Not until we reach the ocean. They're not fond of the Jalenus Sea." Alaric pointed. "There's a school of fish trailing us, though."

Sienne leaned far forward over the rail. A long mass of purple and red fish, their colors muted by the seawater, paralleled their course, though the fish couldn't quite match the *Wave's Crest's* speed and were falling behind already. "Oh," she breathed, "how beautiful."

"Beautiful, yes, but dangerous too," Alaric said. "Those sea serpents the sailors mentioned aren't as beautiful when they're trying to eat you."

"Now you've gone and spoiled it," Sienne teased. "It can't be more dangerous than the wilderness."

"Dangerous in a different way. Even the coastal waters, which is all I've ever sailed, have their dangers. And the open ocean...you couldn't pay me to make the crossing to the southern continent."

"What if it were the only way to fulfill your quest?"

"Thank Sisyletus that's not the case. All right, I'd make the crossing for that. But I wouldn't be happy about it. There are worse things than sea serpents out there."

"Don't tell me about them. I'll be happier not knowing." She turned her back on the sea and leaned against the rail to watch the sailors going about their business. Some of them clambered up ropes to the bars crossing the masts that held the sails, and she shuddered, thinking of how much falling from those heights would hurt. Many of the sailors were shirtless, and most of the women wore halter tops that barely covered their midriffs. They looked comfortably cool, and Sienne was just considering whether she had a shirt she could sacrifice to make one when Alaric said, "Interesting."

"What is?"

"There's a ship following us."

Sienne turned. A ship with faded blue sails that nearly matched the color of the true summer sky lay some distance behind them, far enough that it looked like a toy Sienne could balance on the palm of her hand. "How do you know it's following?"

"I suppose I don't. It probably just left right after we did, and the run to Sileas isn't uncommon. But I don't believe in coincidence."

"*I* don't believe Master Delucco could have found out about our journey and put together a voyage to follow us that quickly. And who else would care?"

"True. It's unlikely to be pirates after Captain Talvanus's cargo, either." He blew out his breath and put his arms around her. "I'm just used to thinking everyone's out to get us."

"Because usually everyone *is* out to get us. It makes sense." She put her hands over his where they rested on her stomach. "I think we're faster than they are, anyway."

"Is it bad that that relieves my mind?"

A bell jangled nearby, the sound carrying clearly to Sienne's ears. "What's that?"

"Dinner bell, probably." Several of the sailors had left their mysterious jobs and were streaming toward the smaller hole in the deck. "Shall we see what delights the cook has prepared?"

Kalanath, Dianthe, and Perrin were already seated when Sienne and Alaric descended the ladder. They had a table to themselves near their quarters. "I think we are neither fish nor fowl," Perrin said, nodding at the nearest table, which was packed full of sailors. "They are not keen on fraternizing, as Captain Talvanus implied, but the captain dines in her quarters with her officers and we are not invited to join them either. Not that I feel slighted. It is simply an observation."

The door to the opposite cubby opened, and a woman emerged, yawning as if she'd been asleep. She straightened her loose shirt and strolled across to take a seat at their table. "By the looks of you, you're my fellow passengers," she said. She was Omeiran, but spoke Fellic like a native, with only a hint of sibilance to her *th*'s. "My name is Ghrita Chakhorkurda. Have you met the other fellow? He's suffering from seasickness. His name is Harchan or Harchow or something." She swung her leg over the bench and smiled at all of them, making her narrow eyes almost slits above her high, sharp cheekbones. Sienne smiled back to conceal how intimidating she found the woman's brash, open manner.

Alaric made introductions, ending with, "Are you headed for Chirantan, too?"

"What, because I'm Omeiran?" Ghrita chuckled. "I am, actually. Headed home after a few years away. And you, fellow countryman— have you been away from Omeira long?"

"Six years," Kalanath said, curtly enough that Sienne would have taken the hint to back off. Ghrita just laughed.

"That's a long time for someone as young as you," she said. "Homesick?"

Kalanath gave her a long, level stare. "Were you?"

"Not really. I don't feel much attachment to the place. Home is where you make it, right?"

Kalanath spared a swift glance for his companions. "That is true."

Sailors bearing stacks of shallow tin bowls and fistfuls of cutlery passed between the tables, handing them out. The man who served their table did so in silence, without a word of greeting for the strangers, but also without any sign of irritation at having to cater to outsiders. More sailors lugging enormous pots that smelled deliciously of chicken and baskets of hard rolls emerged from the door Ajhital had said was the galley. One of them was Brigit. To Sienne's surprise, she headed directly for their table, bypassing others to get there. The sailor dipped her head in greeting and began ladling out big chunks of chicken in thick golden broth.

"Hope you like chicken and dumplings," she said, handing Dianthe the basket of rolls. "Two each. We eat well the night we leave Fioretti. Most of the time it's boiled salt pork in gravy."

"It smells wonderful," Dianthe said.

"There's fresh fruit for after," Brigit said. "Though we try to keep stocked on that so long as we're doing the coastal run. It's after we leave Chirantan that fresh food is limited. Not a lot of places to stop on the eastern coast."

"You don't have any wizards on board, do you?" Sienne asked.

"Aside from you? No."

"Because a wizard could *jaunt* to and from Fioretti and bring anything you like, if she was familiar enough with the ship."

Brigit leaned the heavy iron pot on the table. "Even though the ship is moving?"

"Everything's moving, all the time, as the world turns. This is just a little more obvious."

"Huh." Brigit hefted the pot. "Interesting. You might could tell the captain. Who knows if there's a need for that?" She nodded again and walked away.

"A wizard?" Ghrita said. "Why are you on a ship? Couldn't you just—" She wiggled her fingers in a way Sienne guessed was meant to be magical.

"I don't have the right spell," Sienne said. She dropped her hard biscuits into the gravy as she saw the sailors do and let them sit there, soaking it up, while she forked up chunks of juicy chicken.

"I hope you did not just volunteer yourself as the captain's personal transportation," Perrin said in a low voice.

"Surely not. Captain Talvanus strikes me as too responsible to go *jaunting* off whenever she feels like it," Sienne said. "And I'm still too tired, anyway. I really should make more of an effort to find *transport*, though. That would let me take up to five people at once. Perfect for us."

"Did you ask at the university?" Dianthe said.

"I did. It's not a common spell outside the scrapper community. Not very common within it, either. But the university wizards didn't know it." She used her fork to break the biscuits into bite-sized pieces, saturated with thick chicken gravy. Heavenly. Leofus wouldn't be ashamed to serve this meal in his own kitchen.

"It will have to wait until we return from Omeira," Alaric said. "I've heard there are wizards in Chirantan, but they're all foreigners and don't do much more than minor wizardry."

"It is true, Omeirans do not have wizard magic," Kalanath said. "We believe it is reserved for those who—pardon me—are not one with God."

"So my doing wizardry won't make anyone angry?" Sienne asked.

"Only in the usual way, which is that you do magic to hurt someone, and I think you will not do this." Kalanath tipped his bowl to his lips and scooped the last drops of gravy into his mouth. Sienne, after a moment's thought, mimicked him, trying not to feel self-conscious about her poor manners.

"That's not entirely true," Ghrita said, mopping up the last of her broth. "There are those in Omeira who believe wizardry offends God. Your existence alone will upset them. But they wouldn't attack you, don't worry about that. They'd just ostracize you."

"I am rather more concerned about how they will view me, a worshipper of Averran," Perrin said. "I do not intend to make a secret of my beliefs."

"I do not know," Kalanath said, glancing at Ghrita. "Where I... used to live, they are...it is when you are gracious to someone you consider lesser, like a child speaking his first words."

"Magnanimous, perhaps," Perrin said. "Or indulgent."

"Yes. They think they are better and do not feel threatened by Rafellish worship. I was taught that worshipping God through another is...weakness. Or it is that the worship is itself weaker, not allowing God full scope to exercise Her will. But also that some need this beginning step." Kalanath shrugged. "It is not a thing I believe anymore, after this last year."

"Understood," Perrin said. "So my worship would not be considered blasphemy?"

"By some," Ghrita said. She nodded at Kalanath. "I don't know where you come from, but that's not a common belief. It's more usual to disdain worshippers of the avatars as not truly believing in God. Some people would go so far as to say your God is false." She shrugged. "That's more likely in the smaller cities than in the capitals of the *rakhyans*."

"The *rakhyans*?" Dianthe said.

"Omeira isn't as unified as Rafellin. It's more a collection of city-states—like your dukedoms, but without a king ruling the lot. A *rakhyan* is one large city and several small towns, all under the protection of the *rakhyanam* or *rakhyani*. Chirantan is the largest of the *rakhyans*." Ghrita stood and stretched as unselfconsciously as a cat. "I think I'll go check on what's-his-name, see if he wants food. Unlikely, but I feel sorry for him. He looked miserable even before he stepped on board." With a smile that lingered longest on Alaric, she walked away. Sienne watched her go, envying her loose-limbed grace, then felt stupid about envying her.

The meal was coming to a close, and someone retrieved their plates and utensils, carrying them back through the door to the galley. Sienne thought about offering to help wash up using the minor magic of summoning water, but decided she was tired enough not to set a precedent she'd regret later. She stepped away from the table, then watched in wonder as it was winched up to the rafters, folding neatly in on itself. "So clever," she said.

"Maybe if we get to know Captain Talvanus better, she'll show you her cabin," Dianthe said. "Ships are designed to be storm-worthy, and they have all sorts of clever ways to stow furniture so it won't fly around and kill someone in a bad squall."

"Some captains have beds rather than hammocks," Alaric said. "They're suspended in frames that move with the ship's motion, like a cradle. Very comfortable."

Sienne eyed him. "And you would know this, how?"

Alaric reddened and wouldn't say any more.

"The captain on that same voyage to New Solis was very apprecia-tive of Alaric's...prowess," Dianthe said with a grin. "After we fought off raiders, I mean."

Sienne smirked and poked Alaric in the side. "You have more stories than I imagined."

"Trust me, you don't want to hear them," Alaric said. "Let's go topside and look for kelpies."

"You're also a master of changing the subject." One of the sailors approached with a basket of fresh peaches, and she took one. "And we can all watch the sunset."

"I will remain here, if you would not mind lighting our quarters," Perrin said. "I should communicate with Cressida, though I have little to say as yet."

"Of course." Sienne poked her head into the cubby and made a handful of lights that she sent flying to the corners of the ceiling. Their cold white light made the small room look bigger, though not by much. Perrin took a seat cross-legged on his bedroll and nodded thanks.

The rest of them climbed the ladder and returned to the spot they'd claimed near the figurehead, which continued to be out of the sailors' way. Sienne bit into her peach and licked up the juice that dribbled down her chin. "I wonder what his communication with Cressida is like," she said, idly taking another bite. "Will they talk to each other?"

"I almost hope not," Dianthe said with a shudder. "I remember having that blessing and how confusing it was, having all your voices in my head."

"But it must be different if there are just two of you. Intimate,

47

maybe." Sienne finished her peach and tossed the pit over the side. "I hope it's not just him telling her things. Don't you wish they could reconcile?"

"If it is a thing they want, yes," Kalanath said. "But I do not think they can marry again if his father is against it. I do not understand how Master Delucco can own his grandchildren."

"Perrin wasn't even his heir," Alaric said. "So it's not like Delphine and Noel are going to inherit the family property. Some people just like controlling others." He wound up and flung his peach pit as far as he could. It sailed away, a dark speck against the amber and pink sunset.

"Alcander will figure something out," Sienne declared, "and once the Delucco children aren't Master Delucco's property anymore, that will free Perrin and Cressida to marry again. If they want."

"Your brother must be remarkable, for you to have such faith in him," Dianthe said.

"He's much smarter than the rest of us, and he's passionate about justice. That will matter more than experience in this case, because I don't imagine most of the people with experience care about overturning the law."

"I think you're right." Dianthe sucked the last of the juice off her own peach pit and tossed it away. "Alaric, what are you looking at?"

"That ship," he said. "It's closer."

"So? It's not a pirate ship. And I doubt Master Delucco is *that* quick off the mark to hire a whole ship to come after us."

Alaric shook his head. "I know. I'm just being paranoid again."

"Your paranoia has saved our lives, so I cannot regret it," Perrin said, coming up to join them. "It is a beautiful evening, is it not?"

"Did you speak with Cressida, or just send her a message?" Sienne asked before she could stop herself.

"We spoke. They had just stopped for the evening, and all is well, though there was no reason to think otherwise." Perrin tied his hair, which whipped around his face in the brisk wind, back from his eyes more securely. "I still wish I had gone with them, and yes, I know it is a selfish wish, so do not remind me of my duty."

"Something else is wrong," Dianthe said, regarding him closely.

Perrin glanced at her and a wry half-smile touched his lips. "Not wrong," he said. "It is just that it is something I have…not wished for, exactly, but allowed myself to idly dream of. My family appearing on my doorstep, that is, rejecting my father's strictures and returning to me. My feelings at the moment are a muddle—anger at my father, joy at seeing my children, humiliation at being able to do so little for them and the satisfaction of having, to some extent, won the day. And now we are separated again. It is a tumultuous time."

"I think it's wonderful that Cressida's first thought was to come to you," Sienne declared.

"That, too, warms my heart," Perrin said. He leaned on the rail and looked off into the distance as if he could see past the horizon to Fioretti and, then, to wherever the Verannus horde had stopped for the night. "That ship is rather close, is it not?"

"It's nothing," Alaric said.

Sienne yawned. "I'm suddenly very tired," she said. "All that food, and…it's been a busy day. I think I'll try to get some sleep. Try not to trip over me when you all come in later."

The small, stuffy room felt even stuffier after the brisk breezes of the deck. Sienne made a few breezes of her own, but succeeded only in moving the warm air from one side to the other. Sighing, she lay down on her bedroll and extinguished her lights. The ship's movement was a gentle rocking that was as good as a lullaby, and between that and the soft creaking of the boards and the distant murmur of voices, she was asleep in minutes.

She woke only briefly, when Alaric settled in beside her, and fell back to dreaming of being an infant cradled in her mother's arms as they flew across the ocean waves, far faster than the *Wave's Crest* could travel, passing sea serpents like jeweled snakes until they reached the southern continent, which in her dream became Omeira. Then she was walking the streets of Chirantan, searching for someone who knew where Ma'tzehar was, only to be told it was actually outside Beneddo and she'd passed it dozens of times in her childhood without knowing.

When she woke for real, it was to a sense of confusion heightened by the impenetrable blackness of her surroundings. She heard Alaric's deep breathing nearby, and Dianthe's snoring, and that reminded her where she was. Breathing slowly, she let the dream fade into memory. Then she rose, careful not to disturb anyone, and made her way out of the cubby and across the mess room, now filled with hammocks. She had no idea what time it was and didn't want to disturb anyone's sleep by making a light to read her watch. Enough light filtered through the net covering the cargo hole above that she didn't run into anyone, and she found the head and used it with only a little trouble.

After her adventure with the nautical facilities, she felt alert and rested. Rather than return to their quarters, she decided to go up on deck and watch the sun rise. It was her favorite time when they were out in the wilderness, when she was on watch in the predawn hours, and this was just a different kind of wilderness.

The sky was overcast, and except for the lanterns winking at the ship's front and back and lashed to the masts, they might have been sailing through a black night sky, warm and damp and comfortably quiet. Sienne fumbled her way to the prow and used her magical sense of true north to get her bearings. They were still sailing southwest, toward Sileas. She turned to face east, but saw not a glimmer of sunrise. She groped for her pocket watch, but decided against making a light again, this time because it felt wrong to disturb the peaceful darkness. Sunrise would come soon enough.

She stood, listened to the footsteps of the sailors and their quiet voices, and swayed with the movement of the ship, until someone approached. "I wondered where you'd gone," Alaric said, coming to stand beside her. "Feel better?"

"Much. It's such a beautiful morning."

"Only you would think that when the sun's not yet up and it's blacker than a crow's heart."

"I like this time of day. It's invigorating."

Alaric took her hand and drew her into his embrace. "Too bad we're not in a position to do anything about how invigorated you are."

"Mmm. You're always more amorous in the mornings."

"Tell me it's not your favorite way to wake up." He kissed her lightly, sending a shiver through her.

"It really is. Too bad we don't have one of those beds you mentioned. You could show me how to use it."

"I'm not going to hear the end of that for a while, am I?"

"I just had no idea your history was so varied and interesting. You shouldn't be ashamed."

"I'm not ashamed. It's just indelicate, talking about former lovers with the woman who holds your heart."

That made her shiver again. "You're so honorable. I love that about you."

"I love your complete lack of jealousy." He kissed her again, more deeply, and she leaned into his kiss and wished the illusion of privacy afforded by the darkness weren't an illusion. "There's that ship again," he said, confusing her briefly. "Or its lights, anyway."

"Maybe we'll leave them behind in Sileas. We're almost there, aren't we?"

"The captain said we'd be arriving around dawn, and it's dawn now."

Sure enough, Sienne saw a thread of gold across the horizon, and the black clouds had turned charcoal gray. Birds flew past, calling to each other in their hoarse voices like housewives shouting news to their neighbors. And far ahead, gleaming like stars fallen to earth, lay the lights of Sileas. The land made a bulge blacker than the clouds across the horizon. "This would have taken us two weeks if we'd gone on foot," she marveled.

"Let's go below," Alaric said. "If we're coming into port, the sailors will be busy, and I don't want to get in their way."

"*Hoy, the ship!*"

The voice was faint, but unmistakable. A few sailors stopped what they were doing to look off to the left, where the mystery ship was approaching, then went back to their business. The voice cried out again. This time, one of the sailors swung down from the rigging and went below. Sienne and Alaric crossed the deck to where they could see the ship more clearly. It was close enough to make out movement on its deck, though not to identify individual people. "I wonder what they want?" Sienne said.

Alaric didn't reply. His face was grim in the low light. "I don't like this," he said.

"It can't possibly be to do with us."

Noise at the ladder made Sienne turn. Captain Talvanus, her head bare and her heavy coat rumpled, stumped up the steps and crossed to where they stood. "What do you want?" she shouted, sounding irritated.

"You're harboring fugitives," the voice said. "Give them up now or face the consequences."

5

Alaric swore. Talvanus immediately turned on him. "Are you fleeing justice?" she asked, her voice deeper and angrier than before. "How dare you—"

"We're not fugitives," Alaric said. "But we may have given someone the impression that we're sheltering fugitives."

"And dragged me into it. Thanks so much." She cupped her hands around her mouth and shouted, "There's no one here doesn't have a right to be. You've got the wrong ship."

"We're going to have to search your ship."

"By Averran, that's too much. Search my ship," Talvanus muttered. "You've no right to search anything," she shouted back. "Back off, or I'll have the law on you."

"That tells us you have something to hide. An honest ship would allow a search."

"For all I know, you're pirates looking to make a quick profit." To the nearby sailors, she said, "Ready the port and starboard cannons. This may get ugly." She strode away, calling out more commands that made no sense to Sienne.

They were close enough now to the mystery ship that they could see the speaker, a short man Sienne didn't recognize. As they watched, he turned away from the rail and disappeared below deck. "So Master Delucco was faster off the mark than we'd thought," Alaric said. "That's unnerving."

"It doesn't make sense," Sienne said. "He'd have had to learn we were leaving town, then that we were taking ship, then which ship. And then he'd have to find another ship leaving the same time and heading the same direction. How could he have managed that in only a few hours?"

"We have to tell the others," Alaric said, heading for the ladder. "And be prepared for a fight."

They found Kalanath awake and Perrin and Dianthe still sleeping. Both roused drearily, with much yawning. "Did anyone think to inquire as to the possibility of coffee?" Perrin asked.

"No time for that," Alaric said. "It seems Master Delucco has found us."

That woke Perrin completely. "Impossible."

"The ship that was following us has demanded we give over our fugitives," Alaric said. "It may be impossible, but it's true."

"What do we do?" Dianthe asked. "We can't hand over people who aren't here. And once they find out Cressida and the children aren't on board, they'll start to search elsewhere."

"The captain won't let them search the ship," Alaric said. "We can keep the illusion going so long as she doesn't give in."

Someone ran past their door, boots tromping hard on the deck, and a door opened and slammed shut nearby. "What was that, I wonder?" Perrin said.

"Let's get up on deck," Alaric said. "We want them to see us and believe the Deluccos are here."

The sky had lightened considerably when they returned to the deck. The mystery ship was much closer. Talvanus paced the deck near the wheel, speaking in a low voice to the helmswoman. "You people are bad luck," she told them as they emerged from below deck. "Whoever that is, they're determined on boarding us and taking you away. Or whoever it is they think I'm harboring. Why couldn't you have picked some other ship? Amely Vispatis's, for preference. That woman can't have enough bad luck as far as I'm concerned."

"Will they open fire?" Alaric said.

"Maybe. We're within sight of Sileas, so it's unlikely. But as desperate as that man is, I wouldn't count on it." Talvanus chewed her lower lip in thought. "If they try to board, will you fight?"

"Of course."

"Good. I'll be damned if I give over control of my ship to somebody who thinks he's got a mandate from God to hunt these fugitives down."

"Captain!" The man on the other ship waved to get Talvanus's attention. "We're preparing to board. We just want our rightful prey. Give them up, and it doesn't have to end in bloodshed."

"There's nobody aboard named Sestura, Chaperi, or Wessil," Talvanus shouted back. "Back off, or I'll have the harbor patrol on you."

Sienne blinked. "What did you say those names were?"

Talvanus said, "It's who they're after. Sestura, Chaperi, and Wessil. Those aren't your friends?"

"No," Alaric said. "Unless they're playing an unnecessarily deep game, they're not after us."

Talvanus turned toward him. "What are you saying? That by some incredible coincidence, you happen to be fleeing justice just as this other ship comes after a different set of fugitives?"

"We're not fleeing. And I don't believe in coincidence."

An explosion shattered the morning air, and Alaric grabbed Sienne and pulled her into the shelter of his body as shards of wood flew everywhere. Talvanus swore. "That's it," she said. "Bring her about, and ready the port cannons!"

"That was a warning, captain! We're coming alongside now," the man shouted.

Sienne stepped away from Alaric and surveyed the other ship's masts and rigging as the *Wave's Crest* swung in a wide arc, turning to meet the mystery ship. Behind her, Ghrita said, "What is going on?"

"We're about to repel boarders," Alaric said. "Do you know how to fight?"

"I can take care of myself, yes."

"Captain Talvanus," Sienne said. "Captain!" The captain ignored her, her eyes on the other ship. Sienne gave up and stepped forward to the rail. The man had said it was a warning shot, and if he'd wanted them dead, he could have followed it up with several more. Well, he wasn't the only one who could fire off a warning. Sienne opened her spellbook to *scorch* and read off the evocation, casting quick glances at the mystery ship to make sure no one was aiming a cannon at her. The *Wave's Crest* continued to swing around, and now it seemed the mystery ship was alert to the danger it was in, because sailors were swarming over the cannons on its deck, bringing them to bear. It didn't matter.

Sienne read off the last syllables of *scorch* and a flickering ball of orange flame shot away from her. It plowed across the enemy ship's deck, burning a furrow through its planks and starting little fires wherever it passed. Sailors screamed and threw themselves out of its way. Sienne backed up, bumped into Alaric, and the *Wave's Crest's* cannons pounded away at the mystery ship's sides.

Alaric grabbed Sienne and bore her to the deck as the other ship returned fire. More sailors screamed, and the air was full of the stink of gunpowder clouds, fogging Sienne's vision. She coughed, tried to rise, and felt Alaric's heavy hand on her shoulder. "Stay down!" he shouted. "They're going to board!"

A great grinding sound rose over the shrieks and the cracking of wood under stress, and dim shapes lurched out of the gunpowder fog, hurtling over the rail with swords and knives drawn. Alaric cursed and reached for a sword that wasn't there. "Perrin!" he shouted, and picked up a length of shattered wood flung free by the last barrage.

Perrin appeared out of the fog, muttering an invocation. Pearly light flared, and a shield radiated out from his left arm. "Go, go!" he said, helping Sienne rise. Sienne let her spellbook fall open to a new spell and began reading, shifting position as she did. The spell built within her, filling her chest with a terrible aching pressure that grew and grew until it burst out of her as the evocation *shout*.

A dozen assailants stumbled away from her, then dropped, paralyzed. One who'd been perched on the rail toppled and fell into the ocean. Sienne screamed and dove for him, but was restrained by Perrin. "You cannot help him!" he said.

"I can," Sienne said, flipping pages and reading as quickly as she dared. Which syllable had to be altered? If she guessed wrong—

Blood filled her mouth as she read the sharp syllables of the summoning, picturing the creature in her mind. For a moment, as she reached the end, she thought she'd failed. Then a pale shape shimmered into being three feet above the water, and with a chattering burst of sound, dove beneath the waves. "Save him!" Sienne commanded the dolphin. It was all she had time for, because Perrin was hauling her away from the melee and maneuvering her behind his shield.

"That is the most ridiculous thing I have ever seen you do," he said, breathing heavily. "I suppose you did not even notice the man who attempted to remove your head from your body?"

"No," Sienne said. "But—"

"No need to explain. I could not have let him drown, either." Perrin's shield popped and vanished. "There is something about this encounter I dislike."

"Me too. If all he wanted was to destroy us, he might have unloaded all those cannons instead of firing just one when we were unprepared. But why not wait until we were both in harbor and negotiate properly, if he has a legitimate right to pursue this fugitive?"

She rose up to cast *shout* again, but had to desist because the *Wave's Crest* sailors, as well as her friends, had engaged with the enemy—if enemy it was. No *shout,* no *scream,* no *fury*—Sienne turned to *force* and blasted a couple of enemy sailors as Perrin once again invoked a shield to defend them both. Alaric had taken someone else's sword and was laying about him with a snarling fury. Talvanus fought near him, her jeweled knife drawn. Despite the shortness of the blade, the captain had no trouble fending off attackers armed with swords. And Ghrita, unarmed, beat back two opponents with hands and feet alone in a way Sienne had only ever seen Kalanath do.

Unexpected movement against the background of the melee drew Sienne's eye. The man who'd first spoken to them was making his way toward Talvanus, shouting things Sienne couldn't hear over the screaming. Sienne saw the spellbook in his hands and fear gripped her. She gabbled out *force* again, feeling time slow to a crawl the way it always did when she knew she would be too late. She was still several syllables from the end when the man cast *shout*, catching Talvanus and Alaric and another dozen or more sailors from both sides in its effect. Sienne screamed, disrupting her spell, and the man turned to face her.

"I'm sorry," he said. "I had to stop it before it went too far."

Sienne looked around, past the pearly gray glow of Perrin's shield. Men and women lay bleeding or dead across the deck, or paralyzed by *shout*. Beyond the wizard, Kalanath slammed the end of his staff into his opponent's head and advanced on the wizard.

"Has it not already gone too far?" Perrin said, not lowering his shield.

"I have a right to pursue justice," the wizard said. "I hoped the captain would see sense."

"You have no right to attack innocents," Perrin said.

"You don't know anything. The men I'm after murdered six people in Fioretti and will likely kill again. I know they're on board this ship."

"There's no one like that here! Why won't you *listen*?" Sienne said. "There's just us, and Ghrita, and the seasick man, and nobody's ever heard of these men before!"

The wizard put away his spellbook and reached into a pocket, withdrawing a glowing stone. "This blessing says otherwise," he said. Then he froze, one hand still outstretched, as Kalanath pressed the end of his staff against his throat.

"You have killed many in pursuit of these fugitives," he said, breathing heavily, "and you still do not have them. Why do you not say all this before?"

"Because your captain's refusal to hand over men I know for a fact are here tells me she's in league with them." The wizard swallowed, making the staff move. "And you attacked us before I was close enough to use *shout*. I can't see how I can construe that as anything but open disregard for the law."

Sienne couldn't keep her eyes off Alaric, who lay as if he were dead, his eyes still open. She knew *shout* didn't last forever, that he was conscious within his paralyzed body, but it still tore at her heart to see him like that. "You're an idiot," she snarled, "and I wish I'd *force*-blasted you when I had the chance."

"Then I'd arrest you for interfering with the law," the wizard replied promptly.

"I think that will be unnecessary," Ghrita said. Sienne jerked in surprise. She'd forgotten the woman was there. Ghrita emerged from the ladder, hauling a struggling form with her that she threw at the wizard's feet. "I found him hiding in the captain's quarters. We know him as Harchan, or Harchow—I can't remember what he claimed."

The wizard darted forward to grab the man's chin. "Martin Sestura," he breathed. "So I was right. You were harboring a fugitive." He stood. "I'm going to have this ship impounded—"

"You will not," Perrin said. His shield vanished, and he took a few steps forward. "Did you not hear that this man gave a false name when he came aboard? No one here knew his true identity. You have no grounds for impounding this ship, and no grounds for the attack you mounted upon it."

"I have a legal right—"

"Sienne is correct. You are an idiot." Perrin's level tone concealed barely checked fury. "You failed to consider the possibility your quarry might have given a false name. You made demands without offering proof that you were who *you* claimed to be. You brought to bear lethal force against a ship that did nothing but refuse to allow strangers to board—strangers who might well have lied about their intent. And now, having used wizardry against *your own people*, you continue to make threats you are in no position to carry out. Whoever you are, I intend to see you brought to justice."

The man withdrew his spellbook from his vest again. "Don't," Sienne said, her book already open. "I can do far worse to you than *force.*"

"You wouldn't dare."

"Watch me."

The wizard eyed her, then slowly closed his spellbook and put it away. "This is all a terrible misunderstanding," he said.

"I think not," Perrin said. "And your ship has left you behind."

The man started and spun around. The mystery ship had drifted away from where it had ground against the *Wave's Crest*. He took a few steps, and Kalanath tripped him with his staff, sending him sprawling.

"Sienne, how long before they recover?" Perrin asked.

Sienne let her spellbook fall and dropped to her knees beside Alaric, taking his hand. The fingers moved slightly when she pressed them. "It's wearing off already. Maybe another fifteen minutes?"

"Then—excuse me, sailor, I'm afraid I don't know your name or rank," Perrin said, approaching the helmswoman. She'd stuck to her post the whole time, though her eyes were wide with terror. "Can you bring us into harbor? Your captain will wake soon, and then we can have this whole affair settled."

"Aye," the woman said. "The captain's not dead?"

"She'll be fine," Sienne assured her.

Sestura rose from where he'd crouched quivering on the deck and ran for the rail. Sienne cried out and went for her spellbook. "I don't think so," Ghrita said, darting after him. With a couple of long strides, she caught up to him, grabbing his arm and spinning him around to meet her fist impacting with his stomach. He bent double, groaning, and she caught hold of his wrist and twisted his arm behind his back. "After all this fuss, you'd better get what's coming to you. Whatever that is." She grinned. "Though I hate to see this fellow—" she pointed at the wizard—"have the satisfaction."

"If you let him go, you really are abetting a criminal," the wizard said.

"Why would I let him go?" Ghrita marched Sestura to Perrin's side. "Do you have any blessings that will lock a door more securely than metal?"

"I do not, but I have yet to pray for blessings this day," Perrin said, "and it surprises me that you, of all people, should be aware of a Rafellish priest's capabilities."

"Just because I don't share your heathen worship doesn't mean I don't know how it works," Ghrita said. "We should lock this fellow up before he can cause any mischief. And probably lock *that* fellow up as well."

"I am an officer of the law!"

"Who is in a good deal of trouble," Perrin said. "I would hate for you to take yourself beyond the law's reach, though I imagine if you had any transportation spells, you would already have used them."

"*Hoy there!* Discharging cannons in Sileas harbor is forbidden!"

A small ship, its single sail bellied out in a wind Sienne couldn't feel, approached the *Wave's Crest* at speed. Several men and women crowded its deck, three of them with spellbooks open. "Harbor guards! Prepare to be boarded!" the same woman shouted.

The wizard got heavily to his feet. "This is a lawful—" he began, and Kalanath whipped his staff around to press against his throat once more. He shut up.

Two sailors busied themselves lowering the rope ladder. Sienne crouched beside Alaric and held his hand, which closed around hers with reassuring firmness. A woman dressed in a bulky robe that didn't impede her movement at all clambered over the side, followed by a wizard with his spellbook tucked inside his jerkin and another man who wore his sword strapped to his back as Alaric usually did. "I want to speak with your captain," the woman said.

"I am afraid that will not be possible for a few minutes," Perrin said, gesturing at the fallen Talvanus. "This man saw fit to board our ship and loose magic on both our people and his own in a blatant disregard for the law."

"I am an *officer* of the law," the wizard insisted. "My name is Thaddeus Romanus and I am in pursuit of that man." He gestured at Ghrita's captive.

"So, this woman is the captain of this vessel. What about the captain of the other?" The woman waved in the direction of Romanus's ship.

"I am the one you should speak to, madam, I have the authority," Romanus said, drawing himself up to his unimpressive height.

"Very well," the woman said. "I'm Mistress Cantero with the Sileas harbormaster's office. Which of you fools shot first?"

Sienne immediately pointed at Romanus. "We told him he didn't have any right to search—"

"Who are you?"

"Sienne Verannus."

"You're no sailor."

"No, but—"

Cantero shook her head. "I want to hear from someone in authority on this ship. Where's the second in command?"

"Killed in action, mistress," said one of the sailors. "I'm Captain Talvanus's other lieutenant."

"Fine. You. What happened?"

The lieutenant, who looked to be all of sixteen, glanced frantically around for someone else to take the burden of speaking. "That man wanted to board us," he said. "Said we was harboring fugitives. We said we ain't, but he wouldn't listen. Shot at us. We defended ourselves, his people boarded us, and we had to fight back. And the captain—" He pointed at Talvanus—"they said she ain't dead, but she looks it to me."

Talvanus chose that moment to twitch and moan faintly, in which the garbled sounds of speech were audible. "I see she's not," Cantero said. She turned to Romanus. "What's your story?"

"I am an officer of the law, in legal pursuit of that man," Romanus said. "This ship harbored a fugitive, and I was within my rights to demand he be handed over. When they failed to do so, I ordered an attack."

"We didn't know nothing about fugitives!" the lieutenant cried out. "He gave us names that didn't match anyone on board and didn't say nothing about what his fugitives looked like. We thought he was pirates, mistress, and the law don't say you have to heave to and be boarded just on anyone's say-so."

"Indeed." Cantero's attention shifted to Sienne. "And you witnessed this?"

"My friends and I did, yes. We're passengers."

"And scrappers." She said it with no hint of disdain, but Sienne bristled anyway.

"We're scrappers, yes," she said. Alaric's hand convulsed on hers.

"Is the lieutenant's story accurate?"

"It is. Master Romanus was criminally negligent in casting spells that caught his own people in their effect."

"How dare you—" Romanus began.

"I'll decide whether Master Romanus was justified, thank you," Cantero said in a cold, cutting tone that shut him up. "*Is* this man a fugitive?"

Sestura, sagging in Ghrita's grasp, looked so much like a fugitive Sienne didn't know why it hadn't been obvious from the beginning. "His name is Martin Sestura, and he is accused with his two accomplices of murdering six people in Fioretti in the course of a robbery. I demand you allow me to search this vessel for his compatriots," Romanus said.

Alaric groaned and rolled onto his side. Near him, Talvanus struggled to sit up. Two sailors rushed to her side, but she waved them off. "You do *not* have permission to search my ship," Talvanus growled. "You can have your fugitive, Averran knows I don't want him. But we took no one else aboard at Fioretti and I'll be damned if I give up my rights just so you can puff out your chest."

"If he is an officer of the law, he has the right to search," Cantero said.

"His behavior has not been that of anyone with a legitimate right to pursue justice," Perrin said. "He failed to show proof of his authority—and I note he still has not done so. I question whether he has the law on his side."

Cantero looked at Romanus. "Well?" she said.

Romanus drew himself up. "The manner in which I left Fioretti—the haste in which I traveled—"

"No officer of the law travels without proof of his or her authority," Cantero said, holding out a hand. Romanus said nothing. "I see," Cantero added, lowering her hand. "Take him into custody. Master Romanus, you're being cited for discharging cannon within the bounds of the harbor and for illegal use of wizardry within city limits. Captain Talvanus, is it? If you returned fire, we'll call it self-defense. You're within your rights to pursue reparations."

"No," Romanus shouted, "no, you can't let him get away!"

Cantero eyed the despondent Sestura. "He hid when Romanus showed up," Ghrita said. "Authority or no, this man certainly has something to hide."

"That's my instinct, too," Cantero said. "We'll take him ashore and interrogate him." She gestured to her armed companion, who took Sestura from Ghrita's hold. "Are you going to give me any trouble?" she asked Romanus. "Because that would make you look very guilty."

Romanus glared at her. Cantero gave him a pleasant smile. "Captain Talvanus, you're to report to the harbormaster's office to give your side of the story," she said. "If it's determined you were an innocent party, you'll be free to go."

Alaric struggled to sit up. "I'm fine," he said to Sienne, and got heavily to his feet. "I didn't understand how powerful *shout* was until just now. Remind me not to piss you off."

"As if I'd use it against you," Sienne said. She watched Cantero guide her captives to the ladder and down to the waiting ship. "That was exciting."

"The rest of you, go below," Talvanus said. "I want you out of the way while I'm dealing with this, not to mention we still have cargo to unload. And...my thanks for fighting alongside us. You didn't have to."

"I promised we would," Alaric said. He popped his neck a couple of times and gestured for Sienne to precede him down the ladder.

When they were all below, Ghrita said, "I don't know about you all, but I want to see what that Sestura fellow left behind." She took a few steps toward her cabin.

Kalanath whipped his staff around and caught her across the stomach, bending her double and sending the breath whooshing out of her. In the next moment he'd thrown his staff down and grabbed the woman, bearing her into the bulkhead and pinning her there. "You are no mere traveler," he snarled.

"Kalanath, what—" Dianthe exclaimed.

Ghrita smiled despite his arm across her throat. "My mistake, fighting so openly," she wheezed. "Should have known...you'd recognize it."

"Who are you?" Kalanath demanded.

"I told you my name. Ghrita Chakhorkurda." She smiled again. "You've already guessed my purpose. I came to find you, Kalanath Oushikdali."

6

Kalanath said, "You will have to kill me. I will not return."

"Your death isn't the desired outcome," Ghrita said. "Release me, and I'll explain."

Kalanath pressed harder, making the woman gasp, then let her go. Ghrita coughed and rubbed her throat. "I should have been more cautious, but I thought we were all about to die, in which case it wouldn't matter what you knew."

"Kalanath, who is this woman?" Sienne asked.

Kalanath retrieved his staff, but didn't relax, standing on the balls of his feet as if prepared to launch himself at Ghrita again. "Temple *nirana*," he said. "It is...part guard, part warrior, part priest. Only the *nirana* fight with hands and feet."

"And the *devesh*," Ghrita said. "You, Kalanath Oushikdali."

Alaric took a step closer. "I see," he said. "And Kalanath fled the temple. If you intend to kill him, you're going to find that difficult, temple *nirana* or not."

"I told you, his death isn't why I'm here," Ghrita said. "I was to observe and protect, if necessary." She smiled, a wry expression. "Though we didn't know he had such loyal companions. I don't think my protection is necessary."

"No more being a mystery," Kalanath said. "Why are you here if not to kill me?"

Ghrita leaned against the wall, casual and languid as a cat. "You know they sought you when you fled," she said, "prayed for guidance in finding you. All those prayers went unanswered. God was deaf to their pleas."

"I thought I had simply put myself beyond their reach," Kalanath said. "Why would God refuse to answer Her divines?"

"Why, indeed?" Ghrita smiled. It wasn't a pleasant expression. "It was a question, once raised, that could not be ignored. If you, a *devesh*, were so important to God's will, why would She allow you to abandon the temple and then hide you from Her own divines?"

"Unless those divines were somehow at fault," Alaric said.

"You're quick, Ansorjan. Unless the *devesh* needed protection from the temple divines. That possibility set the cat among the pigeons, as I'm sure even you heathens can imagine. Certain... irregularities... in the behavior of the divines regarding Kalanath Oushikdali came to light. Specifically, that they had intended to force God's hand in breeding more *deveshi* when they failed to receive the revelation they expected." Ghrita's smile became more pointed. "There was a quiet and tame little war, and when the dust settled, a new order prevailed."

Kalanath's face was like stone. "What new order?"

"Those who would have turned you to their use no longer rule in the temple at Chirantan. All the temples bent their prayers to supplication that God might turn away Her justified wrath at having Her gift—you see a *devesh* is one of God's greatest gifts to Her people—abused. It was more than a year before God relented, and restored Her grace to Her people. Such a trial." Ghrita made it sound more like a festival than a trial.

"How fortunate for you," Alaric said. "What does this have to do with Kalanath?"

"Ah. The great mystery was that even after peace was restored, and the divines once more begged God to reveal the *devesh's* location, every scrying attempt failed. You can imagine the divines' reaction.

All evidence to the contrary, they believed they were still on some level under condemnation. That God's blessing had been taken from them. But they dared not give up hope at someday recovering him. So scrying for young Kalanath became a commonplace—a reflex, even. Something you do when you've given up hope of it ever producing anything. And two weeks ago, their faith and persistence paid off."

Sienne tried to remember where they'd been two weeks before. "Just like that?" she said.

"Just like that. It was cause for rejoicing, or so they told me. I wasn't in the temple—I've been living in Fioretti these many years, pursuing the temple's interests outside Omeira. That's why they tasked me with finding you and bringing you home. That, and I had no connection with those who drove you into exile. They thought that might matter to you."

"But we are going without you," Kalanath said. "You did not make me go."

"Imagine my delight when it turned out you didn't need my prompting," Ghrita said. "My intent was to befriend you, sound you out as to your reasons for returning to Omeira, and then to reveal the truth so it wouldn't be a huge shock when you arrived in Chirantan to a hero's welcome. Or so you wouldn't feel you needed to sneak around, whatever it is you're up to there. Our friend Romanus just accelerated the process."

"Kalanath?" Dianthe said, looking at him with concern. Kalanath's entire body was rigid, his eyes focused on some point beyond Ghrita's head.

"How long ago?" he said.

Ghrita's amused expression softened into something resembling compassion. "The temple war ended five years ago. You were safe to return all that time."

Kalanath turned away, closing his fist on his staff and bowing his head. "Five years," he said. He swept the staff around in an arc that slammed into the bulkhead near Ghrita's face, sending chips of wood flying. *"Five years!"*

No one spoke. Kalanath's shoulders heaved as if he'd run a mile.

Sienne' heart ached for him. Into the silence, Ghrita said, "There's something else. Your mother is alive, Kalanath. I don't know if that makes it better, or worse."

Kalanath's head went up. "Alive?"

"The old divines were afraid to kill a *madhi*. They imprisoned her. She was freed when they were ousted. She has a respected role within the temple at Chirantan, or so they tell me. I've never met her." Ghrita straightened. "I hope you don't think I tell you this as some kind of persuasion to get you to return with me. I think it's kinder for you to know the truth."

"Kinder." Kalanath closed his eyes. "When you know nothing will keep me from the temple now."

"The temple hoped you'd return regardless. I suggested that was optimistic of them. From what I hear, you have no reason to love them, even if the ones who wanted you for breeding purposes are out. So I told them I wasn't going to keep your mother's fate a secret."

"Thank you."

"I didn't do it to be thanked." Ghrita glanced at Alaric, looming nearby. "I don't suppose you're interested in telling me what takes you to Omeira? Given that it certainly has nothing to do with my quest?"

"You're right, we're not interested," Alaric said. "Scrapper business, and none of yours."

"Fair enough." Ghrita approached Kalanath without a trace of fear. "Then I'll ask you straight up—will you come to the temple? Find out what they want of you? I can assure you they won't try to hold you against your will. They learned to their cost five years ago what it means to interfere with a *devesh*."

Kalanath lowered his staff. "I told you, I will go because it is my mother," he said. "That is all."

"That's more than enough." Ghrita made a complicated bow. "With your permission, I'll tell them you're coming. You and your friends—or am I wrong in thinking you won't be separated?"

"Will they allow us into the temple?" Dianthe said.

"The temples of Omeira are sanctuaries for all, even those who are not one with God. There are places you won't be allowed to go, but they will welcome you. As friends of Kalanath, if nothing else."

"We can't stay," Alaric said. "Our journey won't wait."

"As I said, no one will try to stop you leaving." Ghrita turned and walked to her cabin. "I'm relieved to have this off my chest. I didn't relish the idea of finding an appropriate time to tell you. Maybe I should thank Romanus." She disappeared inside the cabin.

Silence fell once more. Finally, Alaric said, "Well. That was unexpected."

"Are you all right?" Sienne asked Kalanath.

He nodded. "My mother is alive," he said. A smile crept across his lips. "I lived with the guilt of killing her—not of killing her, of being why she was killed—for so long, it is like losing a burden I forgot I carried."

"We're so happy for you," Dianthe said, touching his shoulder.

"But we need to decide what to do next," Alaric said.

"I cannot imagine how we can make that decision, absent knowledge of what the divines at the temple intend," Perrin said. "Suppose they wish Kalanath to remain, to fulfil some purpose we cannot know?"

"That's exactly what we need to decide," Alaric said. "Whatever their intent, they likely will want Kalanath to stay, if only to assuage their remaining guilt. I want to know if there's anything about being a *devesh* that might induce you to do as they ask."

Kalanath shook his head. "I feel I do not owe them things. More so now that I know the old divines' treatment of me was not God's will. But they will have knowledge that will help our quest, so maybe what we should ask is, what trade will we allow ourselves to make? If they show us the way to Ma'tzehar in exchange for me?"

"We wouldn't make that deal," Alaric said. "You're one of us, not a bargaining chip."

"I decide, not you, Alaric," Kalanath said. "But I do not think it will come to that. The *nirana*—" he jabbed a finger in the direction of Ghrita's cabin—"said it: interfering with me lost them God's voice for a year. They will not risk it again."

"But they don't have to put pressure on you, they just have to offer you something you want," Sienne pointed out.

"We do not know what that is," Kalanath said, "so I think it is not important to make guesses. But I promise I will not leave you before I have seen this through."

Perrin cleared his throat. "I believe I will petition Averran," he said, "and leave the choice of blessings entirely in his rather crotchety hands. It may give us some better idea of what we are to expect for the coming days."

"The rest of us will leave you to it," Alaric said. "I hate sitting idle, but Captain Talvanus is right that we'd just be in the way above deck."

"Maybe we can help with breakfast," Sienne said. "Or they'll let me use the galley to make our own." Now that the terror of the battle was over, hunger gripped her stomach.

"Coffee," Dianthe moaned. "Why is there never any coffee?"

———

SIENNE STOOD AT THE RAIL SEVEN DAYS LATER, RUNNING HER FINGERS over its rough surface and watching the lights of Chirantan draw nearer. At nearly midnight, there shouldn't have been as many as there were, or at least that would have been the case in Fioretti. Chirantan was big, bigger than Rafellin's capital, and extended far back from the harbor so the lights blended with the skyline and made it seem the stars had fallen to earth, though the lanterns burned gold instead of witchlight blue. No magic in Omeira. It was the strangest notion, making Sienne feel even more alien than just the fact of her being Rafellish.

Her fingers caught on a gouge in the wood, and she picked at it idly, the remnant of a sea serpent attack three days before. It had kept the journey from being monotonous and given them common cause with Ghrita, who until that battle had kept scrupulously to herself. Sienne had felt awkward around her when she wasn't annoyed: awkward because Ghrita had deceived them, annoyed because the woman didn't make a secret of her attraction to Alaric. It wasn't as if it mattered, and jealousy wasn't even on the table, but Ghrita's boldness...yes, she'd stick with "annoyed." Sienne had caught herself acting possessive in response to some comment Ghrita had made, and felt embarrassed at the look Ghrita gave her, amused and slightly pitying as if Sienne weren't mature enough to handle a little friendly competition. Which there wasn't.

"Eager to be off?"

Sienne turned. Talvanus joined her at the rail, her head bare to the night breezes. She found the same gouge Sienne had and ran her fingers across it. "Can't say I'll be glad to see you go, the lot of you. This ship would look far worse if not for your help."

"We saved our own lives as well as yours."

"Still. It's appreciated."

"You're welcome." Sienne gazed out over the distant city again. "We won't go ashore until morning, right?"

"If you want. Chirantan's a deep harbor, and we sail right up to the docks, not like Fioretti, where we have to weigh anchor away from shore. You're like to find inns open even at this hour, but you're welcome to stay aboard until dawn if you'd prefer."

They hadn't mentioned Kalanath's identity, or their destination in Chirantan, to anyone else aboard ship. "I think we'd like that, thanks."

Talvanus nodded and clapped her companionably on the shoulder, then strolled away aft. Sienne cast one last look at Chirantan's warm lights, which gave the illusion of a friendly welcome. Who knew what they'd actually find there? She turned away from the rail and headed for the ladder.

To her surprise, Perrin sat cross-legged outside their cabin, his eyes closed and his hands resting open on his knees. Sienne slowed her steps, not wanting to disturb him, whatever he was doing. A peculiar smile, faint but unmistakably pleased, touched his lips, and as she drew near, it broadened, giving his face such a glow of happiness she felt like an intruder for seeing it.

A board creaked under her foot. She froze. Perrin's eyes opened.

They stared at each other, and Sienne swallowed, searching for something to say. Perrin held up a finger as if to say "wait," and closed his eyes again. Sienne held still, watching Perrin for some evidence that would tell her what he was doing, but his face was still now, with no hint of the pleasure he'd shown before.

Finally, he opened his eyes and stood. "My apologies," he said. "The others are sleeping, and I chose not to disturb them."

"Were you praying? Isn't it a little late for that, even for Averran?"

"I was not. I was in communication with Cressida. For whom it is not so late, given the differences in our respective locations." That smile appeared again, as if Perrin knew a beautiful secret.

"Oh. Is she well?"

"As well as can be expected. My father's men have not appeared, demanding the children's return, and they are settling in with your family quite amicably." The smile became more serious. "I do not think I ever sufficiently thanked you for your intervention on Cressida's behalf."

"You did. But...I hope it helps."

"I am certain it will." Perrin got to his feet. "And what keeps you up so late?"

"Just restless. We're nearly there, and I wanted to see the city. Not that there's much to see in the darkness."

"I, too, am curious about our destination. Until I joined our merry band, I had never been outside Fioretti in my life. This is the farthest I have ever gone from the city of my birth." Perrin gingerly pushed open the door to their cabin. "Morning cannot come soon enough."

Sienne nodded. Stepping carefully over Dianthe, she settled down next to Alaric, who stirred sleepily and put his arm around her. She snuggled in and sighed with pleasure. He gave off a steady warmth that was almost uncomfortable in the muggy confines of their cabin, but it was so nice to be held close she didn't mind.

She'd almost drifted off when a peremptory knock sounded at the door. Alaric's arm over her tensed. "What is it?" he said.

"Captain asks you join her on deck," a voice said. "Someone's waiting on you."

"What?" Alaric rolled to his feet and opened the door as their companions stirred around them. "Who, someone?"

The sailor licked his lips nervously, his gaze shifting from Alaric to Sienne and away again. "Someone important, belike. A whole procession, with lanterns and bells and things."

"You mean at the docks?" Alaric turned away from the sailor to face the others. "Would the temple know we were coming just at this moment?"

"We do not know what Ghrita told them," Kalanath said, "or what they may have seen in vision. It is possible." He yawned. "Though I do not like that they do not give us sleep."

"Me neither." Alaric faced the sailor again. "Tell the captain we'll be up shortly."

Sienne raked through her hair with her fingers and stood. "Should we tell Ghrita?"

"Ghrita knows," Ghrita said, appearing in the doorway. "I didn't expect a welcoming party."

"Who is it?" Dianthe said. "The temple?"

"Yes. At least, I assume so. And no, I don't know why they couldn't wait until morning."

"I think to tell them to wait," Kalanath said. "I do not like this. It is like they say, you there, it is our time you must wait on."

"Let's at least see who they've sent," Alaric said. "We don't have to go with them, if that's what they want."

They made their way up on deck to find the lights of the city much closer and brighter, some of them as large as bonfires. Those burned high in the air, making Sienne wonder about the towers, invisible in the darkness, they must surely be at the top of. She trailed after Alaric, who strode to where Talvanus stood watching the fast-approaching docks. "Who *are* you people?" she said. "I've never received a sending from an Omeiran divine before. 'The scrappers,' it said, like that was some kind of royal title. And that's a delegation from the temple, or I miss my guess. Right where we're intended to dock."

She pointed at one of the docks. A handful of figures waited there, unmoving, beside a curtained palanquin from whose corners large bells hung, sending the faintest of tinkling sounds across the water. Two of the figures carried flambeaux that cast a flickering glow over the scene and turned the figures' dark robes orange. They were too distant to make out more than that, but Sienne felt certain every one of them was staring at the approaching ship.

"Divines," Kalanath said. "Of the highest rank."

"How can you tell?" Dianthe asked.

Kalanath gestured with his staff. "They wear the robe of the first circle...dark green, or midnight blue, I cannot tell. I do not recognize any of them."

"I wonder who is in the palanquin," Ghrita said. "Surely the Hierarch wouldn't come to you? That would be a bit much."

"Who is the Hierarch now?"

"Chakhran Ririkhariyaa."

Kalanath stiffened. "That is a name I know."

"He wasn't consenting to your treatment, Kalanath. He wouldn't still have authority if he did."

"I do not remember that. I remember him giving me a cup to drink before my visions." Kalanath shook his head as if to dislodge a memory. "I do not trust him."

Ghrita shrugged. "You're the one who would know. I wasn't in Chirantan at the time."

"You continue to sound as if the things of your faith matter little to you," Perrin said. "What kind of *nirana* does that make you?"

She smiled. "One who is free to be the temple's left hand in matters of faith. My beliefs are secure enough—that is, those of the *nirana* are secure enough—that we are trusted not to become... corrupted...by your heathen religion. And yet your divines and priests clearly have access to God's power, though you go about it wrongly. The temples wish to understand this better. For me, it means I have a certain flexibility of understanding that most of the divines of Omeira struggle with. I assure you, my devotion to God is undeviating."

Perrin smiled back, shaking his head. "As is mine. I find it curious that God should allow our understanding, so very different, to end in the same results."

"It's not something I understand well myself. *Nirana* are taught to fight so they may defend the temple in times of anarchy, which happens occasionally. Matters of religious doctrine above the general don't much concern us. You should ask the divines—they'd welcome a chance to set you on the right path." Ghrita smiled and winked.

Kalanath had continued to watch the men—it was all men, Sienne could now see—waiting for them. All but one looked like the Omeirans Sienne was familiar with from Fioretti: dark skin, copper-rust hair, high cheekbones and narrow eyes. The one exception had black hair rather than red, but still looked recognizably Omeiran. Three of them were portly, one almost gaunt, but all six of them stood as proud as kings, their heads held high, their faces expressionless.

Sienne looked at Kalanath. His face was as still as theirs, making him look more fiercely handsome than ever, like a ruling duke about to receive a royal delegation. He seemed so much a stranger Sienne reached out to him, touching his hand.

He jerked, and turned toward her, the spell broken. "Are you afraid?" she said in a low voice.

"Yes. And no. They will not hurt me, but this..." He gestured at the waiting delegation. "This, I do not understand. I do not know what they want of me. And that makes me afraid."

"We'll stand by you, whatever happens."

He smiled, a strained expression. "I count on it."

The helmswoman brought the *Wave's Crest* neatly to the dock, barely bumping against it. Sienne heard the captain's commands to weigh anchor and other nautical things in a daze, her attention entirely on the men waiting to receive them. One of the sailors flung the rope ladder over the side. Kalanath moved toward it, but Alaric intercepted him. "I don't want you to be the first one down," he said. "I'll go first, and you can follow. Sienne, you go last, and be prepared for treachery."

"I promise there's no danger," Ghrita said.

"I believe you. But we haven't survived this long without taking precautions." Alaric slung his leg over the side and descended the ladder. Sienne opened her spellbook to *fury* and watched him go, her heart in her throat. If they were wrong...

The divines had been watching the ship's rail where they all stood. When Alaric began his descent, all of them shifted, drew closer together like a flock of dark geese huddling against the storm, and began muttering words too low for Sienne to make out other than that they were speaking Meiric. Alaric reached the dock and took a couple of steps toward them, making them back up into the palanquin. Ghrita, alighting shortly after him, held out her hands in placation and said in Meiric, *"He is the devesh's bodyguard. Show respect."*

Sienne stifled a grin at Alaric's sudden elevation. He'd probably think it a fine joke, given that Kalanath was a deadly fighter who had no need of a bodyguard. She watched all her friends climb down the ladder, then released her spellbook and followed. The thought of using *float* or *jaunt* occurred to her, and she as quickly dismissed it. No magic in Omeira meant these men were likely not used to seeing it done casually, and they seemed nervous enough that she didn't want to push.

When she reached the bottom, sweating and cursing whoever had invented the rope ladder, one of the divines, his rust-red hair falling in a long tail to the middle of his back, had approached Kalanath and stood a few feet from him, his hands pressed palms-together in front of his chest. *"Lord,"* he said in Meiric, *"welcome home. I am Banu Sarvejvaan. We are honored by your presence."*

"Thank you," Kalanath said in the same language. *"Though I'm not sure why this couldn't wait until morning."*

The divine, Banu, bowed his head low. *"We are an honor guard for someone who did not wish to wait to greet you,"* he said, gesturing at the palanquin.

Sienne, standing next to Kalanath, saw him swallow. *"Who...?"* he said, but even Sienne could guess the answer.

The black-haired divine parted the palanquin's curtains, and a woman stepped out. Her red hair was cropped as short as Kalanath's, but even without that detail, the resemblance was uncanny. Kalanath took an involuntary step forward, and said, *"Mother."*

7

"*Oh, my dear,*" the woman said, reaching out to Kalanath. Kalanath hesitated, then with a few quick steps caught the woman up in his arms. Sienne found herself blinking back tears and wiped them away. Kalanath said something Sienne couldn't hear, and the woman laughed, sounding as though she were crying at the same time.

Eventually, Kalanath let her go, but remained at her side, holding her hand. It hadn't been obvious how very small she was until she stood next to her son, who wasn't a tall man, but towered over her. She had the same calm presence Sienne was used to seeing in her friend Octavian, a divine of Kitane and someone obviously touched by the avatar. She also looked far too young to be the mother of someone Kalanath's age, which made Sienne wonder for the first time how young the temples allowed women to become *madhis*, sacred vessels for God's presence.

"Mother, these are my friends," Kalanath said, guiding her to stand near them. He spoke in clearly articulated Fellic, enunciating even more carefully than he usually did. "Alaric, Sienne, Dianthe, and Perrin. We are companions."

Kalanath's mother bowed her head briefly. "It good is, it is that

Kalanath has friends," she said in heavily accented Fellic. "Thank you. Please to me call Manisha."

"We're glad to see you reunited. Together," Alaric amended when a look of puzzlement crossed her face at "reunited."

"*Kalanath has fought beside us often,*" Sienne said in Meiric. "*He has saved our lives.*"

Manisha's face brightened. "*You speak Meiric very well.*"

"*Sienne studied languages in Rafellin,*" Kalanath said. "*I'm afraid the others don't speak it at all.*"

"*There are enough divines who speak Fellic, I'm sure they won't have any trouble communicating,*" Manisha said. "*I'm sorry we disturbed your rest, but I couldn't bear to wait until morning.*"

"*I feel the same,*" Kalanath said, and hugged her again, making her cry once more.

Alaric's hand fell on Sienne's shoulder. "What are they saying?" he murmured.

"Just greetings. Introductions." Sienne felt awkward witnessing this reunion, so long delayed. It didn't seem like the sort of thing that required witnesses. She noted with some satisfaction that the divines looked as uncomfortable as she felt.

Finally, Manisha wiped her eyes and said, "We do not know you have friends. The temple will make room."

"Oh, we couldn't impose," Dianthe began.

Manisha shook her head. "Not impose," she said. "We owe you. They will make room." Her words had the finality of someone pronouncing a great doom. Sienne caught the glances the divines gave each other and concluded the temple would not find it easy to "make room." That satisfied her too. Maybe the ones who'd hurt Kalanath weren't in power anymore, but he'd been in unnecessary exile for five years and she felt that was due some consideration.

Manisha climbed into the palanquin without assistance and gestured to the black-haired divine to tie the curtains back. "*Manisha, it's not seemly,*" he protested.

"*I don't care about seemly. I want to see my son.*" She glared at the man, who, to Sienne's surprise, didn't look cowed. Instead, he smiled, an expression of startling tenderness that came and went so swiftly Sienne doubted having seen it, and fastened the drapes to leave the palanquin open on one side. "*Walk with me,*" she told Kalanath.

"We will go to the temple," Kalanath said to the others. "The divines walk before and after, as an honor."

"They don't have you ride?" Dianthe asked.

"It is for the *madhis* to ride, as God's vessels. We are not God, but Her servants, so we walk." Kalanath gestured. "I mean the we that belongs to the temple. I do not know why I think myself one of them. Because I am not."

"In a sense, we are all God's servants," Perrin said. "Lead on. I find myself curious about this temple."

The divine Banu bowed to Manisha, then strode to the head of the palanquin and said a few words to the bearers. They lifted the palanquin smoothly, as if they had one of Perrin's mind-linking blessings, and set off down the docks. The bells made a sweetly musical sound that almost made sense as a melody. Sienne trailed a few steps behind Kalanath, who walked next to his mother. Alaric walked beside Sienne. "Tired?" he asked in a low voice.

"I'm too excited to be tired. Excited and a little worried. They aren't expecting us."

"Yes, and I hate not knowing what to expect from them. But we could hardly let Kalanath go alone, and take rooms in the city."

"No." Sienne breathed in the warm, damp air. "This place even smells foreign. Exotic." The docks were quiet at this hour, with only one other ship unloading its cargo a few piers away, but the still air hummed with the distant sounds of the city. The scent of cedar and cinnamon and something else Sienne didn't recognize overlaid the ordinary smells of the docks, warm, wet wood and bitter tar and the constant salt air. Even the lanterns were different: fire rather than magic, true, but the lantern glass had a reddish tinge to it that gave the light an orange glow Rafellish lights lacked. Sienne gazed at a lamp burning above a sign that read HARBOR MASTER and silently wished Talvanus a safe journey.

The divines guided the palanquin through darkened streets

Sienne would have called slums if they'd been in Fioretti. Despite their location, they didn't speed up, which was fortunate because the procession was already traveling at a rapid pace. She guessed people in Chirantan were as reluctant to assault a divine as anywhere else, and a *madhi* even less so. The divines certainly didn't behave as if they were worried.

Sienne eyed the falling-down huts, the gaping holes where doors should have been, and gasped when she saw eyes looking back at her. In the next instant, they were gone, but she edged closer to Alaric anyway. There was no reason to think they might be attacked, but she'd been a scrapper long enough to know one didn't take chances.

The huts became sturdier as they walked, and gained doors and fresher paint. A stray dog, thin enough its ribs were visible, trotted out from between two of them and shied at seeing the procession pass. One of the divines peeled away from the pack and approached it, holding out his hand. The dog whined and sniffed it, and then Sienne was past and afraid to turn and watch further, in case she stumbled and fell. Shortly, the divine trotted past and took up his position again. Strange, but nothing she could investigate.

She fell to watching the black-haired divine, who walked just ahead of Kalanath, his left hand resting on the palanquin's roof. He was tall and muscular and looked more like a warrior than a divine. A temple *nirana*, perhaps? He, unlike the others, was alert to the possibility of an attack, his eyes constantly scanning his surroundings. And yet he wasn't easily spooked; when a pair of birds winged past overhead, calling to each other in high, croaking tones, he didn't flinch at all.

The road opened up ahead of them, wide enough to allow three palanquins to travel side by side, so abruptly it felt like entering another city. All Sienne could see of her surroundings were high, pale walls and doors outlined with dark mosaic tiles that were shades of gold and orange in the light of the flambeaux and the occasional tinted flame of hanging lanterns. Arches rose overhead, crossing the wide street, and Sienne heard the rushing sound of flowing water that grew louder every time they passed beneath an arch. No one was abroad at this hour but them. It felt like a dream world, as if all the people were hovering just out of sight, ready to emerge when the divines were gone.

Ahead, a larger building became visible, its domed roof a white bubble against the black sky. Torches burned around the building's square foundation, illuminating the many arched doorways leading to its interior. Sitting atop the dome was a short tower open to the sky where a bonfire burned with a strange blue-tinted light. Sienne was sure it wasn't magic even from this distance, but she didn't know what else might cause the effect—tainted wood, perhaps?

The bearers brought the palanquin to one of these doors, and the black-haired divine helped Manisha to stand. Manisha extended her hand to Kalanath. *"Come with me."*

"This is the temple," Kalanath said to the others. "I think they will find us room."

Sienne followed Kalanath and Manisha, resisting the urge to take Alaric's hand. If they were actually walking into a trap, he'd need his hands free. The divines hadn't insisted the companions disarm, which meant...what? That the temple trusted them? Or that the divines had resources for defending themselves that the companions couldn't fight? It left Sienne wondering, again, what kind of place they'd come to.

She heard water again, this time the bubbling sound of a fountain, as they came through the doorway into a lush garden that smelled of green growing things. The fountain sat at its center, spraying water high into the air that caught the torchlight and sparkled like tinted diamonds. Benches surrounded the fountain and were placed here and there elsewhere in the garden. It would be beautiful to sit in, cool and shady in the heat of true summer.

Manisha skirted the garden and led the way around it to a pillared, covered walkway that ran along three sides of the garden courtyard. Her feet, Sienne realized, were bare. Another reason she couldn't have walked. Her feet made no noise against the stone of the walkway. Sienne cast a last glance at the garden as they went through an archway and proceeded deeper into the temple.

She lost track of where she was as they took turn after turn. Was it intentional? Not to deceive specifically them—she didn't think Manisha would bring them all this way just to deceive them now—but on the part of the temple's builders. Would there be a need to keep enemies confused if they infiltrated this far? It reminded her of how little she knew about Omeira. The *rakhyans* weren't always comfortable allies, but she'd thought that enmity didn't extend to the temples. Maybe she was wrong.

They took another turn, and the hall ended at a room big enough to hold all of them comfortably, including the six divines, who'd kept pace with them. The room was empty of furniture except for a padded kneeler against one wall beneath a large stained glass window. Two torches burned on opposite walls, barely illuminating the window, and Sienne couldn't make out its subject. A man, his red hair streaked with white, knelt facing the window, which put his back to them. He raised his head when they entered, but didn't rise.

"*Chakhran,*" Manisha said, "*I have returned.*"

"*I saw it in vision,*" the man said. He stood and turned, and Sienne held in a gasp. His eyelids were sunken, clearly empty, and a long scar from the crest of his cheekbone to his jaw dragged down his mouth on the left side. "*Kalanath Oushikdali. Welcome home.*" He bowed, his arms spread to the sides and his head lowered.

Kalanath looked profoundly uncomfortable. "*Chakhran,*" he said. "*I don't wish to be rude, but this is not my home.*"

"*We can argue semantics later. We are simply very grateful you have chosen to return.*" Chakhran straightened, turning his head as if listening. "You have friends, not Omeirans," he said in unaccented Fellic. "They, I have seen as well. Be welcome, friends of Kalanath."

"Thank you," Alaric said.

Chakhran smiled. "You do not trust us. That is reasonable. We have done nothing to earn your trust. Allow us to host you this night, and we will discuss further in the morning your reasons for coming to Chirantan."

A mutter went up from the divines. Manisha said, "There are guest places, yes?"

"Indeed," Chakhran said. "Banu, take our guests to the visitors' chambers. Ghrita, stay. I would speak with you before you retire."

"I will stay with my friends," Kalanath said.

Manisha made a pained noise. *"You don't have to,"* she began.

"I'm not comfortable being on my own here, Mother," Kalanath said. *"Just for tonight."*

"It's not an insult, Manisha," the black-haired divine said, touching her hand.

Manisha nodded. *"Tomorrow, then. We will have breakfast together."*

"Of course," Kalanath said, hugging her once more.

Banu gestured to Alaric. "This way," he said, surprising Sienne with his sudden acquisition of Fellic, and led them back through the door and into the maze of twisty passages. This time, it ended at a sparsely decorated room that reminded Sienne of their sitting room in Fioretti, though the two couldn't be more dissimilar in décor. It was furnished with chairs and a couple of long, low sofas with strangely curving backs, a table surrounded by cushions, and two mirrors that reflected one another's images into infinity.

Three doors led off the room, and Banu opened one of them to reveal two thick pallets on the floor, each big enough to hold three people, piled high with blankets and more cushions. "Be welcome," he said in his soft tenor, almost high enough to be a woman's voice. "Food will be brought in the morning." He bowed, the slightest inclination of his head, and left.

Alaric set his bags down in one corner of the bedroom, and Sienne quickly followed suit. "This is nice," she said.

"Pretty enough," Alaric said. "Are there enough beds?"

The other two doors led to bedrooms with two pallets each. Dianthe sank onto one and began removing her boots. "Finally, I won't keep the rest of you up with my snoring," she said. "I'm suddenly very tired."

"As am I," Perrin said. "Tired enough that even my curiosity about this place is blunted."

"Sleep, then, and we'll see what the morning brings," Alaric said.

The pallet was as comfortable as a mattress, though it felt odd having the ceiling so far away. Sienne snuggled up to Alaric and said, "You don't really think we're in danger here, do you?"

"No. But I'm reserving judgment until we learn what they want from Kalanath." Alaric put his arms around her and drew her close. "And I wonder about that black-haired divine."

"You mean, how he's acting like Manisha's lover? Do they let *madhis* have lovers?"

"I wouldn't know. I just don't want Kalanath upset."

"Me neither." Sienne yawned. "More things to find out in the morning."

———

THE WINDOWS IN THE BEDCHAMBERS WERE COVERED, NOT LETTING IN any light, but Sienne woke to some internal signal that told her dawn had come. A little fumbling revealed a long cord that shifted wooden shutters and let her see the morning sky. It looked just the same as the one over Fioretti. Maybe there was symbolism in that, but she didn't care enough to ferret it out.

She left Alaric sleeping and went barefoot into the sitting room, where the pale light of dawn filtered through two windows high in the ceiling. The room smelled dusty, as if it weren't often used. She explored the space—it didn't take long—and opened the main door to see if morning made any difference to her being able to tell where in the temple they were. It didn't.

She closed the door and went back to Alaric's side, sliding in next to him and lying on her back, staring up at the distant ceiling. There were pictures painted on it, a garden scene with animals of every kind and a few Sienne was sure were mythical. No people, which wasn't unusual. She'd learned in school that Omeirans didn't go in for depicting people in their art.

Beside her, Alaric stirred. "That door doesn't have a lock on it, does it?" he murmured.

"I don't think I'd be comfortable having sex in a temple, even if it did."

Alaric slid his hand beneath her shirt, stroking her skin. "If Kalanath is right, they have sex here all the time. It's a holy act."

"Only for the *madhis*." She rolled on her side to face him and traced the outline of his eyebrow and cheek. "I wonder how old Manisha is."

"Meaning, how young do they start? I'm trying not to be judgmental."

"Me, too."

Alaric kissed her. "Just so you know I wanted to, because you're beautiful and desirable, and I love sharing your bed."

"Mmm. Now I'm wondering about the possibility of barring that door."

The sound of the outer door opening made them both freeze. Alaric smiled and kissed her again, lightly this time. "Breakfast," he said as the smells of hot bread and cheese and an unfamiliar aroma wafted through their door. He rolled to his feet and gave Sienne a hand up before opening the door.

In the outer room, two women with trays were arranging food on the low table, under Manisha's watchful eye. Sienne wasn't sure if she was supposed to bow to the *madhi*, so she settled for a respectful nod. Manisha returned the gesture. *"You are together,"* she said, gesturing at Alaric.

"We are," Sienne said, feeling unexpectedly defensive, though Manisha's words hadn't sounded critical.

"He's the biggest man I've ever seen, and the palest. Where is he from?"

"Ansorja."

"Astonishing." In Fellic, she said, "I am sorry to speak wrong. In Meiric, I mean. My Fellic is not good, but I will try."

"Thank you," Alaric said. "I'm afraid most of us don't speak any Meiric."

Sienne went to the other doors and knocked. "Some of us aren't usually early risers, either. What's that delicious smell?"

"Flat breads, and soft cheese. Fruit. And tea." Manisha sat on one of the cushions and poured out a thin dark stream of liquid into a small cup with no handle.

"I've heard of it. Some of the nobles in the capital drink it. It's not as popular as coffee." Sienne accepted the cup and inhaled deeply. "It smells good."

Manisha poured another cup and handed it to Alaric just as Kalanath emerged, his red hair disordered from sleep. She smiled broadly. "Sit, my son. Eat. You do not rise so early as you did before."

"I usually wait for Sienne to make breakfast," Kalanath said. "It is a habit."

"Sienne is you, yes?" Manisha said to Sienne. "I will learn names. Sienne, and Alaric."

"Dianthe and Perrin," Kalanath added.

Perrin came to the door, his eyes squinted nearly shut. "That is a lovely smell, though it is not blessed coffee," he said. "I believe I will try it."

"It will do you good to develop a new vice," Alaric said with a grin.

Sienne spread soft cheese over a round of bread and took a bite. It was tangy and smooth and delicious. "Dianthe, have some of this," she said, preparing another round and handing it to her friend. Dianthe folded it in half around the cheese and took a large bite, nodding her thanks.

They ate in companionable silence for a while. Sienne was just trying to decide what of all her questions she wanted to ask first when Alaric said, "Chakhran is the Hierarch?"

Manisha nodded. "He wants to speak with you today. All of you. I do not know what he sees in vision."

"He will not keep me here," Kalanath said.

Manisha's eyes widened. "No. Not ever. You may leave—but you will not leave, yes?"

Kalanath put his hand over hers. "No. I mean, yes, I must leave, but—"

"*No.* You were gone so long, I do not know if you live, Kalanath. You cannot go."

Kalanath looked uncomfortable. "We came to Omeira seeking knowledge," Alaric said. "Kalanath is part of that quest."

"We will talk about it later," Kalanath said. "I will not go forever, if I go."

Sienne almost protested that "if," but managed to say nothing. Manisha looked to be on the verge of tears. "So much has changed, my son. The ones who hurt you, they are gone. You not have afraid— not fear. They respect you."

"I believe you," Kalanath said. "It is not they that will keep me gone."

"And I..." Manisha's voice trailed off. "I do not stay the same. I am free to..." She withdrew her hand from his and clasped her hands in her lap. "Chakhran helped me. It was a thing I wished, that the divines say is not to be. The old divines. They thought you were..." She scowled, and switched to Meiric. *"The old divines believed you were born of God's will. That not knowing who fathered you was what made you a devesh. I have never believed this."*

Kalanath went still. "What are you saying?"

"You saw him last night. The man who stood with me. Vaishant Dakhshavaan." Manisha drew in a deep breath. "He is your father."

8

Kalanath's eyes went wide. "My..." He swallowed. "How can you know?"

"It is in vision. I wish to know..." Manisha took Kalanath's unre-sisting hand. "A *devesh* has two parents. They give me respect because I am a *madhi*, but what of the other? He is respect—has respect too. And you were lost to me. I think it will you bring back in a small way."

"That is the why," Kalanath said. "But not the how."

Manisha nodded. "I ask this many times of the old divines and they say, it is not a thing to do. But they do not ask God, they only use their own minds. I ask Chakhran, he say, I will ask. And God tells him."

Kalanath still looked as if he'd been struck by his own staff. "Who is he? *Nirana? Rakhyanam?*"

"He was no one of power. A trader of things. Devout in his worship. He became a priest, and later a divine of the temple in Abhisok, after your birth." Manisha smiled in reflection. "I remem-bered him. I do not remember all the men, but some are different. And he remembered me."

"Of course he did," Sienne said without thinking, and Manisha's smile broadened.

"A man visits the *madhi* rarely, and they do not choose which," she said. "It is to keep them from...so they do not confuse the *madhi* with the woman. Falling into error. We are God's vessels and not women. But we, the *madhis*, we see, and we judge. Vaishant was different. His need—that is another, we do not ask what the men want of God that they approach the *madhi*—I remembered that he was sad, and he touch me like he will lose me. I do not forget this. His name mean nothing to me, when Chakhran say it, but when I see his face, it returns."

"And he is part of the temple now," Kalanath said.

"He come to Chirantan after we find him. A divine, like the others. But he is father to the *devesh* and worthy of respect because he is God's will in flesh, like me. Like you." Manisha drew in a deep breath. "And he and I are one."

Kalanath's eyes widened. "But you are *madhi*."

"The old divines say it is not for me to be God's vessel to men when I have borne the *devesh*. I do not be *madhi* while you are here— I am *madhi* still—" She scowled, and switched to Meiric. "*I am still a madhi, but I do not welcome supplicants to my bed, not since I gave birth. Being your mother is how I am God's vessel, which is why I am madhi. Do you understand?*" In Fellic, she added, "Chakhran say I can choose, and I find in me a desire for one man. It is a pull, here." She put her free hand over her heart. "It is that two of us make one—make you, Kalanath—and I wish to know my other part."

"But...he might have been anyone. Might have married and had a family. Mother—" Kalanath sounded plaintive, like someone reaching for meaning in the midst of confusion.

"I think only to meet him. To tell him of you. Also to know what man is he. I do not think we are to be one." She smiled again, that same peaceful, reflective smile. "*Madhis* do not love men, they love God. I do not expect—did not expect love. But Vaishant is one it is easy to love. You will see."

Kalanath swallowed. "How long?"

"Nearly four years."

"So you have not been alone."

"No, my son, I am not alone."

Kalanath nodded. "Then I am grateful to him in that." He still looked stunned, and Sienne's heart went out to him.

"You will meet him later. First Chakhran will speak to you. All of you," Manisha said. "I do not know what he see in vision, but he say it is important."

"He saw *us* in vision?" Alaric said. He set his teacup down with a *tink*. It looked tiny in his massive hands. "Why would he even think to look for us there?"

Manisha shrugged. "I do not know the mind of the Hierarch. Because he cannot see with eyes he sees most in mind—in vision. I do not think he sees you all, just Kalanath, because we he did not tell to expect more. But that was yesterday. Today, who knows?"

"Then let's not delay any longer," Alaric said, rising. "Will you take us to him?"

"*Not* right away," Dianthe said. "I want to at least wash my face, and relieve myself. Are there facilities, Manisha?"

Manisha looked puzzled, so Sienne repeated the request in Meiric. "Of course," Manisha said. "Back this way."

There was a little room, just off the hall outside their quarters, with a tiled floor and a seat with a hole in it. Manisha showed them how to pump water into a pitcher and then pour it into the hole after relieving themselves. Sienne took her turn with some bemusement. Where did it all go? It didn't smell as awful as the privies of Fioretti, but it had to go *somewhere*, and that place probably stank to the skies.

She wished she had something nice to change into for meeting the Hierarch, but had to settle for wearing the cleaner of her two shirts and brushing her boots until they shone. Alaric picked up his sword and examined the flat of the blade. He sheathed it and set it aside. "I don't think they mind if you go armed," Sienne said.

"I'm pretty sure those *niranas* could give me a fight regardless," Alaric said. "But the sword changes the tone of the discussion. And my instincts tell me we're not in any danger."

"I'm not leaving my spellbook."

"Your spellbook isn't a purely offensive weapon. I don't think you should."

The others had spruced up as best they were able. Dianthe had also left her sword in her room. Kalanath gripped his staff as if it were all that stood between him and a watery death. Manisha stood when Alaric and Sienne entered, and said, "You do not fear. Chakhran is a good man."

"I'm sure he is," Alaric said.

Sienne, watching Kalanath, wasn't sure Kalanath agreed with this. Chakhran, Sienne recalled, had been among those who had participated in Kalanath's vision, the one that had been flawed. Yet Ghrita had said he hadn't consented to the old divines' plan to breed Kalanath like a prize dog. Sienne felt nervous on Kalanath's behalf. It had to feel a little like walking back into the lion's den.

Manisha led them through the windowless passages, which didn't look any different in daytime. If she had to live here, Sienne was sure she'd completely lose track of time. The air was silent, dry, and odorless, and made Sienne's skin feel parched. When they emerged from the passages into the pillared walkway surrounding the garden, she breathed in the moist air with relief.

The garden was even more beautiful in daylight than she'd imagined. Cypress trees like living pillars cast narrow shadows across the short grass, sheltering benches and throwing stripes of darkness over the bubbling fountain. The water in its shallow, broad basin rippled with the spray from the trumpet perched atop its tall spire and made Sienne think longingly of a bath.

Aside from themselves, the garden was empty. Manisha gestured at the benches. "Sit," she said. "Chakhran joins us soon."

Sienne crossed to the fountain and breathed in the cool mist. It was only an hour or so after sunrise, but the air was already warm, and the cloudless sky hinted at a scorcher of a day. "Where is everyone?" she asked.

"The *niranas* practice," Manisha said. "The *madhis* prepare for the day. The divines pray."

"The garden is for meditation after noon," Kalanath said. "For when it is hottest."

"Perhaps not the best place for it," a voice said. Chakhran walked toward them, unaccompanied, avoiding benches and trees as if he could see them. His sunken eyes were two pools of shadow. "There are many distractions. I was taught, when I was young, that learning to ignore distractions brought one closer to God, but I wonder now if God does not give us the world to see what we will dismiss as mere distractions." He found his way to the fountain and swished his hand in the water, then sniffed it, and smiled. "Like this fountain. I can still remember how beautiful it is, even thirty years from the last time I saw it."

"You've been blind thirty years?" Sienne asked.

"Thirty-two this winter." Chakhran reached out and put his hand on her arm, gently feeling his way to her shoulder. "You are the wizard."

"Yes. Did you...see me in vision?"

"I feel the strap of your spellbook," Chakhran said with another smile. "Please, all of you, make yourselves comfortable." He settled cross-legged on the ground beside the fountain. Sienne sat next to Alaric on a bench and tried not to fidget. Chakhran's stillness made her feel as if even normal movement was manic. She ran her fingers over the cool marble and stilled her tapping foot.

"You have been companions—that is the term, yes?—for over a year," Chakhran said. "Companions, and friends."

"We have," Kalanath said, glancing at Alaric, who made no move to speak.

"And before that, Kalanath, you supported yourself alone," Chakhran said.

"I had to." Kalanath's reply was curt, and he looked everywhere but at Chakhran.

"You resent me," Chakhran said.

"You were there, and did nothing," Kalanath said. "I do not see why I should trust you."

"Kalanath," Manisha began.

"It is fair, Manisha," Chakhran said. "He was kept uninformed then. Do you wish to know the truth now?"

"What truth?" Kalanath said.

"The word of God about Her *devesh* is written in many places," Chakhran said. "It is not long. It says the *devesh* is Her voice to Her people and explains what must be done to hear that voice. We followed that instruction, and received revelation we could not understand. The Hierarch at the time believed this was because the *devesh* was tainted. There was disagreement on this point. Some of us, myself included, believed it was we who were unworthy. We were in the minority, and the Hierarch devised the plan to create more *deveshi* by force."

"I know this."

"What you do not know is that your escape had our help. It was not a perfect plan. We could not simply spirit you away, and when you were nearly caught, we could not justify allowing Manisha to escape with you. And we did not expect God to turn Her face from us regardless. But we did our best. And when it became clear that God's displeasure had fallen on us, we took advantage of the turmoil to reveal what the Hierarch had intended for you—a thing that never had the support of most of the divines. He was ousted, and we set about regaining God's favor."

"And you gained power."

"Be respectful, Kalanath," Manisha warned.

"He has a point," Chakhran said. "I was associated with those who tried to thwart God's will. How did I end up in power when the others were dismissed?" He folded his hands in his lap. "We always leave it to God to choose Her Hierarch. I cannot reveal the nature of that choosing, because it is sacred, but every divine witnessed my calling. I assure you, it was not something I sought."

"So how much of my life was false?" Kalanath exclaimed, rising from his seat. "The rules that bound me, the foods I ate and the lessons I learned—"

"All prescribed by God, not by man," Chakhran said. "I can show you where it is written. But those rules did not make you a *devesh*. You would have been a *devesh* had you lived your entire life outside the temple. That was the thing we did not understand—that God's word for you was meant to guide you, not to create something that already existed. I am sorry we did not understand that before."

"I have a father."

"You do. He is a good man."

Kalanath resumed his seat. "I will not stay."

Manisha gasped.

"This I have seen in vision," Chakhran said. "You have far to go before you regain your home. You seek Ma'tzehar."

Alaric shifted. "You've seen that?" he asked. "How much have you seen, I wonder?"

"More than you suspect." Chakhran leaned forward and rested his hands on his knees. "Enough to know you are not human."

Sienne sucked in a startled breath. Alaric went very still. "You are close enough," Chakhran went on, "and your desires and regrets are all very human. But you are shadowed by the creature that is your other self. Don't be afraid. I have no intention of telling anyone."

Sienne couldn't help stealing a glance at Manisha. She looked placid, not shocked or horrified. Did she lack the language skills to know what Chakhran had said, or was she already aware of the truth?

"You have the advantage of me," Alaric said. "That's not something I share with everyone."

"It was not something I sought out," Chakhran said, "or at any rate, I did not descend into vision in search of secrets I could hold over you. I believe God gave me that vision so I would not treat your quest lightly. You seek to free your people, and you believe Ma'tzehar is the key to that freedom. And you intend to ask our help in finding it."

Sienne stared at Alaric. His expression was unreadable, the way it got when he was thinking hard about a problem. "We'd intended to search for Ma'tzehar ourselves," he said, "but that was before you people tracked Kalanath down. Now..." He narrowed his eyes in thought. "You seem to know everything else—tell me why we're after Ma'tzehar at all."

"The temple," Chakhran said promptly. "You believe the key to the ritual you seek is in the temple in Ma'tzehar."

Alaric nodded. "Are we right that the city still exists?"

"It certainly exists. Finding it is difficult for those not of the temple. Reaching it is even more so. But it exists." Chakhran frowned. "Scrying for it is pointless, as there are no landmarks to identify its location. And queries about it tend to fail."

"Why is that?" Dianthe asked.

"It is under a doom," Chakhran said, as casually as if she'd asked about the weather. "We believe God wanted it to disappear. Mahem-netzehar, as it once was, defied God, and was punished."

"I read that the city was once the jewel of Omeira," Sienne said.

"That may or may not be true. I suspect that legend has its roots in the human tendency to romanticize the past. But it was definitely a powerful city."

"Then...is it true there were wizards there?"

"That, we also have no knowledge of. Omeira has no wizards."

"I don't understand that," Sienne said. "Wizards are born, not made. How could Omeira happen to be the one place in the world that doesn't have them?"

"I have no answer for you. When a child is born, we petition God for a blessing upon it, and among the things we ask is that it be free from corruption—that is, anything that might keep it from being one with God. Magic is one of those things. And no Omeiran child has ever been touched by magic." He inclined his head in her direction. "I mean no offense. We do not consider it evil, just not for us."

"I see," Sienne said, though she was a little offended. "So this blessing...removes magic from a child who might otherwise be a wizard?"

"Perhaps. We have never asked God the details." Chakhran tilted his head in Perrin's direction. "You, priest. You have been silent this whole time. Nothing to say?"

Perrin stirred. "I did not believe," he said, "my contribution was needed. God speaks to you in ways different than She does to me."

"And yet you believe they are the same God."

"I see no reason to doubt it. No one has ever claimed God was twofold."

"And yet you worship Her in human form. That seems contradictory." Chakhran's lips curved in a slight smile.

"It is your temple we sit in," Perrin said. "Far be it from me to challenge you on your beliefs in this place."

"But...?"

"But I, too, have heard the voice of God, as She speaks to us through Her avatars. I am not wise enough to know why She chooses to speak with you directly. But I will not deny the evidence of my own mind and my own ears. I have hope that one day I may understand more."

"Well said. Give me your name. My visions did not reveal such."

"Perrin Delucco."

"Perrin Delucco, we do not understand the mysteries of God either. Our tradition is that speaking with God through an intermediary diminishes Her blessings, but what I have seen of you suggests that this tradition is...incomplete." Chakhran smiled again. "Is it true you chose God over your family?"

Perrin's face went rigid. "That is an oversimplification that is nevertheless true."

"Then I hope She blesses you for your sacrifice." Chakhran let out a breath in a long, slow hiss, and fell silent. The burbling of the fountain filled the stillness. Sienne shifted her weight, and rested one hand on Alaric's knee. The sun had risen high enough to shine into her eyes, and she blinked and looked away. No one spoke. She felt as if they were waiting for something, some response from Chakhran that would shape everything that came next.

"I will give you guides, to take you to Ma'tzehar," Chakhran finally said. "And to make sure you survive the journey. The desert is not a gentle place."

"And what do you want in return?" Alaric said.

Chakhran smiled, an expression that made him look as delighted as a child. "You think I want something?"

"I think you're being far too cooperative just to be acting out of residual guilt."

"You do not trust easily, do you, man who is not human?"

"Alaric," Alaric said, "and no, I don't."

"Very well." Chakhran nodded. "But it is not in exchange, I do for you, you do for me. It is a favor only. You seek the temple in Ma'tzehar, and there is a thing there I would like retrieved. A thing I have seen in vision. I ask only that you return with it, since you are going there anyway. But I will help you whether or not you agree."

"Fair enough," Alaric said. "What thing?"

"A feather," Chakhran said. "The feather of a phoenix, made gold by a divine of Ma'tzehar centuries ago."

"Gold?" Dianthe said. "Why didn't they take it with them when they left?"

"We do not know. Only that it was touched by God to write Her words. We think it contains a revelation and we would like to know what it is."

"Forgive me," Perrin said, "but if you already receive God's words, what more do you expect to gain from this?"

"We believe the secret to Ma'tzehar's doom is contained within it. And we do not have so much of God's word that we reject gaining more of it."

Perrin nodded, caught himself, and said, "I understand."

"Is the feather somewhere in the temple?" Alaric asked.

"It is."

"Then I don't see why we can't help you."

"Thank you. It is a small thing, I know, but has meaning for us." Chakhran's sunken eyelids fluttered.

"And then you return here," Manisha said to Kalanath.

"I...you mean, to stay," Kalanath said, looking uncomfortable.

"Yes. To stay with me. To be *devesh* to Omeira." Manisha moved swiftly to sit beside her son. "You do not leave."

Kalanath looked at Alaric. "I...do not know," he said. "I have things I must do."

Manisha shook her head. "*Kalanath, you have been gone too long,*" she said, dropping into Meiric. *"You have a destiny. You are God's voice to her people. And you have a family now. Don't tell me you have things to do. This is where your life is."*

"Mother, I made a life for myself outside Omeira," Kalanath replied. *"I can't just set it aside."*

"Then bring it to an end. I can't bear to lose you again."

"Manisha, now is not the time," Chakhran said. *"Kalanath has much to think about. And he has yet to meet Vaishant."*

Manisha took Kalanath's hands. *"I want you to meet your father. You can't leave today, at any rate. It takes time to prepare for such a journey."*

"What are they saying?" Alaric murmured to Sienne.

"Manisha doesn't want Kalanath to leave when this is over," Sienne said. "And—"

"I will send your guides to you," Chakhran said. "They will accompany you into the city to purchase what you will need for the journey. Two days, and you will be ready to leave."

"But Kalanath come with me, to meet Vaishant," Manisha said, still clutching Kalanath's hands. Kalanath looked like a skittish horse, ready to bolt but afraid of hurting the small woman.

"It is a good idea," Chakhran said. "Do not be afraid, Kalanath."

"It is not afraid I am," Kalanath said. Sienne was sure he was lying.

"Thank you," Alaric said, rising and prompting the others to follow his lead. "How long a journey is it?"

"Nine days, without storms," Chakhran said.

"That's remarkably precise a number," Dianthe said. "I thought Ma'tzehar was impossible to find. At least, the scrappers we talked to all said it was."

"And most of the teams who set out to find it never returned," Perrin said.

"They did not have an Omeiran divine with them," Chakhran said. "We know the way, but we do not share it with outsiders, and we do not take the trip ourselves. It is quite dangerous."

Sienne, about to ask why the temple hadn't retrieved the phoenix feather already, bit back her question. She would have thought the promise of God's word enough to justify a trip to get it, however dangerous, but it wasn't her faith. And maybe it was more dangerous than she imagined. Not that she'd been able to imagine much; she had no idea what the desert looked like, whether it was sandy dunes or rough, rocky soil. She looked up at the clear, cloudless sky and tried to picture it stretching from horizon to horizon, interrupted by nothing but empty waste. Two days, and she wouldn't have to use her imagination.

9

Sienne tilted her head back to look up at the night sky. Half an hour before dawn, the midnight color began shading to soft blue, and the crystal flecks of the stars faded and softened around the edges. Behind her, the dome of the temple rose bulbous and smooth to where the fire burned atop its tower. This close, she saw someone moving in the tower, though she couldn't make out details. It was more likely to be someone tending the fire than a guard standing sentinel over the temple. In the three days they'd been in residence, she'd never seen any evidence that the divines were worried about attacks.

It made her wonder if Omeiran priests and divines received blessings the way Perrin and his fellow worshippers did. In those same three days, she also hadn't seen the divines do more than pray silently, stopping mid-stride sometimes, at what to Sienne seemed random times. They were far more private about their worship than Sienne was used to, and she didn't know if that was because it was a temple, or if it was an Omeiran practice in general. She never felt quite comfortable asking.

She straightened her long, pale blue robe, which she wore over loose linen trousers with a drawstring waist and a sleeveless shirt.

Her head scarf, a length of soft, shapeless white cotton, remained balled in her hands. She hadn't been able to figure out how to put it on. No doubt after a few days it would become second nature, but for now, she'd have to depend on Ghrita.

Ghrita. Sienne scowled. The woman hadn't let up on flirting with Alaric despite Sienne's glares or Alaric's continuing indifference. He'd have to say something to her.

"Sorry?" Alaric said.

Sienne realized she'd said that aloud. "I'm tired of Ghrita treating you like her property. You need to tell her to back off."

"It doesn't bother me. And it's not like I find her attractive."

"I'm not worried about you taking her up on her thinly-veiled offers. It's just disrespectful of me. She always looks at me when she says something suggestive to you, like she knows I hate it. I'm starting to wonder if that's not the point, except why would she want to harass me? It's not like we even know each other." Sienne scowled harder. "Why did the Hierarch make her one of our guides?"

"Because she's one of the few *niranas* who speaks Fellic, and she understands desert survival better than most."

"After who knows how many years in civilization, though?"

Alaric put his arm around her. "I'll tell her to stop. And if that doesn't work, I think you'd be within your rights to *force*-blast her."

"Don't tempt me."

"You are not encouraging Sienne to execute vigilante justice, are you?" Perrin said, strolling up beside them. "Because I would have to insist she demur until I am in a position to watch."

"Yes, but you like Ghrita."

Perrin shrugged. "'Like' is perhaps the wrong word. I find her interesting. She is devout in her own faith, yet asks questions about mine like someone preparing to enter into Averran's worship. She does, however, seem bent on tormenting you, and I have no idea why."

"See? It's not just me, Alaric."

"I never said it was, sweetlove." He kissed the top of her head. "Don't worry. I'll take care of it."

Perrin turned as someone else entered the garden. He nudged Dianthe, who lay snoring on one of the narrow marble benches. "We should be leaving soon."

Sienne followed his gaze to where Kalanath stood, speaking quietly to Manisha. Vaishant was a darker shape behind the *madhi*, his attention focused on Kalanath. Vaishant fascinated Sienne. She'd only seen him a handful of times, but couldn't stop wondering about him. What would it be like, learning fifteen years too late that you had a son? And that your son was blessed by God? Vaishant's dark head nodded at something Manisha said. Kalanath hugged his mother, then stepped aside for Vaishant to do the same. Vaishant held Manisha rather longer than Kalanath had, and Kalanath looked away, shifting his staff from one hand to the other. "Is this really a good idea?" Sienne murmured. "Vaishant being our guide, I mean."

"Kalanath has to come to terms with him sometime," Alaric said, "and Vaishant knows the way to Ma'tzehar."

"I just wish I felt confident that Chakhran would have chosen him even if he wasn't Kalanath's father. I'm not so certain of our abilities that I don't want the very best desert guide we can have."

"Chakhran would not send us off with less," Perrin said.

Dianthe sat up, blinking. "Kitane have mercy," she mumbled. "It's still dark. Whose idea was this?"

"Yours, as I recall," Perrin said. "There was some talk of traveling before the sun could, and these were your exact words, 'boil us like a three-minute egg.'"

"Damn. That was what I said, wasn't it?" Dianthe stood and stretched. "Where's Ghrita?"

"She went ahead to the stables, to ready our mounts," Alaric said. "Good morning," he added as Kalanath and Vaishant approached. "We're ready if you are."

"I am," Vaishant said. His Fellic was nearly as good as Kalanath's, and Sienne recalled that he'd been a trader, traveling the world, before becoming a priest. "It is a good morning for it."

"Lead on, then," Alaric said.

Chirantan was waking up around them as they crossed the city to the stables. Sienne had gone the day before with Alaric and Dianthe to purchase supplies, aided by Ghrita, and had been struck by how the city's layout was both random and regular. Random, in that streets followed some pattern that wasn't obvious at ground level, but regular, because they all radiated out from small round plazas featuring grassy spots and brass or granite fountains.

They passed through one of those plazas now, with merchants setting up booths in preparation for a long, hot day of selling pots or shoes or candied dates. Sienne, accustomed to Fioretti's grand market that sprawled across the city, found these little markets charming, particularly the ones that sold clothing.

She'd bought her new desert apparel at one of these and spent a cheerful fifteen minutes haggling with the shopkeeper, who'd been thrilled to meet a Rafellish woman who spoke his language. He'd thrown in a pendant on a leather thong for free, another tradition Sienne loved. "*Good luck,*" he'd said, and while it wasn't magical, it was engraved with abstract curves and dots that appealed to Sienne. She fingered it now and silently wished the man good luck of his own.

The stables were even busier than the streets, with men and women saddling horses and loading up pack animals. It seemed they shared Dianthe's idea of traveling before the heat of the day struck. The long, low stables, plastered white with deep stalls that would shelter the horses from even the hottest sun, even had room for the strange humped beasts Ghrita called camels. "Better for desert travel," she'd said, "but since none of you have ridden them before, we'd have to take servants to help care for them. I think we want to keep this expedition small, don't you?" She'd followed it up with a long, slow smile in Alaric's direction that had made Sienne want to hit her. Why was the woman bent on turning every comment into innuendo?

Now the woman herself approached from where she'd been leaning against the wall. "We're almost loaded up," she said. Sienne wondered about that "we," given that Ghrita didn't appear to have done any work. She ground her back teeth together and resolved not to be drawn by anything Ghrita might do.

"Let me help you with your head scarves," Ghrita added, approaching Sienne with her hand out. Sienne gave her the wadded cloth, which Ghrita shook out. "You'll need to learn to do this yourself eventually."

She swiftly wrapped the cloth around Sienne's head in a complicated fashion that Sienne was sure she wouldn't be able to replicate. It covered her head and neck and draped loosely across the lower half of her face. "You raise it to cover your mouth and nose when the sand blows," Ghrita said, and turned away to help Dianthe. Vaishant was doing the same for Alaric. Sienne watched Ghrita closely, but the woman wrapped Dianthe's scarf in exactly the way she had Sienne's, so she hadn't tried to sabotage Sienne. Maybe she could behave like a professional, after all.

The stable hands led their pack horses out, all of them laden, then a string of saddled and bridled horses. They were, with one exception, smaller than the horses Sienne was used to, with narrow flanks and fine, short hair. Sienne approached the bay mare that would be hers for the next few weeks and stroked her mane. "I'm sure we'll be friends, but I miss my horse Spark," she whispered. "Though you're probably better at desert travel than she would be."

Alaric mounted the one horse that looked normal-sized. It had taken some doing to find a desert horse big enough to carry him. With his hair covered by the head scarf, only his eyes gave away his race, a startling pale blue in his sunburned face. "Vaishant?" he said.

Vaishant nodded. "One moment," he said, bowing his head and closing his eyes. Sienne watched him, once again feeling uncomfortable at his devotions. She hadn't realized how inclusive the worship of Averran was until she'd witnessed the Omeiran divines in their silent prayers, how comforting it was to hear Perrin speak his prayers aloud as if inviting his hearers to take part. Or maybe it was just that she'd gone from a respectful agnosticism to worshipping Averran herself without noticing the change. She closed her eyes and said a silent prayer: *O Lord Averran, I don't know if I'm doing this right, but if you don't mind, watch out for us in our journeys.*

Peace touched her heart, a feeling of warmth that spread over her.

Was this how Perrin felt all the time? No wonder he'd chosen to give up everything to serve his avatar.

Vaishant raised his head and nodded. He mounted his horse in one smooth motion and said, "We will ride until noon, rest for a few hours, then continue to the first haven. Does everyone have water? Drink freely at this stage. You should not become sick."

Sienne checked that her waterskin was attached to her saddle, ready to hand. Thanks to her small magic, water was not something they needed to conserve, though she didn't intend to be profligate regardless. She could even keep it cool, a luxury she was sure she'd appreciate during the heat of the day.

Vaishant turned his horse and trotted out of the stable yard, followed by the two pack horses. Sienne fell into line behind Alaric. She felt the rush of pleasure she always did the first moment of a journey, the first few steps that marked the line between staying home and setting out on an adventure. Especially one as foreign and mysterious as this. Desert travel, a lost city—she'd never been happier to be a scrapper.

Traffic in the streets was light enough that they drew attention from the men and women going to work or setting up stalls. Sienne wondered if it was obvious, in the dim pre-dawn light, that most of their procession weren't Omeiran. Her harness jingled a merry tune as she trotted along, one that sounded different from Spark's tack. Or maybe she was imagining things, romanticizing their journey. Probably a few days of sand getting into everything would dull her excitement. But for now, she felt like singing.

They left Chirantan by its northern gate, a heavy brass-studded thing that reminded Sienne that Chirantan was, despite all other appearances, built to withstand the attack of another *rakhyan*. At the moment, packed sand driven against its foot suggested it had been a while since the gates were closed. No guards were visible at the gate, either. Maybe it wasn't so ready for an attack, after all.

The road spooled away northward into scrubland, not true sandy desert, but still arid, the ground hard, cracked white clay that would be blinding when the sun fully rose. Scruffy gray-green bushes clung to life within those cracks, drinking up water not visible on the surface. A few gnarled trees, equally dusty, spread low branches in wide canopies that would provide scant shelter in a few hours. Birds chirped and twittered, swooping from tree to bush and eating Sienne didn't know what. Insects, maybe. It was hard to imagine anything living out here, despite the birds.

"It is a few hours before we reach true desert," Vaishant called out. "Then we will make our journey between havens. They are... places of refuge, yes? With water and shade. The *pakhshani* use them too. Though at this season we are unlikely to see them. They travel north, where it is cooler."

"Is that a polite way of saying we're crazy for making this trip now?" Alaric said.

Vaishant laughed. He had a nice laugh, hearty and open. "The desert is not a friendly place at any time. You will see this. God teaches us that no journey is without risk, because it is in the journey we are made to change. A bird who fights free of the egg is a bird strong enough to fly one day."

"And hardship makes us strong?" Kalanath said. There was an edge to his voice that surprised Sienne.

"Do you disagree?" Vaishant said. He wasn't laughing anymore.

"I do not think looking for hardship is good. That is what those who worship God as destroyer think. I would rather not have fled. I do—did things I wish I had not because I must."

"And yet you are the man you are because you do these things. Because of all you have endured. What would you give up if it meant losing who you are now?" Vaishant's voice was gentle, but he didn't look at Kalanath, riding well behind him.

Kalanath scowled, but said nothing. Sienne said, "It's not just the bad things that shape us, it's everything we experience. Wouldn't you rather have known you were Kalanath's father years ago, and not missed all those years?"

She knew immediately it was a mistake. Kalanath's silence spread outward from him until it encompassed all of them. Vaishant's back went rigid. "At least in that I had no choice," he said, so quietly Sienne almost couldn't hear him. "I could not even suspect..."

"I'm sorry," Sienne began.

"There is nothing to be sorry for," Vaishant said, and lapsed into silence again. Sienne, her face flaming, caught Ghrita's mocking eye and cursed herself. Of course Vaishant had regrets, and most of them he couldn't do anything about. It was none of her business.

They rode on. The sun rose, turning the grays and browns of the wasteland a dozen shades of white. Sienne developed a headache from the reflected glare almost immediately. There was nowhere to look to relieve the brightness. Even the sky felt bleached to near-whiteness, as pale as Alaric's eyes but more merciless. Sweat pooled beneath Sienne's arms and breasts and trickled down her back. She took a drink of cool water and tried to come up with reasons to be grateful. She wasn't walking, that was something. She wasn't alone. She had plenty of water. It was an adventure. That last made her want to laugh. How quickly the adventure had palled.

By the time the sun rode highest in the sky, they'd left the road behind and were well and truly surrounded by sand dunes. Vaishant and Ghrita directed them in erecting the tents. They were bigger than the ones the companions usually used on a job, with many poles that held up the heavy canvas and sides that rolled up to allow the desert breezes to cool their occupants. Sienne laid out rugs over the sand and sat down next to Alaric. It was too hot for cuddling, but he took her hand and held it loosely in his. "Still glad you came?" he said.

"We've barely been out here half a day. It's too early to complain."

"True. It's all so different, though. The land, the desert...even our goal. I'm trying not to be too hopeful. What if we reach Ma'tzehar, and there's nothing there?"

"Then we figure out the next step. But there will be something. I'm certain of it."

"I'll lean on your confidence." He looked so exotic, dressed in desert robes, that Sienne wished they were somewhere cooler and more private. She settled for squeezing his hand and reveling in the smile he gave her in return.

After a few hours in which Sienne napped fitfully, Vaishant had them break camp, and they moved on. It was hot enough that Sienne couldn't imagine how much worse it would have been if they'd kept traveling instead of camping briefly. Waves of heat radiated off the horizon like a distant lake, and she found herself looking forward to the desert winds Chakhran had warned them of. She didn't want to discount the effect of being scoured by sand, but a breeze would be nice.

When the sun began to slip behind the horizon, Sienne started looking to Vaishant for the signal to halt. But they kept going until after full dark, despite the moonless night. Sienne made magical lights that didn't do much to dispel the darkness; in fact, the lights made the darkness outside their circle deeper and more impenetrable. The air cooled, and kept cooling, until Sienne felt chilly despite her several layers. She was grateful for the warmth of her head scarf and the horse's body heat. They hadn't brought fuel for a fire, which would have meant hauling twice the load, and Sienne had seen the sense in that. Now she regretted the lack.

"Shelter, and then food," Vaishant said. He dismounted, but instead of going to the pack horse to unload the tent, he led his horse forward into the darkness. Sienne jogged her horse's ribs to follow, and came up short as a squat gray building loomed out of the shadows ahead. She got down and walked forward, feeling as if the thing had appeared by magic and might disappear the same way if she weren't cautious.

Vaishant returned, without his horse. "Come, come," he said. "The haven is unoccupied. It is just us."

Sienne gathered her lights into one place and sent them to hover over the building. It looked like a squared-off clay brick, with small ventilation holes surrounding the roof and one larger hole for a door. Sienne ducked to enter—Alaric was going to have real trouble—and found herself in a room that looked like it went the entire length of the building. There were no furnishings, and the walls were unpainted, giving it the appearance of a prison. Two interior doorways opened on darkness, but when Sienne investigated, she found nothing but two smaller rooms just as bare and unappealing as the first.

"We sleep here," Vaishant said, startling her. "Cook outside. I will light a fire and you will unload the horses."

Sienne nodded and went back to where her horse stood. Now that her eyes had adjusted, she could see a structure that might be a stable and a fire pit where Vaishant crouched. Beyond those was the low, humped shape of a well. She led her horse to the stable and set about removing her saddle. Beside her, Dianthe said, "This isn't what I expected when he called it a haven. I was thinking more along the lines of a desert oasis like they have in stories."

"I suppose that was never very likely, huh?" Sienne said with a smile.

"It could happen!" Dianthe said, laughing.

"What could happen?" Alaric said, leading his horse up beside them.

"Magical desert oases," Dianthe said. "Cool ponds under palm trees."

"Scorpions in your boots," Alaric said. "Sand in your—"

"Go ahead, ruin my fantasy," Dianthe said.

"What, you don't think this place is beautiful even without ponds and palm trees?" Alaric unfastened his horse's saddle and set it on the ground. "And it smells so fresh. Though some of that is the rice Vaishant is cooking."

"Real Omeiran desert cuisine," Sienne said. "All part of the adventure."

When they'd finished unloading the horses, Vaishant had produced a meal that smelled deliciously of spices and coconut, served over soft, sticky rice and eaten with cold flat breads. "They should be hot, but that takes time," he said.

"It's wonderful," Dianthe said. "I'm never so hungry as when I'm in the wilderness."

"Travel is indeed a fine spice," Perrin said. He helped himself to another piece of bread and conveyed a dripping morsel to his mouth. "Though spice is also a very fine spice."

Sienne kept an eye on Kalanath. He ate steadily and in silence, responding only with nods when addressed directly. He didn't meet Vaishant's eye and sat as far from the man as the fire would allow. When he finished, he stood and said, "I will wash tonight."

"Oh, I can do that, Kalanath," Sienne said.

"I would like to." He held out a hand for her tin plate. She handed it to him and watched him walk away in the direction of the well.

"What's wrong with him?" Alaric said in a low voice.

"He's probably just tired," Sienne said, horribly conscious of Vaishant listening.

"He does not like me," Vaishant said.

"Oh, I'm sure that's not true," Dianthe said.

Vaishant shook his head. "We are not father and son in the usual way. He does not like me taking his mother's time. And he thinks I have no right to him. To his affection."

"Three days ago he didn't know he had a father," Alaric said. "He needs time."

"Some things don't happen no matter how much time you have," Ghrita said, stretching out her long legs.

"You don't know that," Sienne snapped.

"I'm not saying this is one of them," Ghrita replied, unperturbed by Sienne's tone. "Just that you can't compel love."

"You ought to keep that in mind," Sienne said, rising. Ghrita smiled at her with that mocking expression Sienne had come to hate.

Vaishant rose as well. "We will leave at first light," he said. "Rest well. I must pray now." He walked away out of the circle of firelight and disappeared to view.

Sienne collected plates and carried them to where Kalanath had drawn water and was scrubbing the plates with handfuls of sand. "Let me help, it'll go faster," she said. Kalanath only nodded.

They scrubbed for a while in silence. Sienne breathed in the cool night air and felt the tiredness of the day's travel seep into her bones. "I'll sleep well tonight," she said.

"I think I will dream. I do not wish to," Kalanath said.

"I didn't think you could control it that well."

"I cannot. But I can feel it when a dream is coming. And I have dreamed every night since we arrived in Omeira. Always dreams of something coming, something that watches. Something I do not see."

"That sounds unpleasant. Can we do anything?"

"I think not. But I am glad you care."

She caught his sidelong smile, and it relieved her mind. It was enough to make her say, "About Vaishant..."

The smile vanished. "What about him?"

"What do you think he wants from you?" It wasn't what she wanted to ask, which was *Will you ever see him as your father?* But it felt like the right question.

Kalanath relaxed. "I do not know. I think he wishes for those lost years. He does not have other children and believed he was incapable." He grimaced. "My birth was miraculous for him as well, I think."

"I get the feeling he doesn't know how to be a father. But...I think he's trying. Does that matter?"

Kalanath sat back on his haunches, a plate forgotten in his hand. "I did not feel I need a father, all my life," he said. "I do not want one now. It is that he loves my mother, and they are one. I am not a part of that one. I should not be angry at her happiness, but I am. I feel anger, and guilt, and shame, and I do not like to look at him because I remember all those things when I do."

"He's going to be with us for weeks, Kalanath. You can't not look at him that whole time."

"Can I not?" He smiled to show it was a joke. "He is not a bad man. I will learn what I want from him, and then it will be easier. But I do not know if I will ever call him Father."

"I think that's up to you," Sienne said. She collected the plates and added, "I hope you're wrong, and you don't dream tonight."

"It is my hope also," Kalanath said. "I think I will sit outside for a while."

Sienne nodded and carried the plates back to the fire, which Dianthe had banked for the night. Alaric still sat there, watching the embers. "Did you talk to him?" he said.

"He's struggling. And he's been dreaming again. But I think he'll be all right."

Alaric drew her down to sit next to him. "It'll be a very long trip if some of us aren't speaking to the others."

"He knows."

Alaric kissed her, a light gesture that rapidly became something more serious. Sienne put her arms around him and kissed him back, tasting the spices of the meal and breathing in the musky scent that was his alone. "Damn," she said when he released her. "No privacy."

"We could *ferry* back home for the night and return in the morning," Alaric said, his eyes twinkling.

"Oh, that's tempting. But you know if we started doing that, it would destroy morale."

"Morale, yes. We wouldn't want to do that." He kissed her again, his lips giving his words the lie. Sienne sighed, then slid her hand between their mouths. Alaric kissed her palm once, then hugged her and stood. "This is going to be a damned long trip."

Sienne nodded. Between Kalanath's moodiness, Ghrita's antagonism, and the complete lack of privacy, it was going to be a very long trip indeed.

10

The second day was exactly like the first: rising early, camping mid-day, sleeping at another of the havens. This time, they reached the haven before sunset, but Vaishant called a halt anyway. "We will sleep rough soon enough," he said. Sienne, lying in the darkness on the hard floor of the haven's shelter, thought it was more than rough enough.

Talking as they rode through the desert heat was exhausting, and Sienne spent the next few days daydreaming, her mind ranging far from the brutal heat and unending sand. Kalanath had said once Omeiran temples were all mostly identical, so she pictured the Ma'tzehar temple like the one in Chirantan, but run-down and neglected, maybe with its garden courtyard desiccated by the sun and sand-scoured air. When she got tired of that, she imagined being back in Fioretti, and then in Beneddo, which led her to think about the Deluccos and wonder if Alcander had found a solution yet.

Sometimes she rode beside Perrin, the two of them riding as was customary at the center of the group, and occasionally tried to strike up a conversation. His responses were terse, and eventually she gave up. She couldn't help watching him, though. He made the strangest faces, smiling for no reason and then furrowing his brow in thought.

Sometimes he drew his scarf up over his mouth when there wasn't any wind, and Sienne was sure he was concealing a laugh. Finally, unable to contain her curiosity, she said, "Perrin, what's so funny?"

He startled, glanced at her, and said, "I did not realize...it is not a joke I can share without a great deal of explanation."

"You looked like you were telling yourself a funny story."

"Close. I was speaking with Cressida, and she was telling me of something Noel did yesterday."

"I didn't realize you had that blessing again."

Perrin smiled. "I have had that blessing every day since we left Fioretti, unasked for but marvelously welcome. It is..." He ducked his head. "I did not know how much I longed for my wife until I was reunited with her, even in this small way. Averran has been generous beyond anything I could have imagined."

"That's beautiful. Are you...reconciled?"

He shook his head. "It is not an easy thing, gaining forgiveness. We each said and did things that wounded the other terribly. Much of what we speak of concerns our children, and our daily routine—nothing of deep or abiding interest. But I have hope that when we meet again, we may have learned to forgive each other. And...is it too optimistic of me to say I can imagine us a family again?"

"No. Not at all."

Perrin sighed. "For now, I continue to be grateful for Averran's intervention. And pray that your brother will be successful. It would break my heart to lose them again."

"We'll figure something out. I promise."

He looked off into the distance. "I hope you do not regret that promise...what, I wonder, is that?"

Sienne looked where he pointed. A large gray boulder, scoured to a matte finish by the relentless winds, emerged from the sand some hundred feet away. Patches of sand near it were darker than the rest, making interesting swirls that relieved Sienne's sun-blinded eyes. "That's strange," she said.

At the head of the line, Vaishant waved to them, gesturing to stay wide of the stone. "Is it dangerous?" Sienne asked.

She hadn't spoken to anyone in particular, but Ghrita, riding behind her, said, "Scorpions may nest in the shade of such rocks. There's no—"

An earsplitting wail shook the air, and something big and sand-colored erupted from the ground near the boulder. It shook itself, sending sand flying, and raced toward them.

Sienne whipped her book open to *force* and read as rapidly as she dared. The thing looked like a giant lizard, but with too many legs, all of them digging into the sand and sending up great gouts of it as the lizard ran. Its oversized head bellowed a challenge. The horses' shrill cries of panic mingled with its wail until Sienne wished she dared cover her ears.

Force leaped from her when the thing was only twenty feet away. It smashed into the creature, making it stagger, and then Alaric was there, sword in hand, with Dianthe running to the side to take advantage of the distraction. Alaric's first blow glanced off the beast's pebbly hide, but the second bit deep into its left foreleg, sending black blood streaming. It howled again, and reared up on its hind legs to strike. Fierce claws raked at Alaric, who leaped back and nearly fell into his horse, whose reins Vaishant held. The divine yanked on the reins, dragging the panicking horse away. Alaric regained his balance and struck again.

Sienne cast *force* twice more, driving the creature back and into Dianthe's sword. Kalanath and Ghrita, both armed with staffs, took up positions on its other side, but neither weapon seemed effective against the thing's hide except as an annoyance. That was more than enough, as it snapped and clawed at them, twisting as it tried to reach all its assailants at once. "Dianthe!" Alaric shouted, and took a different position, driving his sword toward the thing's throat.

It twisted to avoid the blow, swinging its head around—and Dianthe's sword took it in the eye, all the way to the hilt. It thrashed, ripping the sword out of Dianthe's hand. Dianthe vaulted backward, away from its death throes. Sienne lowered her book. Her heart was pounding, and her hands shook. "Is that—"

"*Look out!*" Perrin shouted, ramming his horse into hers. A giant clawed limb slashed down where she'd been standing. Sienne screamed and fumbled for the reins. She heard Perrin shout something that cut off mid-word, turned, and saw another many-legged lizard rearing up for another blow. Sienne kicked her horse into motion, wheeling and running away. Shield, where was Perrin's shield?

"Sienne!" Alaric shouted. She began reading *force* as Alaric ran past her, his sword gory with black blood. The thing raked its claws across his chest, making him cry out in pain, but he kept going, swinging the massive sword around in an arc that could take a lesser creature's head off. *Force* blasted the thing, which recoiled, and Alaric drove his sword into the softer flesh of its throat. Black blood gushed out, and it wailed. Alaric thrust harder, leaning on the sword with all his weight. The thing shuddered, and collapsed.

Breathing heavily, Sienne lowered her spellbook. "Perrin, why didn't you invoke the shield?" she said.

Perrin was silent. Sienne turned to look at him and bit back a scream. He was frozen in the act of pointing, his riffle of blessings in one hand and a loose blessing in the other. His skin glittered like mica in the bright desert sun, and his eyes, not blinking, were filmy white. "What happened?" she exclaimed.

"Basilisks," Ghrita said. "Big ones. We don't have much time."

"What do we—" Alaric began, then clutched his chest and went to his knees. "I can't breathe," he said, and went into convulsions. Sienne cried out and ran to kneel next to him, putting her arms around him.

Vaishant dismounted and knelt by his side. "I will care for him," he said. "You must help Perrin. Ghrita will tell you what to do."

"Strip him," Ghrita said. "Cut the clothes off if you must." She grabbed the hem of Perrin's outer robe and yanked it off over his head. Sienne gave one last agonized look at Alaric, thrashing on the ground, then ran to help.

Perrin's body was as rigid as stone, and as heavy. Sienne helped Kalanath and Ghrita remove Perrin's clothes while Dianthe, her face white and set with fear, collected the horses. Soon, Perrin was naked, but Sienne was too terrified to feel embarrassed for him.

"Drag him to the basilisk," Ghrita said. Sienne and Kalanath did so, though Sienne wasn't strong enough to do more than steer his inert body. Ghrita drew her belt knife, swore, and thrust it back into its sheath. She picked up Alaric's greatsword in both hands. "He needs to be underneath."

Confused, Sienne did as Ghrita instructed. She and Kalanath positioned Perrin near the fatal wound Alaric had dealt. Ghrita inserted the sword into the wound and widened the gash. Black blood spurted, coating Perrin's head and chest. "Spread it over his body, and quickly," Ghrita said. "It must cover all of him."

Sienne caught handfuls of the blood and smeared it on her friend. It reeked, not of the coppery scent of human blood, but something foul and bitter like old smoke and charcoal. Ghrita, with some effort, made another wound that gushed blood. Some of it fell steaming on the sand, and Sienne cursed the loss. She ran her hands down Perrin's legs, coating herself in blood to the wrists. Beside her, Kalanath worked in feverish silence. How quickly was quickly enough? Ghrita wouldn't make them do this gory service if it didn't work, right?

The blood was clotting fast, and each new wound produced less of it. There was a second basilisk—but what if it had to be the blood of the one who'd petrified him? Sienne let her mind go blank, focusing on the task at hand. She would never be able to explain this to Cressida. With that thought she rubbed blood onto Perrin's foot, and he was completely covered in it. He looked like a streaky marble statue, with flecks of mica showing through the black blood.

In the next instant, all the blood soaked into his skin at once like water absorbed by a dry cloth. The bright glittering sparks vanished, leaving behind smooth, tan skin. Perrin exhaled like someone who'd been holding his breath for a long time. "—grant me this..." he said, blinked, and sat up. "Where is it, and...dear Averran, why am I naked?"

Now Sienne felt embarrassed. She averted her eyes.

"The basilisk's gaze caught your eye," Ghrita said. "A man petrified by it can be cured by being bathed in its fresh blood. It must happen immediately, before the petrification kills him. Your friends have quick hands."

"Thank you," Perrin said. "I am sorry to have put you to the trouble. I was in the act of shielding Sienne from the second monster when it caught me."

The second monster. Sienne gasped and ran to where Alaric was just sitting up, shaking his head like someone coming out of deep water. "He is well," Vaishant said. "The poison has run its course."

Sienne went to put her arms around him, caught sight of her bloody hands, and changed her mind. "That was bracing," she said, feeling her voice shake despite her brave words. She took a few steps away and thrust her hands into the sand to scrub away most of the basilisk's blood. Behind her, Perrin retrieved his clothes and dressed.

"It is wrong," Vaishant said. "The giant basilisk does not hunt in the south. These should not be here."

Kalanath squatted beside Sienne and rubbed his hands with sand. "Why are they, then?" he asked. His voice lacked the veiled animosity Sienne was used to when he addressed Vaishant.

Vaishant looked northward. "The *pakhshani* hunt them. They use the blood and eat the flesh in their adulthood rituals. They do not let them roam far from the hunting grounds."

"So...what does that mean?" Dianthe said. She held Alaric's and her horses' reins and stood looking in the same direction Vaishant was. "There's something wrong with the *pakhshani*?"

"I cannot tell. If they fight a different battle...but there is nothing and no one for them to fight, save..." He shook his head. "I do not want to guess."

"Guess," Alaric said flatly. "It sounds like you have a suspicion."

"Not anything solid. It is just a thought. If they fight, it must be something no one knows is a threat. Abhisok is north, but they would not venture into the *pakhshani's* territory to fight a war they cannot win. But I think imagining monsters is foolish."

"Something watching," Kalanath said. "Something we cannot see."

Vaishant regarded him narrowly. "What have you dreamed?"

Kalanath's lips tightened. "Nothing of value to us now. But...if there is something in the north we do not know, it will not surprise me."

Alaric stood and fingered the bloody rents in his robe. "Sienne," he said, "can you do something about this?"

Sienne ran a hand over his chest and focused a little magic there. The tears in his robe came together and vanished. She poured water over the stains, making him gasp. "Sorry, that was colder than I intended," she said. "I'm afraid I can't get this entirely clean."

"Just so there's no dried blood," he said. He took hold of her hand. "You're shaking. You didn't cast too many spells, did you?"

She shook her head and put her arms around him. "It's just the aftermath. We nearly lost you and Perrin." She half-turned so she could see Ghrita and Vaishant. "Thank you both. Your knowledge saved their lives."

"His sword saved ours," Ghrita said. For once, it didn't sound suggestive. "It's what we do for each other."

Kalanath extended his hands. "Will you wash them?" he said to Sienne. "The blood is gone, but I feel it still."

Sienne felt a little grimy herself. She summoned water to rinse them both off. "Shouldn't we be going?" Dianthe said. "I can't imagine there aren't scavengers waiting to pick these two clean."

"True," Ghrita said. "How much farther to the next haven?"

"Too far for tonight," Vaishant said. "We will ride another three hours and camp in the open. It is not good, but better than we travel until midnight."

Alaric mounted his horse. "I still feel weak. Is that normal?"

"Normal enough. You will need these hours to recover fully." Vaishant smiled. "It is the best thing that we are not attacked by basilisks, but if it must be so, perhaps it is better that you were the one struck by their poison and not small Sienne."

Alaric's eyes met Sienne's. "I agree," he said, his gaze bleak with some imagined horror. Sienne found she was shaking again, and closed her fingers tightly on her spellbook.

Three hours brought them to sunset, and they made camp in silence, pitching the tents and then handing out cold food with no unnecessary talk. Sienne felt drained of energy, as if she'd walked all those miles instead of riding. She leaned against Alaric, who seemed fully recovered from his bout with the basilisk's poisoned claws. "Should we post watches tonight?" she said.

"What do you think, Vaishant?" Alaric asked.

The divine nodded. "We do not have the shelter of a haven, and night is when the desert animals come out to hunt. Best if we do not make ourselves a target."

"All right," Alaric said. "Standard watch rotation, but Ghrita and Vaishant will take first and last watch—if that's all right with you," he said to Vaishant. The divine nodded. Ghrita shrugged her approval.

Sienne went to her bedroll in the women's tent and lay in the chilly darkness, reflecting again on how the desert was such a land of extremes. That probably said something about the people who lived there, but she was too tired for philosophy. Beside her, Dianthe let out a gentle snore. For once, Sienne felt she might sleep as quickly as her friend. But as she was drifting off, she heard someone say in Meiric, *"If you've been dreaming, you should tell us what you see."* It was Vaishant.

"It's not your business," Kalanath replied.

"Normally, I'd agree with you. But the devesh's gifts are not his alone."

"That's how the old divines got into trouble, isn't it? Assuming my gifts were theirs to use as they felt like it."

"I don't want this for myself. This is for all of us. I'm worried about the pakhshani. If they've run into something that keeps them from the hunt—"

"Do you really think that's the problem?"

"I don't know what to think. My instincts tell me we could be walking into trouble. So, again, I ask you to share what you see. If not with me, then with Alaric."

Kalanath made an impatient noise. *"You think I'd be so...so petty?"*

"Is it pettiness not to share secrets with someone you don't trust?"

A pause. *"It's not about trust,"* Kalanath said, but even Sienne could tell he was lying.

"I'm not going to demand that you treat me like a father," Vaishant said. *"But I mean you no harm. Your mother and I—"*

"Let's leave her out of it, shall we? I know you don't mean me harm. And...I'm sorry I don't trust you."

"It's understandable. I wish you'd tell me what I can do to earn your trust."

A longer pause. *"It's my problem, not yours,"* Kalanath finally said. *"In my dreams, I'm in an empty city—no, not a real city, but a giant model. As if a child had built it with bricks. There are no people, but something watches me. Something powerful. I'm searching for something, and the longer the dream goes on, the longer I search, the closer I come to understanding the thing that watches me. And then I wake."*

"What are you searching for?"

"The answer to Alaric's quest, I think. I'm not sure."

"I don't know what that is. Chakhran wasn't very forthcoming."

"Ask Alaric. It's his story to tell, not mine."

"I will."

They both went silent. Sienne strained to hear more. Eavesdropping was wrong, but she hated not knowing things.

Finally, Vaishant said, *"Do you wish your mother had never found me?"*

"She's happy," Kalanath said curtly. *"I can't wish her unhappy."*

"I'm happy too, not that I expect that to matter to you. My point is that I never expected my life to take this turn. To find I have a son, and such a son as you...Kalanath, I don't expect anything from you, but I would like us to be friends."

Kalanath said nothing. As the silence stretched, Sienne wondered if he'd managed to walk away without disturbing the sand. Eventually, he said, *"I'll keep it in mind. And...I don't hate you."*

"That's enough for me," Vaishant said. One of them walked away, his feet crunching across the soft sand. Sienne wondered who still stood behind her tent. Finally, the other left, and Sienne was alone with Dianthe's snoring. She rolled onto her back and stared up at the

invisible tent roof. Had that been a promising start, or evidence that Kalanath was never going to come to terms with his father? She knew better than to try to decide what would make Kalanath happy, but Vaishant seemed like a good man who was doing his best in an awkward situation, and Sienne couldn't help hoping Kalanath would come to see that, in time.

11

More days passed. For the first two, Sienne rode with her spellbook open, her eyes scanning the middle distance for threats. Nothing attacked. The desert was so empty she went from worrying about basilisks to fearing the complete lack of desert life meant something just as dire. When she brought it up, Vaishant said, "You are not wrong. But we cannot know what it is that is wrong. We can only go on as we have, and pray God will protect us."

A sandstorm came up the fourth day after the basilisk attack, and Vaishant made them stop to cover the horses' large eyes. They stood huddled against the animals for more than an hour, faces covered, sand stinging foreheads and hands. Sienne pressed her face against her horse's warm back and tried to think of anything that would take her attention from the feeling of being scoured with a stiff-bristled brush. *Jaunting* home had never been so appealing. Or *jaunting* to Beneddo to talk to Alcander. Perrin hadn't said anything about his progress, so either Cressida didn't talk about it, or Alcander hadn't made any progress. She chose to believe the former.

She was still wondering the next day when she noticed Perrin making faces again. She nearly asked him about it, but feared disrupting his communication. So she waited until his face stilled, and he stretched. "Did Cressida say anything about the legal situation?" she asked.

"Was it that obvious, what I was doing?" Perrin smiled. "She has not said, and I have not asked, for fear her silence means something negative. I do not want to add to her burden by importuning her on a topic she has little control over. But I take heart in knowing, if my father had taken the children, she would certainly have told me, which means there is still hope."

"Alcander will figure something out. He's smarter than I am."

"Then he must be a prodigy indeed."

"I'm not that—"

"There it is," Vaishant called out, pointing. A gray, fuzzy blotch on the horizon wavered in the heat haze bleeding off the sand. "Ma'tzehar."

"We should reach it well before sunset," Alaric said. "Let's ride."

But the blotch never seemed to get any closer. When they stopped for their midday rest, Sienne squinted at it. "Chakhran said it used to have another name. Why is that?" she asked.

Ghrita replied, "Mahemnetzehar was its name before it was lost. You speak Meiric—what does that name mean?"

Her faintly mocking tone put Sienne's back up. "Well, *maa* is 'city,' *hemnet* means 'holy,' *tza* is either 'blessed' or 'consecrated'—"

"Consecrated is more accurate."

"And *ehar* means 'journey.' So...Mahemnetzehar would be 'holy city consecrated to the journey.' A pilgrimage site."

"Very good!" It was the verbal equivalent of a pat on the head. Sienne bristled. "Omeirans used to come to Mahemnetzehar from all over, to pray in its temple and pay homage to its ruler. It was the closest thing we had to a capital. But the story has it that the residents of Mahemnetzehar grew prideful, and God caused the sands to rise up over it."

"Say, rather, that God stopped keeping the sands from rising," Vaishant said. "She withdrew Her protection, and a city without God's protection cannot stand long."

"They began calling it Ma'tzehar as a reminder that it was no longer a holy place," Ghrita said. "The mark is so we will not forget that holiness was taken from it."

"So the *pakhshani* don't live there?" Dianthe said.

"No one lives there," Vaishant said. "There is no water ready to hand, and beasts roam its empty streets. Travelers who happen upon it often do not return home. We do not say curse, because we believe God does not punish us for the sins of another, but it is not a lucky place."

"But it's no more dangerous than anywhere else in the desert," Alaric said, "at least, that's what Chakhran gave me to understand. We won't be cursed for going there."

"No," Vaishant said, "but we should not stay long anyway. What do you mean to do there?"

"Yes, you haven't said what you expect to find," Ghrita said. "I'm in favor of allowing people their privacy, but not if it could get me killed."

"That's unlikely," Alaric said, "but I take your point." He stood and paced beneath the tent, his feet in their soft desert shoes scuffing the rugs. "We're looking for a particular ritual. Or, more accurately, a connection between the Ma'tzehar temple and the ritual we have, the one we've named the coming of age ritual. Kalanath's dream led us here, so that's as much as we know. We hope it will be clearer when we get there."

"And Chakhran asked us to bring back a gold phoenix feather from the temple," Sienne added.

"So the temple is all that interests you," Vaishant said. "That seems very simple."

"Which means it will probably get complicated fast, knowing our previous jobs," Dianthe said.

"Even so," Ghrita said. "The temple is near the center of the city, so we may have to fight off animals, but after the basilisks, those will be easy."

"Though we will still travel with care," Vaishant warned. "Complacency is our enemy." He stood and brushed himself off. "Let us go on."

Brassy sunlight beat down on Sienne from a white sky as they rode northward. She felt sorry for her horse, though it didn't seem bothered by the heat, just kept plodding along as if it knew its destination and didn't need Vaishant's guidance. She drank some water and focused on the city in the distance. Surely it should grow nearer, or larger—anything to show they'd made progress?

The heat ripples intensified, and between one step and the next, the city came into focus, tiny and perfect. Sienne stared. It didn't look like Chirantan, which she thought of as a typical Omeiran city with domes and white walls. Ma'tzehar was bright with color, its tall, narrow buildings painted bright blue or grass green or red like the heart of a rose, and the onion-shaped domes atop most of its buildings gleamed gold and copper in the bright afternoon light. It looked like the model of a city rather than the real thing, particularly with distance making it miniature. "It's beautiful," Sienne said, then realized they'd stopped. She reined in her horse. "Is something wrong?"

"That is not Ma'tzehar," Vaishant said. "Not as we know it."

"Are you saying there's some other city out here?" Alaric asked.

"There aren't any cities in the desert except Ma'tzehar," Ghrita said. "That has to be it."

"But it is new," Vaishant said. "That city, whatever it is, has not seen the passing of years to scour away its paint and gilding. No one lives in Ma'tzehar to care for it like that."

"Let's think about this," Dianthe said. "Either there's another city in the desert no one knows about, that happens to be near where Ma'tzehar is supposed to be, or Ma'tzehar has been mysteriously refurbished. Which is more likely?"

"I will say neither, but that is not possible," Vaishant said. "Even if this is some other city, that does not explain where Ma'tzehar went. So it must be Ma'tzehar itself."

"And it's inhabited," Alaric said.

"How do you know?" Perrin asked.

"I don't, but it's logical. It didn't paint itself, and unless we're talking about a magical, thinking city—"

"Oh, I wish you hadn't said that," Sienne said. "Now I'm thinking about walking around inside something living."

"Is that even possible?"

Sienne shook her head. "Not with any magic we have access to. The ancients might have managed it, but if they'd made Ma'tzehar a living city, they would have done it hundreds of years ago and someone would have noticed. So it's unlikely, thank Averran."

"All right," Alaric said, shielding his eyes to gaze at the distant, tiny city. "So it didn't paint itself, which means someone had to do it, and why paint something if you're not going to live there? I think it's reasonable to say Ma'tzehar is no longer uninhabited."

"But it cannot be lived in. There is not enough water," Vaishant insisted. "And nowhere to grow food or raise animals."

"You said the *pakhshani* live in the desert. Couldn't they, I don't know, make the city a permanent home and go on surviving as they usually do?" Dianthe was looking off in the direction of tiny Ma'tzehar too, and her hands were closed tight on her reins.

"They could, but that's even more unlikely than a living city," Ghrita said. "They're disdainful of city dwellers and only ever come to the outskirts of Chirantan to do their trading. We have to go to them if we want to sell our goods."

"But you said it was unusual that the *pakhshani* didn't keep the basilisks in check," Sienne said. "What if this is why? That they've left their usual territory for Ma'tzehar?"

"It could be," Vaishant said. "I do not like to guess."

"Then we must continue on," Kalanath said. "And we will know and not guess."

"We need to have a plan," Alaric said. "I don't like riding into the unknown. Is there any way for us to get close without being observed, assuming there are people in the city to do the observing?"

"Ma'tzehar used to have a city wall," Vaishant said. "It is mostly fallen."

"Unless they rebuilt it when they painted," Dianthe pointed out.

"If it is, that will only help us some. There is nothing but dunes surrounding the city, nothing to hide our approach. But if we go on the southeast...it is opposite where the city gate used to be, and if they rebuilt the wall, they might keep the gate instead of tearing down walls for a new one. Anyone watching will be looking at the gate."

"We hope," Kalanath said.

Vaishant nodded agreement.

"I believe," Perrin said, flicking through his riffle of blessings, "I may be able to...yes, I received one scrying blessing today. I can at least verify our hypothesis, and perhaps learn more than that."

"Do it," Alaric said. "We're in no hurry now."

Perrin walked a few paces away and settled on the sand cross-legged. He withdrew a blue-smudged square of rice paper from the little bundle and held it in front of his closed eyes. "O Lord, have patience in your crankiness, and grant me this blessing," he said. Blue light flickered behind his eyelids, and when he opened his eyes, they were solid blue, the whites and iris completely covered. Sienne watched Vaishant, but he looked only normally interested, not repulsed or disdainful, so she returned her attention to Perrin.

Perrin blinked slowly a few times. "I see the city," he said. "From a very great height, as of a bird flying overhead. Now I circle inward, and down. The highest towers seem made of gold, and it is fresh— there are no cracks or peels, nothing to say it was not gilded yester- day." He wetted his lips with his tongue, and Sienne uncorked her waterskin and handed it to him. "Thank you." He drank deeply, then said, "I am closer now. There are people in the streets. Many people. It looks like an ordinary city, men and women buying and selling, walking from place to place—I see no animals in the streets, no horses, no dogs or cats."

"Can you see the wall?" Alaric said.

"I am attempting to do so now." Perrin went silent for a few moments. "The wall is intact, and I see the gate. Let me...yes, I believe it is on the northwest. I will circle the city now. Men stand outside the gate and above it, on the wall, but there are no sentinels elsewhere. More to the point, I see no traffic outside the city, no one approaching the gate in either direction. When I return to the gate, I do not see that there is any interest in it despite the many pedestrians who pass close by. It is almost as if something keeps them away from it."

"See if you can find the temple," Sienne suggested. Alaric caught her eye and nodded approval.

"It looks like the one in Chirantan, yes?" Perrin closed his eyes briefly. The blue wasn't so bright as it had been. "Many streets, many men and women. They are dressed rather more colorfully than their counterparts in Chirantan. I see a small boy steal an apple from a cart and run away. The cart owner sees, but does nothing, says nothing. Interesting."

"Very interesting," Alaric agreed. "What else?"

"There is a large, colorful building I take to be a palace. Giant crystals, the size of a man's head, ornament its towers and roofs. Beside it...that must be the temple, but it is strangely plain and looks much older than the rest of the city. Its domed roof is not gilded, and there is no beacon fire laid in its tower. I—" He blinked rapidly. "My sight is fading."

"That was more than enough," Alaric said. "So the temple is there, but didn't get the same treatment as the rest of the city. Does that mean the new inhabitants don't care about God?"

"I do not want to guess," Vaishant said. "But for an Omeiran not to care about God...it is unthinkable. It is who we are."

"And where did they get apples in the middle of the desert?" Dianthe said. "More to the point, what merchant in his right mind would let an urchin get away with that kind of theft? He'd be pegged as a soft touch and lose half his produce in a day."

"More mysteries," Ghrita said. "I'm eager to find the answers."

"I don't like mysteries," Alaric said. "Mysteries can get you killed. But at least we know we can safely approach from the southeast."

"But there is no other way in but the gate on the northwest," Kalanath said.

"We'll worry about that when we get there," Alaric said. "For all we know, this is all perfectly innocent, and we can walk through the gate with no one batting an eyelash."

"You don't believe that," Sienne said.

"No, I don't, but I was trying to build some of that morale you're so fond of." He winked at her and added, "If the wall is short enough, we might be able to get in that way. If not...well, how many times can you cast *vanish*?"

"It won't exhaust me to make us all invisible, if that's what you're asking. But you know how hard it is to stay together when we can't see each other."

"I did not request a blessing to grant us such sight," Perrin said.

"I think I can do that," Vaishant said. "God has often granted me Her sight in the past, and I believe She will extend her gift to all of you."

Alaric nodded. "Then that's our next step. At the very least, I'd like to know more about this situation before giving away our presence. Let's ride on, and pray we haven't missed anything important."

It took another two hours to reach the city. It was even more impressive close up than it had been as a tiny model, its buildings more vertical than horizontal and running to towers and spires and onion-shaped domes. This close, Sienne could see the walls were painted in patterns, not solid colors, their designs made to draw the eye toward the center of the city where the palace lay. It glittered with a thousand crystals reflecting the afternoon sun. It would be blinding at noon. Chirantan had nothing like it.

They huddled in the shelter of the wall. "It's too high to climb," Dianthe said, "even for me."

"We'll leave the horses hobbled here," Alaric said, "and work our way around to the gate. Then Sienne will cast *vanish* and we'll sneak through. Any questions?"

"We are going to the temple, yes?" Vaishant said.

"Can you lead us there?"

"If the city's layout has not changed in its miraculous transformation, yes."

"Then that's where we're going," Alaric said. He shrugged his shoulders to settle his sword more securely. "Dianthe, I want you in front a ways in case we're wrong and someone goes for a stroll outside the city. Everyone else, stay close."

"With pleasure," Ghrita said with a slow smile, and stepped closer to him. Sienne ground her teeth. Alaric eyed Ghrita, but clearly concluded what Sienne had—this was not the time to call her on her flirtatious behavior. Sienne fell into place behind Alaric and thought about *force*-blasting Ghrita in the back of the head. Tempting.

Despite everything, she hadn't realized how big Ma'tzehar was until they'd walked for half an hour without reaching the gate. The wall was plastered over with a white substance that sparkled like Perrin had after the basilisk attack. Glittering wall, sparkling crystal, gilded towers...it was like a city out of a fairy tale, something too beautiful to be real. And yet the wall, when she touched it, felt solid and dry and not at all imaginary. The soft crunching sound of her desert shoes on the sand, the whisper of breezes that occasionally touched her face, were all that kept her from feeling she'd fallen into a vivid dream.

Ahead, Dianthe gestured for them to stop, then trotted back toward them. "We're close," she said in a low voice. "Time for some wizardry."

Sienne opened her spellbook, then hesitated. "Are you going to have a problem with this?" she asked Vaishant. "You've never had a spell cast on you before, have you?"

"I have not," Vaishant said. He didn't look at all nervous. "But I trust you."

"Thank you," Sienne said. "Ghrita?"

"Wizardry intrigues me," Ghrita said. "And I've never been invisible before." Despite her casual words, she did look nervous, her hands clenched into fists, and she looked at Alaric, not Sienne.

"It's not as fun as it sounds," Sienne said. "It only lasts for two hours, so we have to move quickly. Vaishant, usually we have Perrin invoke the sight blessing before I make each of us invisible, so..."

"Clasp hands," Vaishant said, and stood in the middle of the circle they formed. He bowed his head and said nothing. Sienne watched him, but he didn't even move his lips, just stood there with his eyes closed. She became intensely aware of Alaric's hand in her right one, hard and warm, and Dianthe's smoother, cooler hand in her left, how the flesh felt firm and yet yielding, with the beginnings of sweat forming in her right hand because Alaric's skin was so warm—

She blinked. Vaishant's image was fading and intensifying at the same time, becoming an outline drawing of his shape, black and stark. She blinked several more times, but the effect didn't fade. Then, with a snap, the outline flared and vanished, and Vaishant looked normal again. He raised his head. "I do not know how long it will last, so we should hurry."

Sienne didn't waste time asking irrelevant questions about whether he'd actually done anything. She let the spellbook fall open to *vanish* and began reading, focusing first on Alaric, then the others in turn, and finally on herself. With the influence of Vaishant's blessing, or whatever you called an Omeiran prayer, her friends were visible as shimmering outlines of themselves, with light beading along the lines that traced out their forms. The effect was identical to Perrin's blessing of the same type, which intrigued Sienne. More evidence that they really did worship the same God.

12

Alaric turned slowly to survey all of them, then made a "follow me" gesture and set off toward the gate. Sienne tucked her spellbook, which wasn't affected by *vanish*, into her robe and followed him. The sound of her breathing sounded abnormally loud, and when she looked down, she saw the sand disturbed by her footsteps, little holes dug by her invisible feet. How alert were those guards, anyway?

She looked up, searching the top of the wall for the sentries Perrin had said stood there. The white heat of midafternoon beat down on her face, blinding her, and she blinked away tears and raised her hand to shield her eyes before remembering it was invisible and would do her no good. She looked again, and suddenly there the guard was—a man dressed in desert robes wearing a head scarf like hers, but black instead of white. He stood atop the wall like a statue, motionless except for his head, which moved as he scanned the distance.

Sienne watched him long enough to determine he wasn't going to look at the base of the wall, then turned her attention on Alaric, who had reached the gate and was beckoning her to join him. It wasn't actually a gate, Sienne found, just a gap in the wall, flanked by two more sentries. Strangely, they faced inward rather than outward, their hands resting on large curved swords. Despite the heat, they wore leather breastplates studded with iron and spiked helmets over their head scarves, and their dark Omeiran faces were shiny with sweat.

Once they were all gathered in front of the gap, Alaric strode through, ignoring the sentries. Sienne followed more slowly, eyeing them for signs that they'd been detected. The sentries on the ground were even more motionless than the one on the wall, with only their eyes roving the streets before them. Sienne found she was holding her breath and let it out slowly, just in case the sentries had good hearing.

Perrin's description had been inadequate in one respect: there was a wide, empty space between the wall and the first street that looked as if nothing had ever been built there. People thronged the street bordering it, but no one so much as stepped off the road, not even the children who threaded through the crowds, following parents or... Sienne stared in amazement as a little girl no more than eight dipped her hand into a passerby's belt pouch and came out with a handful of coins. The woman glanced down at the urchin, who made a face and trotted away, not very rapidly. The woman watched her go without raising a cry.

Then Alaric reached the street and hesitated. It did look daunting, all those people. Sienne knew from experience how hard it was to navigate a crowded street when you were invisible. Alaric gestured to them to draw back away from the crowds and pitched his voice low to be barely audible over the sounds of people walking, talking, laughing, and calling out to others to sample their wares. "Vaishant, you'll need to go first. Don't move too quickly or we'll get separated. Everyone, stay close. Remember the longer you stay in contact with someone, the greater the chance they'll see through *vanish*. How far is it to the temple?"

"A mile, maybe," Vaishant said. "It is near the center of the city."

"That's not bad. If you do get separated, head for the city center." Alaric took Sienne's hand. "Good luck."

It felt like diving into the sea, entering the crowd, a sea that moved in every direction and smelled of sweat and oils and a dozen clashing fragrances. Sienne let Alaric choose a path and divided her attention between the people surrounding her and Vaishant's figure, made smaller by distance. The few people Alaric bumped into didn't even look puzzled, probably because the crush was bad enough it was reasonable to expect people to bump into you, but Sienne thought it was strange that none of them checked their belongings afterward to make sure they hadn't been the victim of theft. None of them reacted to anyone else at all.

They passed through a marketplace filled with colorful awnings throwing geometric shadows on the hard-packed earth. Here, people interacted with each other, bartering in loud voices that turned the background hum of the city into a gentle roar. It took a few moments for Sienne to realize that despite the shouting and the wild gesticulation of both vendors and customers, no one was actually buying anything. It looked like a picture, like someone's idea of what an Omeiran market looked like.

More children raced between the stalls, some of them stealing right from under the owners' watchful eyes. Sienne dodged out of the way of two of these laughing children, carrying a copper pan between them, and had to dodge again as a woman dressed in vivid green with a blue head scarf covering her mouth and nose nearly walked into her. She stopped watching the people and paid closer attention to Vaishant, whom Alaric was hurrying to catch up to.

Vaishant led them out of the main thoroughfare and into narrower, less-trafficked streets. The houses there were rundown, with doorways little more than openings hung with tan or black curtains and cracks in their plastered surfaces. Soon, they were alone, and Alaric beckoned to the others. "No one got lost, that's good," he said.

"There is something very wrong about this city," Perrin said. "Did you note how no business was transacted in the marketplace?"

"And much of the shouting made no sense," Ghrita said. "As if they all wanted to make noise, but ran out of things to say."

"We just have to finish our business with the temple, and then we can get out of here," Alaric said.

"Unless there is someone guarding the temple," Ghrita said. "Do we have a plan for that?"

"Sneak past, subdue anyone we can't bypass, make it as quick as possible," Alaric said.

"Good plan," Ghrita replied.

"I think we can go behind the big streets," Vaishant said. "It will take longer, but we will not encounter people."

"Do that," Alaric said. "But hurry. *Vanish* won't last much longer."

They went more rapidly now that the streets were clear. Sienne couldn't tell if Vaishant knew where he was going, or if he was guessing, but he moved with such confidence it was impossible not to trust his guidance. He reminded her of Alaric, though where Alaric was forceful, Vaishant simply had a calm certainty that reassured her.

She gripped her spellbook through her shirt, reassured further by its smooth surface rubbing against her stomach. Everything was going so perfectly she had to make herself stay alert. This was the most dangerous time, when it felt like nothing could go wrong.

They came out of the narrow back streets into what Sienne thought of as the public face of Ma'tzehar, the new-looking buildings painted bright colors, the crowds of people all ignoring each other. The main street pointed arrow-straight at a towering structure that could only be a palace. Sparkling crystals embedded in the walls caught the afternoon sunlight and reflected it back in blinding brilliance, making Sienne's eyes water again. The crystals made the vibrant blues and greens and reds of the palace walls look dim by comparison.

Towers at each corner were painted in blue and yellow stripes spiraling up to the golden pointed domes capping them. More gold and copper domes dotted the roofs, stretching back until they vanished from sight. Sienne thought of the palace in Fioretti, with its white and red lights that made it look like a delicate confection at night. Whoever had decorated this place had had abysmal taste.

They dodged pedestrians—that was something nice about

Ma'tzehar; no animals in the street meant no animal waste to dodge as well—until they reached the shallow, curved stairs leading to the palace door. It was gilded like the domes and large enough to admit four of those camels side by side, not that anyone would let camels into such an opulent building. Sienne had enough time to observe this before Alaric tugged on her hand, and they continued to the left, paralleling the palace.

The temple was immediately recognizable from the description Perrin had given in his scrying. It looked decrepit next to the gaudy palace, its unadorned white walls cracked and blistered from long exposure to the sun, its roof sagging in places. Sienne could easily imagine this building sitting there for hundreds of years, uncared for and untenanted except by wild beasts. Doorways like the ones at the temple in Chirantan lined its façade, sheltered by broad roofs that put them in deep shadow. Vaishant stopped near one of these and waited for the others to catch up. "I do not know where you want to go from here," he murmured.

"Neither do we. Is there some kind of sanctum, or secret place? Kalanath, what did you see in your dream?" Alaric asked.

Kalanath shot a quick look at Vaishant. "It was a bare room. Circular. The floor was tiled with many tiny squares, but no pattern, just a dark color. Black or blue or maybe green. The walls were painted very light brown, and the ceiling was a dome with things painted on it. Birds, I think. It was dark enough not to see clearly. I have not seen one like it in the Chirantan temple."

"That is the place where the divines worship," Vaishant said. "There is one in every temple, though its decoration is always different. If this temple is the same, I know where the room is."

"Let's go there first," Alaric said, "and see what's there. Then look for the phoenix feather."

This time, Alaric led the way through the doorway and into the courtyard. It was as decrepit as Sienne had imagined, its fountain cracked with half the stone lying in the basin, its trees dead or dying, the ground covered with dry yellow weeds. Sienne's heart ached at all that beauty turned to dust. Why hadn't this been restored with the rest of the city? Surely no Omeiran would have wanted such a holy place to stay ruined.

Several dark doorways opened off the courtyard. Vaishant took one that looked no different from the others. It led to more of the narrow, winding corridors Sienne remembered from the Chirantan temple, but darker, more ominous. Without being asked, Sienne made several lights and set them to hovering above her friends' shoulders. They made strange shadows on the walls that did nothing to dispel the eerie aura permeating the place. She resisted the urge to light the hall to a noonday brilliance and took her place behind Alaric as they moved on.

Ancient dust that smelled dry and bitter rose up wherever she stepped, more evidence that no one had come this way for a very long time. She followed a crack in the plaster with her eyes from the floor to spider across the ceiling, and prayed the roof wouldn't decide now was a perfect time to collapse. Was it appropriate to pray to an avatar in a temple consecrated to...well, they were both God, so maybe it didn't matter. And maybe the place wasn't still consecrated after all these centuries. Vaishant would know, but she felt wary of speaking in this quiet, still place.

They passed doorways containing the splintered remnants of wooden doors, all painted white to match the walls. Vaishant didn't so much as slow to examine them. Sienne followed him around a corner to find him halted before a doorway at the end of the hall. Her magic lights illuminated enough of what lay beyond to show the room had a floor of thousands of inch-square tiles of midnight blue. "The divines' chamber," Vaishant said. His voice was only just audible, something Sienne understood. He, too, must feel this was not a place where speaking loudly felt appropriate.

Alaric nodded and stepped through the doorway. Sienne followed him, drawing her spellbook out of her shirt so it appeared to float in midair. The round room was some forty feet across and half that in height, rising another ten feet to the top of its domed ceiling. It looked as Kalanath had described it, down to the paintings on the dome.

Sienne sent more lights to illuminate the paintings. Birds of all kinds painted in bright gold that gleamed in the lights flew or perched around the dome, peacocks and doves and strange birds Sienne had never seen that she concluded were Omeiran natives. The artist had rendered some of them realistically, and others in an abstract, blocky style that nevertheless left them both easily recognizable and filled with tight energy, as if they might go flapping off the ceiling at any moment.

A shudder passed through Sienne, and the shimmering outlines of her friends went solid. She looked down at her hands and saw them waver back into focus. "I'll need to cast it again to get us out of here," she said. "But that will leave me at the end of my reserves."

"We'll deal with that when we come to it," Alaric said. "If we wait until dark, we might be able to leave without using *vanish*."

"Now what?" Dianthe said. "I don't see a symbol." She was studying the floor, which bore no markings and was surprisingly free of dust.

"In my dream, the symbol hangs in the air," Kalanath said. "I think it is that we must do the ritual."

"Which ritual, I wonder," Perrin said. "Performing the unaltered ritual does not help us know how to invert the binding and free the Sassaven."

"We know the original, though," Alaric said. "The coming of age ritual, the one that creates a full Sassaven. That's the place to start." He set his pack down and rummaged through it. "I have the flask with the potion, the goblet, the knife...Sienne, you know the spells."

"I do. But I don't know how to make the symbol appear. Unless..." She turned pages in her spellbook. "*Mirage* might do it, if Kalanath can draw the symbol for me."

"Shh," Dianthe said, moving to the door. "I hear something."

The room went silent. Sienne strained to hear whatever Dianthe had, but heard only her own breathing. Dianthe turned and gestured them all away from the door, toward the walls.

"*Hands against the wall!*" someone shouted in Meiric, and now Sienne heard running footsteps as a dozen slim figures in black desert garb, their heads bare, ran into the room, long knives at the ready. *"Drop your weapons or die where you stand!"*

Alaric reached for his sword, and two of them tackled him, kicking his legs out from beneath him and forcing him to the floor. Sienne turned to *fury* and tried to read, but in the next moment someone spun her around and yanked the harness off over her head, shoving her down. She cried out as she landed too hard on her wrist. Alaric shouted her name and rose up, tossing his captors aside before three more of them dove atop him and pinned him. Sienne raised her head and saw more dark-clad figures pouring into the room, subduing her friends and taking their weapons. Kalanath was backed against the wall, his staff in an enemy's hand, and as she watched he feinted left, moved right, and grabbed his opponent in a complicated hold. *"Release them, or I kill him!"* he shouted.

Someone grabbed Sienne's hair and pulled her head back, laying the sharp edge of a knife against her throat. *"Which of us do you think is faster?"* the man holding the knife said.

"Alaric, don't change!" Sienne screamed, feeling the edge bite into her throat. She had no doubt if a unicorn suddenly appeared among them, that knife would find its mark.

Kalanath grimaced, then shoved his captive away. The knife withdrew. *"You will come with us,"* another man said. Sienne's captor wrenched her hands behind her back and withdrew manacles from his belt, securing her wrists firmly but not too tightly. He patted her down briskly and took her belt knife and then, to her dismay, her well-hidden boot knife. Then he hauled her up with one hand under her elbow and pushed her, more gently this time, toward the center of the room.

Sienne hurried to Alaric's side. "Did they hurt you?" he said. He, too, was manacled, but his captors hovered nearby as if they thought he might be capable of breaking iron chains. It was a reasonable fear, Sienne thought.

"I'm fine," she said.

"What language is that?" one of their captors said. *"Stop talking immediately!"*

"It's *Fellic*," Sienne said. "*Most of us don't speak Meiric. And you'd better let us go.*"

"*Fellic? Never heard of it,*" the man said.

"*How did you know we were here?*" Kalanath asked.

The man sneered. "*Our lord has great powers of discernment. Nothing is hidden from his eye. You'd better pray for mercy. Our rakhyanam is a cruel and pitiless lord, and he won't like that you came sneaking into his city.*"

Sienne said nothing. They had been sneaking, after all, and in hindsight they probably should have guessed that where there was a palace, there would be a ruler. But how had anyone known of their presence? Only a priest could scry, and if the temple was dilapidated, she doubted the *rakhyanam* was a priest.

"What did you say?" Alaric said. A dark-clad man prodded Alaric in the vicinity of his kidneys with his so-sharp knife, and Alaric went silent.

"They don't want us talking Fellic," Sienne said to the room at large, then in Meiric added, "*I just told them what you told me, not to speak our language, so don't go jabbing that knife in my direction.*"

Another man walked up to Sienne, dangling her spellbook in its harness. "*What is this?*"

"*A book.*"

"*We were told it was a weapon. How is that so?*"

"*It's magic. Have you heard of magic? You should give it back before it hurts you.*"

The man grinned, displaying very white teeth, the canines filed to a point. "*Our lord has magic of his own, foreigner. You must be weak to need a book to contain yours. The rakhyanam wishes us to bring it to him.*"

Sienne bared her teeth at him, which made him smile more broadly. Someone shoved her, enough to get her moving, and the black-clad men maneuvered them out of the chamber and into the narrow little hall, where they had to go single file. Sienne kept a close eye on her spellbook. If only they'd hold it by the harness straps instead of the book itself, she could maybe use her invisible fingers to snatch it back. But the man carrying it tucked it under one arm, where it taunted her with its unattainable nearness.

They emerged into the dead courtyard, where their captors arranged them in the center of several black-clad men. Sienne once again was near Alaric, whose shoulders were tense in the way that said he was thinking hard about a problem. This was certainly the worst problem they'd faced in a long time. Captured, taken before the *rakhyanam*, unarmed and...well, not exactly helpless, but certainly at a disadvantage. She hoped Alaric would come up with something.

13

They left the temple and, as Sienne had guessed, marched straight for the palace. She thought they might be taken around to the side, but no, their captors led them up the front stairs and through the massive double doors that shone bright as gold. It chilled Sienne to know that someone had known not only that they'd entered the temple, but that Sienne's spellbook was a dangerous weapon. It spoke to a level of awareness Sienne didn't think they could counter. And if the person knew that much, who could say how much else they might know?

The double doors opened on a vast hall, pillared down both its long sides, with a floor patterned in green and gold tiles Sienne thought might be actual gold. The ceiling rose to an elongated dome of some translucent material that filled the hall with a diffuse light. The room felt much cooler than the outdoors, far cooler than Sienne had expected, and she smelled the distinct hot-metal tang of a lot of magic hovering in the background. The only places she'd smelled magic this strongly were wizardry schools; nowhere else had a high concentration of magical residue from people doing many, many spells all at once. She sneezed, and one of her captors gave her a glare that she returned.

Stairs went up at the far end of the hall, rising more than twenty feet to the next floor. Sienne trod carefully, not wanting to trip and go rolling to the bottom, unable to catch herself with her bound hands. The stairs were painted a brownish-red that reminded her of dried blood, an image she tried to shake. Their rough surface clung reassuringly to her soles. Tripping was unlikely, but the idea still made her nervous.

Two more gilded doors the size of the main entrance awaited them at the top of the stairs. These were open, swung inward as if welcoming guests. Sienne didn't feel very welcomed. The manacles might have had something to do with that. She walked forward, feeling comforted, a little, at being surrounded by her friends. Alaric was ahead of her, as usual, and the sight of his broad shoulders and back comforted her further.

She took a step to the side so she could see around him. The walls of this room were solid gold as if someone had slathered the gilding on with a paintbrush, with sheets of mother of pearl at least five feet long hanging like mirrors at intervals. Four other doorways revealed only darkness beyond. More of the soft, diffuse light came from the ceiling, making the gilded walls and the mother of pearl glow as if lit from within. The floor tiles were as small as the ones in the entry, but tinted dark blue and crimson in a chessboard pattern that, when Sienne looked it out of the corner of her eye, made the floor look violet. More men dressed in dark desert clothes stood at attention near each of the mother of pearl panels, armed with long knives and curved swords.

At the far end of the room, on a raised dais, stood a golden throne, and one look at it told Sienne that it wasn't gilded, but made of solid gold, because its creator wouldn't have stood for anything less. Faceted gems that winked dully in the soft light made patterns, spirals and curves, around the throne's base and arms, and outlined an elongated fan across the high back. Golden snakes wreathed the armrests and coiled along the foot, their eyes enormous rubies or sapphires. *This* was the gaudiest thing Sienne had ever seen, putting the palace in the shade.

A man lounged on the throne, his legs disposed over one armrest and his elbow propping him up on the other. His red hair was long for an Omeiran, curling around his shoulders, and his short beard outlined a firm jaw and a shapely mouth. He sat up as they entered and adjusted the golden crown he wore. It was encrusted with gems and would have looked unspeakably tasteless if it wasn't in proximity to the throne.

"*Well,*" he said in Meiric. "*Intruders.*"

No one spoke. Sienne caught Vaishant looking at her and cursed inwardly. She stepped forward and said, "*We meant no harm,*" just as Ghrita said, "*How did you know we were here?*"

"*I don't speak to women,*" the *rakhyanam* said. "*Be silent.*"

Sienne didn't need to see Alaric's face to know he was close to exploding. "*We didn't want to disrupt your city,*" Kalanath said. "*Since some of us are not Omeiran.*"

"*What do you mean, not Omeiran?*" The *rakhyanam* stood and descended the dais steps, bouncing in a frivolous way. He skipped to Alaric's side and grabbed his chin, forcing the big man to look at him. He seemed not at all afraid of Alaric's furious glower. The *rakhyanam* snapped his fingers toward the man holding Sienne's spellbook. The man handed it to him, and the *rakhyanam* released Alaric roughly and held the spellbook up to his face. "*This looks like nothing, but it's a weapon. What is it?*"

"*It is powerful magic, and you should release us before we use it on you,*" Kalanath said.

The *rakhyanam* laughed and returned to his throne, flopping down on it and setting the spellbook on his lap. "*You'd have used it already if you could,*" he said, toying with the ring he wore on his right hand. His eyes grew distant, as if he were listening to someone Sienne couldn't hear. "*You're not the leader,*" he said to Kalanath. "*I think...he is.*" He pointed at Alaric, and said, "*I would like to speak his language.*"

Sienne and Kalanath looked at each other, mystified. The *rakhyanam* worked his jaw as if chewing a particularly stringy piece of meat, yawned, and said in Fellic, "Is this it? This strange tongue that feels like coughing?"

"We understand you, if that's what you're asking," Alaric said.

The *rakhyanam's* face lit with delight. "Astonishing! And do you all understand me?"

Sienne nodded with the rest.

"It's truly amazing. My name is Darinikh Mekhalgohti, and I am the *rakhyanam* of Jamidaara. Now, tell me, why have you come here, and why did you sneak around like thieves instead of entering openly?" He addressed Alaric, who remained silent. The delight left Darinikh's face. "You came to steal from me, didn't you? Admit it!"

Alaric continued in his stony-faced silence. Darinikh made a gesture, and one of the black-clad men approached, sword drawn. "Kill the small one," Darinikh said.

"*No!*" Alaric shouted, turning as the man advanced on Sienne. She backed away into Alaric and wished more fervently than ever for her spellbook.

"So you're capable of speech when you're properly motivated. I wondered," Darinikh said. "It's a simple question. Answer, and nobody has to die."

Alaric stayed close to Sienne. "We came looking for Ma'tzehar," he said.

"That's an old name. Not one that applies anymore." Darinikh leaned forward. "Jamidaara is so much nicer a name, don't you think? Oh, but you don't speak my language. It means 'happiness', more or less. I gave the city a new name when I rebuilt it. And why did you want to find Ma'tzehar?"

Sienne, pressed against Alaric's side, could feel his chest moving with each heavy breath. "We wanted something from the temple," Alaric said. "We thought the city was uninhabited."

"The temple?" Darinikh sounded as appalled as if Alaric had suggested he eat puppies. "The temple is destroyed, unconsecrated."

"Then you won't mind if we finish what we came for," Alaric said.

"Of course I mind! You could have entered openly, like normal people, but you chose to sneak about. I don't think you're telling me the whole truth." Darinikh snapped his fingers again, and one of the black-clad fighters came forward to go to one knee before the throne.

"Take the men to the dungeon. Let's give them time to think about what's in their best interests. The women...they can go to the harem with the others."

Alaric snarled and rushed the throne. Black-clad men tackled him and brought him down on the dais steps. Darinikh hadn't so much as flinched. He laughed. "You're attached to the small one, aren't you? Don't worry, I won't hurt her. But you might want to think about your best interests quickly."

Kalanath leaped into the air, bringing his knees close to his chest and his bound arms down and around so they were in front of him. Ghrita, half a breath behind him, did the same. In total silence, the two attacked the nearest guards with feet and hands. Sienne hurried to put herself back to back with Perrin, who was closest. "They did not take my blessing papers," he said, "but I cannot reach them."

The *rakhyanam* was sitting upright on the throne, watching the fight with avid amusement. The spellbook sat untended on his lap. Sienne grabbed it with her invisible fingers and pulled it toward herself, willing it open to *force* as it came. She saw Darinikh stand and shout something, and then the book hovered in front of her and she read as rapidly as she dared.

Something smashed into the side of her head, something hard that made her bite her tongue and sent her vision swimming. Her spellbook fell to the floor with a crack. Dizzy, she blinked tears out of her eyes and reached for the book again with invisible fingers. It resisted, and she blinked again and saw one of the black-clad guards had picked it up and was holding it tightly at arm's length as if it were a venomous snake. She switched targets and yanked at his robe, hoping to distract him. He let go with one hand and beat at his chest, swearing. She pulled on the spellbook again and this time freed it from his grasp.

"*Enough!*" Darinikh shouted, clapping his hands together once. A thunderous roar shook the throne room, accompanied by a tremor that knocked everyone except Darinikh to the floor. Sienne pressed her spellbook close to her chest as she struggled upright. The guards were faster. Two held her while a third wrenched the spellbook away, several more secured Kalanath and Ghrita, and the rest restrained her other friends. Alaric still lay pinned, struggling, under the weight of five guards. Sienne screamed as one reversed his sword and struck Alaric across the temple, leaving him limp and motionless.

"Interesting," Darinikh said. His voice was higher-pitched than before, and he was breathing heavily, though he didn't look frightened. "Lock them up as I directed. And give me that book. I want to examine it."

Sienne watched helplessly as Darinikh tucked her spellbook inside his jewel-embroidered robes. Two guards took her by the arms and marched her away despite her struggles. The last thing she saw was Alaric's limp body, hoisted between several guards and dragged in the opposite direction.

She was barely aware of the elegant halls the guards led her down, all of which were nearly as opulent as the throne room. She couldn't see Dianthe or Ghrita, though she could hear their footsteps. How were they going to get out of this? Her mind skittered back and forth between hopeless plans for escape and her last sight of Alaric. The latter threw her into a panic. What if they'd killed him with that blow?

She became conscious that the halls were narrower and their ceilings lower just before they stopped in front of a door with a latticed upper half. It was normal sized, which made it look minuscule in this vast palace, and the diamonds of the lattice revealed little of what lay beyond except that it was well-lit. A key hung from a peg on the wall about five feet from the door, and one of the guards used it to open the door. Sienne's guards unfastened the manacles and shoved her inside so she tripped and fell, catching herself on the wrist she'd injured earlier and making her cry out in pain. Beside her, Ghrita and Dianthe hit the floor somewhat more gracefully. The guards did this in total silence, which frightened Sienne more than leering or cursing would have. Then the door shut, the key scraped in the lock, and the guards' footsteps retreated.

"*Who are you?*" a woman asked.

Sienne looked up, cradling her wrist. A woman dressed in blue silk robes that covered her from head to toe, leaving only her face exposed, came toward her. Several other women dressed as she was hovered in the background, watching the newcomers curiously. "*You're not Omeiran,*" the woman continued. She had a sharp, keen-eyed face with thin lips and the typically narrow eyes of an Omeiran. "*Did the bastard capture you, too, travelers?*"

"What's she saying?" Dianthe said.

"She wants to know who we are," Ghrita said just as the woman said, "*What language is that?*"

"*We're from the land west of the mountains,*" Sienne said. "*The rakhyanam captured us. Our friends are in the dungeon, and...is this the harem?*"

The woman scowled, an expression that made her look capable of disemboweling someone with nothing but a dinner knife. "*The bastard thinks women are unimportant. I hope to prove him wrong on his dead body. My name is Lashwanti Haliankhoti, and he has enslaved my people through his foul magics.*"

Sienne quickly translated for Dianthe, who said, "Her people? Do you suppose these are the *pakhshani*?"

Playing go-between was going to get old, fast. Sienne repeated this question to Lashwanti, who nodded. "*I am chief of chiefs,*" the woman said, "*and he keeps me here through threatening them. But I can't stay here forever. My sisters and I intend to escape. Will you join us?*"

"*I can probably make it easy,*" Sienne said. "*Will Darinikh come soon?*"

Lashwanti laughed. "*He never comes to the harem. We think he is incapable of...*" She made a crude gesture that made Sienne blush and Dianthe and Ghrita laugh. "*And the guards...they were ours, too, but they seem to have forgotten us. They fear him too much to trifle with the women of the harem, though.*"

"*Well,*" Sienne said. "*That helps. Now, does anyone have a mirror?*"

———

"Damn," Sienne said. "That was a really good idea."

"It's a mirror," Ghrita said. "You wanted a mirror."

"Yes, but I need a glass mirror. Something that will break. It has to fit through the lattice of the door." Sienne examined her reflection in the polished steel mirror. Her head scarf was askew and her hair straggled around her face because the guards had pushed her around. "I was going to use magic to retrieve the key and unlock the door. But I have to be able to see or touch the object. Even pressing my face flat against the lattice doesn't work."

Ghrita pursed her lips in thought. "*Are there guards anywhere near?*" she asked Lashwanti.

Lashwanti shook her head. "*We tried to break the door down, and no one came despite the noise we made. We think Darinikh has no regard for women, that he doesn't post guards. He thinks we're helpless.*" Her scowl said she felt helpless, and was furious about it.

Ghrita strode to the door. "Stand back," she said, and repeated herself in Meiric. Sienne stood to one side, where she could still see the woman's face. Ghrita closed her eyes and breathed in and out, slow and rhythmic. She clasped her hands in front of her face, one balled up and pressed against the other's palm. Then, in one swift movement, she drew back her fist and slammed it against the lattice, letting out a sharp *hah!* as she did so.

The lattice shattered, spraying outward in a cloud of sharp pieces. Ghrita opened her eyes and shook out her hand, which was undamaged. Sienne gasped. Ghrita glanced at her. One corner of her mouth twitched upward in a mocking smile. "Not something your magic can do, eh?"

Sienne's awe turned to irritation. "Thank you," she said, suppressing an angry retort. Ghrita's smile widened. "Now, unless you're capable of fitting yourself through that hole, let me take a turn."

Ghrita stepped aside, and Sienne stuck her head through the smashed remains of the lattice. It was a tight fit, and the sharp edges of the broken wood scraped her cheek and tangled in her hair, but she was barely able to see the key, hanging on its peg five feet away. It was almost too easy. With her invisible fingers, she lifted the key off the peg and drew it toward her, withdrawing into the room at the cost of a few more scrapes. The key landed in her hand, and she swiftly unlocked the door.

Lashwanti immediately made for the exit, followed by the other women. "*My thanks,*" she said. "*Will you join us? Turn your fists and your magic to defeating Darinikh?*"

"We have to find our companions. They're in the dungeon," Sienne said.

"*My male chiefs may be there as well,*" Lashwanti said. "*Or they may have been turned like the guards. We will come with you to the dungeon. Though we don't know where it is.*"

"I've already got a sense for how this place is laid out," Dianthe said when this conversation was relayed. "There are three doors between here and the throne room that might lead down—I assume the dungeon is below ground. It's possible the stairs are on the far side, but we should try those three first."

"Lead the way," Sienne said.

There were too many of them, with Lashwanti and her six companions, to remain perfectly silent, but the *pakhshani* were barefoot, and they didn't sound like a herd of rampaging camels. Sienne had no idea how Dianthe was able to keep track of all the turnings. The halls all looked the same to her, though some were more gilded than others. Dianthe stopped before a door and tried the handle.

It opened smoothly on a room Sienne at first thought was painted in a thousand random colors that radiated magic blinding to her inner eye. A second look showed her it was full of— "Rugs," she said, stepping inside to examine them more closely. "Rugs, hanging from the ceiling." Each was about ten feet long and six feet wide, with tassels dangling in a fringe on the shorter sides.

Lashwanti followed her, tugging on one of the rugs and making it sway. "*Flying carpets,*" she said. "*Worth a fortune.*"

"*Flying carpets? Like in the stories?*" Sienne realized the rugs weren't hanging from anything; they simply floated vertically in midair. To her eyes, they glowed with magic. "*Why are they stored here instead of being used?*"

Lashwanti shrugged. "*Who knows why that bastard does what he does,*" she said. "*They're useless to us now. They'd only hamper our escape.*"

"They're actual flying carpets," Sienne told Dianthe. "I wish—"

"I know, but they'd just get in the way. It's not like we know how to use them."

Sienne scowled and shut the door. "I always wanted a flying carpet."

"Don't take this the wrong way, but I hope you don't get your wish," Dianthe said, "because it would probably mean failure."

They proceeded down the hall. The complete absence of other people, guards or servants or even Darinikh himself, made Sienne nervous. It was an enormous palace, true, but not so enormous that all its inhabitants could vanish into it so completely. Dianthe tried another door, which was locked. She grinned, and pulled her lock picks out of her left boot. "Sloppy," she commented. Sienne patted her sides and discovered she still had the hazard deck. That might be useful if she were desperate. Though with her increasing anxiety over Alaric, desperation might be just around the corner.

The lock clicked open, and Dianthe opened the door, revealing stairs...going up. Dianthe swore. "I was sure that was it."

"Next door," Sienne said.

Dianthe nodded and trotted off around a corner, and immediately said, "Guards! Run!" She and Ghrita took off down the corridor to the right.

Sienne shouted, *"Run!"* in Meiric and put her own command into action, turning and fleeing back the way they'd come. She immediately realized how stupid that was, separating their little group, and tried to turn around, but the *pakhshani* crowded the hall, and fighting through them was pointless. So she let them sweep her along, taking turn after turn until she found a cross-corridor, where she shoved through to the side and let them pass her. Then she trotted back the way she'd come.

The corridor was as empty and silent as it had been before Dianthe's warning. Sienne slowed her steps, fearing running into more guards. Nothing looked familiar. She wished for once they had Perrin's blessing that let them speak to each other mind to mind. She was lost and had nothing but questions. Where had Dianthe and Ghrita gone? They'd vanished as thoroughly as the guards had.

She was positive she'd never been in the hall she currently found herself in. It was long and had a high ceiling, dim because its only light came from the translucent roof. A few doors at irregular intervals lined the walls. If only she knew which way the front door was, or even the throne room! That thought made her feel stupid, and she worked the small magic that told her which way was north. The entrance was on the west, so if she kept heading to her left, that should eventually bring her to it.

She continued down the hallway, her soft desert shoes making almost no noise on the tiled floor. The gilded walls glimmered, reflecting her image as a shadowy, unformed blob pacing her as she walked. She couldn't imagine living in this place, however opulent. Everything was hard and sharp-edged without any softening influences. Even the solid gold throne couldn't possibly be comfortable. And it smelled of nothing at all, which was more unnerving than if it had stunk of refuse or acid.

She neared the end of the hall and froze. Booted footsteps approached from that direction, distant yet unmistakable. Sienne turned and hurried back the way she'd come only to hear more booted footsteps approaching from the other direction. Trapped. It was almost funny.

She tried the nearest door, but it was locked. So was the next. The footsteps were growing louder. In a panic, she took hold of a third door and wrenched the handle. It turned, and the door swung open. She bolted inside and shut the door firmly but quietly behind her.

Breathing heavily, she leaned against the door and surveyed her surroundings. Filmy drapes dividing the room in half hung from the low ceiling, moving in an intangible breeze. Giant pillows lay on the floor, which was thickly carpeted over the ubiquitous tile. It had all the softness Sienne had believed absent from the palace. Formless shapes lay beyond the gauzy curtains. Sienne tiptoed forward and pushed one of the drapes aside. It was a bedroom, with a bed tall enough to require the little stepladder propped beside it and a dressing table with a mirror, not steel but fine glass, mounted above it.

The bed was also occupied. A slim figure lay atop the blankets, curled loosely with its knees pulled up under its chin. It wore a loose robe, nearly transparent, stitched all over with silver peacocks. Despite this, Sienne couldn't tell if it were male or female. She hesitated beside the bed, then took half a step back as the person's eyes opened. They were bright silver, without pupil or iris, but blinked at Sienne in a way that said they saw her.

The person sat up, a graceful, languid movement like water flowing, and folded his, or her, legs beneath her, or him. "Who," it said in a voice that shimmered like morning dew, "are you?"

14

"You speak my language," Sienne said. It was the only thing that came to mind.

"I speak all languages," the person said. Its voice was low for a woman or high for a man. Its face was beautiful, but in the way a statue's would be, not like anything human. Black hair curled softly around its face, making its pale skin, paler than Alaric's, seem almost white. Sienne tried not to stare at its body, which lacked both the curves of a woman and the muscles of a man. "But I have not seen your kind in centuries. You are Ginatese?"

"No. Rafellish."

"I don't recognize that."

"Then...how can you speak Fellic?"

"I draw your knowledge of your own language from your mind. Don't worry, it doesn't hurt, and I can't read your thoughts." The person smiled. The smile was friendly, but the silver eyes, devoid of emotion, made it a menacing expression. Sienne kept from retreating another step through sheer willpower.

"There haven't been Ginatese in five hundred years," she said. "Who...what are you?"

The smile vanished. "You're afraid of me," the creature said. "I haven't done anything to hurt you. You shouldn't be afraid."

"I'm sorry. Everything in this place is trying to kill me."

The creature laughed. It was an unexpectedly pleasant sound, and Sienne relaxed. "I promise I won't try to kill you," it said. "You must have met Dari. Darinikh, I mean."

"He has my friends captive."

"He has a lot of things captive." The creature frowned. "I beg your pardon. You asked a question. My name is Jenani, and I am an ashwar. The Ginatese called me yfrit."

"I've never heard those names before. You must be very old if you knew the Ginatese." She supposed in some respects she was Ginatese, since the Rafellish and Ansorjans and Wrathen all descended from them, but she had a feeling the ashwar meant something more literal when he referred to that lost civilization.

"Millennia," Jenani said. "I was lost for many centuries, until...but sit, please. I don't have anything to offer you, as I don't eat anything you would find nourishing."

"That's all right. Thanks. My name is Sienne." Sienne looked around, saw no chairs, and settled on a large cushion on the floor. Jenani flowed off the bed and settled on another cushion nearby. As the robe shifted around it, Sienne couldn't help seeing that it had no male organs, no breasts—it really wasn't male or female. She tried and failed to come up with a way to gracefully ask about it, then realized it didn't matter what sex it was or wasn't.

"So, you said Darinikh has many captives. Are you one of them?" she said instead.

Anger flitted across Jenani's face. "I am," it said. "His first captive, and responsible for the others."

"I don't understand."

"Ashwara have access to great magical power—you do have magic among your people, yes? The Omeirans don't."

"I know. They do something to prevent their children becoming wizards."

Jenani smiled. "I didn't know that. Interesting. What is a wizard?"

"Someone who knows how to read the spell languages. Someone born with the ability to do magic."

"You mean that not all Rafellish are...wizards?"

"Yes. But I am."

"Then you have power. Can you show me?"

"Darinikh took my spellbook. I can do small magics without it." Sienne made a couple of lights and sent them flying around the room. Jenani watched, its mouth slightly open in fascination.

"What are you capable of with your...spellbook, I wonder?" it said.

"Much more. Transportation across great distances, creating fire or magical force, making images that fool the eyes, turning things into other things. My spellbook is my dearest possession."

"Then you will understand my plight, to a degree. Ashwara are beings of magic, capable of great deeds. But many of us were captured by Ginatese who hoped to use our magic for themselves. Imprisoned in objects, rings, brooches, even a lamp once. And the possessor of that object has total control over our magic."

"And Darinikh has your object."

"You're quick. Yes. There is a ring to which I am bound, and Dari —Darinikh found it. He commanded me to rebuild this place and to fill it with servants for him, forced me to bring the *pakhshani* from the desert to populate the city, insisted I make him a *rakhyanam*...that was only the beginning."

"We wondered how Ma'tzehar could have been rebuilt so thoroughly."

"It was a ruin when I found it," Jenani said. "I should apologize. I was the one who revealed your presence to Darinikh. He commanded me to tell him if anyone enters or leaves the city."

"It's not your fault, if he forced you."

"I also told him about the book you carry, that it radiates power. I should have kept that to myself, but I'd never seen anything like it and my surprise slipped out. Would it have allowed you to free yourselves?"

Sienne tried not to feel irritation at the creature's carelessness. "It would. Maybe. But there's no sense falling into regret."

"So, why did you come here? You and your friends?"

"We needed something from the temple. Why wasn't it rebuilt?"

"Darinikh has no use for religion, and he didn't want to provide the *pakhshani* a place to worship." Jenani shook its head. "I am not religious either, but it seemed wrong to me to leave it uncared for. But I am at Darinikh's mercy. I cannot use my magic on my own behalf, or in any way save at his command."

"That's so unfair!" Sienne exclaimed. "You shouldn't be a captive."

"I can't free myself. I've been a slave of the ring for a very long time, so long I've forgotten what it felt like to be free."

Sienne scowled. "That's even worse. Is there anything I can do?"

Jenani frowned. "You mean, take control of the ring from Darinikh?"

"No, I mean free you."

Jenani's laughter filled the room. "You would not do it. You would want my power for yourself."

"I don't have any interest in your power. I just don't want Darinikh to have it."

"So many people have said that over the centuries, Sienne. All in the same way, too. They make bold promises about freeing me, then, when they have the ring, they want me to do just one small thing before releasing me. Then another. And then they 'forget' their promise to me. When they die, or the ring is stolen, the cycle begins again. So forgive me if I don't believe you. I'm sure you mean it now. They all do. But that won't last."

"It will for me. I have more than enough magic at my command to satisfy me, and you can't give me what I want." The second the words left her lips, though, she thought of the Sassaven, and the wizard who had them enslaved. If an ashwar could build a city with magic, what else could it do? Break the binding that held the Sassaven captive?

"You see? You're already thinking about it," Jenani said with a sad smile.

"All right, I thought about it, but I swear I'll find a way to set you free, and I keep my vows." Sienne stood and paced. "How do I do it?"

Jenani shrugged as if to say *I'll go along with this for now.* "You must destroy the ring," it said. "It constrains my power and allows its wearer to direct it. It won't be easy."

"I'll figure something out." Sienne looked down at Jenani, who was watching her with that same sad smile. "You must have been disappointed so many times," she said. "I'm sorry."

"Are you always like this?" Jenani asked. "So determined to see right done?"

Sienne blushed. "One of my companions says I have an overdeveloped sense of justice," she said. "I don't think that's a bad thing."

"Neither do I," Jenani said, standing. It was the same height as Sienne, and delicately built despite its lack of feminine curves. "I almost believe you might be able to do it."

"Of course I can. How destroyed does the ring have to be? Is it enough that it be twisted so it can't be worn, or does it have to be disintegrated or something?" She remembered an emerald falcon artifact and for the first time in her life wished she still had it.

"Melted would be best. But I think smashing it will work. I've never seen it done before."

"All right. I need to find my friends. Do you know where the dungeon is?"

"I built this palace. I know where *everything* is. But I'm forbidden to leave this room."

"Damn." Sienne scowled. "Can you give me directions?"

Jenani pushed through the drapes and opened the lid of a writing desk, removing paper and a stick of charcoal. It sketched a map with bold, black lines, then drew a path through it. "You'll have to watch out for guards," it said. "They usually stay near Darinikh, but sometimes he has them patrol the corridors. I think it makes him feel like a real ruler."

"So he wasn't noble before he found your ring?"

"Not at all." Jenani smiled reflectively. "He wasn't much of anything except very lucky." It handed her the map.

"Thank you," Sienne said. "We'll destroy Darinikh and the ring, I promise."

"Forgive me if I don't hold my breath," Jenani said, with a smile to show it wasn't serious.

Sienne opened the door and peered out. The hall was silent and empty. She saluted Jenani with the map and eased through the doorway, letting the door close quietly behind her.

She studied the map, getting a sense for how the palace was designed. The route Jenani had drawn for her took her back the way she'd come, she thought, certainly away from the throne room. East, according to her inner sense, and then north. Map in hand, she ran down the corridor to the first turning.

She needed to consult the map more than once as she ran, and twice nearly ran into guards patrolling the halls. She'd never realized how much she'd come to depend on wizardry in her scrapping career. *Vanish* would have made this journey easy, or *imitate,* though that had its own hazards if she tried to impersonate a guard.

She paused at a corner when she heard someone coming toward her, someone whose footsteps weren't as loud as the guards. Breathing quietly, she concentrated, and from the far end of the corridor, someone said in Meiric, "*You there! Come here!*"

The footsteps stopped, and she heard shuffling. "*What...?*" a man said. Sienne peeked around the corner to see a young man in desert robes, bearing a tray, with his back to her, peering down the corridor. "*I said come here!*" her phantom voice said.

The man began walking toward the sound, and when he was about halfway there, Sienne slipped from concealment and ran for the next intersection, which lay between her and the man. The man stopped and turned, saying, "*Who's there?*" but Sienne was already gone. He'd probably seen some of her, but she looked Omeiran in her robe, and with luck he had some errand too important to interrupt by looking for an intruder, if that's what he thought she was.

The corridors she now entered were small, smaller even than those leading to the harem. She checked the map again. Two more intersections, then the first left. She moved as slowly as she could bear, trying to stay silent. Being captured so close to her goal would be devastating. She heard nothing but her own quiet footsteps and the sound of her breathing, which felt hard and fast even though she hadn't exerted herself much.

Two intersections, then the first left. There was only one door on the left, but it was heavy, made of solid oak—where did they get oak in the desert? That only proved, again, how immensely powerful Jenani must be—and banded with iron. It also hung slightly ajar.

Sienne stopped and considered it for a moment. She had expected it to be closed, probably locked, and this made her nervous. Maybe her friends had already made their escape, and she would have to search the entire palace for them. And she wasn't going to find out if she stood there dithering. She opened the door to find steps leading down into darkness.

Not daring to make a light, she edged forward to the top of the stairs and let the door swing shut behind her, closing but not latching. Absolute darkness unrelieved by any hint of illumination swallowed her. She tried to think rationally. This meant there probably weren't any guards there, but why wouldn't they leave the prisoners even a little light? It meant nothing good. Possibly that the prisoners were already gone.

She took a step forward, feeling for the top step and balancing with one hand on the wall. It was cold as nothing else had been in the sundrenched desert, made of rough stones, and surprisingly damp. It felt exactly as she imagined a dungeon ought to feel—a dungeon in Rafellin, not Omeira. How would Darinikh, who knew nothing of Rafellin or its people, know to create a dungeon from her nightmares? Or was this Jenani's work, imitating the Ginatese he'd once known?

Sienne took another step, and her foot slipped, setting her heart racing. There was nothing for it—she'd have to make light, and risk the consequences if she was wrong and there were guards waiting at the bottom. She made one white light and set it hovering at her right shoulder. The dungeon stairs were even more frightening when they were visible: irregularly shaped, descending to a tiny landing and making a right turn she couldn't see past. Slowly, because the stairs were slick, she descended.

The stairs made two more turns before she heard voices. She stopped, straining to hear, but they echoed enough that she couldn't even make out what language they spoke. With luck, it would be her friends. She refused to think of all the many unlucky possibilities.

She continued down the steps toward an arched doorway only a foot or so taller than herself. She couldn't imagine how they'd fit Alaric through it. Thinking of him made her heart ache. He wasn't dead, he couldn't be. They'd just knocked him unconscious.

The voices cut off as she approached the doorway. Horribly aware that she was a clear target, she stepped through and looked around. The dungeon was a smallish room with a very high ceiling that rose past the range of her light. Manacles dangled from the walls at a height that would painfully stretch the arms of anyone chained with them. Dianthe stood on tiptoe, picking the lock on Perrin's chains, while Ghrita stood next to Vaishant, who was similarly manacled. Sienne relaxed, then let out a squeak as Kalanath appeared beside her from where he'd been hiding next to the doorway. "We thought it was you," he said, embracing her tightly. "Your light is white and not fire, like the guards."

"I'm so glad to see you all," Sienne said. "But...where's Alaric?"

Kalanath released her. He looked grim. "They took him," he said. "An hour ago, I think. We cannot tell time here."

Dianthe stepped back, and Perrin lowered his arms and massaged his wrists. "Ghrita and I stayed together when the guards appeared," she said, moving to begin on Vaishant's manacles. "We only just got here. What happened to you?"

"I got lost. And I found—but where did they take Alaric? *What happened?*"

"Calm down, Sienne," Dianthe said. "We'll find him." She didn't sound certain. Sienne paced the small chamber, fists clenched. Taken...did that mean torture? She'd believe Darinikh capable of anything.

"I met a creature," she said, trying to distract herself. "It's a magical being Darinikh holds captive. It's responsible for all this—I mean, its magic is. Darinikh tells it what to do, and it does it. Built the palace, restored the city, captured the *pakhshani*. We need to free it, and to do that, we need to defeat Darinikh."

"I am in favor of this, Sienne," Perrin said, "but we are at a disadvantage. You have no spellbook, and the rest of us have no weapons. And I have no more scrying blessings to tell us where to find Alaric."

Vaishant stepped away from the wall, rubbing his wrists as Perrin had. "I do not know Alaric well, but perhaps God will grant me sight of him," he said. "Though I am not certain how well it will work. The sight frequently shows only the thing you seek, without detail of its surroundings. But it is worth trying."

"I will watch the door," Kalanath said, and trotted up the stairs out of sight.

Vaishant lowered himself to his knees, kneeling upright, and clasped his hands before him. With his head bowed, he closed his eyes and brought his clasped hands to chest height. Sienne watched him for any sign that he was doing anything. He might as well have been asleep, if anyone could sleep kneeling up. Sienne looked at Perrin, who shrugged. He removed his riffle of blessings from inside his robe and sorted through them.

Sienne went back to watching Vaishant. Would it be appropriate to pray to Averran that Vaishant would be successful? Not for the first time, she wished she understood the relationship between Vaishant's God and her own. If they were the same being, why had God come to earth in the form of avatars rather than just asking humans to worship Her as Herself? Frustration, and unexpected shame at not knowing enough, filled Sienne.

Vaishant's head snapped up, and his eyes opened. Sienne held back a gasp. Vaishant's eyes were solid blue from white to pupil. *"He is here,"* he said in Meiric, then seemed to remember himself and repeated the words in Fellic. "They are...it is not important."

"They're what?" Sienne demanded. "Are they hurting him?"

"Not yet," Vaishant said, in a voice that said there was nothing she could do to force him to explain further. "I will try to see the room...

oh, that is simple, it is the throne room. Guards, Darinikh, a few servants with…" He blinked, and the light faded. "That is all."

"We have to go *now*," Sienne insisted. "If they're going to torture him…they've had him for over an hour—"

"We need a plan, Sienne," Dianthe said. "If we go bursting in there, with all those guards, they'll just capture us."

"I hesitate to say this, but Alaric generally comes up with our plans," Perrin said.

"But we're not stupid," Sienne said. "We can think of something." She paced the room again. "If we could disguise ourselves…damn it, everything I can think of requires me to have my spellbook."

"And that's another thing," Dianthe said. "We need to retrieve our things, wherever they've been taken. I can always get another sword, but Kalanath and Ghrita—"

"My staff was a gift from my mother," Ghrita said. "I would prefer not to leave it."

"And that spellbook is priceless," Perrin said. "Not to mention that, as you say, we stand a better chance of survival if we have it."

Footsteps sounded on the stairs. "There are guards coming," Kalanath whispered. "We must attack."

15

"Quick, everyone, back to where you were," Dianthe said. "Sienne and Ghrita, beside the door. Sienne, put that light out!"

Sienne waited for everyone to reach their positions, then stood close beside Ghrita and doused the light. Immediately a warmer light became visible, the faintest of glows that gradually grew stronger as the torch or lantern approached. Sienne pressed as hard into the wall as she could. The guards would see them almost immediately—unless they had a distraction. Without her spellbook, she couldn't cast *mirage* or *imitate*, to fool the eye into believing something was there when it wasn't or that someone looked like someone else. But she did have a small magic at her command, and while it wasn't powerful, it might confuse the issue long enough to turn the tables in their favor.

She concentrated, and a wispy form coalesced opposite the door, midway between Perrin and Vaishant. She couldn't remember what Omeirans thought about ghosts, whether they were as afraid of them as the Rafellish were, but all that mattered was that the figure draw the guards fully into the room without noticing the women stationed on either side of the door. She put more detail into it, giving it Alaric's face and size and trying not to think about the real Alaric, suffering who knew what kinds of torture. It grew more solid as the light brightened, standing with its arms crossed over its chest, the perfect image of the man sculpted out of mist.

The light went abruptly brighter as the unseen guards rounded the last corner. Sienne let out the breath she'd been holding. A guard dressed in dark robes came through the door. "*What is that?*" he exclaimed, stopping a few feet inside the door.

Alaric's image stretched, and his arm pointed at the guard. "You," it said in hollow tones. It sounded nothing like Alaric, because her small magic wasn't capable of that, but it still chilled her.

The guard drew his curved sword. Another guard, this one holding a torch, followed him into the room. Neither noticed the women, nor that none of the prisoners were bound. The first guard approached the ghostly form as a third man entered the dungeon. Sienne looked at Kalanath, who nodded. That was all the guards there were. She nudged Ghrita. Ghrita glanced at her, and she gestured, hoping Ghrita would interpret it as she meant it, to attack. The third guard reached for his sword, and Ghrita detached herself silently from the wall and took him from behind.

Kalanath leaped for the torch bearer. Sienne made Alaric's image dart forward, enveloping the first guard in white mist. The man screamed and flailed with his sword. Perrin called out an invocation, and pearly light flared around his left arm. He slid into place across from the first guard, bringing up the shield to block the flailing blow and shove the man back. Vaishant held up a hand, palm first, and took two steps toward the guard. The man flung his head back and screamed, then dropped.

Ghrita had her man on the ground. "Take his sword," she panted, and Sienne snatched it from its sheath, forcing Ghrita to lean back to avoid being slashed. "More careful?" she said, and Sienne flushed. Kalanath shoved the torch bearer against the wall, making him drop the torch. Dianthe retrieved it before it could go out. Then Vaishant was there, his palm upraised, and the torch bearer screamed like the first guard and sagged unconscious in Kalanath's hands.

Kalanath dropped the man, not gently, and said, "What was that?"

"It is...energy, shaped and directed through the mind," Vaishant said. "Like Sienne's *shout*, as she described it."

"I have wielded such power myself before," Perrin said. "It is effective."

Vaishant nodded and turned to where Ghrita crouched, pinning the third guard to the ground. "Don't," she said when Vaishant raised his hand again. "This man wants to talk to us. *Where are our belongings?*" she asked in Meiric.

The man sneered at her. Ghrita smiled. "Dianthe, bring that torch over here," she said. "Sienne, can you make the fire move?"

"A little, with a magic breeze," Sienne said. "You want—"

"Yes," Ghrita said.

Dianthe held the torch close to the man's head. He flinched, his eyes flicking between the fire and Ghrita's face. With the firelight falling on her, Ghrita looked demonic. "*Where are our belongings?*" she repeated.

"*You're prisoners. I won't help you,*" the man said. Beads of sweat appeared on his forehead.

"*We're not prisoners any longer. Talk, and this one won't burn your face off,*" Ghrita said. Sienne concentrated and raised a little breeze just where the torch was, gesturing in what she hoped looked like a mystical way

. The fire went mad, with licking tongues of flame darting in every direction. They looked like tiny arms, reaching for the man. He tried to break Ghrita's hold, but succeeded only in jerking away from the torch. Sienne made the torch burn higher. One of the tongues of flame brushed the guard's forehead, and he screamed, though it couldn't have burned him much.

"*The guard post! Across from the dungeon!*" he shouted. "*Stop, please, stop!*"

Ghrita nodded. Vaishant held his hand in front of the man's face.

The guard convulsed, and fell unconscious. "A choke hold is not as elegant," Ghrita said. "Now what?"

"Disguises," Sienne said. "We'll pretend to be guards, or at least some of us will. The rest of us will be captives, summoned to the throne room."

"Sienne, that is too risky," Perrin said. "We do not know if these guards have recognition signals, or if they are all known to each other. We may be attacked before we can reach the throne room."

"I don't think we have a better idea," Sienne said. "And we can't afford to wait for another opportunity to drop into our laps. Alaric…" She didn't know how to finish that sentence.

"It will work," Dianthe said. "It has to." She jammed the torch into a bracket on the wall, then bent and began pulling the black robes off the torch bearer. "Let's move quickly. They could wake at any moment."

Sienne helped Ghrita disrobe her fallen victim. "Good work," she said.

"It is what I am trained for," Ghrita said. "That, and avoiding being decapitated by my companion."

Sienne flushed again. "Sorry."

Ghrita shrugged. "You think fast," she said. "This plan might actually work. What are we going to do when we reach the throne room?"

She'd addressed Sienne, but Dianthe answered, "Everyone should stay back until Sienne casts her spell to disable as many people as possible. We'll almost certainly be outnumbered, so we want to even the odds. Then we attack. If Alaric is still chained, I'll free him."

"We have to get Darinikh's ring away from him, and destroy it," Sienne said. "I promised Jenani I'd free it—the creature I mentioned. Maybe it can fight on our side once it's freed. At the very least, it will mean Darinikh can't use its magic against us. I was thinking, if I can hit him with *grease*, and then use invisible fingers to grab the ring—"

"That could work," Dianthe said. "Damn it, I wish Alaric were here. I'm sure there are all sorts of details we haven't thought of."

"We still have not achieved our original goal," Perrin said. "How are we to access the temple if we are chased by Darinikh's guards? Because I cannot believe we will be allowed to do whatever we wish simply because we have defeated him. And defeating him is still not certain."

"Let's focus on getting Alaric and the ring," Dianthe said. "Then we'll make a new plan. Alaric always says there's no point in planning too far ahead when other people are involved." She held out a handful of dark cloth to Vaishant. "The fake guards need to speak Meiric for this to work."

"I shouldn't be disguised," Ghrita said. "We haven't seen any female guards, and based on Darinikh's attitude toward women, I think I would look suspicious."

"Kalanath and Vaishant, then," Dianthe said, "and we'll just have to take our chances at not being bound, because the only manacles are the ones attached to the wall."

They waited for Kalanath and Vaishant to dress in the guards' robes. In identical clothes, frowning as they buckled on the curved swords, they looked so much alike it was impossible not to see them as father and son. Vaishant, like Manisha, looked far too young to have a son Kalanath's age, which would work to their advantage now. He still looked a little too old to be a guard, but a casual observer wouldn't notice anything strange.

They trooped up the stairs, Kalanath in the lead, Dianthe bearing the torch in the middle of their group. At the top, Kalanath peered out into the hallway. "No one," he said, and the rest hurried out.

Perrin stopped them before they could go farther. "I think," he said, "we should take precautions," and removed a blessing from the riffle of papers. He pressed it flat against the dungeon door and muttered an invocation. A warm light like melted butter welled up in the grain of the door, outlining the metal bands and hinges. The next moment, it vanished as if soaked up by the wood. "That will prevent them opening it for an hour or so," Perrin said. "Now, which is the guard post?"

There was another door, not immediately opposite the dungeon, but across the way and to the right some fifteen feet. It was the only door in that wall. Kalanath gestured for them to stand back out of sight and opened the door. "*The rakhyanam wants the prisoners' belongings,*" Sienne heard him say.

"*I have no orders,*" an unseen man said.

"*I'm giving you your orders now,*" Kalanath said. "*Hurry up. You know what he's like when he gets tired of waiting.*"

There was a pause. "*I don't recognize you,*" the man said. "*Who are you?*"

Kalanath stepped fully into the guard post, letting the door swing shut behind him. Sienne and Dianthe exchanged helpless glances. If he needed help...but if he succeeded in bluffing the man, would their intervention ruin his plan? And what if there was more than one man?

Ghrita let out an exasperated sigh and flung open the door. Sienne crowded after her. Kalanath was lowering the unconscious guard to the floor. "Find our things," he said, sounding not at all breathless.

The guard post was practically empty. There were two tall stools next to a table where the remnants of the guard's meal lay, reminding Sienne that it was nearly suppertime. She had no appetite, though the food smelled unexpectedly delicious. A couple of chests lay against the back wall, along with a weapons rack half-full of curved swords. Alaric's greatsword dwarfed its neighbors. The thought of him without it...he wasn't exactly helpless, but it was so much a part of him Sienne's heart ached again.

Kalanath took his staff from where it leaned against the wall near the rack and examined it closely. "I cannot carry this and look like a guard," he said.

"Hold it crosswise, like a baby," Sienne suggested. "And Vaishant can carry the others the same way. Then it will look like a burden and not like a weapon."

"We just need a few seconds' distraction, not to fool anyone long-term," Dianthe said.

"Sienne," Perrin said, "your spellbook is not here."

A chill went through her. "It has to be."

"Darinikh was intrigued by it," Perrin said. "He could very well have kept it with him."

The chill vanished, replaced by red-hot anger—anger that this upstart nobody had enslaved an innocent magical being, that he probably meant to torture Alaric, and that he'd dared to steal her spellbook. "New plan," she said. "You all distract Darinikh and his guards, and I find my spellbook and blast the bastard until he forgets his own name."

"Sounds fair," Dianthe said. "What if he's holding it?"

"I will attack him," Kalanath said. "He has magic we know not what, but a blow to the head will make him as confused as anyone."

"It's not his magic, it's Jenani's, but that's irrelevant so long as Darinikh is the one using it," Sienne said.

"I do not think I can find the throne room again," Kalanath said.

"I can," Dianthe said. "Follow me."

Sienne wasn't any more able to remember the path the second time. She depended on Dianthe's guidance and her own magical inner sense of direction to know they were headed west, toward the front of the palace. They passed real guards twice, both in pairs. The first ignored them completely. The second gave the "prisoners" a sharp look, but said nothing, and Sienne breathed out in relief. Either the guards were incompetent, or didn't care, or maybe Darinikh didn't like his servants acting on their own initiative.

The halls seemed dimmer than they had earlier. Sienne had lost track of time other than her general sense that evening was approaching, but if the light came from the sun, it made sense that it was diminishing now. How did they light the halls at night? She saw nothing she recognized as lights, no frosted glass bulbs like they had in Fioretti, no lanterns or torches as they had in Chirantan.

Just as she thought this, the hall brightened considerably. It took Sienne a moment to figure out the light was coming from the walls themselves, glowing softly like sheets of thin gold wrapped around a steadily burning fire. It would be a fire that gave off no heat, though, because the hall didn't feel any warmer. Sienne veered off to touch the wall and found it cool. The radiance outlined her fingers and turned her skin a dull, unattractive orange. She returned to her place in their little group and said, "This place is unnatural. I hate it."

"I will be happier when we are free of it," Perrin said. He held his riffle of blessings loosely in one hand, ready for use. Vaishant, immediately behind him, carried his armload of weapons as if they were a bundle of sticks, but Sienne noticed Ghrita's staff was topmost and his other hand gripped it in readiness to hand it off to the woman, who walked nearby. Sienne felt naked and awkward without the comforting weight of her spellbook on her shoulder. If they were lucky, it would be sitting unattended all by itself in a place where she could whisk it to her side. She decided not to count on luck.

Dianthe led them to a stair, narrow and without a rail, that went up one wall to an open doorway at the top. Sienne finally recognized where they were: one of the four doorways in the throne room, between the throne and the grand entrance. Dianthe gestured to the others to hang back while she ascended silently to the landing and pressed herself against the door frame, peering inside. Sienne, immediately behind her, saw her eyes widen. Then Dianthe's face went so still it frightened Sienne. She turned and gestured to the others to join her.

Sienne caught only a glimpse of the throne room, and the barest sight of a handful of guards gathered around something, before Dianthe hustled her behind her. "Darinikh is holding the spellbook," she whispered. "Alaric is facing him, and he's surrounded by guards. He's unbound, but I saw guards with whips and I think it's just a matter of time before they use them on him."

"I will attack Darinikh," Kalanath said. "Ghrita and Dianthe, do what you can to free Alaric. Sienne, stay with me. Vaishant and Perrin—"

"Are there more guards than those surrounding Alaric?" Perrin asked.

Dianthe nodded. "All around the edges of the room. An honor guard near the great door and others beside the throne."

Perrin and Vaishant exchanged glances. "We can shield the room to keep those guards away," Vaishant said. "It is a small thing only."

"A small thing that might make the difference between success and failure," Dianthe said. "Let's go before I figure out this is a stupid plan."

Sienne took up a position behind Kalanath, with Dianthe behind her and Perrin after that. Ghrita stayed close to Vaishant, who brought up the rear. Kalanath quickly checked to see that they were ready, then walked forward into the room.

"So you insist—what is this?" Darinikh said, turning his attention from Alaric. Sienne studied Alaric with avid eyes. He looked about two seconds from erupting into violence, but bore no marks of torture. It would have relieved her mind if she hadn't been so worried about the success of their tattered, probably stupid plan.

Alaric saw her and his eyes went wide. He shifted his weight, preparing to throw a punch.

"*We have brought the prisoners as ordered,*" Kalanath said.

Darinikh took a step toward them. "*I didn't order any such thing.*"

Alaric roared and swung a heavy fist at the nearest guard, who dropped like a sack of rocks. "Now!" Kalanath shouted, and spun his staff into a fighting position. Ghrita snatched her staff from Vaishant seconds before Dianthe retrieved her sword. A pearly gray shield dome went up all around them, cutting off half the guards from their *rakhyanam*. Kalanath ran at Darinikh, and Sienne sped after him. All her attention was on the book he held tucked under one arm.

She'd never seen Kalanath move faster. Darinikh squealed, an unexpectedly childish sound, and backed away rapidly, switching his grip on the book from his arm to his hand. He pointed at Kalanath, and a bolt of white lightning shot at the Omeiran. Kalanath spun out of the way, and Sienne heard a scream as the bolt impacted against someone beyond them. Hoping it wasn't one of her friends, she hovered, waiting for her moment.

Kalanath's staff spun and cracked Darinikh across one temple. The *rakhyanam* cried out in pain and, to Sienne's delight, dropped the spellbook. She shouted and whisked it to herself, already open to *force.* Darinikh backed away from Kalanath again and clapped his hands together.

A shock wave like an earthquake in midair blasted Kalanath and Sienne. It took Sienne completely off her feet to skid backward across the slick tiled floor and impact with someone else. Sienne shook her head to dispel dizziness and then had to fling herself to one side to avoid the sword of the guard she'd slammed into. Rolling, she came to one knee and read off *force*, months of experience keeping her voice steady as the guard charged at her. The *force* bolt took him off his feet much as the blast had Sienne, but unlike her, he fell and didn't rise again.

Standing, Sienne looked for Darinikh and found him still battling Kalanath, blasting the young man with lightning Kalanath barely dodged. Then someone grabbed her from behind, and she shrieked and twisted, trying to get in a position to blast them. "It's me," Alaric shouted, swiveling her around. "We need those guards disabled! Use *shout!*"

She flipped pages. "I'll catch Ghrita and Perrin in the effect!"

"I've warned them. Signal when you're almost done!"

She read as rapidly as she dared, feeling the spell build inside her chest and behind her throat to a painful crescendo. Raising one arm, she waved frantically, and Alaric shouted, *"Drop!"*

Ghrita and Perrin, in her line of fire, hit the floor and flattened themselves just as Sienne spat out the last acid-etched syllables. A burst of sound erupted from her, catching ten guards in its blast and dropping all of them in that instant.

Sienne coughed and looked for Kalanath and Darinikh again. She was just in time to see a cloud gather in the air above the throne, a misty whiteness that turned gradually into Jenani. The ashwar floated midair near Darinikh, its silver eyes cold and remote. It was much bigger now, twice as tall as Alaric and more heavily muscled.

"Jenani! Destroy them!" Darinikh shouted.

A look of terrible sadness crossed its face. "As you command, master," it said. It raised a hand, and wind whipped through the throne room, a whirling cyclone whose calm heart centered on Darinikh and Jenani. It snatched the breath from Sienne's lungs and carried her off her feet.

She covered her face with her spellbook, making a tiny space of clear air so she could breathe, and struggled to rise. The wind was too powerful for her to fight. She crawled backward, hoping to find the limits of the whirlwind and put herself outside its reach. Effectively blind, she turned pages anyway, though it would be impossible for her to cast spells with any accuracy in this storm.

The wind died away as abruptly as it had started, leaving her gasping for air. She lowered her spellbook. Jenani had Alaric by the throat and held him struggling with his feet dangling a few inches above the ground. Desperate, Sienne flipped to *force* and read off the evocation, her heart screaming at her to hurry. Jenani's expression was remote, as if it had put itself somewhere far away from the hands that were choking the life out of Alaric.

Sienne spat out the final syllables of *force*. The bolt of magical energy shot away from her, just missing Jenani's head and striking Darinikh full in the chest. The *rakhyanam* let out an explosive grunt and shot backwards, landing in a dazed heap some three feet away. Jenani didn't let go of Alaric, but Sienne didn't hesitate. She ran, turning the pages to *grease* as she went and spitting out the sharp, painful syllables of the spell.

Blood flecked her lips as she came to the end of the spell. Darinikh groaned as silvery grease sprang up all over his body, coating his skin and clothes and making his face a shiny mask. Sienne reached out with her invisible fingers and tugged on the ring. It slid a fraction of an inch and stopped. Darinikh's hand was curled into a loose fist, rigid from *force* and too tight for her invisible fingers to break open.

Sienne dropped her spellbook, which hit the floor with a sharp crack, and grabbed the *rakhyanam's* greasy hand. With a scream, she slammed it against the tiled floor, her fist forcing it down. The fingers twitched open.

Sienne grasped the ring, closing her fingers tightly around it heedless of the grease, and yanked. The ring slipped off easily, nearly sliding free of her hand, and she clutched it tighter. Swiftly she jammed it on the middle finger of her left hand and screamed, "Jenani! *Stop!*"

16

She turned in time to see Jenani release Alaric, who fell in a lifeless heap on the floor. Sienne ran to his side, falling to her knees and trying to lift him. It was like trying to lift a boulder. "Perrin!" she shouted, and then Perrin was beside her, holding a square of rice paper to Alaric's forehead.

"O my gracious Lord, have patience in your crankiness, and heal this man," he cried.

Green flames burst from the blessing paper, and an emerald light rose up from Alaric's body. Alaric convulsed, tearing away from Sienne's embrace, and she cried out wordlessly and flung herself on him. Alaric coughed, a long, hacking sound, then drew in a deep breath that rattled in his throat. Sienne lay against his chest and breathed in tandem with him, feeling obscurely that so long as she could do that, he would be all right.

Alaric's large hand came up to cover Sienne's. "...all right..." he said. "Need...to fight..."

"Just lie still for a minute," Sienne said, sitting up and pressing against his chest. She wasn't capable of preventing him from getting up, but she hoped he'd take the hint. Guards, most of them paralyzed by *shout*, lay on the floor. A few were still up and fighting Ghrita and

Dianthe, while Kalanath guarded Darinikh's fallen body, snarling at the guards who hacked at the pearly shield across from him. Vaishant stood near the center of the room, his hands clasped and head lowered in prayer. Sienne couldn't see what effect it had, if any.

She looked up. Jenani hovered in midair, its beautiful face haunting in its sorrow. "What would you have me do, master?" it asked.

Sienne shuddered. "I'm not your master, Jenani. I promised I wouldn't use the ring, remember?"

"You ordered me to stop."

"I—that's different, though. I couldn't let you kill Alaric. And I know you didn't want to."

Jenani shook its head. "That's how it begins, Sienne. One justification after another."

Sienne wrenched the ring from her finger. She'd thought it was too big even for her biggest finger, but she must have been wrong, because it fit snugly and took a little effort to wriggle it off, even with the lingering traces of *grease*. "I said I wouldn't use it," she said, and tucked it into her belt pouch.

"Sienne," Alaric said, his voice raspy, "can you control that thing?"

"Its name is Jenani, and it's an ashwar, not a thing."

"Right now I'm more concerned that the shield is about to come down, and there are still more than a dozen guards eager to tear us apart." He struggled to sit up, with Perrin assisting him.

Sienne stood. "But we have an excellent hostage," she said, walking to where Darinikh still lay. He twitched occasionally, but otherwise seemed incapable of movement. Large, dark eyes blinked up at her when she crouched near his head. "Can you speak yet?"

Darinikh's lips moved fractionally, and a sound like a low whistle emerged. "So, no," Sienne said. She stood and opened her spellbook to *shout*. "Kalanath, you might want to move," she said. Kalanath glanced at her, looked down at Darinikh, and took a few steps that put him behind Sienne. Sienne eyed the shield, which was visibly shaking from the force of the guards' blows, and counted down silently. She began reading the evocation just before the shield came down and the guards ran at her, shouting and waving their swords. Her heart raced faster, as it always did no matter how many times she did this—faced down a screaming adversary who would kill her if her timing was the least bit off.

The guard in front was close enough that she could see the bloodshot whites of his eyes when the evocation tore out of her in a burst of sound that cut across the remaining shouts of the enemy. She had to step back to avoid his falling body and nearly tripped over Darinikh. The sight of men dropping like stones satisfied her immensely.

Behind her, Kalanath moved to intercept a final guard who'd been outside her range. She turned to watch, and the room turned with her, dizzying her. She hadn't realized how close she was to the end of her reserves...but then, she'd cast *vanish* all those times and hadn't rested since then, so that made sense. Still, sitting down felt like a good course of action. She sat rather faster than she'd planned next to Darinikh's head and drew in a deep breath. This was the hard part, watching the others fight and restraining herself from joining in and becoming a liability.

She kept an eye on Alaric, who'd risen while she was casting *shout* and had repossessed his sword. To her, he still looked unsteady, but guards who came up against him decided to find an easier target. Not that there were any of those. Ghrita was as deadly with the staff as Kalanath, and Dianthe picked off enemies who were preoccupied with Ghrita and Kalanath. As Sienne watched, Vaishant raised his head and swept his right arm in front of him as if clearing a counter by shoving all its contents to the ground.

Instantly, the remaining guards lowered their weapons, blinking as if coming from a dark room into the light. Ghrita swept her staff at one of them, and he shouted and backed away, dropping his sword and shouting, *"Wait! Please, don't kill me! This is a mistake!"*

The others picked up his cry, dropping their swords and waving their hands to fend off their attackers. Dianthe lowered her sword and said, "What are they saying?"

"They wish to surrender," Ghrita said. *"Lie face down on the floor and you won't be harmed,*" she said in Meiric. "What did you do, Vaishant?"

"They were under an influence," Vaishant said. "They believed I do not know what. That they are to guard that one with their lives, I think." He pointed at Darinikh, who'd started moaning sometime during the surrenders.

Sienne eyed Jenani, who was impassive. "Did you do that? Make them believe they were the *rakhyanam's* guards?"

"It was Darinikh's wish, to be a true *rakhyanam,*" Jenani said. "That includes the palace, the city, guards, everything."

"But you had to...did you cast *dominate* on them?" The thought of Jenani being capable of casting that evil spell made his silver eyes look threatening, though his face showed no sign of anger or malice.

"I don't know what that is. Ashwara are creatures of magic. We will a thing, and it happens. If your magic is capable of doing the same, it is by a different method." Jenani suddenly looked sad again. "I have no control over what my master does with my magic."

Sienne's heart ached with sympathy for it. "That's evil," she said. "We have to figure out how to free you."

"I'm beginning to think you can," Jenani said. It floated down until its feet touched the floor, though Sienne noticed it didn't put any weight on them.

Ghrita approached. "I've spoken to the guards. They don't remember anything but a strange storm coming across the sands toward their caravan, then waking up here."

"Darinikh wanted servants, and I took those closest to him." Jenani didn't look embarrassed at this admission. Sienne, looking at him, wondered if he felt any responsibility for the uses Darinikh had put his magic to.

"But what of the ones Sienne paralyzed?" Perrin said. "They will wake in a few minutes. Will we have to fight them again?"

"God's blessing extends to all in this room," Vaishant said. "They will wake and remember nothing. But we should take the swords. They are not theirs, in any case."

Sienne looked at Jenani, who shrugged. "Creating things is simple if you know how," it said.

She sat beside Darinikh, watching him regain control of his body, while the others collected swords and arranged the paralyzed ones in more comfortable positions. Sienne was almost grateful they wouldn't remember *shout*. She felt a little bad about attacking people who hadn't been in their right minds, even if they had been trying to kill her and her friends.

Darinikh's mouth opened, and this time, she heard, "Don't kill me, please..."

"You tried to have us killed. Why should we spare you?" she said.

His mouth opened and closed a few times before he said, "I wouldn't have...killed you...just wanted the truth...big one scares me..."

"He should. He can rip your arm off and beat you to death with it," Sienne improvised. Darinikh's dark face went a few shades paler. "What made you think you had the right to kidnap the *pakhshani* and force them to serve you?"

His head twitched, the barest movement side to side in negation. "Just...part of it all...I wanted to be a *rakhyanam*...this is what Jenani found."

"Well, it was wrong. And now you're going to be nothing again. We ought to turn you over to Lashwanti and let her execute justice. You certainly wronged her enough."

Darinikh's forehead puckered. "Who is Lashwanti?"

"The chief of chiefs of the *pakhshani*? You stuck her in the harem because you don't think women are worth speaking to?"

"They have...a woman leader? I didn't know." Darinikh struggled to sit up and Sienne pushed him down easily. "Just let me go, please. I'll leave and you'll never see me again."

"That's not good enough. Alaric would be dead now if Perrin hadn't had the right blessing. I can't forgive you for that."

"But that was Jenani who hurt him, not me."

"Jenani already told me it can't use its own power except at its master's discretion. So you're the one I blame."

Tears trickled down Darinikh's cheeks. "Please, spare me," he begged. "I'm not who you think I am. I'm not a man. I'm just a street rat. You wouldn't kill a child, would you?"

Sienne stared at him. "You're what?"

Darinikh closed his eyes. "I wanted to be powerful. Jenani made me powerful. Except it thought that meant I should be a full-grown man."

"So you're...a little kid?"

"I don't know my age. My mother didn't keep track because she was always chin-deep in a bottle. But I think I'm nine or ten."

That explained why Darinikh didn't ever visit the harem. Sienne looked up at Jenani. "Is this true?"

"His name is Dari. He found my ring in a scrap heap outside Abhisok," Jenani said. "I have fulfilled his every wish."

"Except I didn't know what it meant!" Darinikh—Dari—shouted, or tried to; it came out as a hoarse whisper. "I just wanted not to have to live on the midden anymore! You took my words and twisted them!"

"I did as I was asked," Jenani said with a tiny smile Sienne was sure was mocking. "It's not my fault you weren't more specific."

"All right, enough," Alaric said. Sienne looked up, startled. She hadn't heard him approach. "Do I understand correctly that Darinikh isn't what he appears to be?"

"So they say," Sienne said. "I don't know what to believe, though there's no reason for either of them to lie."

"You've got the ring," Dari said. "Make Jenani put everything back the way it was."

"I can't do that," Sienne said.

"Why not?" Alaric asked. "It's the obvious solution."

"Because I promised," Sienne said.

The others drew close, attracted by the conversation. Perrin said, "This man is under a spell? I believe I have a blessing that can fix that. It is similar to the one Vaishant used to break the...ashwar's... spell over those men."

"Do it," Alaric said. "I want some real answers."

Perrin crouched and pressed a square of paper to Dari's head. He bowed his head and muttered an invocation.

Orange fire flared, making Dari cry out, and a flash of orange light temporarily blinded Sienne. In the next instant, someone shoved her away, making her fall back, and she opened her eyes to see Dari leap to his feet and dash for the exit. Kalanath threw down his staff, took three running steps, and tackled the fleeing man. Who wasn't a man any longer, Sienne realized: he was a good two feet shorter than he had been, and the robes that had fit his athletic frame now swamped his skinny, undersized body.

Kalanath wrestled with him briefly before putting him in a complicated hold and marching him back to the others. A murmur went up from the guards, who'd gone from lying flat on the floor to kneeling. Sienne wasn't sure if they were responding to the transformation, or to Perrin's divine blessings, so different from their own. Either way, she hoped none of them would do anything stupid.

"So it's true," Alaric said. "Damn. I was going to break all your limbs and leave you for the basilisks to devour."

Sienne knew he was joking, but Dari paled again. "I just want to go home," he whined. "I wouldn't have hurt you."

"My throat says otherwise," Alaric said. "I think we should turn you over to the *pakhshani*. You wronged them more thoroughly than you did us."

"But they'll kill me! I'm just a kid! I can't be expected to make smart choices."

Dianthe snorted. "For a kid, you're quick with an argument. I agree that Lashwanti should have the chance to dispense justice."

"No!" Dari struggled in Kalanath's implacable grip.

"We'll have to find her first. I wonder where she is." Sienne stood. "Did you or Ghrita see where she went, Dianthe?"

"She and her chiefs ran the same way you did," Dianthe said, "away from us. I assumed, since we haven't seen her, that she left the palace rather than try to kill the *rakhyanam*. Would she have tried to free her people from the ashwar's spell?"

"That is impossible," Jenani said. "My magic is far too potent. She would only have succeeded in making herself a target for those Dari ordered me to enthrall."

"So when will they stop being enthralled?" Sienne asked.

Jenani regarded her with emotionless silver eyes. "Only my magic can free them," it said. "And I can't use my magic unless I'm commanded."

Sienne blinked. "Oh," she said. "But—oh. Jenani...wait, what about Vaishant's blessing? He freed the guards!"

"It is limited in scope," Vaishant said. "The *pakhshani* are far too many for it to be effective."

"But—I can't. I promised!"

Jenani was silent. Alaric said, "I don't think you have a choice. The *pakhshani* can't go on like this. It's not fair to them."

Sienne slid her hand into her belt pouch. The ring was cool to the touch and free from grease now. "I hope you get what you deserve," she snarled at Dari, who cringed, and slipped the ring onto her middle finger. It fit as if it had been made for her.

"I won't do more than I absolutely have to," she said.

"Don't command it to undo all its magic, or we might find ourselves in the middle of a collapsing palace," Alaric said.

"I...hadn't thought of that. Thanks." She turned to face Jenani. "I want you to free the *pakhshani* from whatever magic you put on them."

Jenani bowed its head. "As you wish...master," it said. "It is done."

"It is?" Sienne said. "That was quick."

"How can we know if it is done?" Vaishant said. "I do not mean to doubt this creature, but it is clear it can only do magic according to the literal word of its master. We should learn if your wish was successful."

"Let's go find out," Sienne said.

With Dari still Kalanath's captive, their little group went down the long, wide stairs to the vast entry hall. The walls here glowed like living gold, too. No guards remained at the doors, which Sienne thought was a hopeful sign. Jenani drifted beside her, moving its legs as if the ground actually propelled it along, though the way it bobbed up and down told her it was floating. She couldn't bring herself to look directly at it. She'd made a promise and kept it only so long as it was convenient for her. That was untrue, and probably unfair, but she felt so guilty it burned within her.

The sun was setting, and the air already cooler, when they emerged from the palace. They stopped at the top of the shallow, curving steps leading up to the wide door. The streets were completely empty, though Sienne saw movement far ahead, in the direction of the city gate. Her fingers twitched toward her spellbook, then stilled. She might cast *sharpen*, improve her distance vision, but the thought of casting spells made her feel dizzy again.

"Sienne. How close are you to collapse?" Alaric murmured in her ear.

She shook her head. She didn't want to reveal to Dari or Jenani that she had maybe one more *force*-bolt or *shout* in her, and make herself look weak. Dari might be powerless, and Jenani an ally, but they were still strangers. "I'm fine," she said, willing Alaric not to push.

He eyed her skeptically, but said nothing more. It was even true— her vision was clear, her stomach settled, and so long as she didn't cast any more spells, she'd be fine.

"I think they're leaving," Dianthe said, shielding her eyes and peering off into the distance. "I'd need to be closer to be sure."

"We should explain to Lashwanti what happened," Sienne said. "Why weren't she and the female chiefs affected?"

"Who listens to a woman?" Dari said with some contempt.

Ghrita slapped him across the ear. "You are young, so I won't follow that up with a knife to the belly," she said as he moaned. "But I suggest you adjust your thinking quickly."

"Dari's command was specifically that I command the male warriors to obey him," Jenani said. "And for those who were not warriors to be the city's inhabitants, behaving as city dwellers. Though he also specified that children could not be punished for theft."

"Typical of a street rat, to live out his personal fantasy," Alaric said. "What other commands did he give?"

"He wanted a *rakhyan* to rule, but he did not specify which one, so I created one rather than destroying an existing city," Jenani said. "He wanted to be powerful, rich, and handsome. And the throne was of his design."

"I suppose we should have guessed only a child could have imagined that monstrosity," Perrin said, unmoved by Dari's glare. "Shall we go? I imagine the *pakhshani* will not linger."

With its streets empty, the city seemed a different world. Now the brightly-colored buildings seemed more like a model of a city than before. Doors hung open as if the houses' owners had just stepped out for a moment and would return immediately. The smell of food hung in the air, tantalizing Sienne, whose appetite returned full force the first time she smelled roasted meat. The broad thoroughfare looked as if it extended the full length of the city from the palace to the gates, and Jenani agreed this was true when Sienne asked.

"I completed only what the *pakhshani* would need," it said. "The rest is rebuilt, but in no particular fashion. And I judged Dari's... consequence... would be flattered by having this road he could parade up and down."

Sienne was starting to get a feel for how the ashwar's mind worked. What would it be like to live your life in such a state of sophistry, constantly looking for ways to subvert the demands placed on you? It made her even more determined to free the creature.

"I thought you were my friend," Dari said. "All this time, you were looking for ways to disobey me."

"I am a slave. Slaves and masters are never friends." Jenani sounded so disdainful it made Dari look like he might burst into tears. Sienne felt no pity for him.

As they neared the gate, they finally saw people, men and women and children pressing forward in near-silence. No one spoke, but this time Sienne saw people holding hands, or with their arms around each other. It looked like the biggest funeral procession Sienne could imagine. Her initial impulse, to speak to one of them and ask if they knew where Lashwanti was, died in the face of all these mourners.

Alaric stepped forward, then seemed to remember he didn't speak their language. "Kalanath, would you...?" he said, gesturing.

Kalanath nodded. He handed off Dari to Ghrita and went to the nearest little group, a man and woman and three small children who were probably a family. They were too far away for Sienne to hear what they were saying, though Kalanath was gesturing in the direction of the gate and the man kept looking back at the rest of them as if wondering who the pale strangers were.

Finally, Kalanath nodded and returned to the others. "He says the chief of chiefs is outside, directing all to join their clans. Though he thinks it is unnecessary, because he knows his clan from birth. But he is shaken, they all are, by what has happened. He says it is like a dream, being city dwellers, and now the dream is over and he wants to go back to the desert."

"Let's hope that's the only side effect," Alaric said. "We'll take this one—" He prodded Dari with his finger and was unmoved when the boy snarled at him—"to their chief of chiefs for judgment. And then we'll see about setting Jenani free."

17

They trailed along at the end of the procession, following the mass of people pressing forward to the gap in the wall. Impatience gripped Sienne, a desire to be finished with Dari and in a position to free Jenani, but Alaric shook his head when she tried to push through the crowds. "We're not in a hurry," he said in a low voice, "and I don't want to disturb these people any more than we already have." Sienne had to admit this made sense.

The *pakhshani* eyed them curiously, particularly tall, blond Alaric, but kept their distance. It was possible they knew each other so well that they realized Kalanath, Ghrita, and Vaishant weren't *pakhshani*. In any case, they didn't try to strike up a conversation even with those who were likely to speak their language, and among themselves they were mostly silent. The resemblance to a funeral procession was stronger than ever.

Beside her, Dari tried to jerk away from Ghrita's hold, and Ghrita twisted his arm behind his back, making him yelp. "Please, just let me go," he begged. "I won't cause trouble. Look, it's miles to Abhisok. I might die before I get there. That's punishment enough, don't you think?"

"I think you have a strange idea of what punishment is," Ghrita said. "This isn't about retribution. It's about you making amends. Which, granted, might mean retribution, if that's how Lashwanti feels about it."

Dari scowled and went silent. Sienne said, "You don't think she'd execute a child, do you?"

"The *pakhshani* live by different rules than us soft city-dwellers," Ghrita said. "Life in the desert is unforgiving. They can't afford mercy the way we understand it."

Sienne watched Dari's face, and despite herself felt a pang of guilt. She made herself remember Alaric choking in Jenani's grasp, but the guilt didn't fade. She was a soft city-dweller.

Finally, they reached the gate, and Sienne breathed more easily. The city hadn't felt oppressive until she knew it was full of slaves. The crowd moved more quickly once it was past the bottleneck, and Alaric's pace accelerated. "So, which of these people is Lashwanti?" he said. "Not that I expect you to recognize anyone in this throng."

Sienne almost offered to cast *float*, to raise herself above the heads of the *pakhshani* for a better view, but realized she would only incapacitate herself. "I think we should keep moving forward. Lashwanti might be at the center of all of this, if she's directing them."

"I'll forge ahead," Ghrita said. "Not too far," she added, as Alaric opened his mouth to protest. "But I know what she looks like, and I think I can break a path more readily even than you, Ansorjan."

Alaric nodded. Ghrita passed Dari to Kalanath and strode forward, using her staff to nudge people aside. Those moved in that way glared at her, but said nothing. Then they saw Alaric and the other non-Omeirans and moved with greater alacrity. Alaric put his hand on Sienne's lower back. "Truth, now. How close are you?" he murmured in her ear.

"Close. I might have one more emergency spell in me. But I don't want that public knowledge."

"Understood." He guided her to walk before him, sheltering her with his body, and her heart swelled within her.

Ghrita began moving faster. "I see her," she called over her shoulder.

In another few minutes, they reached a place where the crowds were thinner. Sienne recognized one of the women from the harem, speaking to a slender, short man whose head scarf was bright blue. Then she saw Lashwanti a few paces away. Lashwanti recognized her, and her brow furrowed. *"You,"* she said when Sienne approached. Then she noticed Alaric, and her eyes widened. *"Who in God's name is that?"*

"This is Alaric. These are our friends," Sienne said.

"What is he? Sometimes white ones are born to us, but never anyone so large." Lashwanti couldn't take her eyes off Alaric, who regarded her with curious incomprehension.

"He's from the north. All his people look like him." This was either lie or truth depending on who she was willing to claim as Alaric's people, but Sienne didn't feel like losing control of the conversation. *"We broke the spell on your people, and captured the one responsible."*

Lashwanti's gaze traveled to Jenani, who had shrunk down to Sienne's size again. *"Another white one,"* she said. *"I will take her head."*

"That's not the one," Sienne said, once again opting for the most straightforward conversational option. *"This is."*

Kalanath dragged Dari forward. Lashwanti's eyes widened. *"This... child? Where is the man who imprisoned us?"*

"This child transformed himself into an adult," Ghrita said. *"That spell is broken, too."*

"I do not know what a spell is," Lashwanti said. *"Is it magic?"*

"Yes," Sienne said.

"Then he is powerful indeed. How can we stop him enslaving us again? I cannot kill a child."

Sienne felt unexpected relief. *"His magic is gone. He won't enslave anyone ever again."*

"You are sure of this?"

"Positive."

Lashwanti regarded Dari closely. He shrank from her, as far as he was capable in Kalanath's grasp. *"You, child. Where are you from? You are not one of us."*

"Abhisok," Dari said. *"Let me go."*

"You would die before you reached your home. And I think that death will not satisfy us." Lashwanti turned to Ghrita. *"I demand the right to justice. Give him to me."*

Ghrita looked at Alaric. "You're sure we want to hand him over?" she said.

"Is that what she asked?" Alaric nodded. "It's her right."

Kalanath released Dari to Lashwanti, who held him in a competent grip despite his struggles. *"Child, you must make restitution,"* she said. *"It may take you the rest of your life. You will live with us and learn what it is to be pakhshani. And you will learn why what you did was evil. Understand?"*

"I'll just run away," Dari said, pouting.

"I think not," Lashwanti said. *"We owe you thanks,"* she said to Sienne. *"I regret that we can't offer you hospitality now. We must return to our caravans. But—"* She signaled to the slender, short *pakhshan* man who stood nearby. *"I will give you a token you can show to any pakhshan, as a sign that you are friends, and we will treat you as our own."*

The man patted his robes in a gesture so like an absent-minded professor Sienne had once had she nearly laughed. He reached inside his robe and pulled out a palm-sized copper disk, stippled all over with hammer marks. A hole had been cut out of its center, and a flat, faceted yellow stone, translucent and irregular in shape, was wired into place there. The man hesitated, looking at all of them, then offered the disk to Ghrita. Ghrita bowed. *"We're very grateful."*

Lashwanti returned the bow. *"We are the grateful ones. Where do you journey?"*

"We will return to Chirantan soon."

"Then—good fortune to you." Lashwanti saluted them Omeiran-style, with her palm extended, and Ghrita pressed her palm against the woman's without hesitation. Sienne followed suit, and then the others, even the ones who'd been following this conversation in silent incomprehension.

"We should go," Ghrita said in a low voice, though Lashwanti had turned away and couldn't understand Fellic in any case. "It cost her her pride to admit to owing outsiders anything."

Sienne took one last look at Dari, who had been passed off to another *pakhshan* chief. "I wonder what will happen to him."

"What did Lashwanti say they'd do to him?" Alaric asked.

"That they'd teach him to be one of them, and he would make restitution."

"Then I hope they turn him into a man," Alaric said. "Let's go. We need food, and rest, and I hope there's some of both still in the palace. And then—the temple."

———

JENANI'S INABILITY TO USE ITS OWN MAGIC DIDN'T EXTEND TO ITS willingness to help in other ways. Without its guidance, they'd have taken at least an hour to find the kitchen. Kitchens. The palace was the biggest building Sienne had ever seen, even bigger than the palace in Fioretti, and it seemed to have more than one of everything.

Unfortunately, none of the kitchens resembled the ones Sienne was familiar with. There were fireplaces, not stoves, and the ovens were made of clay and looked like giant beehives with round iron doors. She stood before one of these and felt despair creep over her.

"Don't worry," Ghrita said, startling her. "I know how to cook."

"Really? Because you may be the only one of us who knows how to work this thing," Sienne replied.

"It's not hard." Ghrita's smile was mocking, but Sienne was too tired and hungry to rise to the bait. She turned away, not waiting to hear what other insults Ghrita might come up with. Dianthe and Kalanath were searching the pantry, which was itself the size of the kitchen, looking for foods that would cook quickly.

"Rice," Dianthe said, prodding a bulging sack on the ground, "and flour. Spices, most of which I've never seen before."

"I can cook rice," Sienne said. "But we'll want something more than just rice and flatbreads."

"That, I can provide," Perrin said from the doorway. He held up two dead chickens by the ankles. "There is a very cold room in which these are stored. Some of the meat smells bad, but this appears fresher."

"I wonder why they stored meat when Dari only had to tell Jenani to make it?" Sienne said. "See what Ghrita wants done with that, and I'll start the water boiling for rice."

The small magic that let her create water didn't tap her reserves, and she filled a large pot and set it over the fire to boil. Then she sat beside the fireplace and closed her eyes, welcoming the warmth. The desert heat had begun to drain away when they walked back to the palace, and that along with her diminished magical reserves made her feel cold. The sound of the fire filled the quiet kitchen, joined by the noises Kalanath and Perrin made while plucking the chickens, soft grunts of effort and the sliding sound of the chickens against the table, and Ghrita murmuring instructions to Dianthe as they rolled out rounds of dough.

"Can I ask you something?" Kalanath said in a low voice. Sienne opened her eyes. He'd addressed Perrin, who looked at him in inquiry. "It is that I would like to know what it is like to be a father."

Perrin's eyes widened. "That...may be a question with no answer," he said. "Or too many answers, perhaps. I know only my own experience."

"But you are a good father, so I think it is a good experience."

Perrin smiled. "I thank you for the compliment. I am not certain it is entirely deserved. I have failed my children in the past year and more, in being forbidden to see them, and thus I have not been the father to them I would wish."

"That is not your fault. It is the fault of another. You did not want to not see them."

"That is entirely true." Perrin swept feathers into the sack nearby and sighed. "I remember when we learned Cressida was first with child. I was twenty-four, and we had only been married a few months. I have never been so afraid in my life, not even facing monsters, as when I knew I would be a father. My own father is a cold man, lacking in natural affection, and I feared being like him. But when I held Delphine for the first time...it felt as if my heart opened up, and I knew I would do anything for her."

"And you feel that way even though you have not seen them in over a year."

"I feel that way even more *because* I did not see them. I watched them secretly, and prayed for their safety, and cursed my father that he kept me from them." Perrin laughed. "Did you see that Noel had lost a tooth? His first, I believe. And when I saw him, I had the ridiculous thought that I should have been there to witness it. A tooth, Kalanath! But it represents what I believe is a father's most vital role —to be a support and a guide to his children in their trials, however small."

Kalanath lowered the animal he held. "Then it is not a father who is not there for his child."

"Would you say I was less a father because they were kept from me?" Perrin shook his head. "A father's desire counts for much, Kalanath. And I believe, if both hearts are willing, it is never too late to build that bond."

"And now we talk about me," Kalanath said, smiling—a little sadly, Sienne thought.

"I think," Perrin said, "we were always talking about you."

Kalanath ducked his head. "I do not think of a father while I am in the temple. The old divines...they often spoke as if the will of God was my father, not a man. And then I leave the temple, and I see families, fathers and mothers and children, but it is as if they are a different world. And then your father...I think he is an evil man, but he is still a father. And Sienne's father, who keeps her from us and then releases her, he too is a father. I do not know if I want a father, if all fathers are different. I am a man grown, not young like your Noel, so Vaishant cannot be a father like you. Maybe it is too late for us."

"Too late for him to be a father to the child you once were," Perrin agreed. "But not too late to learn to be a father to the man you are." He leaned forward. "If you could choose, what would you want your father to be? What would you want from him?"

Kalanath looked thoughtful. "I...did not think I wanted anything," he said, "but...I am glad he makes my mother happy. I am selfish because I do not want to share her, but that is wrong. And if I must share her, I think it is good that it is with him and not someone who is not part of us."

"That is how your mother benefits. I want to know what *you* want."

"I—"

Footsteps sounded in the hall. "We tried the smithy fire," Alaric said. He tossed the ring at Sienne, who fumbled with it before clasping it tightly. "Whatever it's made of, the forge couldn't burn hot enough to melt it."

"I may just be out of practice," Vaishant said. "It has been many years since I was called on to exercise that youthful apprenticeship."

"You were doing all right. It's the ring that's impervious to heat."

Sienne looked past them to Jenani, who stood in the doorway, its silver eyes once more blank and almost malevolent. "I'm sorry," she said.

"I didn't think it would be so difficult," Jenani said. "Maybe I'm wrong, and there's no way to destroy it."

"Haven't other ashwara been freed?"

"I thought so. But those are stories—I've only ever heard of it at second- or third-hand."

Sienne stood and went to Alaric, who put his arms around her. "We'll have to come up with something else, then."

"I take it you have no spell that will unmake the ring," Perrin said, rising from the table and going to the sink to pump water over his sticky hands.

"None that I can think of. *Change* only works on living things, and even if it didn't, I don't think transforming the ring into something else will remove the bond. *Burn* and *scorch* aren't hot enough, and it's not made of stone, so *sculpt* won't work. If I had *run*—that liquefies anything inorganic, but I don't know it."

"Then perhaps we need a divine solution." Perrin dried his hands and returned to his seat. "Vaishant?"

"I know of nothing I can ask God to do," Vaishant said. "She will not unmake something, nor will she destroy at a man's request—which is to say that God chooses of Her will what to turn Her power against. To give that power to a human, even temporarily, would invite disaster."

"Couldn't you pray for a solution? You know, ask God what She thinks we should do?" Sienne asked.

Vaishant shook his head. "I am not so far along in my worship to do such a thing."

"But Perrin does it all the time," Dianthe said, then blushed. "I mean—I don't mean to imply—oh, let's forget I said that, all right?"

"The worship of avatars is different from mine," Vaishant said with a smile, "and no one knows the full extent of those differences. It is entirely possible that things forbidden to me are allowed to you."

Perrin cleared his throat. "I, also, know of no solution to this problem. But Averran in his wisdom sees farther than we do, and I have no doubt he knows what it will take to destroy this ring. Whether he will share his wisdom with us, I have no idea, but I am willing to attempt it in the morning. The late morning. Which reminds me, did any of you find coffee in that mansion of a pantry?"

Ghrita produced a dinner of roasted chicken turned bright red by its seasonings that, with steaming rice and fragrant flatbreads, filled all of them to satisfaction. Sienne leaned against Alaric and sighed. "It's so nice to have a meal not flavored with sand."

"I was going to suggest that we tackle the temple again this evening, but I'm too full," he replied. "And I think we could all use the rest."

"I can show you where the bedrooms are," Jenani said. It had sat with them through the meal, but ate nothing and spoke little. Sienne thought it looked tired, too, though probably ashwara didn't feel fatigue the way humans did. "There are many."

"Whose design was the palace?" Dianthe said. "The dungeon didn't seem Omeiran."

"I entertained myself in drawing from many different palaces I've seen over the years." Jenani floated off its seat and drifted toward the fireplace. "I have so few avenues for entertainment. And Dari didn't forbid it, just asked for a palace."

"But you could have left much of it unfinished, the way you did the city," Sienne said.

Jenani shrugged. "I built the palace first, and by the time I came to build the city, I was bored. And it seemed such a waste by then, building things that no one would use. Dari's imagination was naturally that of a nine-year-old boy—he knew nothing of architecture or craftsmanship. Tedious."

Sienne fiddled with the ring on her finger. "Is that better, or worse, than if you have a master who does know those things and puts more constraints on you?" The ring on her finger. When had she put it on? She slipped it off and tucked it away in her belt pouch.

Jenani regarded her closely. "Better not to have a master at all, but you know that. I don't know. I suppose I enjoyed serving men or women who had imagination. The worst were the ones whose only thought was war, or conquering others. Evil is really quite banal, if you think about it—every person with a dark soul ultimately comes up with the same ways of hurting others. It's probably a good thing. The last thing the world needs is a creative villain."

"No villains at all would suit me," Alaric said. "Many bedrooms, you said?"

They followed Jenani out of the kitchen wing and past the dungeons, up the stairs Dianthe had discovered in their escape from the harem, and into a luxurious interconnected set of corridors. "Many" turned out to be an understatement; there were at least a dozen suites, all resplendent with gilding and rich fabrics, all uniquely decorated. "Jenani, these are beautiful," Sienne exclaimed. "You have a wonderful imagination."

Jenani smiled. "Rest well, and...is it too eager to ask when you will pray for this blessing?"

"Not at all," Perrin said. "After breakfast, probably well after breakfast. Averran does not respond well to requests made before ten o'clock in the morning, and for this, I think we should not impose upon his rather crotchety good nature."

"I will join you then. And...thank you, all of you." Jenani's body faded, dissipated, and was gone.

"That should have been more unsettling than it was," Perrin said. "I daresay one may become accustomed to anything, yes?"

"Then I think we should investigate the temple before Perrin prays in the morning," Dianthe said. "If nothing else, I'd like to find the phoenix feather."

"I should see if *mirage* really will work," Sienne said. "But I don't know how much more preparation the ritual will require."

"Then we have a plan," Alaric said. He took Sienne's hand and drew her through the door of the suite they'd chosen. "Good night, everyone."

Sienne closed the door behind them and squeaked as Alaric pushed her up against it, kissing her breathless. "Everyone knows what we're doing," she said between kisses.

"I don't give a damn what they know," he murmured, gathering up her robe so he could pull it off over her head, then tearing off his own. "We have a bed, we have privacy, we have nothing but time, and I've never wanted you more than I do right now."

She shivered at the intensity in his voice. "In that case," she said, her hands moving to the front of his trousers, "you are wearing *far* too many clothes."

18

———

Sienne left Alaric sleeping the next morning and found her way, with only a few false turns, back to the kitchens. She built up the fire and set water heating for porridge and coffee, grinding the latter in a coffee grinder bigger than she'd ever seen before. Whoever had originally used the kitchen Jenani had drawn his inspiration from must have been used to cooking for an army.

"Is this something you do all the time?" Jenani said. Sienne let out a squeak of surprise and turned to see the ashwar floating near the fireplace.

"You mean, breakfast? When we're out in the wilderness, I usually do. It's a habit now."

"Where is the wilderness?"

"Mmm? Oh. It's...well, outside civilization. The Empty Lands. Not everything was resettled after civilization collapsed all those centuries ago."

Jenani drifted nearer. "You say such strange things. What civilization collapsed? Is that why there are no more Ginatese?"

"Yes. All that's left of their civilization are some ruins and parts of their language. And the monsters created by their wars."

"I have been gone so long..." Jenani sat on a chair near Sienne and folded its arms on the table top. "I don't remember the Ginatese using spellbooks like yours. Their magic was different."

"We don't know much about how they cast spells, except that they used the four—I mean five—spell languages. Sometimes we, I mean the Rafellish, not our team, find lost spells. Though our team did find one recently. But—you've seen the ancients! You probably know far more than I do."

"Not as much as you think. I never had a wizard like you as a master. How do you become a wizard?"

"You have to be born able to do magic. And then you go to school to learn wizardry—the spell languages, and how to control them."

"I see." It was hard to read the silver eyes, but Jenani appeared to be looking far into the distance rather than at Sienne. "And no one who isn't born wielding magic can become a wizard."

"Right. Why do you ask? Were the Ginatese different?"

"Oh—no, no different, as far as I know. They cast spells, used rituals. What is this ritual you intend to perform?"

Startled at the sudden change of subject, Sienne hesitated. She was used to thinking of Alaric's quest as a secret, but Ghrita and Vaishant knew about it, and it wasn't as if Jenani were going to tell anyone. "It will make Alaric a full Sassaven," she said. "That's his race, Sassaven. They're enslaved by an evil wizard and we're trying to free them, and this is the next step."

"I've never heard of the Sassaven." Jenani's quiet curiosity relieved Sienne's mind. "What is a full Sassaven?"

"It means he'll have access to magical powers. All the adults of his race go through the ritual, but for them, it's combined with binding magic to tie them to the wizard."

"Interesting. So it will open his magical potential."

"I...guess you could call it that, yes." Jenani was once more looking off into the distance. Sienne got up and stirred the porridge, wishing she knew what the ashwar was thinking. "Anyway, once we do that, we have to figure out how to break the binding ritual, so the Sassaven keep their magical abilities, but aren't slaves."

"What does the binding ritual look like?"

"It's too complicated for me to describe in detail. The two participants draw symbols on each other's hands, in blood, and they're joined by something symbolic, like a silver chain. Then there are words they have to say, and a cup they drink from."

"I've seen it done. The Ginatese used many different binding rituals, or maybe you could say they had many variations on the binding ritual—"

"You've seen it done?" Sienne exclaimed, dropping her spoon into the porridge, where it sank out of sight. "But—do you know how to break it?"

Jenani shook its head. "In theory, you would need to recreate the binding ritual, and then break it—cut the chain and speak words of releasing rather than binding. But that's just an informed guess. Though I do have some experience with binding magic." Its smile went crooked, self-deprecating.

"That's more than we've ever had before. Thank you."

"It's a small thing I can do to repay you if you free me."

Sienne used another long-handled spoon to fish the first out of the depths of the porridge. "We will. I'm sure Averran will grant us the right blessing."

"You have great faith in your God."

"Not really. I've only become a worshipper in the last few months, and I don't know how devout I am. I just know Averran has saved my life, and my friends' lives, time and again, and I feel I've been touched by his presence when I pray."

"I imagine that's how faith begins. Ashwara don't have gods."

"So who created you? Wasn't that God?"

Jenani shrugged. "I'm not interested in the answer to that question. Whoever created us made us vulnerable to being trapped, and I feel no loyalty toward whoever could do that."

"I...guess that makes sense. Though Perrin would say God probably had a reason for it."

"What would Perrin say?" Perrin said, following Dianthe through the door. "Praise Averran, you have made coffee. May you be thrice blessed."

"I was just saying you'd say God has reasons for the things She does, even when we think they're hard on us."

Perrin poured himself a steaming cup of coffee and drank it down, pitch black. "That is true. God's will is sometimes difficult to ascertain, and She gives humans free will with which to thwart Hers, to an extent. She will never force us to follow Her plan, however much happier we will be in the end. Is there something in particular you had in mind?"

"Please, for the love of Kitane, no theological discussions before breakfast," Dianthe moaned.

"We were talking about whether the ashwara were created by God." Sienne hauled out a frying pan and set it on to heat.

"That, I would not care to speculate on," Perrin said. "So many creatures came into being due to human intervention, or arose spontaneously from the residual magic of the wars, that the best anyone can say is that God permitted those creatures to be created. But I do not think that puts them beyond God's mercy. Think of the werebears."

"What are werebears?" Jenani said.

Sienne perked up. "That's a good example. They're intelligent magical creatures, like you, Jenani, and Averran blessed them with healing when they needed it. Which is like saying God cares about them, too."

"And you think God cares about me," Jenani said.

"I think it's possible. So maybe it doesn't matter who created you. Maybe it's more about what you do with your life. Once you're free, I mean."

Jenani frowned. "I...wish to think about that," it said, and turned cloudy and then vanished.

"Heavy discussion for the start of a new day," Perrin said.

"It didn't start out that way." Sienne cracked eggs into the hot pan. "I hope I didn't offend it. I still don't understand religion very well myself."

"It did not look offended, though I realize it's hard to tell." Perrin poured another cup of coffee. "I have not seen Vaishant or Kalanath. Or Ghrita."

"Kalanath and Ghrita are probably practicing, and it wouldn't surprise me if Vaishant were praying somewhere." Dianthe scooped up a bowlful of porridge and returned to her seat. "Though Alaric must have had quite a night, not to be awake yet."

Sienne blushed, but said nothing. Dianthe grinned.

Kalanath and Ghrita appeared in the doorway. "Ah, porridge, thank you, Sienne," Kalanath said, heading for the pot.

"Yes, thank you, Sienne," Ghrita said, helping herself to two eggs from the frying pan.

"Those are for Alaric," Sienne said.

"He's not here. And I'm sure he'd prefer fresh ones." Ghrita smiled, her eyes alight with a hint of malice. It felt like an insult, but one so subtle Sienne couldn't figure out what. Fuming at not being able to respond, she cracked more eggs and ignored Ghrita. She couldn't react without Ghrita pretending innocence and making Sienne look foolish, but the instant the woman said something directly cutting, Sienne was going to tear her apart. Until then...she tried not to feel too relieved at the thought that Alaric might do it for her.

Alaric entered the room at that moment and came directly to her side. "Eggs," he said in a tone of deep satisfaction, and put his arm around Sienne's waist and kissed the side of her head. "None of your goopy porridge for me, thanks."

Sienne drew his head down and kissed him on the lips. "There's no bacon. Sorry." She deliberately didn't look at Ghrita.

"Eggs are fine. It's a glorious morning, isn't it?" He took a seat at the table across from Kalanath. Kalanath raised an eyebrow at him, but continued eating in silence. Sienne wanted to laugh, and then rub Ghrita's face in Alaric's obvious satisfaction with how his night had gone.

Vaishant appeared in the doorway. "I am sorry to be so late," he said. "Porridge only for me, thank you. It is...we say *prakrhuti bhagyar khem donakhoti*, which is that it sticks to your ribs."

Kalanath looked up at this, surprised. "It is what I tell them as well," he said.

Vaishant smiled. "Then we are in agreement in this."

A faint smile touched Kalanath's lips. "I think we are."

Sienne met Alaric's eyes, stopping her from drawing attention to father and son's moment of accord. "I almost forgot," she said instead. "Jenani gave me an idea for reversing the binding ritual. We'll still need to work out the details, but it thought breaking the chain would work."

"I agree," Alaric said. "Eat up, and we'll search the temple. I'm impatient to get to the ritual, but I'd like this other task out of the way before we do."

Sienne sat next to Alaric and ate her porridge hastily. There was plenty of time, true, but she found herself eager to take the next step. She'd worked out most of the missing details on the journey, both on the ship and riding through the desert, and she had a feeling the rest would become obvious as they performed each step. She hoped. No one had ever cast *change* the way the ritual demanded, for example— at least, no one in the last five hundred years. She hoped, at worst, it would just fail if she did it wrong, as opposed to killing its target. The thought turned her eagerness into worry, and she made herself think of something else.

Breakfast over, and the kitchen cleaned, they found their way out of the palace. Jenani didn't appear, but they managed not to get lost, and ended up on the street outside the palace at nearly nine o'clock, according to Sienne's watch. Was it only that she knew the *pakhshani* were gone, that the city felt so empty? Or was there a background hum to a living city that was absent when all its people were? She shivered, and rubbed her arms to quell the goose pimples that had sprung up at the thought.

The temple looked no different than it had the day before. This time, Alaric halted them in the decrepit courtyard. "Let's split up and see if we can't find that phoenix feather," he said.

"Because splitting the party is such a wise move," Dianthe drawled.

Alaric grinned. "This place is empty, and it didn't hold any terrors when it wasn't. I think we're safe to split into two groups. Sienne, you and Kalanath come with me. The rest of you, with Dianthe. We'll each cover half the temple and meet in the divines' chamber."

With Kalanath leading the way, they inspected every room they passed. All were empty of furnishings—"They had plenty of warning to leave before the sands rose," Alaric said—and looked just as any hundreds of years-old building would look: cracked walls and floors, with sand in the corners of the rooms with windows. Remnants of paint, blue and green, still decorated the walls of the corridors, though the rooms were a patchy dull white. In all the important respects, it was a ruin like dozens of others they'd investigated in the past year, and Sienne said so.

"It's tempting to fall into reflections about mortality, and the impermanence of human creations, when you're in the wilderness," Alaric said. "But that leads too easily to feeling hopeless. Why build anything if it's destined to turn out like this?" He made a sweeping gesture with one hand. "And nothing would ever happen if people thought like that."

"Fioretti is four hundred years old," Kalanath said. "Chirantan is older even."

"Exactly," Alaric said. "And parts of those cities have fallen into disrepair, and been destroyed, and new construction took their place. It's part of what it means to be human—to face destruction and choose to build atop it."

"Jenani did make a beautiful city," Sienne said. "It wouldn't take much to keep it going. All Dari had to do was ask for a water supply." She fingered the ring absently, then froze.

"What's wrong?" Alaric said.

"I don't remember putting on the ring. Was I wearing it last night?"

"I wasn't looking at your hands, Sienne," Alaric said, making Kalanath turn away, blushing.

Sienne removed the ring and put it away. "It's unsettling. Like it wants me to use it. Wouldn't Jenani have said if the ring was sentient?

And if it had that kind of power, it would be an artifact, and I'd see its magic. But it's just an ordinary ring."

"That can't be melted by any human fire," Alaric said.

"Maybe you do not remember because it makes you forget," Kalanath said. "Maybe it survives by being not noticed. Jenani said it was lost for many years before Dari finds it."

"I don't know if that's comforting, or unsettling." Sienne tightened the strings of her belt pouch. "Let's keep looking."

They searched every room they could find, with Kalanath commenting that the temple really was identical in layout to the one he'd grown up in. All the rooms were empty. By the time they worked their way to the divines' chamber, Sienne was tired and irritable and more than ready to sit, even if it was on the floor. "Are we sure the feather is here?" she said. "Maybe some other scrappers came through here years ago and took it."

"That is possible, yes," Kalanath said. He joined Sienne on the floor, laying his staff down next to him. "Maybe we need a scrying blessing."

"I'm starting to think we should have done that first," Alaric said. He remained standing, pacing around the center of the room and gazing up at the birds.

"Averran likes it when people use their own talents before coming to him," Sienne said. "We haven't wasted time. It just feels like it."

"Then you, too, have found nothing," Perrin said as he and the others entered the room. "I believe I will ask for a locator blessing. It is unlikely Averran will grant it, as we have never seen this phoenix feather, but he has never yet chastised me for asking."

"Should we try the ritual first?" Dianthe said. "It's not yet noon."

All eyes turned to Sienne. "Why are you all looking at me?" she said, feeling defensive.

"Because you are at the heart of both our endeavors," Perrin said. "It is you who must cast the spells for the ritual, and you who are Jenani's champion."

"Oh." She hadn't thought of herself in those terms before, and it was an unexpected burden. "I think...we should free Jenani first. The ritual came from the ancients, and Jenani knew them, so maybe it could help with the ritual. It might need its magic for that."

"Where is it?" Alaric said.

"I don't know." Sienne hesitated, then put on the ring and said, "Jenani, come here."

The air thickened, became an amorphous cloud and then coalesced into Jenani's lithe shape. "Yes, master?"

"I'm not your master, Jenani."

"You wore the ring. You summoned me." Jenani's eyes were cold and remote again.

Sienne flushed and wrenched the ring off her finger. Was it her imagination that it resisted her pull? "I didn't know where you were. We're going to ask for the blessing that will free you. You wanted to be here for that, right?"

Jenani's face softened. "Yes," it said. "Thank you."

Perrin settled on the floor and laid a handful of rice paper squares in his lap. "Quiet, if you don't mind," he said. "I can pray amidst distractions, but I prefer not to."

Sienne stepped backward and felt Alaric take her hand. It comforted her, which made her realize how tense she'd been without knowing it. Perrin closed his eyes and fell into the rhythmic breathing pattern she was so familiar with, that made her breathe in tandem with him. She closed her eyes and prayed, *O Lord, please have mercy on this creature. It's been trapped for so long.*

A chill touched her heart, unexpected and frightening. Her eyes flew open, and she scanned the room for a threat, but saw no one but her friends and Jenani. Her gaze lingered on the ashwar. It floated nearby, regarding Perrin curiously. Sienne blinked, and the feeling was gone. She felt sure it was a warning, but a warning against what? If she were more experienced in her worship, maybe it would have been clearer. But she didn't want to ignore it.

She opened her mouth to ask Perrin's opinion just as he said, "O mighty Lord of crotchets, forgive my importuning you at this early hour. I hope you will find it in your heart to hear my plea regardless." He went silent, then smiled, a half-curve of his lips that made him look boyish. "My many thanks for your communication blessings, o Lord, and Cressida thanks—has she? Forgive my surprise, but—yes, there is no reason she should not, since she is now your worshipper, but I did not expect it."

Perrin settled himself more comfortably on the tiled floor. "I have only two requests, most cantankerous Lord. We have been tasked to retrieve something for the Hierarch at Chirantan. A phoenix feather. It is supposed to be in this temple, but we have failed to find it after much diligent searching. If it be your will, I would ask a blessing to guide our search.

"The other request is more vital, o Lord of ill humor. You see before you a creature made a slave by men thousands of years ago. We wish to free it from its binding. Lord, in your wisdom you—"

Perrin paused. A look of consternation crossed his face. "I fail to understand your meaning, Lord. Of course we are not immune from the consequences of our actions. Do you mean to say we are wrong to ask this boon?" He went silent for a long time, his brow furrowed in intense thought. Finally, he said, "If it is a matter of repercussions from destroying a powerful object, I assure you we will take precautions, and thank you for—" He went silent again. "I apologize, but I still do not understand. Please forgive my ignorance. We feel strongly that this creature should be freed."

A sizzle of white smoke that smelled of jasmine and mint went up from the papers on Perrin's lap. "Thank you, o mighty Lord," Perrin said, and opened his eyes.

"Did he..." Sienne said.

Perrin examined the papers. "Two blessings," he said. "One variation on a scrying, not a locator blessing, but that is as much as I could have hoped for. And this one..." He lifted the second paper by the very corner as if hesitant to touch it. "I have never seen anything so complex, and so potent. Averran's warning is generous: I believe using this blessing will unleash powerful energies that might well injure or even kill us if we do not take precautions."

He looked at Vaishant, whose face was very still and expressionless. "What do you think?" he said.

Vaishant moistened his lips. "I have never seen the like," he said. "Is it that your avatar is not fully God in Her glory, that you dare speak to God so...familiarly?"

"Haven't you seen Perrin pray before?" Sienne asked.

"I have always been engaged in my own prayers in the past." Vaishant smiled. "I still do not understand why our worship differs, but had I ever in the past dismissed yours as being unworthy, I would not be able to do so now."

"I am grateful that you are not averse to joining your faith with mine," Perrin said, "because I have no way of shielding us from the effects of this blessing, whatever they may be."

"That should be no problem," Vaishant said.

Jenani said, "You mean... just like that? I will be free?"

"If I understand Averran correctly, yes," Perrin said.

"Wait," Sienne said. "Are we doing the right thing?"

"Of course." Perrin's brow furrowed. "Why should we not?"

Everyone was staring at her. The memory of that chill touch on her heart had faded, leaving Sienne uncertain that she'd felt anything at all. "Your half of the conversation made it sound like Averran was concerned," she improvised. "Did he tell you not to do it?"

"He said to be prepared for the consequences, that destroying the ring would loose tremendous powers. I think with the proper shield, we need not fear." Perrin was still looking at her with concern. She made herself smile, and removed the ring from her finger, setting it down on the floor directly below the dome.

"Let's do it," she said.

"Back up," Perrin said, and everyone but him retreated to the wall. Perrin crouched and set the blessing down on the tiles, then laid the ring atop it. "I hope I can invoke it from a distance. I have no desire to be within its range when it is destroyed."

He nodded at Vaishant. The Omeiran divine came forward and clasped his hands below his chin, bowing his head in prayer. A shimmering gray wall rose up around the ring and curved inward to form a dome a foot high and twice that around. Perrin laid his hand flat atop the curve of the dome. He drew in a deep breath, let it out, and said, "O Lord, have patience in your crankiness, and grant me this blessing."

The dome went white, brilliant enough that Sienne, who'd been watching Perrin's hand, went briefly blind. She threw up her arm to shield her eyes, too late, and blinked away pained tears. Exclamations from all around her told her she wasn't the only one suffering. Gradually, her vision returned, though she saw the black inverse of the dome behind her eyelids whenever she closed her eyes. Perrin was crouched beside the dome, whose light was fading. He had both hands over his eyes. Sienne felt a moment's relief that he still had two hands.

Alaric walked past her to the dome. It had been translucent before Perrin invoked the blessing, and now it was cloudy, making the ring invisible. Alaric drew his belt knife and, crouching, drove it hilt-deep into the dome. The shield parted, not popping as a broken shield usually did, but separating like a wilting flower to fall in two halves to the floor. Sienne moved forward to look over his shoulder.

The ring sat in the middle of a blackened circle, completely unharmed.

"No!" Sienne exclaimed, diving to pick it up. Alaric cried out a warning, but it was in her hand before she realized touching it might be a bad idea. It was cool to the touch and as smooth and shiny as ever, unmarred by whatever that explosion had been.

Sienne turned to look at Jenani, whose face was as expressionless as she'd ever seen it. "I'm sorry," she said.

"Give me an order," it said.

"No. I promised. Look, we'll try something else—"

"Put it on and order me to do something. Order me to make this an oasis in the desert."

She realized the ring was on her finger. "No, Jenani."

"Please. If this is my destiny, I will embrace it."

Sienne closed her eyes. "Jenani, make this an oasis."

Nothing happened. She opened her eyes and saw Jenani still floating there. "Is it done?" she asked.

Jenani smiled. It was an expression of pure happiness. "It is not. The binding is broken. I am free!"

"Oh, Jenani! I'm so glad!"

Jenani turned its attention on her. It floated closer. Its smile changed, became something dark and menacing. Sienne stepped back, and it followed her. "I am free," it said again. "I have been a slave for thousands of years. Thousands of years of humiliation. I have not forgotten a single one of those years. Humanity will pay for what it did to me. Starting with you."

19

S ienne took another step back. "What are you talking about? Jenani, we freed you!"

"I swore I would kill the man who did that, as my first act of free will. My powers are diminished without the ring, but I'm still capable of that." Jenani drifted closer. Sienne felt hands close on her shoulders, and Alaric put himself in front of her.

"You're going to find that hard," Alaric said. "I don't care how powerful you are, you're outnumbered and we're not weak."

Jenani laughed. The sound was so cheerful, so at odds with the ashwar's menacing demeanor, it filled Sienne with fear. "So bold, in defense of your love," it said. "She's remarkable. The ring exerts a powerful influence on its bearer, encouraging him to command me, and she resisted every time." It stopped moving toward Alaric and Sienne. "I never believed you would succeed, or that you'd want to. I think that's worthy of some consideration."

A strong wind came out of nowhere, blasting them all and knocking them off their feet, even Alaric. Sienne found herself flattened against the wall, unable to breathe. She gasped, covered her face with her arms, and shouted, "Jenani, stop! We wanted to help you! How can you possibly—"

"Betray you?" Jenani said, its voice carrying above the wind. "The more fool you, for believing I could possibly feel any obligation to worthless humans. But, as I said, you did what no one in millennia has been capable of, and you deserve something for that. I won't kill you. I'll just leave you here to die."

The ground shuddered. A roar greater than the wind's voice deafened Sienne, coming from everywhere at once. Dust filled the whirlwind, stinging her face and hands. Something grabbed her spellbook and yanked it off her shoulder, snapping the strap as if it were paper and making her cry out in pain.

She clutched the book, but it was snatched from her fingers. Dust clogged her nostrils, and she had to cover her face again. Then the wind died, and the pressure released her to fall in a heap. She sneezed and drew in a breath still silty with dirt, coughed and choked until her lungs were clear. Blinking, she opened her eyes and looked around.

Her friends were all picking themselves up off the floor, coughing as she was. Alaric, nearest her, sat up and said, "Is everyone all right? Sienne?"

"I'm fine," Sienne said.

"I think we are unharmed," Perrin said. "Jenani is gone."

Sienne scanned the room, though she already knew it was hopeless. "It took my spellbook."

Dianthe ran through the door only to come up short a few steps down the hallway. "It's caved in," she said. "The way is completely blocked."

Kalanath went to join her, prodding the wreckage with his staff. "There is most of the temple roof fallen," he said. "We cannot escape this way."

"Is there magic on it, Sienne?" Alaric asked.

Sienne went to look. "No. Just rubble."

"So I can't break through the way I did with that keep last year." Alaric put his shoulder to the mass. It shifted, and a rumble went through the room. "I think that's a bad idea," he said, stepping back. "Damn it."

"It did not kill us," Vaishant said, "as it promised. I am not sure whether this is not a more terrible fate."

"We're alive, and that's what matters," Alaric said. "We've been in worse situations."

"Really? I can't think of any," Dianthe said.

"Neither can I. I was building morale again." Alaric leaned against the wall and ran his fingers through his hair, which was dark with dust. "Any ideas?"

"Everything I can think of requires my spellbook." Sienne crossed the room and put her arms around him, felt him return her embrace. "I'm sorry. This is my fault. If I hadn't insisted on freeing it... and I think Averran tried to warn me..."

"There is no blame in wanting to do the right thing," Perrin said. "And Averran warned me as well. I simply did not understand. I thought his words about loosing a great power referred to the effects of the blessing, but..." He sighed. "I should have paid closer attention."

"This isn't getting us anywhere," Alaric said. "Sienne, what can you do without your spellbook?"

"We've already seen that moving the blockage will bring the roof down on us, so even if my invisible fingers were strong enough, they wouldn't help. I can't make the building invulnerable and stop it caving in because it's too big. I can keep the lights burning so we can see how hopeless it is."

"I have a feeling Averran will not respond to any further petitions of mine," Perrin said. "He seemed rather more irritable than usual, possibly because I ignored his warnings."

"But Vaishant may pray," Kalanath said.

"I cannot imagine...no." Vaishant stopped himself mid-sentence and held up a finger for silence as he closed his eyes in thought. After a few seconds, he said, "There is a thing I may try. It is dangerous, and may have no effect on us now. But it is permitted the divines to attempt to see as God sees."

"I have done that in the past," Perrin said. "You are correct, it is dangerous."

"More dangerous than staying here and doing nothing, and dying?" Kalanath said. "I think you should try."

Vaishant smiled. "I appreciate that you have faith in me," he said, and Kalanath ducked his head. "You will stop me if I am overwhelmed?"

"You trust me to know that?" Kalanath's head came up in surprise.

"I do," Vaishant said.

The two men looked at each other for several moments. Then Kalanath nodded. "I will," he said.

Vaishant took off his outer robe and rolled it up for a pillow. He lay on the dirty floor in his sleeveless black shirt and loose trousers with his hands clasped loosely on his stomach. "I may not remember what I see," he said, "so it is for you to listen."

"That is how it worked for me," Perrin said. "We are prepared."

Kalanath took a position near Vaishant's head. The others gathered around, not too close. Vaishant closed his eyes and let out a long, slow breath, then inhaled, equally slowly. Sienne found herself breathing in rhythm with him. It relaxed her, drew the tension out of her shoulders and back.

Nothing happened. Vaishant continued to breathe deeply. Sienne shifted her weight and Alaric's arm went around her waist. His warm bulk comforted her further even as she cringed inside, remembering Jenani's face as it threatened her. How could she have been so stupid? Then again, not one of them had suspected treachery. It had been so helpful, so friendly, right up until it wasn't. She felt stupid, and angry, and sad—sad that it wasn't who she'd thought it was. And, running beneath those feelings like a subterranean stream, she felt fear. What was Jenani capable of now that it was free? And if it hated humanity for what a few men and women had done to it, what did it plan to do to the innocents in its path?

"*I see,*" Vaishant said in Meiric. "*So many things—some are past, some are future, some are now. There I am, as a young man, and Manisha—*" He smiled, and shook his head. "*Kalanath as a baby, and as an old man, and everything in between—but that is an indulgence. O God, hear my prayer, and guide my eye. Show me how we may escape.*"

Sienne realized she was holding her breath. She'd seen Perrin do this once, but Vaishant's face was so still and tight, as if he were exerting himself to a great feat of endurance, his communion felt far more serious. Or maybe it was just that their lives were at stake. She let out her breath and took Alaric's hand.

Vaishant's face clouded over, and his lips went thin as if something disturbed him. "*I see Chirantan in flames,*" he said. "*The divines flee. The harbor is a sheet of fire. Horses with horns, racing across a valley. A man with glowing yellow eyes. We sit in a circle beneath the dome, in a card game I don't recognize. Sienne, screaming in terrible pain.*" He licked his lips. "*The images come faster now. I have—no, that can't be—blood, streaming down my hands—the ashwar choking Alaric in the throne room—Dianthe wading through a sea of white—*"

His eyes flew open. Blood trickled from the corners like tears. "*God have mercy,*" he cried, "*I can see everything—She is near—*"

With a swift movement, Kalanath whipped his staff around and cracked the divine across the skull. Vaishant cried out again and lay still. Kalanath flung down his staff and knelt beside Vaishant, taking his wrist and feeling for a pulse. "I think I am in time," he said.

Perrin offered Kalanath a handkerchief, and Kalanath blotted the blood from Vaishant's face. Ghrita knelt on the divine's other side. "He's still breathing," she said.

Vaishant's eyelids fluttered, and he looked up at the faces surrounding him. "I remember blood," he said. "Chirantan in flames. That does not seem useful."

"There were other things," Kalanath said. "Some were in the past. I think you saw a creature we fought once."

"And unicorns," Sienne said, glancing at Alaric. They'd been open about his quest, but had said nothing about his true race or that his other self was a unicorn. Alaric made a tiny motion with his head. Now was not the time for that discussion.

"You saw me in pain, and yourself with bloody hands," Sienne went on. "Dianthe in a white sea. All of us playing cards—oh!" She patted her sides and felt, with relief, the hard, angular shape of the hazard deck. "I forgot I had this."

"A hazard deck?" Ghrita said, her brow furrowed. "You want us to play cards?"

"It's magical. Once a day, the cards, if you draw them the right way, do things. Make you smarter, or maybe stronger...I can't remember all the effects, not that anyone knows most of them. But it's possible their magic can do something to get us out of here."

"Show me," Vaishant said, pushing himself up on his elbows. Kalanath put an arm behind him for support. Sienne opened the box and tipped the hazard deck into her hand, extending it to Vaishant. With a look for permission, he touched the cards, fanning them slightly. "It is familiar, but I do not remember the details of what I saw."

"It's worth a try," Alaric said.

"Should we all draw cards, or just one of us?" Sienne asked.

"I think we want as much help as we can get." Alaric turned up the front card, which displayed the three of crowns. "How does it work?"

Sienne directed everyone to sit in a circle near the blackened spot beneath the dome. "This could be dangerous. Some of the cards are supposed to have negative effects."

"The alternative is dying in here," Alaric said. "Show us what to do."

Sienne split the deck and shuffled, somewhat awkwardly. "Three times," she said. "Then you cut the deck like this." She made three stacks, then put the center one on the left-hand pile and both of those atop the right-hand one. "Then you just...draw the top card." She hesitated, said a silent prayer, and lifted the card.

Dianthe drew in a breath. Sienne's hand shook. A bone-white skull stared back at her, its eye sockets faintly glowing against a dark background. "The Skull," she said. "That can't be—"

A whoosh of air rattled the card in her hand, bringing with it the smell of decay. Alaric was instantly on his feet, scanning the room for danger, with Kalanath and Dianthe close behind. Sienne glanced at the card again, then took a longer look. "It's changing," she exclaimed.

The image on the card bulged as if something were emerging from it, stretching out in a translucent blur. Sienne held it at arm's length, obscurely fearing what might happen if she let go. Or was it worse to be in contact with it? She opened her fingers, but the card stuck to them, even when she waved her hand vigorously to detach it.

"Don't touch it," she said when Dianthe moved to help. "If we're both stuck to it—"

The bulge had turned into a miniature skull, the size of Sienne's two fists together, and it was solid, no longer a translucent image. It stayed fast attached to the card no matter how Sienne shook it. "Mortal," a deep, mournful voice intoned, "speak your—stop shaking me! Stop it!"

Sienne held the card where it was level with her eyes. "Did you... say something?"

"I did. Really, it's beneath my dignity to have to endure such treatment. I am a powerful, omniscient spirit, and you are but a mortal, fleeting and impermanent upon this world. Speak your question, and let me be."

"Question?" Sienne looked at her friends. "Any question?"

"You don't have one in mind? I can offer suggestions. Wealth, that's a popular one. I can direct you to any treasure you care to name. Or if it's love you're interested in, I can tell you the name of your soulmate, or the location of the nearest brothel—it's all in the asking. I can find anything, speak with your beloved ancestors, guide you places. But I hate waiting around, so if you wouldn't mind hurrying it up a bit..."

"How do we get out of here?" Sienne said.

"How do we get out of here," the spirit repeated thoughtfully. "Give me a minute to look around." Its eye sockets, which gleamed with a faint blue light, dimmed to almost nothing. Sienne watched it avidly, afraid to say anything that might interrupt its search.

The light brightened. "You just have to go through the door," the spirit said. "Good luck." The skull sagged and began to melt back into the card.

"Wait!" Sienne exclaimed. "The door is blocked. How can we go through it?"

"One question," the spirit said, its voice fainter. "One answer. Use your head." The skull disappeared entirely, leaving Sienne holding a hazard card by one corner.

Sienne let her hand fall. The card slipped from her fingers. "That was worse than unhelpful," she said. "We can't use the door."

Alaric held out his hand for the deck. "My turn," he said. "We'll go around the circle."

He shuffled, cut, and drew a card. "The Key," he said, examining it closely. The card shimmered, and a key fell from it to land with a chiming clatter on the tiled floor. Alaric picked up the iron key and turned it over. It looked dainty in his huge hand. "If we had a door, this might be helpful." He tucked the key into his belt pouch, then gathered the cards and handed the deck to Dianthe.

Dianthe drew the four of staves. Four little staffs ornamented with crystals, looking more like magical artifacts than Kalanath's weapon, glimmered from the card. Dianthe furrowed her brow. "I don't see anything," she began, then gasped.

"What? What's wrong?" Alaric said.

"Nothing's wrong," Dianthe said, her eyes narrowed. "It's just that everything makes so much more sense now. I can remember things I thought I'd forgotten. Ask me something I don't know. Something mathematical."

"Um...what's the square root of 2,569?" Sienne said.

"It's about 50.6853. See?"

"I'm terrible at math. I don't know if it's right."

Dianthe smiled. "I promise it is. I feel so much more...it's like everything is sharper."

"The wizard who investigated the deck said staves is the suit associated with intelligence," Sienne said. "I remember now I drew a staves card and it made me a lot smarter for a while."

"Well, I don't know how useful this will be," Dianthe said, her face radiant, "but it feels amazing." She handed the deck to Ghrita. "Your turn."

Ghrita drew the four of coins, and had to duck as a shower of gold rained down on her. "Ow!" she exclaimed. "Gold is heavy!"

"I do not recognize this coin," Kalanath said, retrieving one where it had rolled next to his foot and holding it up to the light. "It looks new."

"They were minted during the reign of Zysztad III, also known as Zysztad the Capricious," Dianthe said, looking at another coin. "The stad, as it was called, was worth about a quarter of a larus because the currency was debased with other metals."

"How do you know that?" Alaric said.

"I have no idea." Dianthe handed the coin to Ghrita. "I'd like to say you could get a bundle for those from the right collector, but I don't know that anyone will believe those coins are three hundred and twenty years old."

"For all we know, they'll disappear in a few hours," Ghrita said, but tucked the handful of coins away in her robes somewhere.

Perrin took the deck with no hesitation, shuffling and cutting expertly. "I was particularly skilled at the card game Sovereign States," he said to their obvious surprise, "though I am not as good at hazard as Dianthe, whom I would suspect of cheating were she anyone else." He closed his eyes and murmured, "O Lord, we are in a bind, so if you would see fit to influence this deck, it will be much appreciated." He flipped over the top card. The perky blond image of the duke of crowns smiled up at them.

Sienne leaned over to look at it, not touching the card. She didn't think touching someone else's draw influenced the outcome, but after the morning she'd had, she didn't feel like taking chances. "I wonder," she said, looking up at Perrin, and the words died on her lips. Perrin was looking back at her, one eyebrow slightly raised. She took in his well-defined cheekbones, his soft, dark eyes, his shapely lips, and her breath caught. She'd never realized how attractive he was.

"Kitane help me," Dianthe said. She, too, stared at Perrin as if she'd never seen him before. "I think I know what the card does."

"What?" Alaric said. He glanced at Perrin, then at Dianthe. "I don't see anything different."

"You probably wouldn't," Ghrita said. She rested her hand on Perrin's knee and leaned toward him. "At least, I hope you don't." She swept his hair away from his face with her other hand and leaned in closer, her mouth drawing up for a kiss.

Perrin shot backward, out of her reach. "Ghrita, what are you doing?" he said, his voice breaking in the middle.

"Just what we're all thinking," Ghrita purred. She crawled toward him, a slow, sensual movement.

Sienne felt a flash of jealousy, followed almost immediately by the sensation of being dashed in the face with icy water. "Ghrita, stop, it's the card!" she exclaimed.

Ghrita sat up and shook her head as if she'd been doused in water too. "I—" she said, then sat back on her haunches. "I apologize," she said to Perrin, scooting backward. "You were suddenly intensely attractive, and I forgot myself. It is nothing *they* weren't thinking as well," she added somewhat defensively, swiping her arm toward Sienne and Dianthe.

"Yes, but *we* didn't act on it," Sienne said, feeling smug. She looked at Perrin, whose face was a mask of astonishment, and wondered what it would feel like to kiss those amazing lips. She closed her eyes and gripped Alaric's knee. "But I hope it wears off soon." If it was powerful enough to make her consider attacking Perrin with Alaric sitting right there, no wonder Ghrita hadn't been able to resist.

"I think I should sit over here," Ghrita said, moving to a spot behind Sienne.

Sienne tried not to feel uncomfortable at Ghrita's nearness and focused on Kalanath, who now took his turn with the deck. He looked as uncomfortable as she felt. Carefully, he turned over the top card. "The Eclipse," he said.

The card showed a man and a woman looking up into a dark sun with a bright corona. "They don't look happy," she said, turning to face Kalanath, and gasped. A pale film covered Kalanath's dark eyes.

He blinked, and blinked again. The film grew brighter and less translucent.

"The lights are dimming," he said. "Sienne, should you make more?"

Sienne's hand closed hard on Alaric's knee. "It's not the lights," she said, feeling faint.

Kalanath swallowed. His eyes were solid white. "I see nothing," he said.

20

Dianthe leaned across the circle and waved her hand in Kalanath's face. He didn't react except to lean back slightly. "I feel air on my face," he said, "and I think it is a hand waving, but I cannot see it."

"You're completely blind?" Alaric said.

Kalanath nodded.

No one spoke. Sienne felt numb, her face and hands tingling as if they'd fallen asleep and were just beginning to wake. Finally, Alaric said, "Is this something you can heal, Vaishant?"

Vaishant knelt before Kalanath and thumbed open his left eye, then his right. "I can ask," he said, "but I do not think this is ordinary blindness. It seems to be a cover to his eyes, which is good because it means the eyes themselves are undamaged."

"But bad because it's not something healing can fix," Alaric said.

Vaishant nodded. He gently pressed Kalanath's eyes closed and rested his thumbs atop them. He closed his eyes and bowed his head. Silence descended, the only noise the occasional creak of the beams settling more firmly over—Sienne refused to think of it as their tomb, but it was hard to stick to that vow when the place was so quiet, and smelled so strongly of dust.

She took Alaric's hand again and gripped it tightly, unable to take her eyes from Vaishant and Kalanath. Kalanath sat perfectly still, his legs still crossed beneath him and his hands resting on his knees. He didn't look at all afraid, and the peacefulness of his countenance touched her heart, easing it somewhat. She couldn't help feeling guilty over his condition. It had been her suggestion, and even though she'd warned them bad things could happen, she hadn't expected anything like this.

Vaishant sat back and removed his hands. Kalanath's eyes opened. Sienne controlled a gasp—his eyes were still filmed over with solid white. "God tells me it is not permanent," Vaishant said. "She was not specific about how long it will last. But time will cure it."

"But what if it's months? Years?" Sienne burst out.

"This is not your fault, Sienne," Kalanath said, turning his blind head to face her. "I chose this. It is a risk I take for all our sakes." The faintest smile touched his lips. "I hope we are attacked so I can learn if I remember all I was taught about fighting blind. Though it has been years since I practiced, so maybe I do not want it, after all."

"I don't think we should draw any more cards," Sienne said. "What if it happens again?"

"We still don't have a way out," Dianthe said.

"I am not afraid to try," Vaishant said. He took the cards from where they lay in front of Kalanath, shuffled, and cut the deck.

"Alaric—"

"Vaishant knows what he's doing, Sienne. Let him take the chance."

Sienne subsided. Vaishant drew the top card and laid it down on the floor next to the deck. "The Fool," he said. "I do not know this game. Is it good, or bad?"

"In a hazard reading, it means new beginnings," Dianthe said. "But it can also mean randomness, the unexpected, depending on the other cards in the reading. I...don't think it's bad."

"Does it do anything?" Kalanath said. He had his head tilted up as if straining to make up for his lack of sight with hearing.

"It hasn't had an effect yet," Alaric said. "As far as we're aware."

Vaishant rose, taking the Fool card in his hand. "I wonder," he said, and walked to the doorway. "New beginnings. New journeys. A safe road, perhaps?" He held the card at arm's length and began circling the room, walking slowly as if taking a bearing with a compass. Sienne and the others watched him in silence. Despair crept over Sienne. They'd taken their best chance and it wasn't enough. Now Kalanath was blind and they were still trapped.

She cursed Jenani and wished with all her heart she had her spellbook. She still couldn't *ferry* everyone, she didn't have the reserves, but she could *ferry* most of them, and bring the rest out tomorrow. It would have been a nearly ideal solution if she only had her spellbook. Why did magic have to be so damned *hard*? If she were capable of memorizing spells...her memory was excellent for languages, but magic was slippery and powerful and no human could keep a spell in memory, or even remember individual syllables, for more than a few seconds. She could barely imagine what it would be like if things were different.

About two-thirds of the way around the room from the collapsed door, Vaishant stopped. "Something is here," he said, just as the card glowed brilliant scarlet for a few seconds and then faded back to an ordinary card. Everyone but Kalanath came to join him.

"It looks like the rest of the wall," Perrin said. Sienne had to make herself stop staring at his lips. That effect couldn't wear off soon enough.

Ghrita, who'd been eyeing Perrin with an avidity that made Sienne uncomfortable, said, "Is there something concealed there?"

Dianthe stepped up and examined the wall. "I don't think so. It looks like a wall."

"But I am certain the card indicates that this spot is the beginning," Vaishant said. "The beginning of our next journey."

"And the skull said to go through the door," Dianthe said. "*And* we have a key." She stepped back with her hands on her hips, staring at the wall and chewing her bottom lip in thought. "Go through the door..."

"Maybe we need to examine the fallen—" Sienne began.

Dianthe snapped her fingers. "Got it. Perrin, I need your pastels."

"You may have them with my blessing," Perrin said, removing the grubby packet and handing it over. Dianthe selected a dark gray stick of pigment and sketched rapidly over the spot Vaishant had indicated, long, straight lines for the verticals, shorter ones for a lintel. In less than a minute, she had drawn a slightly lopsided door, complete with a lock plate and handle. The lock plate bore a very large keyhole, larger than a door that size would typically have.

"See? Walk through the door," she said.

Alaric rested his hand on the flat surface of the wall, over the handle. "Dianthe," he began.

Dianthe rolled her eyes. "It's simple. We're not at the center of the temple here—"

"How do you know? It is true, but I do not think you see it," Vaishant said.

"I remembered how many steps we took and which turns went where," Dianthe said. "This effect is incredible. It's like the best coffee in the world, injected straight into my veins. Anyway, I know where we are in relation to the temple dome, and the collapse wouldn't have been even on all sides, which means we're not evenly covered here. The point being that there are places where there's going to be less rubble, or none at all. This—" She rapped on the wall as if knocking on a real door—"is the spot where breaking through is easiest."

"You know that?" Sienne said.

"No, but the card does. And now we have a door. Alaric, use the key."

Alaric dug in his belt pouch and came out with the key. It looked even smaller than Sienne remembered, small enough that if Dianthe's keyhole were real, it would disappear inside it. "It's worth trying," he said, and pressed the tip of the key to the wall.

It sank into the plaster until the shank disappeared.

Alaric drew in a startled breath. He turned the key to the right. There was a click, faint but still audible in the room's sudden silence. The wall shimmered, and cracks formed along the lines Dianthe had drawn. With a groan, the door pulled away from the wall and opened inward. Dusty air swirled in from the space beyond.

Sienne went to look past Alaric's arm. It wasn't the outdoors, but that would have been too much of a coincidence even for their magic-aided escape. Instead, it opened on a passage clear of rubble that extended into darkness. Sienne sent lights spinning down to where it turned a corner. "It's empty."

"Let's go," Alaric said. "Vaishant, lead the way."

Sienne took Kalanath's arm as he rose, feeling about him for his staff. "How can we help you?" she said. "Should we...I don't know... lead you? Hold your hand?"

"I must walk in front or I will trip over your heels," Kalanath said. "If Vaishant tells me directions, I will be fine."

Sienne had looked in Vaishant's direction when Kalanath said his name, so she saw the look that passed over his face when he heard this—a look equal parts yearning and sorrow. She pretended she hadn't seen anything and guided Kalanath to stand beside Vaishant. Vaishant touched Kalanath's elbow and turned him to face the right way. "I will say left or right," he said, "and you will feel with your staff."

"Thank you," Kalanath said, and clasped Vaishant's hand firmly for a moment before switching his staff to his right hand. Sienne made her lights gather around them, and they set off.

It was only her knowledge that the temple dome had collapsed, and that much of the temple was in ruins, that made Sienne so nervous. As far as she could tell, the passages were as safe as ever, still windowless and dark, still patchy with the remnants of paint worn away over the centuries. She stayed close behind Alaric anyway, listening to Vaishant's murmured instructions to Kalanath.

Kalanath, after the first minute of tentative feeling-about with his staff, walked as confidently as if he could see, only blundering into walls a few times. It reassured her, made her feel less guilty, though she tried not to think of it as a good thing that Kalanath, of all of them, had been the one struck blind. She'd have preferred it to be

Ghrita if she'd been able to choose. It was an ignoble thought that gave her guilty pleasure.

It felt like no time at all before natural light gleamed ahead, and they came out of the passages into the ruined courtyard. Sienne breathed in the smell of sand and hot air and felt she'd never appreciated those smells enough. Alaric took the lead. "We need to get to the horses," he said. "It's probably too late, but we have to try."

"Try what?" Dianthe said.

"You heard what Vaishant saw. Chirantan in flames." Alaric removed his head scarf from where it hung around his neck and began wrapping it sloppily around his head. He tore it off and started over, more neatly this time. "I don't think it's coincidence and I don't think that's some future prophecy. Jenani wanted to destroy humans, and it's not unlikely it would start with one of the oldest cities in the world, and the biggest."

"It will take us nine days to get there," Dianthe protested. "I realize this sounds defeatist, but don't you think he'll have destroyed it and moved on by then?"

Alaric's lips thinned in anger. "We have to do something. We can't race around the world trying to guess where Jenani will go next. We freed him. That makes defeating him our responsibility. Do you have a better option?"

Dianthe shook her head. "I just wish we weren't so helpless."

"We're not helpless. We can't think like that or we really will have failed."

Sienne reached to adjust the strap of her spellbook and remembered too late it wasn't there anymore. She felt so miserable she wanted to cry. "There's not much I can do against Jenani," she said.

Perrin swore and reached into his robes. "I have one more blessing," he said. "A kind of scrying."

"But that was for the phoenix feather." Another thing they'd failed at. She was two seconds away from sitting down and bursting into tears, curling up on the sand and lying there until it covered her completely.

"It is not a locator blessing, which would be for a specific object, but a scrying to reveal a location," Perrin said. "Whatever location I choose. And I think Averran, in his wisdom, chose this blessing deliberately." He withdrew the paper square from his robe and held it up, murmuring an invocation.

A blue globe that shimmered like water appeared in front of Perrin at chest height. Sienne stepped forward to look at it. Cloudy shapes floated within it, shapes Sienne felt she could almost recognize. Perrin put his hand against the globe, as tenderly as if it were a baby. "Show us Sienne's spellbook," he said.

The cloudy shapes firmed, became a view of a city from above. By the bright colors, Sienne recognized Ma'tzehar. The view swooped sickeningly, rotating and pulling away from the city, then diving toward the palace. If this was a bird's eye view, Sienne wanted never to leave the ground.

The movement slowed, spun once more, and Sienne let out a small scream, because the vision was centered on her spellbook, which lay... "That bastard," she said. "It dropped it on the temple dome."

"I imagine Jenani attempted to destroy it and became frustrated when it could not," Perrin said. "I believe it is...I see it."

He pointed, and Sienne looked up toward where the temple dome lay collapsed over the building. It took her a moment to pick the outline of her precious book out from the rubble. She held out her hands, and the spellbook flew into them, slapping her palms and making them sting from the force of its flight. She hugged it to herself, then opened to *ferry*. "I can get some of us to Chirantan," she said. "But I'll be useless after that."

"Can you transport the horses as well?" Vaishant asked.

She'd forgotten the horses. "No. If some of us...but who would stay behind?"

"Let's see that they're all right, first," Alaric said. "We left them with enough food and water for the night, but they'll need caring for."

They ran down the long, wide road at the center of Ma'tzehar. Sienne was kicking herself for not having thought of the horses sooner. They'd left them hobbled, for Averran's sake, helpless to flee if something threatened them. It was small comfort to think she'd have remembered if it had been Spark—or maybe that only made it worse.

They had to slow to a walk when they left the city, with the soft desert sands shifting uncomfortably if they tried moving faster. Sienne trudged along behind Alaric, wishing she could fly. The spell *fly* would be faster, and the movement of the air would cool her. It was not quite noon and already the sun was working toward its full blistering heat. When this was over, they could go to Beneddo, which was much cooler even in true summer.

Then Sienne remembered Jenani, its sinister face and mocking smile, and her fantasy evaporated. Even if they could *ferry* to Chirantan, it wouldn't be all of them, and Sienne would be helpless to participate in the fight. Worse, suppose they couldn't fight Jenani at all? It was powerful enough to rebuild a city and make an entire people forget themselves, and though it had said its powers were less without the ring, that might not mean much. What might it be capable of now it was free?

Alaric cursed and broke into a run. Sienne, her heart in her throat, followed him. He crouched and came up with a couple of leather straps. "They're gone," he said. "The hobbles look like they just stepped right out of them."

"You think it was Jenani?" Dianthe said.

"I can't think of any way they could have freed themselves." Alaric threw the straps down with some force. "I hope Jenani didn't kill them."

"Unlikely," Ghrita said. "It would have left bodies to taunt us, on the chance we escaped."

Vaishant, leading Kalanath by the elbow, came up beside them. "Then we need not worry about them," he said, "and can worry about ourselves."

"But that leaves us with nothing but what we were carrying," Dianthe said. "Now I'm mad."

"Let's think of it as a blessing in disguise," Alaric said. "Sienne, how many of us can you get to Chirantan with *ferry*?"

"Five."

"But that leaves you incapable of casting spells," Dianthe said, "and if we're going to fight Jenani, we'll almost certainly need you."

"I have to use *ferry* regardless," Sienne said. "We can't exactly walk back to Chirantan."

"And who is it will go back?" Vaishant said. "Perhaps Kalanath and I should stay."

"I am not helpless, though I am blind," Kalanath insisted.

Ghrita flicked her staff and knocked Kalanath's staff out from under him, making him stagger until Vaishant bore him up. "You are a liability," she said. "You stay."

"Then Sienne, I want you to stay with Vaishant and Kalanath," Alaric said. "You'll return here after you take the last of us—"

"I will not!"

"You'll be helpless. I can't fight if I'm worried about what's happening to you."

"I can still do things—warn the divines—"

"The city is probably already under attack. They know there's danger."

Sienne scowled and turned away. "You can't force me to go."

"I shouldn't have to. You're not stupid, Sienne. This is the smartest course of action."

Smartest course. "Dianthe, what do you think we should do?" Sienne asked.

Dianthe frowned. "Why are you asking me? Alaric's the leader."

"Because you're the smartest of us right now. Is there a better plan?"

Dianthe's eyes went unfocused as she stared into the distance. Her face shifted as she thought. Finally, she shook her head. "If you had *transport*, obviously that would change things. Even *fly* wouldn't make a difference, or at least that's what you said the last time I brought it up as an option."

"No, *fly* is as hard to cast as *ferry*. And we'd probably be exhausted when we got there." Sienne kicked the sand, which shifted unsatis-factorily. "Though it might give us an advantage against Jenani. It can probably fly as well as float."

"How unfortunate that we cannot harness the birds to carry us through the air," Vaishant said with a smile. His hand was still on Kalanath's elbow, his vibrant red robe shifting in the desert air like—

Sienne's breath caught. There *was* something they could harness. Maybe. And there was no knowing how fast it would go, or if they could even make it work. But it would take no more than an hour to find out, and if it did work—

"Let's go," she said. "I have an idea."

21

"You have *got* to be kidding," Alaric said. "There's no way."

Sienne pushed one of the floating carpets, which shifted slightly before returning to its original position. "It's worth trying," she said. "Dianthe can figure out how to make them fly—"

"Are you sure Dianthe is up to that?" Dianthe said with a laugh. "I'm not sure phenomenal intelligence is useful in situations like this."

"I was thinking more of your ability to figure out how a trap works, even if it's part artifact," Sienne said. "These can't be that difficult to use, and I doubt you have to be a wizard to use them. We just have to figure out the...the command words, or whatever it is. Maybe you steer with your legs, like a horse."

"I have just imagined Sienne atop one of these wearing riding boots and wielding a crop," Perrin murmured.

"You're not funny. Come on, time is slipping away from us. Half an hour, and if we can't make it work, I'll *ferry* you to Chirantan without argument."

"That, I don't believe," Alaric said.

"Of course I will!"

"I meant the no argument part." Alaric sighed and took hold of the nearest rug, brightly patterned in an eye-watering green and pink. "They're not heavy, just bulky and hard to maneuver."

They steered the carpet out of the storage room and down the hall to the grand pillared entry chamber at the base of the throne room. Alaric had insisted that if they were going to experiment with an unknown form of transportation, it should be in an enclosed space where it couldn't take off for the horizon with one of them aboard. It took some doing to get the thing horizontal, and more work to pull it down to waist height, but eventually the rug floated there as placidly as a brightly colored cow. Sienne went to climb atop it, but was restrained by Alaric. "If it crashes, we can't afford for you to be hurt," he said. "You're the backup plan."

Dianthe put her hands on the rug and pulled herself up. It dipped a little, not enough to throw her off balance, and she was able to stand and even take a few steps on its smooth surface. "Hmm," she said, going to her knees and examining the edges. "It's got a couple of irregular spots on this edge. Darker than the rest." She rested her palms on the rug's surface and curled her fingers around its tasseled shorter edge.

The rug shivered. Then it...Sienne could only think of it as coming to attention, if an inanimate object could do such a thing. But it wasn't exactly inanimate, was it? In any case, it had a look about it that, if it had been a dog, Sienne would have called alert helpfulness.

Then it moved. Slowly, and at no more than crawling speed, but it definitely moved. Dianthe's face was set with concentration. "Are you doing that?" Alaric asked, keeping pace with her.

"Yes. Shut up, mountain, this is harder than it looks." The rug turned in a slow curve to the left, away from Alaric and the others, then curved in the opposite direction. Sienne held her breath as the rug proceeded to rise, still moving slowly, until it was close enough to the ceiling that Dianthe could touch it if she dared move her hands.

Then she did move her hands, sitting up and waving to them. Sienne let out a shriek. But the rug didn't plummet to the ground, just hovered where Dianthe had stopped it. "Just one more thing to try," Dianthe shouted, and dropped back to lie on the carpet. It curved, losing height rapidly and going faster and faster until it sped past, forcing them to dodge and, in Perrin's case, flatten himself on the floor as it passed over him. Sienne heard Dianthe laugh like a madwoman as she flew past.

"Kitane's left arm, but that was fun," Dianthe said, making the rug wheel about and return to its starting position. "It corners like a pig in wallow, but I bet it can go faster than that. A *lot* faster."

"So how does it work?" Alaric said.

"You'll have to try it yourself to understand. When I put my hands on those marks, it was like making a connection with the power that moves the rug. Like harnessing a horse to a wagon. And then it did whatever I willed it to do. The hard part was staying focused and not getting distracted by things like how high I was in the air." Dianthe hopped off and gestured to Alaric to take a turn. He looked at her skeptically, then at the rug, but climbed on less gracefully than she had and put his hands where she directed him.

Sienne half expected the rug to lift more slowly under the Sassaven's weight, but it floated even more swiftly to the ceiling than it had for Dianthe, spun around, and dove at an astonishing speed. Alaric sat up and said, "We need these. Everyone take one."

"Kalanath has to be a passenger," Sienne said. "But they look big enough to carry two people."

"He can ride with me," Vaishant said. "It will be no trouble."

"Let's make sure it's possible before we do that," Alaric said.

Vaishant, with Kalanath lying prone beside him, took the garish rug for a swing around the room. Now it moved more slowly, but Sienne thought Vaishant was being especially careful. When he came back down to floor level, Kalanath sat up and said, "That feels strange when I cannot see. I will be happier when I touch the ground again."

"The question is, can they go fast enough?" Sienne asked. "All our camping gear was on the horses, and they carried it away with them. If this takes longer than a day…"

Dianthe smiled. "Wait until you try it yourself," she said. "I could feel how fast I was capable of going, the way you know how fast you can run. And I didn't come close to its top speed. I think those things can really move."

"Then let's put that to the test," Alaric said.

It was easier to shepherd the rugs along when they were vertical, so they didn't bother turning them, just hauled rug after rug out of the storage room until there were six of them lined up in the hallway like heavy curtains. Sienne's was deep red and royal purple, a combination she liked better than Dianthe's pink and green rug. She gently guided it through the halls and around to the front doors. Outside, she found that if she gripped it by the short side near the markings, it swung down into a horizontal position without any trouble and hovered just below waist height.

She got one knee on its flat surface and pulled herself up. It dipped slightly, but otherwise remained steady. Its fibers were smooth and soft, making a pattern like a rose garden bordered by geometric shapes. She liked the contrast between the hard edges and the soft curves. She swept a palm across the roses briefly, then crawled forward—she wasn't all that confident about standing on the thing—to look at the dark patches on the forward edge. With only a slight hesitation, she rested her palms against the marks and curled her fingers over the edge of the rug.

Something tickled the edge of her mind, like the rising sun just peeping over the horizon, or a friend seen out of the corner of her eye. She relaxed and welcomed it, reasoning that it hadn't hurt anyone else and she was more likely to find success if she didn't fight. Gradually she became aware of the carpet as an extension of her, spread wide to catch the air, and discovered she'd started drifting forward without consciously intending to. She focused, and...it felt like flexing a muscle, though not one she'd ever had before, and the carpet stopped.

She looked up. They'd reached the front gate without her realizing it. Her friends were all drifting along near her, bobbing at varying heights. They were also all looking at her. "What?" she said, feeling unexpectedly nervous.

"You're the one who can sense true north," Alaric said. "You have to lead."

"Oh. That makes sense." She worked her small magic and oriented the rug so she was pointed southeast. "I hope I don't get us lost."

"It is a straight line southeast from here to Chirantan," Vaishant said. Kalanath, lying beside him with his staff held flat by his side, had his unsettling eyes closed and his cheek pressed against the carpet. "You cannot be too far off if you stay on the line."

"Then...let's go," Sienne said, crouching lower. She gripped the carpet firmly and imagined herself moving faster.

The rug moved forward at a slightly better than walking speed, staying level regardless of the irregularity of the sandy ground. "Faster," Alaric called, and Sienne obliged. Soon, they were traveling as fast as she could run, then as fast as Kalanath could run, then they'd outpaced a theoretical Spark and still Sienne knew the carpet had more speed in it.

Her eyes burned as the air blew against them, drying them out. She lowered her head and closed her eyes before realizing this was a bad idea at the speed they were going. She turned her thoughts inward, reaching for her sense of the thing that was the carpet. It wasn't alive in any conventional sense, but it still radiated that sense of alertness she'd observed when Dianthe took her first ride. *What do I do?* she thought, picturing herself sandblasted by the desert air.

The carpet's attention came to rest on her. She felt herself being observed from head to toe, analyzed the way a tailor might inspect someone who came to her for a fitting. The air in front of Sienne's face shimmered, becoming clearer as if it were a lens she could view the desert through. A rainbow sheen passed over it. Then, with a snap, the shimmering spread from side to side.

The wind blowing sand into her face cut off instantly. Sienne blinked. It was like a sheet of glass had sprung up before her, but one that wasn't harmed by the blowing sand. She drew in a breath that smelled of heat and sand, squirmed until she lay flat on the carpet with only her head and shoulders raised, and thought *Let's see what you can do.*

The carpet took off, jerking her head back unexpectedly. It accelerated until she was flying faster than a horse could run, faster than a bird could fly. Without the invisible glass, sand would have scoured her skin from her skull. She didn't dare look behind her to see if her friends were keeping pace, just hoped they'd figured out the trick. Nothing in the world had ever gone as fast as she was moving now. She laughed with delight and willed it faster, and the carpet responded as if it, too, loved skimming along the tops of the dunes faster than thought.

Minutes passed, turned into hours. Sienne's neck and upper back ached from the position she lay in, propped on her elbows with her head raised to watch for obstacles. She didn't like to think what might happen if she ran into something at this speed. Every so often she checked her inner sense and adjusted her course if necessary. Southeast in a straight line. She hoped Vaishant was right, and it wasn't actually south-southeast or something like that, something that on horse you could easily correct for, but on a flying carpet would make you overshoot your mark and end up over the ocean. Could the carpets fly over water? She didn't want to find out.

More time passed. Sienne guessed it was mid-afternoon, both by the sun's position and by her stomach's complaint of hunger. She glanced around. There was another boulder like the one the basilisks had hidden by. Off in the distance to the west lay a shimmer that might be an oasis of the kind Dianthe had wanted to see. And directly ahead, on the distant horizon, was a blotch that grew steadily larger. She wished she could see it clearly—and with that wish, the invisible shield contracted, thickened, and a patch before her eyes turned into a lens through which Chirantan was clearly visible.

She stared at the great city in horror. Plumes of dark smoke rose from its tall towers, turning the southern sky gray. Even with the lens, she couldn't tell what the movement near the open gate was, but she guessed it must be people fleeing the destruction. And from what she'd already seen Jenani do, it would be terrible destruction.

The city drew ever nearer, growing larger with every mile and making Sienne feel it was a vast, monstrous creature creeping up on her. She shook her head to break the illusion and realized Alaric's carpet now flew beside hers. Alaric shouted something and jerked his chin up and toward the city. "What?" Sienne screamed.

He steered his rug closer and shouted, "...go...overhead..." That time, Sienne got it. He wanted her to rise higher, to go over the wall and avoid the crowds. She nodded, and Alaric pulled into the lead. It felt good seeing him there, a reminder that she wasn't alone.

The dark moving mass was now visible as tiny individuals, ant-like in size and movement. She couldn't tell if any of them noticed the colored flying specks racing toward them. Probably the citizens were too preoccupied with their own flight. Then the carpets were over the wall, which flashed past thirty feet below them in an insubstantial blur, like a line in the sand. Alaric banked his carpet, then rose again, fifty feet, a hundred.

The towers clustered around them like long-stemmed flowers, their gleaming domes gilded roses or tulips on the verge of blooming. Fire licked at their bases, sending black clouds skyward that the carpets soared through, making Sienne cough. Alaric slowed to avoid hitting the towers, though he was still going faster than a horse could run. Sienne slowed to match him and found Dianthe coming up beside her. Her friend shouted, "Some ride, huh!"

"I'm not sure I can bear to go back to walking," Sienne shouted back.

"No reason we can't keep these things. Let's destroy this monster and get down to business." Dianthe steered her carpet wide around a narrow tower and returned to Sienne's side.

Now that the wild wind wasn't blowing over her body, cooling it, the sun beat down on Sienne again, and sweat prickled beneath her arms and down the small of her back. She was aware of it as a distant annoyance, because all her attention was on the streets of the city, scanning for sight of Jenani. Screams drifted toward her on the wind, and she saw occasional collapsed buildings, but at this height, people were too small to distinguish male from female or even child from adult.

Alaric, on the other hand, seemed to have a destination in mind. Just as Sienne realized the destruction was more widespread, and that there were fewer people in the streets—fewer that were still moving; there were more and more figures that lay too still below her —they came out from between the towers into an open space made wider by the shattered buildings surrounding it. Sienne recognized one of the great round plazas that were hubs for Chirantan's many streets. The green park at its heart had been torn up, the fountain shattered and spraying water randomly in the air. More motionless people lay beside it, these all in red, like uniforms.

Alaric shouted something Sienne couldn't make out, then dove. Instinctively she matched him, not knowing what he had in mind but certain that following him was the smart thing to do. Then she saw Jenani, standing near the shattered fountain. It was large again, twice Alaric's height and more heavily muscled. It looked up as they sped toward it. Sienne was close enough to see its expression of total bewilderment before it brought its hands up and clapped them together.

The air shattered around them like an earthquake, shaking the carpets until Sienne's teeth rattled. One of her hands slipped off the carpet. Instantly it slowed to a stop, and Sienne screamed as she slid forward down the slope created by her descent. Frantically she groped for the handhold, and found it just as she would have slid over the front of the carpet and fallen twenty feet to the ground. The carpet moved again, and she flew past Jenani's head, swiftly coming level with the ground and tumbling off in an irrational fear that the carpet would buck her off if she didn't.

She got to her feet and ran, not stopping to look back at Jenani, just certain she needed to find cover before it hit her with some other attack. The destruction surrounding the plaza left plenty of places for her to hide behind shattered walls. She tried not to feel grateful for it. She swerved around a body wearing the red uniform—did Chirantan have a city guard?—and dove for what was left of a wall.

Breathless, she peeked out from behind the fragment of masonry that shielded her body and looked around. Alaric and Dianthe were facing Jenani with their swords drawn, and Ghrita was circling around behind it. Perrin, off to her right, had had the same idea she had and sheltered behind what was left of a different wall. Sienne couldn't see Kalanath or Vaishant.

Jenani regarded its tiny opponents with a look of complete disdain. "I can't believe you escaped," it said. "Don't think I'll be so generous a second time."

"We're not going to be generous at all," Alaric said, and leaped, sword raised.

22

Jenani shimmered and grew fainter, as if it weren't entirely there. Alaric swung, and overbalanced as his sword went through misty air. The ashwar passed through him, making Alaric stumble nearly into the path of Dianthe's sword. Sienne opened her spellbook to *fury* and began reading, as slowly as she dared. She wasn't sure *fury* would work on something that was only semi-corporeal, but if Jenani could do that whenever it liked, she wouldn't have time to cast the spell if she waited to start when it resumed physical form.

Jenani shimmered again, growing solid just as Sienne reached the end of the spell. Half a dozen *force* bolts shot away from her, shaking her to her core. They struck Jenani in its chest, making it scream in pain. Sienne swallowed. Six *force* bolts ought to be enough to stagger even the biggest creature. They had scared off the second sea monster they'd faced on the way to Omeira. But Jenani didn't look staggered. It looked furious. It swung around to face Sienne and pointed a finger at her hiding place.

A bolt of lightning leapt from its hand and sizzled through the air to strike her concealing wall. Sienne yelped and ducked away, scurrying to find a new place as rocks scattered, some of them striking her painfully on the back and shoulders. Perrin darted toward her, joining her in her new shelter. It was a fragment of wall that still had a window hole in it. The rest of the wall lay in pieces all around, making running difficult. "You should—" he began.

Wind came up all around them, battering them, stealing their breath. Sienne turned and pressed her face against the wall, gasping. Dizziness overwhelmed her, made her vision blurry, but she turned pages by memory and ducked her head over her spellbook. The syllables of the confusion *mirror* poured out of her, increasing her dizziness and giving rainbow edges to her spellbook pages. Beside her, Perrin shifted as if peering out from around their shelter, but she didn't have attention to spare for him. She reached the end of the spell and closed her eyes.

Perrin exclaimed, "You—what was that?"

She opened her eyes and looked around the side of the wall. Three Siennes darted away in three different directions, heading for cover. A lightning bolt flashed after one of them, missing her by inches. "*Mirror*," she said. "Three duplicates of me. They all do the same thing, but they're more or less autonomous. And it's impossible to tell the difference between them and the real thing. It should keep Jenani busy while the others attack."

"Very good choice," Perrin said. He peered over the top of the wall. "I fear I will be useless in this fight."

"If it wasn't affected by *fury*, I don't know that I'll be much use either." Sienne rose to look through the window. Jenani's attention was on one of the Siennes, and Alaric took advantage of its distraction to attack it from behind, skewering it. Jenani roared and twisted, taking Alaric's sword out of his hands and slamming its enormous fist into Alaric's face. Alaric flew backward, and Sienne screamed. He landed, his sword spinning away from him, and didn't get up. Jenani advanced on him.

With a shout, Dianthe launched herself at Jenani from the shadows, slashing at its legs. Ghrita, silent but just as terrifying, ran at it from the other side, twirling her staff almost too quickly to follow.

They battered at Jenani, who brushed at them, fending them off, before continuing its approach toward Alaric.

Sienne cast *force,* making Jenani stagger again, but it kept moving. Alaric didn't rise. Perrin grabbed Sienne's hands, startling her. "Pray with me," he said. "O Lord, forgive my importunity, but if ever you were willing to overlook my weakness, now would be the time. Heed the faith of your servants, and grant me your power according to my need!"

A rush of power surged over Sienne, leaving behind the smell of jasmine and mint. Perrin dropped her hands and stood where he could be easily seen. He stretched out a hand toward Alaric, with Jenani looming over him. "Now," he said.

Jenani raised one huge fist to bring it crashing down on Alaric. In the same instant, a pearly gray shield flickered into life, surrounding Alaric entirely. Jenani's fist smashed down on it. White light flared, and Jenani was hurled backward into one of the remaining intact buildings, smashing through the wall and disappearing into its interior.

Sienne let out a sharp breath. "How did you do that?"

"I did nothing. It was entirely Averran. I was his hand," Perrin said. "It is...I do not know how far I can reach, but I am grateful for anything he gives me."

Alaric was stirring beneath the shield dome. He propped himself on his elbows and shook his head as if dispelling a nightmare. Blood covered his lower face from what might have been a broken nose. Sienne started toward him and Perrin yanked her back into hiding. "Jenani will return at any moment," he said. "It will almost certainly come after us."

Dianthe and Ghrita were approaching the hole Jenani had made, taking very slow steps. Sienne was sure neither of them was stupid enough to follow it inside. They neared the building, which appeared to be a tavern, and went to both sides of the hole, holding their weapons at the ready.

The walls exploded outward, knocking Dianthe and Ghrita down and covering them with shattered chunks of brick and mortar. Jenani emerged, brushing off its fists. It stepped over Dianthe as it walked away. She lay still, one arm flung out and her sword fallen some inches from her hand. On the other side, Ghrita struggled to rise, then collapsed again.

Sienne flipped to *shout* and stepped out of her hiding place, ignoring Perrin's cries of warning. Jenani turned and saw her, then its gaze flicked toward another Sienne standing some distance away, also reading from a spellbook. Jenani shimmered, and Sienne's concentration almost broke. This time, it was because she wanted to laugh. *Not much good against sound*, she thought, and *shout* built within her chest until it burst from her and slammed into the ashwar.

That one, it felt. Jenani was knocked back again, not as solidly as when it had collided with Perrin's shield, but a good three or four steps. It shimmered back into solidity and appeared dazed, actually coming to rest on the ground instead of floating.

In that moment of inattention, Kalanath attacked. Sienne hadn't seen him at all, but there he was, bringing his staff around as readily as if he weren't blind. It took Jenani off its feet, and Kalanath followed the move up with a smash of the steel-shod staff to the ashwar's chest. Jenani screamed and rolled out of the way, once more shimmering into semi-corporeality. Kalanath's next blow met empty air as the ashwar sped away from him toward one of Sienne's doubles. It went solid in time to smash "Sienne" in the face. The *mirror* image popped like a shield blessing. Sienne rejoiced at Jenani's look of bewilderment at its lack of a target.

Beyond it, Alaric had gotten fully to his feet and was pushing against the shield, hacking at it with his belt knife. Jenani spun, appearing to size up its opponents. Alaric, trapped. Dianthe and Ghrita, down. Kalanath, turning in place with his head upraised, scenting for an enemy. And Sienne and Perrin, still up and still dangerous. Jenani smiled, a nasty, terrifying expression. Perrin grabbed Sienne and pulled her close, throwing up a hand to bring a shield dome into place in time for another lightning bolt to impact against it, making it sizzle with the smell of jasmine and mint.

Jenani advanced on them, still smiling. Perrin released Sienne and stood with his hand pressed against the inside of the shield. "I do not know how long it will stand against lightning," he panted.

"I have to leave sometime if I'm going to do anything," Sienne said. Beyond Jenani, Alaric appeared to be shouting as he tried to break the shield surrounding him.

"Forgive me, but your attacks seem only to be annoying the creature." Perrin had his gaze fixed on Jenani. "I think we need a different approach."

Jenani was only feet away. "I'm listening," Sienne said, backing toward the rear of the shield dome.

"I have no ideas. I am rather too terrified to think beyond the exigencies of the moment."

Jenani raised a hand and slammed it down on the shield. The shield shook, and quivered the way they did when they were close to collapse, but didn't fling the ashwar away.

"Be ready to run," Perrin said, still touching the shield as if that alone could keep it intact.

Sienne looked in Alaric's direction. Her mouth fell open. "Here comes our different approach," she said, and a unicorn slammed into Jenani from behind.

Jenani screamed, arcing its back to get away from Alaric, whose horn dripped with pale blue ichor. The shield popped, and Sienne and Perrin backed away quickly. The ashwar turned and swung at Alaric, who dodged, reared up, and struck with razor-sharp hooves, raking a gash across Jenani's pale chest.

Feet pounded behind Sienne, and Dianthe staggered past, her sword upraised and blood streaming down her face. Perrin grabbed her arm and swung her in an arc back toward him. He splayed a hand across her bloody temple, and green light glowed from her wound. Dianthe blinked at him in amazement. "I don't want to know," she said when the light faded. "Just keep doing it."

Ghrita came running up. "Is that—"

"We can talk about it when we all survive this," Sienne said. Ghrita shrugged and ran toward where Dianthe had just joined the fight, taking advantage of the unicorn's impressive distraction. Across the plaza, Kalanath trotted toward them, sweeping his staff before him and dodging debris almost as easily as ever. Vaishant followed him more slowly, terrifying Sienne at how he ran in the open, unprotected against Jenani's attacks.

But maybe it didn't matter. Alaric and Jenani fought soundlessly now, fists against horn and hooves. Jenani seemed to have forgotten it could work magic, didn't care that Dianthe and Ghrita were harrying it on both sides. All its attention was on Alaric, whose horn shone like black oil in the hot afternoon sun. Jenani's body was covered with gashes that trickled blue blood, but Alaric wasn't unscathed, his sides stippled with dark marks that showed where Jenani had struck him, one cheek split and bleeding.

Alaric lowered his head and ran at Jenani, goring it low in the side. Jenani shoved away from him and sped away, bowling over Kalanath, who realized too late what was coming toward him. Jenani swung its massive fist and took Kalanath beneath the chin, snapping his head back and dropping him like a stone.

Sienne screamed and began reading *fury* again, as fast as she dared, hoping her friends would be smart enough to stay back. Acid-edged syllables spat from her lips, burning her, and six *force* bolts erupted from her body, flying at Jenani. Five of them struck the ashwar. The sixth hit Vaishant, crouching over Kalanath. Sienne gasped as the divine fell beside Kalanath. In the next instant, a pearly gray shield dome sprang up over both men before Jenani could hammer Kalanath again.

"Keep it contained!" Alaric shouted. She hadn't seen him transform. He ran for his sword, but sheathed it once he'd picked it up and kept going, circling around the drifting ashwar. Dianthe and Ghrita followed more slowly. Everyone was tiring, but Jenani, though it was wounded, seemed much less weary than they were. It brought up its hands again, and the air shattered around Sienne and Perrin, knocking them off their feet. Sienne lay there, dazed, until Perrin helped her stand. "We must help them!" he said, gesturing.

Sienne looked where he pointed. Alaric had changed to his other self and the unicorn was once more pressing the attack. He and

Jenani stood practically on top of the shield protecting Kalanath and Vaishant. Kalanath, to Sienne's relief, had rolled over and gotten to his knees. Ghrita and Dianthe once more flanked the ashwar, preventing it from backing away from Alaric. Sienne and Perrin approached cautiously, Sienne with her spellbook open to *force*, though she didn't know if it would help. But she couldn't stand by and do nothing.

Jenani screamed, a terrible sound that shook Sienne as badly as the airquake had. "You are nothing!" it shouted. "I will not be humiliated by you!"

A quivering, nauseating feeling struck Sienne. It felt as if her bones had turned to jelly, and she fell, unable to support herself. Something took hold of her and *pulled*, drawing her out as if she were soft wax and then crushing her together into a ball. She screamed, and heard answering screams all around her. The lights went out, then flickered back on, and she smelled dust and sand and, more distantly, the hot metal scent of too much magic in one place.

She blinked away blurriness, and the world slid into focus around her. She lay on the floor of the palace in Ma'tzehar, the cool tiles of the throne room growing rapidly warm from her body heat. Groans all around her told her she wasn't alone. She hoped it was her friends, and hoped even more that none of them were seriously injured. She pushed herself onto her knees and crouched there, breathing as heavily as if she'd run five miles without stopping.

A terrible wind struck her. She was so tired she only thought, *Damn it, Jenani, not again*, before it picked her up and flung her against the wall, where it held her pinned. Her spellbook fell to the floor at her feet. Then the wind was gone, and she collapsed, gasping for air.

"No," Jenani said. "You follow me like bad luck. All of you?"

Sienne raised her head. Across the room from her, Alaric said, "You meant to escape, and drew us with you. You're slipping, Jenani." He was gory with blood and held his shoulders as if he were exhausted.

"No more," Jenani said. It was back to being Sienne's size and looked hopelessly ragged, its robe in shreds stained blue with its blood, its chest and arms a mass of wounds. One deep gash in its side looked as if Alaric's horn had torn a chunk out of it. How it was still standing, Sienne couldn't understand. "I will finish you for good, and then I will conquer this petty human world. I will make them pay for what was done to me."

"None of those people deserve that fate!" Sienne exclaimed. "It was wrong of men to make you a slave, but those people who harmed you are long dead." She hoped it wouldn't remember Dari. "Think how much good you could do with your power. Humankind will respect and honor you if you don't turn to evil."

"What do I care for the honors of men?" Jenani shouted. "Even you couldn't resist the lure of the ring entirely. Someone will find a way to enslave me again, and it will start over. I will make it impossible for anyone to do that."

Sienne tried not to stare at Perrin, who was directly across from her and behind Jenani. He'd risen to his feet and had his head bowed, and Sienne could see his lips moving, then stilling, then moving again as if in conversation with some invisible person. "I wouldn't let that happen. I swear it."

Jenani laughed. "You're young and idealistic. I believe you'd try. You just wouldn't be able to stop it, not even if your conduit was open. You have no idea what lengths people will go to to gain power. And when it's power like mine..." It brought its arm up to point at her. "No. You'll all have to die."

Alaric rushed it as the lightning bolt left its finger. Sienne screamed and dropped, and felt the lightning course past just inches from her head, frizzing her hair. Alaric didn't bother with his sword, just tackled Jenani and bore it to the ground.

Jenani exploded upward and outward, regaining its size in a second. Sienne retrieved her spellbook and hesitated, unsure what attack to make. Ghrita came at Jenani from the other side, and Dianthe hovered as Sienne did, hesitant, with her left arm hanging useless at her side. Kalanath rose from where he crouched beside Vaishant and came forward, feeling his way with his staff. Jenani fought like the wind, and a lucky blow took Ghrita off her feet to collapse unconscious, where her body got in the way of her allies.

Alaric got his hands around Jenani's throat, which seemed to have no effect. Jenani pummeled him in the kidneys until he let go and backed away. Jenani swayed, blue blood trickling into its eyes. "I won't give up," it said, "and you will all die."

"I think not," Perrin said. Jenani's head swung around to face him as he approached, one hand raised. "We will kill you, and the world will be a safer place—and a much poorer one. Averran taught that even the wasp has a role to play, and should be treated with respect and not fear."

"I don't believe in your stupid God," Jenani snarled.

"She believes in you," Perrin said. "And She grants you rest."

He clenched his fist. White light radiated from Jenani's many wounds, making Dianthe and Alaric, who were in contact with it, wince and back away as if the light's touch hurt. Jenani, though, seemed to feel no pain. It stood very still, staring at Perrin in wonder. The white light surged to cover it until it seemed made of light, radiant and cold. Sienne threw up an arm to shield her eyes. The light faded, and she lowered her arm, blinking back tears.

Jenani was gone.

Alaric stepped forward into the space where it had been. "Perrin," he said, "what did you do?"

"As I told Sienne, this was all Averran's doing," Perrin said. "I am but his tool. When I asked him what we might do to defeat the ashwar, he told me it was not up to us to pass judgment on it by way of killing it. He said we were to leave that to God. I choose not to argue with an avatar." He smiled ruefully. "At least, not today."

Dianthe lowered her sword. "But where did it go?"

"My understanding is that it went to join others of its kind, in a place where it might heal both physically and spiritually. It was deeply wounded by millennia of slavery, as I am certain you can imagine, and God chose to give it a chance to choose differently."

"I don't think that will be much comfort to the people it killed in

Chirantan," Alaric said. "Or to the thousands more whose homes and livelihoods it destroyed."

"That is beyond my comprehension. Though I agree it is poor consolation for those people." Perrin turned and strode toward Vaishant, who lay motionless on the floor. "I believe he is uninjured save for the *force* bolt he sustained."

"He ran in at the last minute," Sienne said. "I'm sorry."

"It is not your fault," Kalanath said. "He came to protect me." His eyes looked less white than before, Sienne thought, and he moved as if he could see a little. The thought eased her inappropriate guilt.

Alaric turned, and winced. "I'm starting to feel the pummeling," he said. "It takes a while for the pain to transfer from my other self. And I think it broke my nose."

"I believe I can fix that," Perrin said. "And probably should, before Averran's grace is withdrawn."

"You think this won't last?" Sienne said. "That you'll go back to needing paper blessings?"

"I have no idea," Perrin said. He laid a hand on Alaric's forehead, and green light enfolded the big man in its embrace. "Averran's communication with me back in Chirantan was rather terse, and along the lines of 'if I let you act with my power freely, will you stop pestering me?' But he sounded...proud, I think." Perrin's smile was radiant. "And to think a year ago I was a drunk with no family and no friends."

"You had us," Sienne said. "It's been more than a year since we first worked together."

"This is true." Perrin lowered his hand. Alaric let out a deep breath and rotated his shoulders. "Ghrita, give me your hand."

Ghrita, who'd just sat up, took Perrin's hand without a word. As green light surrounded her, Sienne said, "You fought well."

Ghrita glanced up at her. "So did you," she said. "For a skinny little thing."

"Oh, for Averran's sake, will you lay off?" Sienne exclaimed. "What is *wrong* with you? Did I injure you somehow, or are you convinced that goading me will win you Alaric's heart?"

Ghrita blinked. She got easily to her feet and took a few steps to face Sienne. "That was a joke," she said. "But I haven't been very kind to you. You scare me."

"I—what?"

"I can fight everything except magic," Ghrita said, pitching her voice so everyone could hear. "You could tear me apart in seconds and I'd have no defense against it. I think needling you was my way of proving to myself that I'm not weak and defenseless. And Alaric is extremely attractive. But—I'm sorry." She extended a hand to Sienne. After a moment's pause, Sienne took it.

"I wouldn't attack you," she said. "Unless you attacked first."

"I didn't say it made sense." Ghrita released her. "But I know you better now."

Alaric cleared his throat. "That's reassuring," he said. "Perrin, how's Vaishant?"

"Moving on his own," Perrin said. He laid a hand on Dianthe's broken arm, which glowed green.

"I will be well soon," Vaishant mumbled. "Kalanath, are you well?"

"I am well," Kalanath said, kneeling beside the divine to help him sit. "Thank you for guiding me. My vision is returning."

"In that case," Alaric said, "we've got one last thing to do."

23

The temple was no more ruined than before, though as they approached, part of the roof shifted and slid lower into the rubble. Sienne hesitated before the passage entrance, which looked more menacing than she remembered. "If we get trapped in here, it's going to take a long time to get everyone out," she said.

"It's not going to collapse," Alaric said.

"How can you tell?"

"I can't. We just survived a battle with a powerful being capable of destroying a city. I choose to be optimistic."

Vaishant, now mostly recovered from *force*, led the way through the corridors, never taking a false turn. Sienne's nerves inspired her to make more lights than they probably needed. Behind her, Ghrita said, "Are we going to talk about what happened?"

Alaric's shoulders tensed. "About what?" he said, sounding too casual.

"You turned into a mythical being and tore Jenani to ribbons. You can't pretend that didn't happen. We all saw it. Did the rest of you know?"

"They know," Alaric said. "I told you my race is Sassaven, and that we're creatures of magic. That's part of the magic, that transformation into my other self."

"It is strange," Vaishant said. "A good strange. In our stories, the unicorn is a symbol of purity of purpose. Of desire untainted by jealousy or fear. You are a good luck token, my friend."

Alaric chuckled. "I don't know about that. I hope my desire to free my people is pure, if that will make it successful. This ritual is the next step toward that."

"And Jenani did give us a hint about how to undo the binding ritual," Sienne said. "And it..." She fell silent, remembering.

"It what?" Dianthe said.

"It was just...it mentioned a conduit. That I couldn't stop it from being enslaved even if my conduit was open. Doesn't that remind you of anything?"

"The necromancer Ivar Scholten's notes," Perrin said. "But he did not know what a conduit was, or if he did, he failed to write it down."

"It was something he believed people had, that was related to his studies of the human body," Sienne said. "Something he was trying to open. He didn't say why."

"Jenani's words suggest it would give someone power," Perrin said.

"Does that tell you anything about Scholten's notes, Sienne?" Alaric asked.

"No, but here's the strange thing. It also reminds me of the ritual. The coming of age ritual. There's a point where I cast *change* to alter Alaric's body, and it...it's too complicated to explain the details, but you could almost call it turning the person into a conduit for the rest of what the ritual does. It's a strange coincidence."

"I don't believe—"

"—in coincidence. I know, Alaric. But what are the odds that a necromancer who was trying to become a lich would happen on a piece of a ritual relating to a magical race he'd never heard of?"

"The varnwort potion connects both. It's not such a huge stretch." Alaric ducked his head to enter the divines' chamber after Vaishant. "Let's do the ritual, and find out."

"One moment," Vaishant said. "I have been considering the phoenix feather."

"That's got to be a lost cause," Dianthe said. "The rest of the temple is inaccessible."

"Yes, but we searched the whole temple and found nothing. All that is left to search is this chamber." Vaishant made a sweeping gesture encompassing the whole room.

"We can look, but I don't know that we'll find anything," Dianthe said. She walked to the nearest wall and examined it. Ghrita followed her.

"My pardon, but I think you do not see," Vaishant said, and pointed at the dome. "I believe it is there."

They all looked up. "Sienne?" Alaric said, and Sienne sent magic lights sailing toward the dome, making the gold gleam as brightly as if lit from within. Birds of all kinds frozen in mid-flight covered the curved surface.

"I don't know what a phoenix looks like," Dianthe said, scanning the dome.

"I see it," Ghrita said, pointing.

The phoenix was one of the larger birds in the painting, its wing-span nearly six feet across. Its feathers were picked out in great detail in comparison to most of the others, whose outlines ranged from highly representational to swift sketches of wing and claw.

Sienne opened her spellbook. "I can take a look," she said. She read off *float* and rose a few inches into the air. Reaching down with one foot, she gave herself a push off the floor and drifted upward, holding out one hand to keep from banging her head against the dome. Using her fingers to guide her, she worked her way across the dome to the phoenix and ran her hands over its smooth surface, closing her eyes to shut out distractions. The gold was cool to the touch, cooler than the stone surface of the dome, which was also rough in texture by contrast to the smooth metal.

Her hands ran across something bumpy that was smoother than the stone. She opened her eyes. The feathers didn't look any different, but her fingers felt a hair-fine crack she traced to outline one of them, a long feather near the outside of the phoenix's wing. "I found it," she said. "I don't know how to get it out." She tried to fit her nails into the crack, to no effect.

"*Sculpt?*" Alaric suggested.

"I don't want to ruin the dome. It's so beautiful."

"It's probably going to ruin it if you remove the feather," he pointed out. "Leave a big hole."

"We might also need to be concerned about the dome collapsing," Perrin said.

"It's not an artifact," Sienne said. "I can try *fit*." She flipped pages and began reading. Dianthe moved to stand beneath her, her eyes on the feather, ready to catch it if it fell.

Sienne rolled the honey-sweet syllables around her tongue as she came to the end of the spell. The feather quivered, shrank to a third its size, and fell out of the shallow cavity it had been embedded in. Dianthe caught it neatly. "It's heavy," she said, weighing it in her hand. "Even shrunk, it's got some heft to it."

"It's probably solid gold," Alaric said. "I can't imagine there's much of the original feather left after all these years."

Sienne pushed off the ceiling and floated downward, hitting the floor a little too hard and rebounding. Alaric grabbed her wrist, tethering her. "Thanks," she said. "Let me restore it."

Dianthe handed the feather over, and Sienne cast *fit* again, returning it to its original size. "Look," she said, "the tip's already cut into a pen nib."

"It is remarkable," Vaishant said, holding out his hand. Sienne gave it to him, and he examined it closely. "It is supposed to contain a prophecy, but of what, I do not know. And I also do not know why the feather was hidden here when the divines left Ma'tzehar."

"They might have been afraid of what the prophecy said," Ghrita said.

"Possibly. Or it is dangerous, and they thought to hide it away." Vaishant offered it to Sienne.

"No, I think you should hold onto it," Sienne said. "You're a divine, and it seems appropriate."

"I will care for it well," Vaishant said, tucking it away inside his robe.

"Well," Alaric said, looking at Sienne. "Should we wait for *float* to wear off?"

"It will only be a few minutes. We can start preparations now." Sienne closed her spellbook.

Alaric released her and removed his backpack. Kneeling near the wall, he opened it and removed several objects: a brass goblet, an ancient knife with a red stone in the pommel, and a metal flask. "Ghrita, Vaishant, if you'd step over near the door," he said.

"We can leave, if it's private," Ghrita said.

"The ritual requires witnesses. I don't think it will hurt anything for you to watch. Just don't interfere, whatever you see." Alaric uncorked the flask and poured a measure of a cloudy yellow liquid, bright like a dandelion, into the goblet. He set the flask aside and turned to Sienne. "Are you—"

With a jolt, Sienne dropped a few inches to the floor. "Yes."

"Then...tell us what to do."

Sienne's heart was beating rapidly. Now that the moment was here, doubt assailed her. Was the potion right? Had she copied the ritual down correctly—more importantly, had she memorized it accurately? Maybe she should read it from her notes. She closed her eyes and willed herself calm. She was being stupid. She'd gone over the ritual in her imagination dozens of times, acting out each step until she could do it without thinking. This would work, and she was wasting time.

She guided Perrin, Dianthe, and Kalanath, whose eyes were still slightly filmy, to stand at points of an equilateral triangle centered on the black spot where Perrin's banishment had broken the ring's hold on Jenani. "Stand here," she told Alaric, indicating a place outside the triangle, opposite Kalanath, and crossed the room to pick up the goblet and knife. "Everyone face outward—no, everyone but you, Alaric. Put your backs to the center."

She eyed her three friends. Would it make a difference who did what? It couldn't hurt to follow her instincts. She handed Perrin the goblet. The liquid inside smelled fruity, like fine wine with a hint of bitterness. Kalanath received the knife, which he held resting on his open palms as if making an offering. Then, hesitating slightly, she removed the hazard deck from her robes and shuffled it three times. "Pick a card," she told Alaric.

"Is this really the time to risk blindness?"

"You have to shuffle and cut the deck yourself for it to have an effect, and besides, it only works once per day. This is... I just want to be sure this will work."

Alaric shrugged and drew a card from the middle of the deck. "The Key again," he said. "Is that significant?"

Sienne let out a deep breath. It was what she'd expected, but seeing it happen gave her confidence. "I hope so," she said. Putting away the rest of the deck, she handed the card to Dianthe. "You'll all need to give me your items when I ask for them, so be prepared. Alaric?"

"I'm ready." He didn't look at all nervous, which made Sienne's nerves tingle. He was trusting her with his life, after all.

She opened her spellbook to a page near the front and read the spell *mirage* in clear, rainbow-hued syllables. A glowing yellow symbol sprang into life, floating at the center of the triangle, and Vaishant sucked in a breath. "It is well," Kalanath said without turning. "This is a powerful thing we do and it needs a powerful protector. God as destroyer brings great change."

"I hope you know what you are doing," Vaishant said.

Sienne walked around the triangle to face Alaric and took the knife from Kalanath's outstretched hand. She pricked her finger and squeezed it to make the blood flow. Swiftly she drew the simple lines that made up the symbol on Alaric's right palm. Handing the knife to him, she said, "Copy the symbol, and give Kalanath the knife. Then clasp hands."

Alaric repeated her gestures. The warm blood cooled quickly in the dry room. Alaric handed back the knife. "Do I clean it?" Kalanath asked. Sienne shook her head. Alaric took her hand in his large one. It enveloped hers almost completely.

"Walk with me," Sienne said, tugging Alaric and walking backward around the triangle, counterclockwise, until she reached Perrin. With her free hand she reached for the goblet. "Last chance to back out," she said with a shaky smile.

Alaric shook his head. "It's this or nothing."

Sienne nodded. "Repeat after me," she said. "From the center, to the heart, to open what is closed."

Alaric nodded. "From the center, to the heart, to open what is closed."

"I am forever faithful."

"I am forever faithful."

Sienne swallowed. "That the center will accept the offering, let this cup by my hand open the...conduit."

Alaric raised his eyebrows, but repeated the sentence. She'd originally translated the last word as "path," but at the last minute, she'd felt strongly that the word should be changed. She prayed briefly that she hadn't just screwed everything up, and held the goblet up. Alaric took it, breathed out deeply, and raised it to his lips. Sienne watched him in tense fear. It was the right recipe, she knew; they'd tested a dozen concoctions before finding this one. But she couldn't help thinking about the possibility they'd gotten the proportions wrong. It was a sedative potion, at least in part, with ingredients like varnwort to provide a calming effect.

It was also a deadly poison.

Forcing herself not to hurry, she took the goblet from Alaric and handed it back to Perrin. With her free hand, she took her spellbook from inside her robe and let it fall open to *change*. Reading slowly, tasting each sweet syllable as it rolled off her lips, she filled her mind with images of things that opened, doors and locks and flowers and hands, and kept the last image firmly in her imagination as the spell came to an end.

Alaric gasped. Sweat broke out on his forehead. He closed his eyes and held his breath, his jaw locked as if in great pain. She felt the shadow of it cross her, an ache that started in her chest and spread outward. The spell, in conjunction with the poison, altered Alaric's body, transforming it subtly. The sedative effects were supposed to make it easier to bear. She couldn't bear to think how much it would hurt without them.

"Walk with me," she said, continuing counterclockwise around the circle at a steady pace, even though her heart was screaming at her to rush to the next step. Hands still clasped, they circled the three motionless figures in the center twice and stopped next to Perrin once more. Sienne let go of Alaric. "Hold out your hands, cupping them," she said.

Alaric extended his hands. Sienne summoned water in a thin stream to pour into his hands until they overflowed, washing away the symbol. "You are washed clean of your former self," she said, "and prepared to become something new." Her chest ached more fiercely, and she ignored it. "Follow me."

She continued to back around the circle. The ache had spread to her thighs and forearms, a dull, tight feeling like her flesh was swelling from a hundred insect bites. She stopped opposite Kalanath and took up the knife again, handing it hilt-first to Alaric. He wrapped his hand around the bone of the hilt. "Close your hand over the blade, and cut," she said.

Alaric pulled the knife across his left hand, then opened it to reveal blood that glittered like mica in Sienne's magic lights, flowing over his hand to drip onto the floor. He was breathing heavily and his eyes had gone unfocused. Sienne quickly gave the knife back to Kalanath. Her head was pounding, something was wrong with her vision, and the dull ache was turning into a sharp agony as if the knife had cut her flesh instead. She made herself breathe calmly. Alaric only had a few more minutes.

She backed away again, circling the triangle twice and ending near Dianthe. "Take...the card," she murmured, trying to ignore the pain that seared through her. "In your bloody hand."

Alaric did so. Blood smeared the edge of the card. Some part of Sienne wondered if it was a good idea, but the rest of her couldn't remember what was so special about the deck that it mattered. She opened her spellbook and, blinking to make the letters stay still, cast the confusion *mirage* again.

A shape shimmered into view, wavery and indistinct. Sienne focused hard and with her last scrap of will forced it to solidify. It was a keyhole, hanging unsupported in midair. "Turn the key in the lock," she gasped.

Alaric pushed the card toward the lock, moving as slowly as if he were forcing his hand through a wall of tar. Sienne whimpered as pain struck her again, and she fell to her knees. Distantly, she was aware that she was dizzy from casting too many spells. She hadn't kept track, damn it, and what if she couldn't cast the all-important final one? Beside her, Dianthe shifted, reaching out, and Sienne shook her head vehemently. So close.

The card touched the image of the keyhole and slid home. Letting out a groan of effort, Alaric turned the key counterclockwise. Both image and card vanished, and Alaric grabbed his head in both hands and screamed, his deep voice harmonizing with Sienne's as she did the same. She'd never felt pain like this before, as if her bones had been yanked out of their sockets and filled with molten metal. She couldn't see anything, couldn't hear anything; there was nothing but pain and a tiny helpless part of her that shrieked at her to do something or Alaric would die.

She fumbled around in her blindness until she felt his broad shoulder. He was shuddering as if something were tearing him apart. The ritual, or the poison? It couldn't be too late. She flung open her spellbook and forced her eyes open. Blank whiteness met her gaze. She grabbed her book and brought it up to her face until the slick invulnerable pages brushed her nose. Still nothing.

She sobbed, and willed the pages to turn to *purge*. It had to be now, before the poison could rot his insides, but she couldn't *see*, not even the faint brown of the paper. He was going to die, and it would be her fault.

She strained her eyes wider. Nothing. She could remember casting *purge* before, to neutralize another poison, and if only she didn't have a stupidly incompetent human brain that couldn't hang on to a damn spell long enough—

Something flickered in memory. A curve, a line, a swooping pen stroke. She sat on a bed whose mattress was too hard with a writing desk over her lap and scribed the smooth curves of a spell. *Purge.* She'd bought it on a whim before knowing it was part of the ritual, thinking at the time it might be useful someday. It had saved Dianthe's life, weeks ago. Now it was useless, trapped in her spell-book that she couldn't read.

She looked at the board and saw the spell written out in her own blood. The transform language was the most beautiful of the five, its curves and delicate lines prettier than the most elegant human calligraphy because they bore pent-up power in every stroke. It was the whole spell, dredged up from memory, and as she began reading it she heard the syllables echoing in her deaf ears, the only sound in the world. She knew it was real because she could taste the sweetness of a transform.

She gripped Alaric's shoulder and willed the spell to transmute the poison flowing through his veins into something harmless, focusing on the spell and ignoring the same little gibbering voice that wanted her to believe what she was doing was impossible.

The last golden syllable left her lips. She convulsed, falling to her hands and knees and vomiting up bile that bore no tinge of sweetness. It stank of something dark and bitter, as if she'd swallowed lamp oil. She vomited until she felt her stomach had turned itself inside out. Agony shot through her with every convulsion, and she screamed, wordlessly begging the pain to stop.

Hands held her up, and she wrenched away from them as every touch felt like a brand on her skin. She took a few crawling steps before collapsing, her body shaking too much to support her. Blind, deaf, unable to move, she screamed again and waited for death to claim her. *O Averran,* she prayed with her last conscious thought, *have mercy on my soul.*

24

Something soft brushed the back of her neck, easing the pain in her head. **I'm not done with you yet,** a thunderous voice said.

It echoed through her skull and set her head aching again, but it was a bearable ache, something that didn't feel as if someone had cracked the bone and poured boiling oil over her brain. She curled in on herself and sobbed, wishing Averran would just take her home to meet her God already. It would mean leaving her friends, her family, Alaric, but if the pain would stop—

She realized as she thought this that the pain had diminished, and her bones no longer felt out of joint. She still couldn't see, but she could hear voices, though they were very faint and faded in and out:

"*...not moving...*"

"*It's not...do this.*"

"*Sienne. Can...feel this?*"

Someone's hand brushed her cheek. With a monumental effort, she raised her hand to touch it and felt hers enveloped in a strong, familiar grip. Alaric was there. Of course he wouldn't leave her. The spell had worked. Her dazed mind insisted there was something important about this, but she still hurt too badly to understand.

Someone else laid a hand on her shoulder. This time, the touch didn't burn. The person rolled her onto her back and gently pressed her eyelids open. Shivering blobs of color moved before her eyes. She was so grateful to be able to see, even blobs, that tears fell once more.

"...still in pain..."

"...but what happened?"

"Need her...up to tell..."

The voices were growing louder, more distinct, until the volume hurt her ears. She opened her mouth to ask them to stop talking, but nothing came out. Alaric's hand tightened on hers. She tried again. "Hurts," she whispered.

"We know," Alaric said, and she winced at how his voice rattled her skull. "You acted like you were being torn apart."

"Quiet," she said. "Voice...too loud."

"Sorry," Alaric said in a whisper. His arm went around her, lifting her into a sitting position propped against his chest. She breathed in the unicorn musk of him and felt her aches subside again, withdrawing to an endurable distance. Alaric's white and tan desert robes were clear to her vision, though nothing else was. Was she permanently blind now, or nearly so?

A moving blur crouched before her, and swam into focus. Vaishant. "Allow me to try," he said, and laid his palm against her forehead. His hand was cool and dry, and in the next moment a rush of coolness like dry water swept over her. Instantly, her vision cleared, and the aches and sharp pains vanished. She drew in a deep breath and realized it no longer hurt to do so.

She put her arms around Alaric and hugged him. "Thank you, Vaishant," she said as Alaric's arms tightened on her. He brushed a kiss across her forehead, and she listened to his heart beat, slow and deep as it always was, the comforting pulse she'd so often fallen asleep to.

"What happened?" Alaric murmured. "It failed, didn't it?"

"I guess so," she said, feeling suddenly weary. "Don't you feel any different?"

"I don't. Sienne, what did it do to you?"

"I don't know." Sienne snuggled closer and closed her eyes. "It hurt like nothing I've ever felt before. Like I was being taken apart, bone by bone. I was barely able to cast *purge*. I didn't realize how close to my limit I was. I..." She sat up and opened her eyes. He looked so worried she kissed him for reassurance. "I don't feel dizzy."

"Vaishant healed you," Dianthe said. "Of whatever it was you suffered."

"Healing can't replenish my magical reserves," Sienne said. "And I know I was at my limit. It's why I threw up. But now..." She stretched, extending both arms, enjoying the feeling of muscles moving smoothly and joints that didn't crack. "I feel perfectly restored. You're well, aren't you?" she asked Alaric, suddenly worried.

"I feel fine. It hurt for a while, but nothing like what you experienced, or at least that was how it looked. I'm certainly not poisoned, so *purge* worked."

"It used the last of my reserves." *Purge.* There was something important about it. She'd been blind, and then she'd remembered—

Sienne sucked in a breath. She felt as if she'd taken a *force* bolt between the eyes. Remembered. That was it. Impossible, and yet she'd done it.

She'd cast a spell from memory.

She scrambled up and looked wildly around. She had to test this, but on what? "Stand still," she told Kalanath, whose eyes were entirely clear and looked at her in dismay. She drew on memory, and let the syllables of *float* roll off her tongue.

When she was young, she'd been required to memorize poetry for recitation, and she'd learned to picture the page and the words and read them aloud as if looking at the actual book. It felt like that now, only for the first time she saw a spell in its entirety and didn't feel it squirm away from her. Speaking faster, she recited the spell until she reached the end and Kalanath, startled, floated a few inches off the floor. "Sorry," she said, not meaning it.

"You cast a spell without your book," Alaric said, rising. His voice was neutral, concealing whatever emotion he might have felt.

Sienne's hands shook. "I did," she said. "I don't know how."

"It seems the ritual did work," Perrin said. "Just not as intended."

"Maybe," Sienne said, "Alaric, have you transformed?"

"In here? It would be very crowded."

"You've said the full Sassaven unicorns have great power. Wouldn't that mean your human self isn't the one the ritual was for? And I know we did it right." Sienne brushed aside qualms about this statement. "Please. Let's try it."

Alaric shrugged. "Back away," he said, and the others all gave him room. Alaric shuddered, and then the unicorn was there, ducking his head even though there was plenty of space. He walked around the room, nosing each of them in turn and butting his face against Sienne's. She laughed and ran her fingers down his cheek, scarred from a long-ago fight.

Alaric stepped away from her and walked to the blocked hallway. He ducked his head again, this time to look farther down it to where rubble made it inaccessible. He snorted, raised his head—and a deep rumble shook the building as the pile of fallen debris shifted, rose, and then flew in all directions. The roof groaned and settled again. Sienne went to Alaric's side. The path was clear.

Alaric shifted into his human self. "It worked," he said, sounding awed. "There's no way I could have done that before."

"So what did it do to Sienne?" Dianthe said. "She's not a Sassaven."

"It must be what Jenani spoke of, and what Scholten was trying to prove," Perrin said. "Whatever this conduit is, it makes a wizard capable of greater magic."

"Capable of remembering spells," Sienne said. "I wonder..."

"Wonder what?" Kalanath said when she remained silent for too long.

Sienne jerked out of her reverie. "Oh...it's just that the ritual, the way it's worded...I don't read Ginatic well, and even with Averran's help in uncovering the altered ritual the wizard uses, there are nuances I don't get. But in hindsight, there were hints that the officiator, the one who conducts the ritual, is supposed to have gone through it already. I thought that was just a formality, but suppose it's literal?"

"I'm not sure what you're getting at," Alaric said.

"It's just a guess, but I'm certain we did everything right, so… suppose the ritual works on both participants at once? It wouldn't do anything to someone who'd already experienced it—had their conduit opened—but if they hadn't…"

"I don't know how you could prove that," Dianthe said. "Well, that's not true. But I have no interest in undergoing that ritual. Besides, I'm not a wizard."

"Neither is Alaric."

"Yes, but he's a creature of magic. And it didn't affect his human self. I don't know that it would do anything to someone who's not a wizard except maybe kill them."

"It was only that painful to me because I didn't drink the sedative."

"It doesn't matter," Alaric said, "because I doubt anyone else wants to go through that. Sienne, are you sure you're all right?"

"I feel fine. Better than fine. I feel as if I haven't cast any spells at all."

"Then I'd like to try an experiment," Alaric said.

————

SIENNE FERRIED EVERYONE BACK TO CHIRANTAN WITHOUT FEELING ANY ill effects. Whatever the ritual had done to her—and she had a feeling she hadn't discovered the extent of the change—it had increased her reserves substantially. By the time she took Alaric's hand to return them to the Chirantan temple, she didn't even have to read the spell off her memories; she knew in her bones how it worked, and even the lacerations the spell left in her mouth couldn't dampen her enthusiasm.

"Don't tell anyone about Sienne," Alaric had said before she'd begun transporting people. "A wizard who doesn't need a spellbook…

maybe it doesn't matter in Omeira, where you don't have wizards, but everywhere else, she'd either be a target or a threat."

"We will not speak of it," Vaishant had said, and Ghrita had nodded. Sienne felt a pang of sadness that Ghrita looked at her with fear once more. She didn't hate the woman the way she once had, but this looked like it might put an end to any chance of them becoming friends.

She tried not to feel afraid of herself. When she thought about it rationally, about how glorious it felt to encompass a spell so completely, fear was the farthest thing from her mind. But when she held her spellbook and pretended to read from it for the sake of the divines watching her *ferry* her friends back, she couldn't help picturing her new ability through their eyes.

The limitation of a spellbook comforted most people, particularly the ones who were afraid of the small magics of lighting a fire or moving small things with the mind. Sienne was sure, though she hadn't timed herself, that her spellcasting was faster without the book, too. She had so many questions. How would she ever be able to reveal what had happened to her? More to the point, should she help others go through the ritual and open conduits for them as well? It was too much to worry about after everything else that had happened that day. She pushed those thoughts aside and concentrated on *ferry*.

"I can't believe you're still conscious," Alaric said as she prepared to cast one last spell. "Ten times you've cast *ferry* and you're not even breathing heavily."

"It's amazing. I hope nobody at the temple realizes this should be beyond me."

"They don't know anything about wizardry. Your secret is safe."

"For now."

Alaric examined her closely. "You think someone will talk?"

"No. But I doubt I can keep up the pretense that I'm reading from my spellbook forever. I'll slip up, and then...actually, I don't know what then."

"Let's not worry about it." He wrapped his arms around her waist and kissed her gently. "Back to Chirantan, and then start for Beneddo in the morning."

Sienne cast *ferry* one last time, and they appeared in the temple courtyard. The others all stood there waiting for them. "You could have gone on," Alaric said.

"It was unanimous that we wished to present ourselves as a team to Chakhran," Perrin said. "Most of the divines are gone, in any case, into the city to help care for the wounded. And to retrieve the carpets." He smiled. "What are we to do with them now? We covered the distance between Ma'tzehar and Chirantan in hours—think how quickly they could take us to Beneddo."

"My sense of time is askew after today. It feels like forever ago we fought Jenani," Dianthe said. "Isn't it awful that a few hours' destruction will take weeks or even months to repair? I wish we could have forced it to fix the damage it did."

"It has much to learn in the place to which it was sent," Perrin said, "or so Averran gave me to believe. It may not be able to make restitution for this attack, but someday, who knows what it may accomplish?"

Kalanath opened his mouth to speak, then shut it again as Manisha entered the garden. She rushed to Kalanath's side, embracing him. He put his arms around his mother and lifted her, making her laugh. When he released her, she turned to Vaishant, whose embrace was no less firm, if less enthusiastic. "You see we are unharmed," he said with a smile.

"It is good, because I think you not stay away from danger," Manisha said.

Kalanath and Vaishant exchanged glances over Manisha's head. "You should not be afraid," Kalanath said. "My father kept me safe."

Vaishant's eyes widened. A small smile touched his lips. "And my son has done the same," he said.

Manisha hugged Vaishant again. "I think you do not tell me all true."

"You will never let us go if we do," Vaishant teased her.

Manisha looked up at Kalanath. "And you?" she said. "Will you stay?"

Kalanath looked at his father again. "I do not know," he said. "My life is not here anymore."

"You have family. Two parents. A destiny."

"I also have friends who need me." Kalanath sighed. "I will think."

"Speak to Chakhran," Manisha said. "He will tell you stay."

"We would all like to speak to Chakhran," Alaric said. "May we see him?"

Manisha nodded and detached herself from Vaishant only to take his hand. "He is waiting."

The little corridors were starting to be familiar to Sienne, though she still couldn't guarantee she could find her way anywhere. Then they passed a turning, and Sienne almost followed it to the divines' chamber. It would be interesting to see if theirs was as beautiful as the one in Ma'tzehar.

This time, no torches burned in Chakhran's room, and Sienne could see the stained glass window clearly, though the skies outside grew dim as the sun set. It depicted a white tower with a bulbous golden top, surrounded by trees and bushes. Sienne had no idea what it was meant to represent. Chakhran sat cross-legged on a cushion, with other cushions scattered about the room. He lifted his eyeless head at their entrance. "Welcome back," he said. "Manisha, please leave us."

"But—" Manisha's grip on Vaishant's hand tightened.

"This is not for your ears, not yet. Please. Stand at the end of the passage and ensure no one enters."

Manisha bowed and, with a final glance at Kalanath, left the room. "Sit," Chakhran said. "There is no one at present in the temple who would disturb us, but I cannot predict the behavior of others."

"But you knew we were coming," Alaric said.

Chakhran nodded. "Before you say anything else," he said, "I think you should know I have been watching you in vision. From the time you fought the demon to now...and everything in between."

Sienne went cold. "You saw...everything?"

Chakhran nodded again. "Saw, and heard. My visions are rather more complete than most, after thirty-two years of practice. I wish to assure you I will say nothing of what I saw unless you instruct me to. I understand the value of a secret, and the meaning of yours."

"My secret is unimportant, as far as it goes," Alaric said. "I just don't want to be seen as a monster."

"But Sienne's could be dangerous to her," Chakhran agreed. "You did not know it would happen, as one result of your ritual?"

"Not at all," Sienne said. "I still don't understand what happened. I've made a lot of guesses. All I'm sure of is the ritual changed me and increased my magical abilities, but only in certain ways. I can't will someone to grow gills, for example; I still have to cast *gills*. And it still uses magical energy. But I feel as if I could go on doing wizardry for days. That's probably not true."

"I know nothing of magic, so I cannot advise you," Chakhran said. "But you could do worse than to seek out a trusted friend to help you investigate. If you choose."

"Thank you. I might do that."

Chakhran nodded. "And you found the phoenix feather. I do not believe that hiding place would have occurred to us."

"It occurred to Vaishant, so technically, it did," Alaric said.

Vaishant reached into his robe and extracted the feather, leaning forward to hand it to Chakhran. The Hierarch ran his fingers over the cool length of the pinion, tested the point of the nib. "Marvelous," he said.

"Is it what you expected?" Dianthe said.

"It is not, but I believe it is more wonderful than that." Chakhran lowered it to his lap. "We thought the Ma'tzehar divines left it behind because it contained God's last prophecy to them, about the destruction of their city. We hoped that in retrieving that prophecy, we might gain an understanding of its fall that might increase our faith and strength. So that it might not happen here, you understand? But I can feel its power, and it speaks to me. This feather does not contain Ma'tzehar's last prophecy. It is...you understand the principle of immanence?"

Alaric shook his head, but Perrin said, "In my faith, it is the idea that God is present in all Her creations. That it is Her immanence that allows the avatars to touch our lives. I do not know what it means to you."

"It is the same, though of course God does not speak to us through intermediaries—I mean no offense." Chakhran ran his fingers along the feather again. "This feather, this pen, has been shaped to contain more of God's presence than usually exists in an object or person. When one writes with it, the words that emerge are a prophecy of sorts, God's message to the writer in that place and time. God's power flows from the pen to the page, and then replenishes itself over time. I imagine Her immanence is strong after so many centuries." He turned his head as if he could see each of them, then settled on Dianthe. "I believe the prophecy is for you," he said, extending the pen to her.

Dianthe shied away, holding up her hands in protest. "I'm not of your faith. It would be inappropriate for me to take your prophecy."

"God's word extends to all, even those of your...heretic faith." He smiled, an unexpectedly mischievous expression. "There will be other prophecies. My heart tells me you are the one to receive the first, on behalf of all of you."

"God has a prophecy for us?" Alaric said.

"Don't sound so surprised, young man. Has not God brought you this far? Supported you in your weakness? Why is it so unlikely that She cares about the outcome of your quest? She cannot approve of the subjugation of your people, but She rarely acts directly, choosing instead to give Her creations the chance to act for good or evil. I am certain She has guided your hands all this time."

His words struck Sienne to the heart. It was beautiful, and terrifying, to think of them as God's agents in freeing the Sassaven. Their quest, which had started almost as a whim that bound her friends together, now seemed so much more serious—but it had been a matter of life and death all along, and maybe she'd just forgotten along the way.

Dianthe took the pen. "Sienne, do you have paper? Ink?"

Sienne opened her pack and withdrew one of the sheets cut to fit her spellbook. She might not need these ever again. What if her new ability meant the end of scribing spells? She handed the page to Dianthe, who smoothed it out on the floor in front of her. "I don't have ink," she said.

"You will not need it," Chakhran said. "Just write."

Dianthe let out a deep breath. "I feel so self-conscious," she said, and touched pen to paper. No one spoke. The sound of the golden nib scratching across the page filled the quiet room. Sienne refrained from craning her neck to see what Dianthe was writing, though she felt curiosity might kill her.

Dianthe breathed out again. The scratching slowed as her hand moved down the page. Finally, she lifted the pen and raised her head. "I can't remember what I wrote," she said, lifting the paper. She gasped. "It's not my handwriting."

Alaric held out a hand. The paper shook as she handed it over. Alaric scanned the lines. "It starts out in your handwriting," he said. "It says, 'I don't know what to write. I hope no one knows—' And then it changes." He cleared his throat, and read on.

"'Everything has an ending, even death. You will lose what is dear to you without the promise of regaining it. Remember in the dark times you chose this path, and let that light guide you. The heart cannot be restored.'" Alaric lowered the page. "That's...not exactly reassuring."

"It is certainly cryptic," Chakhran said. "But in my experience, God's word becomes clear in the moment just before it matters. Perhaps you will be luckier."

"Thank you," Alaric said as Dianthe returned the feather to the Hierarch. Sienne was sure it wasn't her imagination that its luster was dimmed. "You didn't have to do that."

"Your cause has captured my imagination," Chakhran said with a smile. "A valley of unicorns, racing the wind...it is a thing of beauty."

"It is," Alaric agreed.

"I hope you will stay the night," Chakhran said. "Though I will understand if you choose to leave immediately. I think Manisha would prefer one more night with her son."

"Then you know I have to leave," Kalanath said. Sienne was looking at Vaishant when he spoke, and the look of pain that touched the divine's eyes struck her to the heart.

"I know very little where you are concerned, save that you are a part of this quest and must see it through to the end." Chakhran reached out and touched Kalanath's knee. "I hope you have learned that there is a home for you here."

Kalanath glanced at Vaishant, who now looked impassive. "I have," he said, "and while I was blind I saw many things clearly. I... may choose to return."

Sienne suppressed a gasp. Of course Kalanath would want to be with his mother, and get to know his father, but it somehow hadn't occurred to her until just now that meant leaving them. He couldn't go on being a scrapper if he was the *devesh* living in Omeira. She ducked her head so he couldn't see her distress. He didn't need her selfish desires influencing him.

"That is, as always, your choice," Chakhran said. He got easily to his feet, and Sienne scrambled up as the others did the same. "You have all already done much for this city. It grows late, and we would like you to share our evening meal."

"We're happy to join you," Alaric said, "and grateful for your hospitality tonight."

"It is we who are grateful," Chakhran said.

———

SIENNE LAY IN THE QUIET DARKNESS WITH HER HEAD ON ALARIC'S chest, listening to his slow, deep heartbeat. The sound comforted her, not least because it meant neither of them were dead. After the day they'd had, that was not at all a given.

Alaric reached for her hand in the darkness. "You're not asleep," he said.

"I still feel like a violin whose strings are too tightly wound. And my thoughts are going around like a whirlwind. Did I really cast spells without a spellbook?"

"You did. It was astonishing. You looked like something out of myth."

"Did I? I felt as if the magic flowed through me. Maybe that's why it's called a conduit." She cuddled closer. "We've never been closer to death."

"We would have killed Jenani if Perrin—if Averran hadn't intervened."

"Yes, but it would have taken at least one of us with it. Maybe that's part of my problem. I want to check everyone to make sure they're still breathing."

Alaric chuckled. "And now we're headed off to an even greater threat. Not only is the wizard powerful, we can't count on the Sassaven not to turn on us at his orders. You saw what I did today. Imagine hundreds of unicorns all bent on our destruction."

Sienne shivered. "Were you trying to help me relax? Because I can tell you right now that's a bad approach."

"Sorry." He put his arms around her and hugged her close. "We'll succeed. You heard the prophecy. God is on our side."

"Yes, but at what cost? Losing what's dear to us...that sounds dire."

His hands strayed to the hem of her shirt and beneath, stroking her skin. "I choose to believe," he said, brushing his lips against her forehead, "that no loss comes without a different sort of gain. I lost my family, and I gained a new one." He kissed her again, his lips soft on hers. "I gained you."

His words, and his kiss, stilled her fears. She put her arms around his neck. "You did," she told him. "Forever and always."

SIENNE'S SPELLBOOK

Summonings:

Summonings affect the physical world and elements. They include all transportation spells.

Castle—trade places with someone else

Convey—teleport an object

Ferry—teleport with one other person

Fog—obscuring mist

Jaunt—personal teleportation

Slick—conjure grease

Summon companion—summon one of six magical creatures

Evocations:

Evocations deal with intangible elements like fire, air, and lightning.

Barrier—wall of fire or air

Burn—ray of fire

Force—bolt of magical energy, hits with perfect accuracy

Fury—six *force*-bolts, hits whatever is in range

Scorch—fireball

Scream—sonic attack, causes injury

Shout—sonic attack, causes short-term paralysis

Confusions:
Confusions affect what the senses perceive.
Camouflage—disguise an object's shape, color, or texture
Cast—ventriloquism
Echo—auditory hallucinations
Imitate—change someone's entire appearance
Mirage—visual hallucinations
Mirror—creates three identical duplicates of the caster
Shift—small alterations in appearance, such as eye or hair color
Vanish—invisibility
Transforms:
Transforms change an object or creature's state, in small or large ways.
Break—shatters fragile things
Cat's eye—true darkvision
Change—polymorph a living thing
Drift—feather fall
Fit (object)—shrink or enlarge an object; permanent
Fit (person)—shrink or enlarge a person; temporary
Float—levitation
Gills—water breathing
Mud—transform stone to mud
Purge—transmute liquid
Sculpt—shape stone
Sharpen—improve sight or hearing
Voice—sound like someone else
The Small Magics
These can be done by any wizard without a spellbook, with virtually no limits.
Light
Spark
Mend
Create water
Breeze
Chill/warm liquid

Telekinesis (up to 6-7 pound weights) (also known as invisible fingers)

Ghost sound

Ghostly form

Find true north

Open (used to manipulate a spellbook)

Invulnerability

SNEAK PEEK: CALL OF WIZARDRY (COMPANY OF STRANGERS, BOOK 6)

The familiar brown brick of the three-story houses along the gently sloping street welcomed Sienne home. It was early evening, when the cool breezes off the harbor blew away the heat of the true summer day, and the long, slanting rays of the setting sun pointed the way to Master Tersus's back door. Their warmth soothed Sienne's aching back, sore from her lying propped on her elbows for ten hours on her flying carpet.

She could have *ferried* herself and her companions back instantaneously, but the joy of flying had captivated her enough that she didn't want to give it up, regardless of the pain. And it was far superior than riding. Ten hours on horseback would have been painful in a different way. It also would not have gotten them nearly so far. They'd made the entire journey from Chirantan in Omeira to Fioretti in that ten hours—a journey of more than a week by ship or twice that overland by horse. Sienne rubbed her lower back. That lightning travel was worth a little pain.

"Are you all right?" Alaric asked. He walked beside her, toting both their rolled-up carpets. They weighed practically nothing because they floated whether they were rolled or flat, but they looked heavy, and Alaric had pointed out that no one would believe someone her size could carry a carpet that big.

"Just sore," Sienne said. "Aren't you?"

"A little stiff. Next time, we should take more rests."

"I concur heartily with this decision," Perrin said from behind them. He sounded so relieved Sienne pinched her lips against a smile. Perrin hated heights more than she did, and he'd looked so chagrined that morning when Alaric declared they would use that method of transportation Sienne could guess how he felt.

"We might not need to, if Sienne can find *transport*," Dianthe said. "Kitane's eyes, but I'm hungry."

"If we have luck, Leofus has supper still," Kalanath said. He sounded as fresh and unwearied as he had when they'd said goodbye to his parents that morning.

"Let's not count on it," Alaric said. "Sienne, will you get the door?"

Sienne hurried ahead to open Master Tersus's back door, then stood aside for the others to enter with their awkward burdens. She paused for a moment when they'd all passed her to look out over the street that sloped downhill before her. It smelled of dozens of different evening meals that blended together into the scent of hot meat and salt potatoes and, from somewhere nearby, a hint of chocolate. That might be Leofus's cooking. He'd been experimenting with the unusual southern delicacy when they left.

The warm evening light turned the paving stones more golden than usual, burnishing them to a bright radiance. Sienne heard laughter from across the street where one of the neighbors was having a party, judging by the extra lanterns strung around his front door and leading around the house. She breathed in a sigh of contentment. Home. They were all safe, no one had died in Omeira, and their quest was all but complete now that Alaric was a full Sassaven unicorn, and she...

She closed the door and went into the bath house to wash her face. The carpets' magic included an invisible shield that protected their riders' faces from wind blasting them at gale force speeds, but Sienne still felt grimy. Dozens of invulnerable magic lights shed a cold white light over the sink and the pump and the porcelain tub for a rather more thorough cleaning. The whitewashed walls peeled at the corners from the damp, making Sienne itch to pull strips off the walls.

She scrubbed and splashed herself clean, then dried off with the cloth hanging from the wall. Then she used a small magic to heat the water the cloth absorbed, making it evaporate and drying the cloth. Three days ago she wouldn't have bothered because it took her so much time. Now she did it in seconds. Just another way in which she'd been altered by the ritual that had changed Alaric. It exhilarated and unnerved her.

It had been an accident. The ritual had been intended only to unlock Alaric's full potential. They hadn't realized it worked both ways, affecting the one performing the ritual as well as the one undergoing it. Now Sienne no longer needed a spellbook to cast spells, and her magical reserves had increased so dramatically she didn't know what they were anymore, and her so-called small magics were enormous by comparison to what they'd been. She felt like a stranger to herself, and she felt more complete than she'd ever felt before. Strange contrasts. If she looked in a mirror and found her hair had gone as blonde as Alaric's, she wouldn't be surprised.

The door opened. "Looks like we had the same idea," Alaric said, entering the room. Sienne stepped back to give him room at the sink. "Leofus is putting a meal together for us. Complaining noisily the whole time, of course, but if he weren't glad to see us, he wouldn't do it at all."

"I didn't realize how much I missed home until we got back." Sienne thought about leaning against the wall, but remembered in time how damp it always was.

"Me too. I'll be glad to sleep in our own comfortable bed." He held out a hand for the cloth, and Sienne tossed it at him with her small magic called invisible fingers. He dried off and tossed it back to her, and once again she dried it, marveling at how easy it was.

Alaric reached for her hand and drew her close, putting his arms around her. "On the other hand," he continued, "we don't have to sleep."

Sienne ran her fingers over his strong chin and the curve of his neck. "I've been thinking about a back rub since we left the Bramantus Mountains behind."

"Mmm. Yours, or mine?"

"Both, so long as we're naked for it." She pulled his head down for a kiss. He smelled deliciously of pine forests and the heady musk of the unicorn, and his lips were firm and warm on hers.

"I thought you were hungry," Dianthe said from behind them. Sienne, startled, jerked away from Alaric and was brought up short by his encircling arms. Dianthe smirked. "Dinner's ready. Though if you want to keep on with what you're doing, might I suggest the bath house isn't the best place for it?"

"Suggest away," Alaric said, and kissed Sienne once more before letting her go.

Leofus was still complaining when they entered the kitchen and took their usual seats at the table. "No warning," he said, "no advance notice at all, it's like you don't appreciate my genius, don't know what you'd do if I just up and refused to wait on you all—"

"Thank you, Leofus," Sienne said. "I'm amazed you were able to put together a meal this good without any notice." The table was covered with remnants of past meals, cold roast chicken and sliced ham and the tag end of a pork roast, hardboiled eggs already peeled, sliced cooked carrots and baked potatoes still in their jackets, sautéed squash emitting aromatic herbed steam, and a tureen of dumplings floating in golden chicken gravy.

"Don't take advantage," Leofus warned, gesturing with his ubiquitous spoon, but he was smiling.

Sienne sat next to Alaric and heaped her plate high with chicken and squash. "I like Omeiran food, but there's nothing to beat home cooking," she said. Leofus beamed.

"Let's talk about tomorrow," Alaric said. "Sienne has to meet with this—what was her name?"

"Carys Bettega," Sienne said. "Ghrita said she's a retired scrapper wizard who might be willing to sell me some spells. A scrapper is likely to have *transport*, and if I can get that, it will change how we go to Beneddo."

"But we *are* going, correct?" Perrin said. He hadn't taken large portions of anything, and Sienne noticed he'd only picked at what he had taken.

"Of course," Alaric said. "The next step is to make sure your family is still safe, and see what progress Sienne's brother has made on their problem."

Sienne nodded and said, around a mouthful of tender squash, "Alcander will have a plan by now. I'm sure of it."

"When I spoke with Cressida this morning, she indicated all was well," Perrin said, "but I...would like to see for myself."

His uncertainty surprised Sienne. Perrin had spoken with his former wife Cressida almost every day since they set off for Omeira, and Sienne had been sure they were working out their differences and moving toward a much desired (on Sienne's part, at least) reconciliation. Perrin loved Cressida still, and Sienne thought Cressida returned his feelings, so if they could just sit down in the same room for ten minutes and talk things through...but now Perrin sounded doubtful in a way he hadn't throughout their journey. If he was having second thoughts, Sienne didn't know what to do.

Outside, a dog howled, a low, mournful sound like the cry of a lost soul. Leofus groaned and muttered, "Not this again."

Alaric turned toward the window. "Again? Has this been going on long?"

"Four days," Leofus said, scowling. He held his spoon, dripping with chicken gravy, like a spear. "Howls like the undead every night around this time. Some stray dog, like as not, though it might be someone doesn't want to lay claim to the beast and get the neighbors in an uproar after him."

Alaric looked thoughtful. "Odd. I could swear..." He shook his head. "At any rate, we need to stop in Beneddo sooner rather than later."

Dianthe nodded. "We can be on our way day after tomorrow,

either by carpet or by *transport*. Or—I suppose Sienne could use *ferry*, take us one by one."

"We'll need to travel overland once we reach Ansorja, so I don't want to leave the carpets behind," Alaric said. The howl cut across his words, fainter this time as if the dog had run away. "But we have plenty of options for that. At any rate, tomorrow Sienne hunts for spells, the day after that, we go to Beneddo, and then once we know where things stand with Perrin's family, we'll leave for Ansorja."

His final words fell like shards of ice into the sudden silence, broken only by the sound of Kalanath steadily eating his way through the last of the roast. Sienne laid down her fork and knife and pushed her plate away. "And then we confront the wizard," she said. "Are we ready for that?"

"We still don't understand how the unbinding should work," Dianthe said, "and we aren't sure about whether it makes more sense to try to do that, or just kill the wizard and hope that breaks the binding."

"I'm inclined to the latter," Alaric said. He wiped his mouth with his napkin and dropped it on his empty plate. "Subduing the wizard long enough to perform the unbinding could be dangerous."

"But what if the binding persists after his death?" Sienne asked. "That would leave the Sassaven—the adults, anyway—trapped in something they can never break."

"We'll have time in Beneddo to finish working out the details," Alaric said. "I don't want us rushing off without a plan. There's no hurry."

"I am glad of this," Kalanath said. "I do not wish to face this wizard with no plan. It is not what I see."

Alaric frowned. "Did you have a vision?"

"Last night," Kalanath said, nodding. "But I do not say because I do not understand it. I think about it while we fly."

Sienne wasn't used to her friend being so open about his ability as *devesh*, holy child of God, to have prophetic dreams. His time in Omeira, and his growing relationship with the father he never knew, had changed him.

"I see us flying," Kalanath went on, "flying like birds, I mean. And we fly over forests and mountains to a tower. It is too tall—no tower is so tall without falling."

"That sounds like the wizard's tower," Alaric said. "It really is impossibly tall."

Kalanath nodded agreement. "We fly, and fly, but the tower's top is always out of reach. So we fly to the ground and search for an entrance, but there is none. And in my dream I know it is because we must have a plan."

"The wizard's tower is solid stone. No stairs," Alaric said. "There's what we call the walkstone in the base. It's an artifact that transports you to the top. I think I remember how to activate it."

"And we have to worry about the Sassaven attacking us," Dianthe said. "Hard to figure out a strange artifact while a mob is nipping at our heels."

Alaric yawned and stretched. "I'm too tired to think about this now. Let's sleep on it, and discuss it in the morning."

Sienne gathered up her plate and Alaric's and scraped the bones into the scrap bucket. "Thank you again, Leofus," she said as she handed him the plates.

"Taking me for granted," Leofus muttered, but he was smiling.

Alaric trailed Sienne up the stairs to the third floor. The third floor had once been servants' quarters, back before Master Tersus had bought the place, and the bedrooms were plain and plainly furnished. Sienne pushed open the door of the room she shared with Alaric and winced at the heat radiating from it. "I wish I'd left the window open a crack before we went to Omeira," she said. She crossed to the window and got it open with some shoving. Cool evening air breezed past her, bringing with it the smell of the distant harbor, brine and hot tar and a hint of cinnamon. She inhaled, closing her eyes. It reminded her of their sea voyage and how beautiful the waves were.

The bed creaked, and she turned to see Alaric sitting on it, removing his boots. She'd cast *fit* on the bed weeks ago, enlarging it and its bedding enough that Alaric's feet didn't dangle off the end. He had his attention on his boots and his brow was slightly furrowed. "Something wrong?" she asked.

"Hmm?" Alaric looked up, one boot in his hand. "Just thinking about getting into the wizard's tower."

"I thought you said you were too tired to think about that."

"I am. But my brain didn't get the message." He set his boot down and tugged off the second one. "This isn't going to be easy. Avoiding the Sassaven, subduing the wizard, performing the right ritual...there are still too many unknowns."

Sienne sat beside him, sending up her own creak. "We'll figure it out. There are still things we have to do before we can make any concrete plans. If I get new spells tomorrow, that could change things."

Alaric put his arm around her. "How likely is it that this Carys Bettega will want to deal with you?"

"Ghrita thought she'd at least be willing to meet with me. She said Mistress Bettega collects scrapper stories, like as a historian or something. But she's not with the university, so I don't know exactly what that means. If she's not willing to sell or trade, she might know others who would be. I feel confident I'll get something out of meeting her."

"We could come with you."

"I thought about that, but the rest of you will do better to prepare for the journey to Beneddo. Besides, I don't want to overwhelm her." Sienne rested her head on Alaric's shoulder and felt his arm tighten around her. "This is nice."

"I had in mind something a little more intense than 'nice.'" Alaric's hands went to the hem of her shirt. "Unless you're too tired."

"I hope I'm never too tired for that," Sienne said.

Outside, the dog howled again, mournful and loud. Sienne, leaning in to kiss Alaric, found his lips unresponsive. His hands rested unmoving on her hips. "What's wrong?"

"I don't know." He blinked and looked at her. "Nothing. That howl...it sounds familiar."

"All dogs' howls sound the same to me." She kissed him again, and this time he returned her kiss, slow and sweet. She loved his kiss.

The howl went up again, and Alaric stiffened. "I swear I've heard that before," he said. He stood and went to the window. "I don't see anything. I—"

The unseen dog howled again, closer this time. Alaric swore and turned away. "Sorry. That howl is going to drive me mad." He crossed to the door without stopping to put on his boots.

"Wait for me," Sienne exclaimed as he strode out of the room. She hurried after him, the floorboards warm against her bare feet.

Outside, the noise of the neighbor's party drifted toward her on the wind, which had picked up since they returned home. Snatches of laughter, and the music of a fiddle and flute, filled the air with a carnival sound. The howling had stopped. Alaric rounded the corner of the house into the small garden, no more than fifteen feet on a side. Yew hedges taller than Sienne could see over bordered the garden on three sides, with the fourth side being the kitchen wall. Kalanath practiced his fighting routines there in the morning, and Sienne had often watched and admired his flowing, graceful movements. At the moment, it was dark and still.

Alaric said, "I need light."

Sienne made half a dozen magic lights with a thought and sent them spinning into the air to illuminate the garden. Their white light cast strange shadows over the hedges, throwing each tuft of needles into stark relief. The branches needed to be trimmed back; their bushy limbs looked like they were reaching for Sienne with prickly fingers. Sienne looked closely at their bases. Nothing moved. She and Alaric were the only creatures in the garden.

"Maybe it ran away when it heard us coming," she said.

Alaric nodded. "Maybe." He had a distant look in his eye, as if he were thinking hard. Then he shook his head. "It was probably nothing."

Another howl swallowed the word "nothing," longer and louder than before. "Around front," he said, and ran from the garden. Sienne followed him, carefully avoiding the small rocks of the gravel path.

Alaric stood at the edge of the street, looking east toward where the houses rose along the steep incline. Lights burned behind windows and in front of each house—it was each householder's duty to maintain a lantern to light the street—some white with magic, some warm and yellow with real fire. The sound of the party was louder now, and Sienne could barely make out the booming voice of Master Innes, calling for more wine. If not for that, the street would have been its usual quiet, peaceful self.

Sienne looked westward, toward the bottom of the street where it curved away to the north and toward the harbor. The small round paving stones were slick when it rained in winter, but at the moment they were dry and not at all treacherous. Cypress trees grew where the street curved, planted years ago by some overzealous property owner who wanted the neighborhood to look more prosperous than it was. Sienne's eye lingered on the base of the left-hand tree. Was it her imagination, or were the shadows there deeper than they should be?

She opened her mouth to ask Alaric what he thought, and the shadow detached itself from the tree and flung itself toward her.

Sienne gasped and said, "Alaric!" Instinctively she flung up her hands and chanted the spell *force* even though the shadow was moving fast enough it would reach her before she finished.

Alaric grabbed her and slung her roughly out of the way, interrupting her spell. She took a few stumbling steps to regain her balance and saw the shadow was a dog, a lithe black creature built like a greyhound. The dog's mouth was flecked with foam and it growled deep in its throat as it ran. It ignored her and went for Alaric, who crouched, hands at the ready to wrestle the animal to the ground. Sienne took a few more steps to the side and once more began casting *force*.

The dog launched itself at Alaric's throat, knocking him over. Alaric got his hands around its throat, holding its head with those sharp teeth away from him. The dog went still.

Alaric, it said, in a voice that echoed in Sienne's head.

ABOUT THE AUTHOR

In addition to the Company of Strangers series, Melissa McShane is the author of more than twenty-five fantasy novels, including the novels of Tremontane, the first of which is *Servant of the Crown;* The Extraordinaries series, beginning with *Burning Bright;* and *The Book of Secrets,* first book in The Last Oracle series. She lives in the shelter of the mountains out West with her husband, four children and a niece, and four very needy cats. She wrote reviews and critical essays for many years before turning to fiction, which is much more fun than anyone ought to be allowed to have.

You can visit her at **www.melissamcshanewrites.com** for more information on other books.

For news on upcoming releases, bonus material, and other fun stuff, sign up for Melissa's newsletter at http://eepurl.com/brannP

ALSO BY MELISSA MCSHANE

THE CROWN OF TREMONTANE

Servant of the Crown

Rider of the Crown

Agent of the Crown

Voyager of the Crown

THE SAGA OF WILLOW NORTH

Pretender to the Crown

Guardian of the Crown

Champion of the Crown

THE EXTRAORDINARIES

Burning Bright

Wondering Sight

Abounding Might

THE LAST ORACLE

The Book of Secrets

The Book of Peril

The Book of Mayhem

The Book of Lies

The Book of Betrayal

The Book of Havoc (forthcoming)

COMPANY OF STRANGERS

Company of Strangers

www.ingramcontent.com/pod-product-compliance
Lightning Source LLC
Chambersburg PA
CBHW070551260626
47161CB00002B/575

* 9 781949 663303 *